I0646023

Dare You to Choose Truth

THE SETLIST SECRETS SERIES

BOOK ONE

LAUREN LIPP

5 PRINCE PUBLISHING
5PRINCEBOOKS.COM

Copyright © 2025 by Lauren Lipp, DARE YOU TO CHOOSE TRUTH

All rights reserved.

Published by:

5 Prince Publishing and Books, LLC

DBA 5 Prince Publishing

PO Box 865

Arvada, Colorado 80001

No part of this book may be reproduced, stored in a retrieval system, or transmitted in any form or by any means—electronic, mechanical, photocopying, recording, or otherwise—without prior written permission from the publisher. The contents of this book may not be used for the purpose of training artificial intelligence or other machine learning systems without explicit authorization.

This is a work of fiction. Names, characters, places, and incidents are the product of the author's imagination or are used fictitiously. Any resemblance to actual persons, living or dead, events, or locales is entirely coincidental.

Digital ISBN: 978-1-63112-412-9

Print ISBN: 978-1-63112-413-6

Cover design by Marianne Nowicki

Interior design by 5 Prince Publishing

First Edition

F07212025

For more information about this title, visit: www.5PrinceBooks.com

To Poppy, because you're the one who helped me get my first library card and taught me that a trip to the bookstore can fix any bad day. I miss our reading chairs. I miss seeing you use my school picture as a bookmark. I miss reading our favorite book every Christmas together. More than anything, though, I miss you, every single day. I told you I'd write my own, so thank you for always cheering me on toward that dream while you were here. I'll be seeing you in all the old, familiar places.

Acknowledgments

First, I want to give a heartfelt thank you to Bernadette Soehner and 5 Prince Publishing for believing in me and encouraging me. You've changed my life in more ways than one. I've never felt more at home than I have in the 5 Prince family.

Cate, thank you for your expertise in helping me make this story the best it could be. Every author deserves an editor like you.

To my LLA critique group, thank you for being the best group of writing friends I could have ever asked for. Your feedback made this story better, but your continuous support and the safe space you've fostered make *me* better.

Thank you to my beta readers, and a very big thank you to Lori Thorn. You were the first person to read this story in its entirety which I will never forget. Your feedback was incredibly helpful, but your support and friendship were priceless.

Kylie and Laura, thank you for giving me the type of friendship most people only dream about and supporting me on every step of this journey.

Conner, thank you for asking "What if everyone got food poisoning?" when I told you I was writing a book set on a tour bus.

Sis, thank you for sneaking me romance books when I was probably too young to read them.

Dad and Kat, thank you for always encouraging my writing and reminding me it's what I'm meant to do.

Sarah Reichert (and by proxy, Destiny Harrison) this book would not exist without you. While that probably seems dramatic,

I can't even begin to fully unravel the invisible string tying us together. Your friendship, mentorship, and stories have been the catalyst for me standing where I am now: thriving in a job I adore and writing stories about love like I always dreamed. I want to gossip about our favorite Peloton instructor over stinky cheese with you forever. (I also have to thank you for the waterproof notepad because a lot of this book was written mid-shower and without that hydrophobic paper, many of my good ideas would have been lost down the drain.)

Thank you to my beautiful (and wildly strong) girls. You two are constantly teaching me how to be a better mom and a better person. Writing a book while raising toddlers is no easy task, but you made it worth it.

I especially want to thank my husband, John. Thank you for making me laugh harder than anyone ever has and lending your jokes to my stories. Thank you for believing in me and constantly telling me so because it pushed me further than I ever thought possible. Thank you for enthusiastically writing the music for this book when I asked. *A Way*, *Fuck Me Sober*, and *She's Better* are exactly what I wanted but could never write myself. Thank you for listening to my ideas and sending me on writing retreats so I could work on this project. My life is full of romance, not because I write or read it, but because of you. There's no way to completely express how I feel in words. I know because I've been trying over the last 14 years and I still can't get it right. The epilogue in this book is just another one of my many attempts. I'm not sure what entity to thank for your existence and presence in my life, but I really feel like one in infinity to have this life we've built together.

Finally, I want to thank Euterpe, the Muse of Music, because I have never felt more alive than I do when I'm standing in the middle of a crowd at a concert, singing at the top of my lungs with strangers. This story is my love letter to music and how it brings people together.

Dare You to Choose Truth

CHAPTER 1

Prudence

"You want me to party? With a rock band? On their comeback tour?"

I've worked as a reporter at *SubVox* for the last five years, but I've never written a story like this before. I'm a little dumbfounded, honestly, that my boss, Felicia has just assigned me to go on the road with the 90s grunge sensation, Gnasher, on their first tour since 1996.

Felicia walks toward me to perch on the edge of her desk, and the sight drags me from my thoughts again. "Yes, I do want you to party with them. I want you to pull anything you can. If you can figure out why Gnasher broke up in '96," she sucks in a breath and shakes her head, lost in her own thoughts, "Oh, that would be delicious!"

"We're eating the magazine these days?" I mumble mostly to myself.

She rolls her eyes. "You don't have to drink with them, but encourage … rockstar behavior. But maybe do it subtly. Clifford Lee's manager sounds a little uptight."

I narrow my eyes at her. "Does he know I'll be there?"

Her eyes glitter at the way I phrased my question as if I'm for sure going to do this crazy thing she wants me to do.

She grips the edge of her desk and lifts herself to sit completely on top of it, her pantyhose-clad legs swinging like she's a child on a stool. "Probably, but that's not the point. Oh, and they are going on tour with a newer band," she snaps her fingers trying to grasp for the name out of thin air, "It uh …" *snap, snap,* "Cosmic, something. Maybe you can write a smaller story about them as well. I'll see what I can do if you're interested."

"Cosmic Intervention?"

She claps her hands. "That's the one."

Cosmic Intervention declines interviews a lot. I am almost positive they've never interviewed before, now I think about it. The wheels in my head start turning rapidly at the possibility of getting to talk to them, making me almost forget what Felicia is asking me to do.

I swirl my pointer fingers around my temples, forcing my brain to process this. "Okay, Felicia. Can we go back to the manager? It sounds like he doesn't want me there, so I'm confused how you got this approved." Not only am I apprehensive to dig for the answer to one of the music industry's most sought-after secrets, but I also don't feel great walking into a situation where I'm not wanted. The last cover story I wrote completely blew up. On the internet, and unfortunately, in my face. I've always had a talent for getting people to talk to me. It's never been a negative thing before now, not until Torrence Gillman.

"I've been coordinating with the bass player's manager."

"Jazzy P and Clifford Lee have separate managers?" At present, it's admittedly an inconsequential question compared to all the others running through my mind, but I'm starting to feel like this will get messy. Bands usually have one manager overseeing them, but considering the way Gnasher broke up, I can't say I'm surprised. The fact that the two surviving members of the original band, and former best friends, have separate managers makes my skin tingle with an anticipation which used to feel like excitement, but now only feels like dread.

She waves my question away. "Not the point, Prue."

I raise my eyebrows in a silent question my vocal cords can't form at the moment. My skin prickles with the reminder she's *always* telling me what the point is, and that's my biggest problem at present.

"The point is we have the opportunity of a lifetime. *You* have the opportunity of a lifetime. This is a huge story, Prue." She's not wrong, and I can't deny that the chance to go on tour with a band and fully immerse myself in the music and lifestyle is tempting. I wouldn't normally hesitate at an opportunity like this.

I start rolling questions and possibilities around in my head, and the thinking is starting to make me nauseous. I know if I resist, Felicia is going to continue to push. And honestly, this will not only be a career boost for me, but this could potentially be life-changing for more than one reason. Maybe I could use this to shift the negative perspective of me that *SubVox* readers and music fanatics have held since that damn story.

Walking into the office last week on the morning my article was published was like walking up to the firing squad. I thought that's why Felicia pulled me into her office today. I thought I was in trouble for not coming up with a story idea or participating in this morning's monthly meeting. I haven't been participating much at all over the last several days. My mind has been occupied by the story that got published a week ago and got me sitting in this position right now. Hated by many, except by those I made a lot of money for, Felicia included.

Covering up the nervous gurgling from my stomach, I forge ahead and ask the question I need verbal confirmation for. "Why me?" Why would she choose me to write this story? I wait, positive I already know her answer.

She gapes back at me, one eyebrow raised slightly. "Prue, don't be modest. It's not cute."

I simply continue to stare back at her, my eyes now narrowed as I stand my ground. I don't know why, but I need her to say it, to confirm what I'm thinking.

"Prue, this is the biggest story of the year, the decade, even," Felicia says placing her hands on her desk in front of her. "You wrote an amazing exposé for the spring issue, and I know you'll handle this with as much fervor." And there it is. Exactly what I feared. Because of the information I was able to get out of Torrence, she thinks I'll be able to do it again; but this time to find out information people have been foaming at the mouth for since 1996.

"And I certainly would. I just ..."

She splays her hands out to her sides and cuts me off. "Just, what?"

She's exhausted with me, I know it. "People aren't very happy with me right now." My voice comes out low as my head dips down with it.

"Oh, Prue. Don't tell me this is about your boyfriend," Felicia sighs with a dismissive eye roll.

"Well, no," I peer off to the side before adding in a quieter voice, "We broke up, actually, so it's not about him at all." Jake and I broke up about three days ago, officially. He is a huge Torrence Gillman fan, as of about four days ago apparently, and he thought what I wrote was extremely inappropriate and "uncool." Why I was ever dating someone, or rather frequently hooking up with since he never wanted to refer to me as his girl-friend, who used the word "uncool," is beyond me.

"Oh, thank goodness," Felicia clasps her hands together as if her disdain for my situationship ... er, previous situationship, was not something she made abundantly clear already.

I force a smile, nodding along with her excitement over my recent heartache.

"So what is your hold up?" Felicia's voice brings me back to the matter at hand. "It's really unlike you to turn down the oppor-tunity to go to a show, and I'm offering you the chance to go on *tour*."

"Right," I begin, "well, because of the ruckus I caused with my most recently published piece. I have amassed a large following of

..." I pause, searching my brain for the right word, "haters," I settle on, unable to find a more professional word floating around my brain.

Her lips part in a wide, almost clown-like grin as she nods her head excitedly. "You sure did," she exclaims in the same way you'd congratulate someone for winning a major award as opposed to getting non-stop criticism on the internet. Felicia's motto is "All publicity is good publicity," even though I don't exactly share that belief. At least, I don't anymore after experiencing what the "all" can entail.

"I sure did," the inflection of my voice not hinting at sarcasm at all.

"It's going to be great. Honestly, Prue, we've tried multiple times to have artists allow a reporter to go on tour and no one took the bait," Felicia pauses, turning something around in her head before continuing. "Which is fair …" her eyes drift off in thought, "getting to be around them before shows, after shows, in-between shows … they are bound to spill dark secrets. If they enjoy alcohol or drugs, even better." Her eyes light up with her revelations and success at finally getting the kind of story that will unquestionably sell because she'll be putting me in the ideal situation to get the information to write it.

I continue to gawk at my eccentric and demanding boss now pacing across her office, talking to herself in a stream of consciousness.

Felicia claps her hands together and twirls to face me before exclaiming, "Get him drunk, Prue!"

When she says 'him', I know she's referring specifically to Clifford Lee, the supposed reason for Gnasher's break-up. I stare back at her, my mouth surely hanging open wide enough to catch a fly, or three. The thought of getting someone drunk in order to air their dirty laundry makes me queasy after what I've recently gone through.

I consider my options: I could tell her no. Look her dead in the eye and say, "Hell no, lady! And by the way, I'd really like to be in charge of what I write from now on." But I know I won't. And I don't. Instead, I go with option two.

"What are the terms?"

She tilts her head to the side and narrows her eyes at me. "What do you mean?" *Okay, she's on to me.*

I take a breath and force my spine to pull me up straighter to appear as confident as I want her to perceive me. "What are the expectations surrounding my recorded interviews and the topic of my article?" The words leave my mouth a bit faster than I intended, but I don't back down.

She straightens her shoulders and her eyes fall into a neutral expression. It's a bit uncanny, and it makes my skin crawl. She knows I had issues over the last story. I did not want to write it. I even fought her on it until I realized I might lose my job if I pushed back any harder. According to my contract, I have to turn in any recordings of interviews, along with handwritten notes if I take any, and from the evidence I've collected, Felicia will tell me the exact angle of a story I need to write. I write it; but even with my name in the byline, I can't fully take claim over my writing. I never had a huge problem with it until I was told to write a story I desperately didn't want to write.

"The expectations have not changed." Her voice is even, flat. She knows exactly what I'm asking, but is choosing to give me a vague answer anyway.

This doesn't sit right with me, but I also don't know how to turn this down. This story could be life-changing, especially if I do uncover the reason for their breakup. I mean, maybe it's mundane. Maybe they don't even care it's kept so secret and they'll tell me outright. *Yeah, right.*

I settle for trying to make a deal with her. "I want to write reviews of the shows, instead."

"That's not what this story is about, though."

She stares at me for a beat before a smile spreads across her face, and I know what she's about to say before she even says it out loud.

"Fine. If you write this story, your next story can be a review." *SubVox* hardly publishes reviews. They don't sell, according to Felicia, but I know that's not true.

I keep my gaze pressed against hers, searching for the flicker in her eyes to indicate she's lying. "If I write this story," I repeat, "Can I do multiple reviews?" I'd love to shift my role. I don't want to interview musicians and artists anymore with the intent to pull some juicy detail of their lives from them. While I enjoy connecting with them on a deeper level, I don't enjoy facilitating conversations that don't center around the music anymore.

She doesn't love this question, I can tell from the snarl forming on her face, but she relents. "Yes." I don't even have time to consider whether or not she's telling the truth.

Emboldened by the brief glimpse into a bright future I've been dreaming about for as long as I can remember, I lift my head. "How long will I be gone, and when do I leave?" I chirp with the biggest smile I can muster without appearing too fake. *What the fuck have I gotten myself into?*

The smile that spreads across her face is almost sinister. "Four months. And you leave tomorrow morning."

My shoulders drop. *Tomorrow?* I text my best friend, Jessica, on my way out of Felicia's office.

> Can you come over after work? I need help

> Of course! Help with what?

> Packing. I'm going on an extended business trip and I'm leaving tomorrow

I stand over my open suitcase, staring into the mostly empty cavity realizing I have no idea what I'm supposed to pack for a cross-country tour with a rock band, for four months.

"So, you're going to be on an actual tour bus? The entire time?" My best friend, Jessica, giggles from my bed where she's lounging and scrolling her phone.

"Yeah. For four months," I tell her, glancing over at her. She's not looking at her phone anymore, but instead, she's looking at me, smiling.

"What?" I say.

She shakes her head, then goes back to contemplating whatever is on the screen of her phone.

A shuffle of Gnasher's entire music catalog plays from the speaker of my phone. Their most successful song, *A Way* is playing and I can hear Jessica muttering along with the lyrics. It's the song they won a Grammy for in February of 1996. Almost immediately after, they kind of dropped off the face of the planet. I had recently been born, but it's talked about in the music scene a lot. They were on top of the world, and then they stopped making music. Clifford was said to be the cause, which no one has ever confirmed nor denied. It's always been a mystery why they broke up. A mystery Felicia expects me to solve.

"Do you want to know the weirdest part about this entire thing?"

She sits up straighter as a non-verbal, Hell yes, I do!

"When Felicia assigned me the story, she told me Clifford Lee and Jazzy P have separate managers. And apparently," I grab two handfuls of panties and throw them into my open suitcase, "Felicia only spoke with Jazzy's. I don't even think Clifford's manager knows I'll be there. So that will be fun," I say this last part through gritted teeth, already anxious about living on a bus with someone who will possibly be unhappy about my presence.

"Is the manager hot?"

The laugh that tumbles out of me is filled with more disbelief than humor. "I don't know. But I'm done with men and dating for now, so it doesn't really matter."

I hadn't told Jessica immediately after Jake and I broke off whatever it was we were. I didn't love Jake, I'm not even sure I enjoyed his company outside of the bedroom. I've found myself in a constantly repeating cycle of falling into bed with men who treat me like shit, and if I'm being honest, I feel a little bit embarrassed. I finally told her today over text before she came over.

"Well, I think that's a great idea. That's why I bought you a break-up gift."

I turn toward her. "A breakup gift?"

She nods and pulls an oblong satin bag from behind her back.

I eye it, but don't reach to grab it. "What's that?"

"Prue, honey, the best way to start your day is with an orgasm. The best way to end your day is ... you guessed it ... with an orgasm," she uses the package I now assume is a vibrator as a prop, waving it from side to side as she speaks. "So if you don't have a vibrator, you best get yourself one, baby girl, and start living the best days of your life."

"It would appear I don't need to get myself one if what you're holding is what I think it is," I say, immediately regretting my words.

Her mischievous grin is contagious, and I start laughing. She holds it out to me to take, "I got you this. To celebrate."

"Please tell me it's not used," I eye the black satin suspiciously, still not reaching to take it from her hands.

She shakes it impatiently waiting for me to grab it, "No. It's not used, you sicko. It's brand-spankin' new, and it's for youuu," she sings.

I laugh as I reach out and grasp the ... object ... hesitantly. I hold it, afraid to open the drawstring holding it closed at the top, and eye her quizzically.

"Prue, shut up and take it. Also, let's delete Jake's number from your phone." She knows my patterns and has correctly guessed that his number is still stored in my contacts. For what, I don't know. I'm not planning to call him again. Not after our last conversation.

I hand her my phone, knowing she already knows my passcode. "You do it, I'm busy," I laugh and walk over to my closet to start pulling clothes out.

"Do you want to talk about what happened with him?" Jessica loves gossip and details, but I know her question is coming from the place of concern she holds for me, and has over the last twenty years of our friendship.

"Not really," I say, but continue anyway as I fold a pair of black jeans while I talk. "It was the article." I shrug, trying to convey indifference.

I leave out the part where he called me a bitch because if I tell Jessica that, she'll probably fly off the bed and start breathing fire. I'd rather not right now. I'm too stressed about my current situation, and I don't want to think about Jake anymore.

She eyes me with sympathy, knowing I don't want to talk about that either. "Okay, well moving on. What did your mom say?"

My back is to Jessica as I pull more clothes out of my drawer, and her words hit me like a bucket of ice. I freeze, clutching multiple bathing suits I can't imagine I'd need on a tour bus, but you can't be too prepared. Her eyes burn lasers through the layer of ice formed around my body, and I wince from the imaginary pain.

Turning, I lower my eyes and walk to my suitcase, dropping my mismatched clothing inside. Without looking to her, I answer in an almost inaudible whisper, "I didn't tell her yet."

The following silence causes me to cringe. I clench my teeth and brace myself as I turn to face my best friend and her narrowed gaze.

"You need to," is all she says. Jessica and I have been friends since elementary school, and therefore she knows my mom well. She was there with me through the ups and downs in my life. When my mom got married to my stepdad Mark in fourth grade, the awkward moments in middle school, when I got my first period freshman year, my first heartbreak, and the countless that followed, including when my stepdad passed away of cancer about six years ago. Jessica was there to let me cry on her shoulder anytime I needed it.

"Yeah," I reply, knowing she's right, but mentally still trying to ninja my way out of it.

"Right now." I twist to her holding my phone out toward me.

We turn into statues, facing off; her with my phone outstretched in my direction, and me keeping my arms locked by my side. When the loud ring of my phone blares out into the silence between us, we both jump. Jessica starts laughing and I peek down. Even upside-down I can read the name on the screen … it's my mom.

"Her ears were burning," Jessica says with a sly smile, and I roll my eyes as I snatch the phone from her quickly. Pushing away my hesitation, I take it as a sign from the universe and answer.

"Hello?"

"Hi, hun," my mom's sweet voice sings down the line. The genuine happiness in her voice makes the contents of my stomach curdle. I love my mom so much. We're very close. Before she met Mark, it was only the two of us, and then again for the past few years since he's been gone.

"Hey, Mom," I say, turning over in my head how to even approach this conversation with her.

"I haven't heard from you in a couple of days. How are you, baby? Can we get dinner soon? I miss you." I saw her three days ago. We met for lunch.

"I miss you, too," I say running my free hand down my jeans in an attempt to wipe away the nervous sweat clamming up my palm, and not answering her question.

"So, dinner?" She's not letting me off the hook, but I'm grateful for the segue.

"Actually, I got an assignment at work and I'll be going on an extended business trip." All my words fall out of me in a rush. I'm nervous to leave her for so long. Mark has been gone for six years, but the ever-present obligation to keep her company looms over me. Obligation makes it sound like I don't enjoy spending time with her, which is not true. I worry about her, though.

"Extended? How long?"

"Uh, well," I stammer, unsure how to tell her this, "three-ish months." I don't know why I lied.

I am met with dead silence, so quiet I pull my phone away from my ear to make sure we're still connected.

"Three ... ish?"

"Yeah, well, closer to four?" I don't know why it comes out as a question. I'm remarkably unsure today.

"Four?" she yells. "What kind of business trip is this?"

"I'm going on tour with a band I'm writing about." She won't know who Gnasher is, so I keep it simple for her.

My mom is not where I got my love of music from. She listens to music, sure, but it's more passive. She's always supported my love of it, even when it made her nervous to allow her teenage daughter to go to concerts on an almost weekly basis. She came to a few with me, but I could tell she didn't enjoy standing in the middle of a packed crowd with speakers blaring so loudly, you could feel it. Where my mom is all pink and frills, I'm black and chains. I've never related to my mom in a lot of ways, but that's almost what makes us fit so well. I'm the yin to her yang. Most importantly, she's always supported my love of music and my career choice.

"Is that ... normal?" Her question comes out with genuine curiosity.

"It's not, which is what makes this a big story. Career chang-ing. I know it seems like a long time, but it's not a big deal. I travel all the time." I'm trying to ease the underlying worry I can hear in her voice.

"Not for four months, you don't."

"I don't want you to worry," I start.

She breathes out. "Honey, I will worry about you until the day I die. But you're 28, you have a career I'm proud of you for, and I know you can take care of yourself." *Supportive as always.* My nerves about telling her mock me. "Promise you will keep in touch with me? You tend to … check out."

She's not wrong. I get caught up or fall into an anxiety which causes me to close myself off. Sometimes talking to people doesn't come naturally to me, even though it's what I do for a living. It's talking about my own thoughts and feelings that trips me up.

"I'm sorry, Mom. I promise I'll keep in touch with you," and I will. Even if I have to set myself alarms to check in with her frequently, I'll do it because I don't want her to be lonely and worrying about me. "I might not call daily, but I'll at least send you texts to let you know I'm not lying dead by the side of the road."

"Not funny." Her tone is clipped, but I know she's fighting a smile at my dark sense of humor. "Can we have dinner before you leave? When do you leave?"

"Uh, well I leave tomorrow," I say.

"Prudence Marie," she screeches. Damn, she brought out the middle name and all.

Jessica is full-on laughing now, clutching a pillow to her face to muffle the sound. I glare at her and mouth, "Shut up."

"Prue," my mom's voice comes back over the phone, slightly more calm.

"Hmm?"

"Just … don't do anything stupid."

I'm not entirely sure what that is supposed to mean, but I affirm to her I won't. We say our goodbyes and hang up.

"That went well," Jessica says, holding back another fit of giggles.

I roll my eyes and pick up the black, satin bag Jessica so lovingly gifted to me.

"As well as it could have," I blow out a breath and toss the breakup gift into my suitcase as I continue to pile in clothing on top of it.

CHAPTER 2
Macallister

I hate managing rock stars, I think as I stand over Cliff's dilapidated cardboard box held together by duct tape and a prayer. I've been going through his fan mail since he's neglected it for the last almost thirty years, and it's all pretty much been the same shit: a lot of disgruntled fans expressing their grief over him disappearing and not making music anymore. Some even have stories about how his music has helped them in different situations.

The last letter I read, however, is different. I hold the single piece of paper in my hands and the design on the stationery hits me with a wave of nostalgia: blue and purple butterflies. Like something from a stationery store that traveled by Time Machine from the late 90s, it appears aged in aesthetic but otherwise is in pristine condition. The design is a stark contrast to the words of the letter, the bombshell that has my body filling with stress and anxiety.

The pen markings aren't even faded because this piece of paper never saw the light of day since it was folded up, placed into the matching envelope, and sent to Clifford Lee in 1996. I can clearly read every single word, and I want to vomit as I read them for the fifth time. My hands are clammy and I'm concerned I'm going to smear the ink if I grip the letter much longer. I fold it up, following the original creases, place it back in the envelope, and place the envelope into the pocket of my slacks.

What am I supposed to do with this information? I try asking the ceiling for some help when my phone buzzes in my other pocket to the same rhythm as my pounding heart.

I grab it and answer the call without checking the screen. "This is Macallister."

"Yeah, I fucking know. I called you, dumb ass."

Cute. "What's up, Cliff?"

"You know what? Never mind, Mac." Cliff is only one of two people I allow to call me Mac, mostly because it isn't worth the fight with the person signing my paychecks.

"Cliff," there's a hint of warning in my voice, "What do you need?" I ask trying to lighten my tone.

He puffs out a breath of frustration. We've been working on his anger issues. "What are you doing?" he asks.

Oh, just going through the years of fan mail you neglected to open. Guess what? I found something quite interesting you might want to know about …

"Working."

"You hurt my feelings when you're so short with me," Cliff mockingly whines into the phone and I can tell he's joking around, trying to get a rise out of me.

We've somewhat mastered this back and forth since I started working for him over a year ago. He became my client after the many managers he reached out to before me declined him, afraid to touch him with a ten-foot pole. I reluctantly agreed, concluding I could handle a grumpy rockstar with anger issues if it meant boosting my career. Gnasher was one of the biggest bands when they broke up, and this reunion has been setting the music industry abuzz. I can handle Cliff's baggage. At least, I thought I could handle Cliff's baggage, until today.

"Don't care. The fuck do you need, Cliff?" I stare at the box, filled with an enormous pile of envelopes still unopened wondering if I should anticipate any more secrets hidden within them. I dread the thought of continuing to go through them, but I cannot go into this tour blind. I need to know what I'm getting set up for.

"You're such an asshole, Mac." He pauses to chuckle. "That's why I like you." I've found Cliff enjoys bluntness, and he responds well to it. "I just got off the phone with Jazz, and I guess Darrell set something up. I'm not even sure I get it, but apparently there's going to be press."

I pinch the bridge of my nose. Why did I opt to work with a retired rockstar who has been out of the business for nearly thirty years?

"Yeah, Cliff, that's how these things work. There's going to be press. I know there was press back in the Stone Age, but I understand the memories might be a little fuzzy for you."

"Stone Age," he mutters under his breath, "Okay, well this seemed out of the ordinary to me. But I'll go with whatever you say, boss." He's always refused to talk to any press, so I assume he's nervous about the influx. But I'll be there, and my job is to help him navigate his return to the scene. He was known for being a loose cannon, which is why I have no intention of discussing the letter with him. At least not right now.

My skin itches with anxiety. "Great. Anything else?" We leave tomorrow and I have a to-do list with much more on it than I can physically accomplish before then. I don't have time for this.

"No."

"Excellent. I will see you bright and early tomorrow."

"Mac …" Cliff's tone shifts and I wait while he hesitates on his next words. "It's been a while." His voice trails off, and I know which side of Cliff I'm talking to now. This Cliff is a scared mess. Yes, he's got a reputation for being an abrasive asshole with no filter. He isn't that guy anymore, though. He's been a hermit for the last decade and a half and now he's the center of attention again, which is where his apprehension, and almost fear, of the press comes from.

I know Cliff is in a vulnerable state that is textbook each time it happens, and it has happened more than once since we started working together a year and a half ago. He starts grumpy, gets a little aggressive—but not so aggressive I can't call him out—and then crumbles into a man I pity because it's nowhere near the man he used to be.

"Yeah, but you've got this," I assure him, trying to soften my tone realizing he's starting to slip. Even I know the talent Cliff possesses. While I'm mostly using this as an opportunity to help myself up the ladder, I also have a deep-rooted love for music. Gnasher, and more specifically Cliff, made amazing music. It was a shame for the industry to lose him, and I want to help him make history with this comeback.

"I quit for a reason." His words come out harsh and taste bitter, even over the phone.

"And you agreed to do a reunion tour for a reason," I remind him, recalling a long conversation we had back when the concept of a tour was suggested.

"I mean," he scoffs, "the reason being people wouldn't leave me the hell alone about it." He exaggerates, but he's also not entirely wrong. There was a lot of pressure.

Gnasher was *the* band in the mid-90s. In 1996, you couldn't go anywhere without hearing *A Way* on the radio. After winning a Grammy and immediately dropping off the radar, their music persisted. For a time, it waned, but then a deep-cut from their first album titled *Fuck Me Sober* blew up online with the younger generation about a year and a half ago, spurring teens and young adults to start streaming Gnasher's music incessantly. *Fuck Me Sober* even charted the Billboard Hot 100 for the first time since it was written in the early 90s. The fans, new and old, started demanding a reunion tour. Loudly.

The bass player, Jasper, who is more commonly known by his stage name, Jazzy P, agreed immediately. Cliff took more convincing. At first, he outright told everyone no. In truth, he told everyone to fuck off, but more or less the same. When he hired me, he was mostly expecting about a few months of interest in him that he'd need help navigating, and then it would fade and he'd go back to living the life of a recluse. Obviously, that didn't happen. Instead, the attention intensified and we both ended up in positions we weren't expecting to be in.

When they knew they'd be going on tour, and performing again, they needed to start playing together again. The first band practice was the most awkward thing I've ever experienced, right next to getting dumped at my freshman homecoming dance in front of my judgmental peers. It was awkward because of the tension between Jasper and Cliff, but also because of the obvious absence of Constantine, the original drummer. He tragically passed away in 2003 from an overdose.

When a tour was first proposed, Cliff started trying to back out saying it couldn't work without Constantine. However, Darrell, Jasper's manager and cousin, had a solution and brought in Travis, the twenty-something prodigy drummer. They've spent the last six months as a trio practicing and doing a couple of interviews to gear up for this reunion. They even presented an award together at the Grammys and did an interview in which Cliff said only two words; "No comment," when asked about their split in '96. Helping Cliff manage the publicity isn't hard since he keeps himself locked down, iron-clad these days. It's something drastically different from the loud-mouthed loose cannon he used to be.

I'm not entirely sure what happened. Most speculate Cliff is the one who called it quits, and that is the only thing I do know for sure because he told me. That is the furthest he'll go with me on the subject, though. My main job now is to keep his image clean. Of course, now with the discovery of this fucking letter, I am realizing I have my work cut out for me.

A grunt from his side of the phone pulls me from my thoughts.

"Cliff, you're a musician. You've been reminiscing about the 'good old days' on tour, and I even got the tour bus set up as you requested. It's happening. So chill the fuck out, smoke a J if you need to, and be ready tomorrow. You packed?" I keep my voice somewhat light, but also firm.

I hear a deep sigh and know the answer is "No."

"I'll send someone."

He breathes a long breath, but he doesn't protest. He mutters, "Thanks. Bye, Mac."

I end the call and hold my phone wondering what to do with this damn letter. This tour is life-changing for me, and even if I don't continue to represent Cliff, this will catapult my career to the heights I need to establish a solid name for myself in this business on my own terms. I grab the lid of the box, place it back on top, and push the box underneath my desk with my foot. There's enough to worry about with this tour. There can't be anything bigger than this inside.

My hand moves toward my pocket with the letter, then hesitates. I can't leave this where someone can find it, so I decide to take it with me and stash it somewhere a little more safe. I make my way out of the office and step out into the sun. It's the start of summer, and I'm about to live on a bus with four other men for at least four months. The sacrifices we make …

I sigh and tilt my head toward the sky briefly before the light buzz in my pocket starts up again. My head snaps back down and I thrust my hand into my pocket to wrap around my phone. I'm expecting it to be Cliff calling me back. But the name on my screen makes me freeze: Dad. *Shit.*

It's not that my father and I have a bad relationship. Confessedly, we don't have one at all. He was never around much while I grew up, even when my parents were married for the first thirteen years of my life. He's a music producer. Which is why I considered changing my last name from Davis to Blackwood, my mother's maiden name, early on when I started trying to take my place in the music industry. I did not want to be associated with him because I didn't want our relationship to affect whether I didn't get a job, or worse, if I did. The problem is that her last name is as noticeable as his. Plus, I didn't want to wait in line at the social security office.

The underlying fear of bias still burns low inside me, pushing me to be better.

"Son," my father's voice says in my ear without me uttering a greeting at all.

"Hi, Dad," I respond, my vocal cords tightening slightly at the anxiety of speaking with him. He never calls me, so anytime he does puts me on edge.

He clears his throat. "When do you head out tomorrow?" *The tour. Of course, he's only calling me about the tour.* My muscles relax slightly and I have a little more footing in this conversation now.

"The bus is leaving around seven," I kick my feet across the pavement outside my office, feeling juvenile with the way talking to him always makes me retreat inside myself, to a me that is about fifteen years younger.

He grunts in response.

"Is that ... it? Did you need something?" I mentally kick myself for asking, and the small spike of anxiety rises again.

"Yeah. Just wanted to wish you a good trip."

Weird. "Thanks."

"You think you'll be able to handle it all?" *Welp, there it is.*

"Uh, yeah, I think I can handle it." I'm not sure if he thinks I'm incapable, or if he simply thinks I am still a nineteen-year-old kid asking for money to help me get started.

"Tour is different than interviews and appearances, kid." I have literally been on tour with a band before. My previous clients were a smaller band and they went on multiple tours that lasted about a month or two each. There weren't big, fancy tour buses or crowds ... okay, so this was a little different than what I've done before, but he acts like I am brand new to this business. I think I've grown enough to be here at this point.

Part of me wonders if he feels tied to my success and the thought makes my blood boil when I think it. "Yep," I cannot even conjure anything snarky enough to say back to him, and I don't want to give him the room to respond.

At this, I can envision my dad narrowing his eyes and sitting a little straighter. "Right, well … safe travels. Let me know if you need anything."

Absolutely not. "Thanks, will do." I'm hoping this is enough to get him off the phone.

"Bye, son," I hear him say after I've already lowered the phone to push my finger hard up against the glass at the "end call" button.

I let my hand holding the phone fall to my side. I am exhausted, but I need to pack. I need to also make sure someone packs for Cliff. When I took him as a client, I knew he'd be high maintenance. I didn't realize he would be this difficult, though. I walk to my car still debating how to best share the information I've uncovered that sits in my pocket like a hot coal burning through the fabric.

CHAPTER 3

Prudence

I walk up to the giant bus: sleek black with no windows. *Fun*. I drag my giant suitcase behind me. I packed it so full, I had to sit on the top to zip it shut. I get closer and the door opens. Standing in the doorway waving at me is a shorter man, wearing a faded Gnasher T-shirt and jeans. His wardrobe is not what causes me to cringe, however. His hair is a faded yellow, a bad bleach job, I suspect, and there are dark brown ... spots? Are those leopard spots? I know my face is scrunched up, trying to discern what I'm looking at as my suitcase wobbles behind me and I struggle to pull it.

He makes no movement to help me, and as I get closer to him, I realize that, yes, those are supposed to be leopard spots. I know I need to adjust my face, but I'm finding it hard to iron out the wrinkled expression I can only imagine presents as insulting. Maybe he'll assume my face is scrunched up from the weight of my bag. Did I pack bricks?

"Potato!" he exclaims, pointing to his head.

"Excuse me?" I come to an abrupt stop in front of him.

"I use a potato. I cut it in half, dip it in hair dye, then use it like a stamp. Looks exactly like a leopard, don't you think?"

"Wow, indeed it does. That's so ..." I cannot find the right words right now, " …creative." I say, trying to match his unbeliev-ably chipper tone.

He thrusts his arm out in front of him. "I'm Darrell, Jazzy P's manager. I spoke with your boss, Felicia."

I place my hand in his and give it a shake. "Prudence. You can call me Prue."

"Well, welcome aboard, Miss Prue." He turns to the side and uses both hands to gesture me to the four steps leading inside the bus. "Mi casa es su casa."

I move to walk up the steps, fumbling with my suitcase trying to lift it up the first step. Darrell says nothing and patiently watches me struggle. I turn around and grasp the handle with both hands as I bend my knees and summon all my strength to lift, when a dark cloud moves across the sun. Only, I realize as I see two feet step next to my suitcase, it's not a cloud, but a person.

I stand and am met with a tall man, wearing a dark grey suit, which seems a bit overdressed, especially in the heat of early summer. I'm scanning my eyes up toward his face when he moves past me, jumps up the first stair, and grabs my heavy bag like it weighs nothing. He holds it up and I'm appreciative of his chival-rous gesture until he opens his mouth. "Who are you?" he asks, or rather, snarls.

I stand up straight and tilt my head to meet his eyes: Hazel. I realize I stare a little too long, taking in his dark caramel skin peppered with a five o'clock shadow, and full lips pressed in a line when he clears his throat.

"Hi," I answer a bit more dazedly than I normally speak, and I don't answer his question, being lost in taking him in.

Darrell's hand gestures out to me, outstretched, but shaking mid-air. "Mac, that's Prudence. From *SubVox*." His voice quivers on the last word.

"Macallister," the handsome man corrects without taking his squinted eyes off me. Before anyone else can say anything, he snaps out of his trance and turns his head toward Darrell. "From *SubVox*? The magazine?"

"The very same!" *Am I going to have to hear Darrell's overly excited voice for the next four months?*

"And why is she here," Macallister lifts my suitcase even higher with a grunt, "with a fucking suitcase?" *Okay … ouch.*

"Oh, Mac," Darrell laughs, slapping him on the shoulder and turning his back on both of us and away from this conversation as he hops up the stairs in a hurry so clumsy, I'm worried he might trip.

"It's Macallister," I am almost positive I hear him mutter under his breath again. I make a mental note to not call him Mac. At least not to his face.

He turns back to me. I can hardly recognize the hazel color of his irises anymore because his scowl forces his eyes into narrow, angry slits.

"You must be Cliff's manager," I say, recalling Felicia's warning, and replaying her description of him being uptight. "I'm not here to cause—"

"You wrote that story about Torrence Gillman, didn't you?" My eyes fall, out of natural embarrassment, and I notice his grip on my suitcase, his knuckles starting to whiten from the strain.

I bite the side of my cheek but raise my eyes up to meet his. I've had to deal with strong reactions the last week and I've trained myself to not back down, not show the shame I feel for writing it.

"I did."

"You are not coming on this bus." I'm too shocked at his bluntness to speak.

"Yes, she is, Mac," a new voice from an unfamiliar man standing just above Macallister at the top of the stairs says.

He's wearing a black, wide-brimmed hat. His dark brown hair reaches his cheeks and flares out slightly at the end. He's wearing dark sunglasses so his eyes aren't visible. He's standing with his tattoo-covered arms crossed over a silky black button-up shirt, with the top half unbuttoned.

"Cliff," Macallister scolds him. *So that's Clifford Lee.*

Clifford doesn't recoil from the venomous tone but instead tilts his head before pointing a finger at Macallister. "I told you there was going to be press. You said that's normal. Besides, I'm trying to stay on Jazz's good side, and he told me to come … and I quote … 'Call off your guard dog.' So, down boy."

"I didn't know when you said press you meant a fucking reporter from *SubVox* was living on the bus with us." Macallister completely ignores the fact that he got called a dog, and it makes me want to giggle, but I stay quiet wanting to continue to take in this interesting exchange. The pinprick of habit urges me to find a way to start recording this back and forth.

"I told you it seemed out of the ordinary. And you remember what you said?" he asks but doesn't pause long enough for an answer. "You told me to shut up and smoke a J."

I snort and both their heads swivel to me as if remembering I'm present. Macallister is scowling. I'm unsure of the exact expression taking over Clifford's face since he's wearing dark glasses, so I can only assume he is also scowling based on the thin line his mouth is set in. Great, four months with two grumpy men and an overexcited weirdo with leopard hair. *Lucky me.* I shrug and my lips quirk upward in an awkward but apologetic smile. I hope Jazzy P and whoever their new drummer is can balance these two out.

Macallister gestures his hand out toward me. "And this is why it's a bad idea to have a reporter on the bus with us," he seethes. His voice is hushed, directed only toward Clifford, but the bite is there.

"What's your name?" Clifford asks, and I assume he's blatantly ignoring his manager and speaking to me now.

"My name is Prudence Taylor," I respond, forcing my spine to straighten.

I still can't see his eyes, but by the way his head cocks, I wish I could.

When he doesn't respond and a silence too long for my liking stretches between us, I follow up with, "But you can call me Prue."

"No," is all he says before turning and walking out of sight to the center of the bus. *This will be interesting*, I think to myself, trying to navigate how I'm going to approach someone I can hardly get a read on. Hopefully he doesn't wear the sunglasses all the time.

Macallister is still holding my suitcase and now pinching the bridge of his nose with his other hand.

I watch him before breaking his moment of peace with my false assertiveness. "Anyway, I'm not here to cause any problems. I'm only here to report on the tour and interview the band members along the way."

His eyes pierce me in a way I'm not prepared for even though I know they're stunning already. "That *is* a problem."

I keep my eyes on his. I want to grab my suitcase and run away, from this bus, from this man, but I don't. Mostly because my suitcase is heavy as hell, and I'm happy to let him continue holding it for me. I stand straight and raise one of my eyebrows in a challenge.

"I don't trust you," he says.

"That's nice," I don't know what else to respond with. "Thanks for carrying my bag," I say as I step up the first step next to him.

He grumbles and raises my bag a little higher. "The fuck did you pack in here?"

I laugh as I squeeze past him up the steps instead of answering. When I reach the top, the man sitting in the driver's seat looks up from a magazine at me with a smile. "Welcome aboard."

"Thank you," I say as I stretch out my hand to shake his in greeting. "I'm Prudence."

"Harvey," he says, then looks behind me. "We'll get moving here shortly, Macallister."

Macallister grunts in response, but I'm focused on what I'm looking at as I face toward the length of the vehicle. I am in shock that this is actually a bus. This is more luxurious than my apartment. Each surface and piece of furniture is black, maroon, or grey. There are couches on one side and a long table with a bench seat stretching across the other side. Further back behind the couches, there's a cluster of four plush chairs around a smaller, round table. Behind the table, there's a small kitchenette. There's a blood-red curtain, which I assume the beds are behind. All along both sides are windows with adjustable curtains. Huh, it must only look like there are no windows from the outside. I find myself breathing a sigh of relief knowing I won't be deprived of daylight or fresh air.

Sitting on one couch is Jazzy P. He's aged, but I recognize him from watching their recent interviews. Next to him sits a much younger guy I assume is Travis, the new drummer. Darrell is standing up, facing me and he is holding his hands out in a welcoming gesture.

"Ta-da!" he sings, "isn't it great?" I cannot get on board with the enthusiasm from this guy.

I nod, smile, and turn. Clifford Lee is lounging across from the others, with his feet up on the table and his signature baby blue Fender Jaguar propped in his lap. His sunglasses are still on, but his face is turned in my direction as he lazily strums the strings. I feel his still shielded eyes scrutinizing and spearing me.

"Fellas, this is Prue-Prue." *Oh no, the man with leopard hair did not just give me a nickname.*

I immediately jump to correct him, "It's just Prue."

"Prudence," I hear the raspy voice of Clifford slice my words out of the air.

"Darrell, can I speak with you in private?" Macallister's voice says from behind me.

"No can do. We have to get rolling. I need to speak with Harvey," Darrell scurries away panicked as he makes his way to the front of the bus.

"Hi, Prue," the younger man says, standing and holding his hand out to me to shake. "I'm Travis."

"Jazzy P. But you can call me Jasper." The man next to him says, nodding at me. I take in Jasper's appearance. He's wearing a classic red and white flannel shirt, but the sleeves are ripped off and the front is completely unbuttoned, showing off his entire torso. He's wearing tight black jeans cut off right above the knee to create a stringy edge with fraying threads resting on his hairy thighs. He looks exactly like he did in the 90s, but with a slightly aged face.

I grasp Travis's hand and nod to both of them in greeting.

"You ever been on tour?" Jasper asks me.

I fiddle with my fingers before stopping myself and trying to adjust my posture. "No, I haven't."

"Ah, well you and Travvy here are in good company."

I look over to Travis. He's wearing a backward baseball cap, a white T-shirt, and grey sweatpants. He's blushing but nods.

"First time?" I point at him.

The chuckle coming from him releases some pressure and his body visibly unclenches as he says, "Yeah."

I nod and smile realizing he might be someone I could cling to for support during this unconventional adventure I'm about to embark on. He lifts his hat off his head to turn it forward, but not before I can notice his honey-colored hair ruffled and matted in different directions from the confinement of his hat. The front of the hat has a Cubs logo. I internally cringe before realizing I can't hold it against him.

Jasper must spot my reaction and starts laughing. "Not a Cubs fan? Or not a baseball fan?"

"Either, I guess." My words float out on an awkward laugh. "You excited?" I immediately berate myself internally for asking such a stupid question.

He doesn't miss a beat, though, and throws his hands out. "Who wouldn't be? Been far too long."

There's a grunt from behind me and I remember Clifford is still sitting behind me.

"Ah, cheer up, Cliff. I know you missed this," he peers over my shoulder toward Clifford.

"Missed this. Not you," Cliff mumbles from behind me.

I turn sideways so I can let my head swivel between them both. "Well, this will make a great story." My tone is filled with lightheartedness both Jasper and Travis recognize, as noted by their concurrent chuckles and smiles. Clifford stops playing and uses one hand to lower his glasses and reveal his eyes, not a touch of humor in them, though. I worry I struck a nerve unintentionally while simply trying to break the ice.

His bright blue eyes previously hidden behind the dark glass now narrow at me. I wait for him to say something, in another long silence that makes my skin prickle at the length it stretches. I hold my stance, but inside I'm begging Travis or Jasper to say something. They don't. But another voice does.

"No, it won't."

I jerk my head toward the deep voice I already know belongs to Macallister. He's glaring at me and there's a slight twitch in his jaw muscle. I'm starting to crack underneath the number of dark gazes I keep finding myself in the way of when Travis stands up and reaches out to grasp my bag from Macallister.

"Prue, let me show you to your bunk."

"Don't bother. She's not staying," Macallister's voice booms.

"Yes, I am," I declare right at the moment the bus lurches forward. It threatens to throw me off balance when he reaches out and catches my arm. I frown up at him and his hazel eyes spear me with daggers of ice. His hand wrapped around my elbow is warm though, and when he lets go, the skin he'd touched still burns. I yank myself free from his grasp.

Without breaking eye contact with him, I say, "Thanks, Travis. I'd really appreciate that." Turning my gaze to Clifford, I announce, "Since it's a long drive to Washington, we can get your first interview out of the way."

I'm accustomed to exuding confidence and authority. Not all

musicians and artists are willing to talk. Most are, but some ... well, let's just say I've dealt with reluctance before. Especially with a reporter like me: a person who pulls secrets and confessions from the deepest parts of someone. I enjoy that kind of power, it gives the bones in my legs more strength to stand my ground with.

Jasper claps and rubs his hands together. "Sounds fun."

"That won't fit," Macallister points toward my suitcase right as I turn to start walking.

I turn back to him. "Listen, you might not want me here, but—"

"No, he's right. There isn't room," Travis's softer tone interjects.

I glance between them, still trying to keep my balance on a moving bus. "Uh ..." I'm about to ask what they expect me to do when Darrell returns.

He's obviously caught enough of our current conversation because he says, "We can put it in the storage below."

Travis rolls my bag off to the side and nods. "I'll help you carry it and load it in when we stop."

I nod, seriously regretting every single thing I packed the night before. A small wash of panic consumes me, and I wonder if there will be room to at least keep my essentials with me. The realization I'm the only female on this bus dawns on me, and I am helpless to the internal panic seeping into my thoughts about how I'm going to navigate this new living situation. Too late now.

"Right this way," I turn and Travis is holding open the curtain for me.

"Well, see y'all soon," I sing in a voice coated with artificial sweetener. My outside stays strong, but I can't help from crumbling internally knowing I'm the most hated person on this bus. And that's saying a lot, considering Darrell.

I can't let Macallister and Clifford break me. They're merely grumpy. Macallister especially so. He's a grumpy guy trying to protect his client. A grumpy professional, with very large hands ... My elbow burns again as I step through the curtain remembering his hand wrapped around my arm. I turn to him, and his gorgeous face is frozen in a scowl. The flutter of butterflies in my stomach catches me off guard, and I quickly remind myself I'm here for a job. Besides, I'm pretty sure he hates me, or at least he hates my presence on this bus, and I need to figure out how to combat that before allowing his attractiveness to distract me from what I'm here to do.

CHAPTER 4

Macallister

I stand in shock, watching Prudence and Travis disappear behind the red curtain together. I'm supposed to feel anger and annoyance at her presence due to the problems it could cause, which I do, but for some reason, I also find myself more upset with the idea that she is now out of my line of sight, with him. Her blue eyes were so striking when she looked at me, I didn't want to blink. It felt like staring directly into the sun, but I couldn't pull my eyes away no matter how much it hurt to keep hold of her gaze while I was simultaneously filled with frustration at the situation. How am I going to keep Cliff under control when an actual reporter will be on the bus with us ... at all times?

"Looks like we are rockin' and rollin'!" comes Darrell's annoyingly high and enthusiastic voice from behind me. I want to rip him apart because I know he's the reason she's here, and I'm about to when Jasper's voice pulls my attention from my left.

"If you kept your face in that scowl for long enough, I wonder if it would get stuck." He clicks his tongue in a way that makes my blood boil.

I turn to him and his smile is as wide as the Cheshire Cat's. I can hear Cliff scoff from my right side. I am almost positive I can hear his eyes rolling as well.

"It probably already has, Cuz. I don't think I've seen a smile grace his lips ever," Darrell's voice says from behind me and I cringe. "You ever seen him smile, Cliff?"

Cliff doesn't even acknowledge his question. Darrell chuckles nervously as he walks over and plops next to Jasper, joining the smile gallery. I flit my eyes back and forth between the two, not sure my filter is solid enough right now for me to open my mouth and respond.

"Mac," Cliff calls. I turn toward him with a grunt. I'm still angry at him for defending her presence. I know he doesn't want her here either, so I'm not sure why he did that. He's always been able to stand up to Jasper, or at least it's appeared that way since I started working for him over a year ago. I've seen my share of tense and borderline-explosive arguments between them.

He just stares back at me. Or maybe he fell asleep. I wouldn't know since he has his fucking sunglasses back on. I hold my ground, waiting for him to speak, but we find ourselves in a staring contest. One I don't intend to lose.

That is until I get too impatient to hear what he has to say. *Dammit.* "What?" The word slithers out of my mouth like a venomous snake.

He slides the glasses down his nose slightly. "Loosen up. This might be good."

He has to be fucking kidding me right now. "You're giving me whiplash, Cliff."

"Good thing I have you on health insurance, then." He shakes his head and laughs at his own joke.

I continue to hold him in this worthless staring contest and the air around us grows thick.

"This might be a disaster," I spit.

"I trust you." He pushes the glasses back up the bridge of his nose and leans back into his seat with his hands folded in his lap.

Those words slice through the thickness starting to threaten my windpipe and evaporate it. *Trust.* Why does that word cover my anxiety like a salve? *I trust you*. Why does that phrase heal a burn I'd long forgotten about?

I nod at him, unable to acknowledge the three simple words that have thrown my thought process into a tailspin. Instead, I trudge on. "Don't talk to her unless I'm there."

He gives me a salute which causes Jasper to chuckle.

I turn as Jasper gives his knee a slap. "Never thought I'd see the day. Clifford Lee, completely whipped. Gotta say, always thought it would be some pretty blonde, but I guess Mac is a decent choice."

"Macallister," I say under my breath with malice as he winks at me.

"You can talk to her without me, Jazz," Darrell pipes up, and we all look over at him with equal expressions that scream, "What the fuck?"

He shrugs and smiles awkwardly. Fuck this guy, I think, and roll my eyes back over to Cliff.

He's not smiling, and I want to pull him into a private conversation, but I quickly realize those will be few and far between for the duration of this tour within the confines of this bus. I'm starting to feel slightly claustrophobic at the thought. At that moment, the letter tucked into my suit jacket starts burning through to the flesh covering my chest. I narrow my eyes as if trying to reach into Cliff's head.

After getting nothing, I relent and walk over to sit next to him instead. I've been trying to stay balanced on this moving bus, and my leg muscles burn from the strain.

I pull out my phone and start searching. When I find what I'm looking for, I hand over the device with the article shining on the screen. He takes it wordlessly and trails his finger up each time he needs to scroll further through the words.

After a few minutes, he hands it back to me. He bobs his head, then opens his mouth to speak. His eyes glance to the side where Jasper and Darrell sit, and he closes his mouth again. They start talking at a reduced volume to each other in what comes across as a surface-level conversation to keep up the ruse they are not trying to eavesdrop. I know for certain Darrell is trying to keep an ear on our conversation because he never speaks quietly.

Cliff doesn't turn to me but directs his words at me. "I have nothing to hide." *You have no idea,* I think to myself.

I turn my body toward him. "We need to be careful." Cliff turns back to face me, most likely misunderstanding the unspoken words packed into my warning. He thinks I'm only telling him to keep his anger in check. I realize I am leaning more toward keeping this letter a secret from him. This secret could ruin him, and he has no idea. At least, I don't think he does. What he doesn't know, he won't have to hide.

He huffs and falls into the seat further. "Why did I agree to this?" His question is directed at himself, so I don't answer out loud, but instead answer to myself, *because I encouraged you to.* I mentally berate myself for not having foresight on something I could never have seen coming.

When Cliff hired me to help with the increased attention on him after *Fuck Me Sober* went viral, he fought back against the idea of a tour. He said the interest wouldn't last. But instead of dissipating, the attention increased. It increased to the point that Jasper and Cliff were forced back into situations together, and talk of a reunion tour only escalated. I pushed him to agree, thinking I could handle a grumpy rockstar as I helped him reintegrate back into the music industry and spotlight. Never did I imagine I'd be dealing with life-altering information now sitting in my suit jacket like a rock, and a feisty reporter who somehow captivated me and pissed me off at the same time.

I blow out a puff of air, trying to release the tension building inside my chest at the racing thoughts in my head. Just then, Travis swings the curtain open. When he sees or rather feels, the awkwardness filling in the space, he sits in one of the chairs behind the couch with his back facing us. He's silent for a full minute before he turns around, his expression determined.

"Be nice to her," he says with more conviction in his voice than I've ever heard from him since meeting him eight months ago.

No one responds, and my eyebrows knit together. *What the hell were they doing back there?* is my first thought. An image pops into my head of hands tangled in her hair, heavy breathing ... I cut it off.

What the fuck was that?

Cliff chuckles. "Got a crush, drummer boy?" I stiffen even though his words were directed at Travis, not me.

Travis gapes back at Cliff, wide-eyed. "No," he says weakly.

"You don't?" The considerable difference in her voice verbalizing my thoughts makes my eardrum ring and my heart rate pick up speed.

She's standing in the opening of the curtain, popping her hip and smiling. Travis turns his head and looks back at her. The back of his head shakes left and right. I assume he's smiling back at her when his ears pull back slightly. He's maybe even laughing at her obviously flirtatious joke.

I don't like that.

Why don't I like that?

"That's okay, I'm not available, anyway," she says with a flirty, breathy tone akin to the actresses in the 1960s who called their love interest "daddy."

Not available? Again, why would I care if she's available or not? The shred of information about her personal life still grabs my attention.

When she walks past Travis, she places a hand on his shoulder in a comforting gesture and my hand involuntarily clenches into a fist. I'm shocked at how gracefully she walks the aisle of a moving bus. She's beautiful, but she's dangerous, like a succubus and I grit my teeth, waiting for her next move.

She sits at the table placing a notebook and her cell phone, which I assume she uses to record interviews, in front of her. The tension in my jaw loosens slightly as I admire her audacity. She could have sat next to Jasper, or shit, she could have sat in one of the chairs at the back not next to anyone. And yet, she sat with the two people fighting her presence the most. I move to adjust my position like her proximity makes me instantly uncomfortable. Not uncomfortable, more uneasy.

"Let's chat, shall we?" Her pen is poised at the corner of her mouth covered in bright red lipstick and she's not even looking in my direction, but I can feel her blue eyes regardless. I kick myself for wishing she had them pinned on me. *Pull yourself together.* I know I need to sleep. That's all this is. The lack of sleep I've experienced is what's fabricating intrusive and distracting thoughts from my tired brain.

"I'm hungry," I say, out loud instead of inside my head where I meant to.

Everyone turns to me and she starts chuckling at my random outburst. "Got the fridge and pantry all stocked, my friend," calls Darrell as Jasper raises an eyebrow at me.

"Yeah," I say, slapping my thighs and rising to stand. As I walk and hold my balance, I realize I'm not actually hungry. Not for a snack, anyway. Simply a distraction. I survey the contents of the small kitchenette as I realize I didn't even call Darrell out for calling me 'friend'. Too late now.

"Let's talk about the Grammys in 1996." I watch as her bright red nail taps a green icon on the screen of her phone as she speaks, which I'm assuming means she's started recording. I'm almost too distracted by the fact that the color on her nail perfectly matches the color spread across her lips to truly feel stunned again by her nerve. She is not seriously trying to conduct an interview already?

I pause before speaking, knowing whatever I say will be captured for her to listen back to and incriminate me with. "Let's not." *Shit, that was stupid.*

When she turns toward me, her dark hair shifts with her movement. My gaze lingers on her shoulder where the brown, almost black, tresses splay. She's wearing a white tank top, and the contrast of her hair against her creamy skin holds my gaze longer than it should. She must observe how my attention shifts, because she gathers all her hair up, and flips it into an elastic, pulling it up into a ponytail. My hand resting on my thigh now grips into a fist.

Cliff's voice interrupts. "Best night of my life. Next question."

We both turn to him in surprise and Jasper barks out a humorless laugh.

"Something to add, Jazz?" Cliff's words are filled with ice.

"Nope," Jasper says, popping the P.

Prudence flicks her gaze back and forth between the two, smiling. *Great*, I think. I'm not sure how I'm going to prevent her from capturing moments like this: tense and filled with heavy secrets. Secrets even I don't fully know or understand. Decades-old secrets that kept two friends apart.

"What made it the best night of your life?" She asks sweetly, clearly trying to turn on the charm that probably works on most people, but I know won't work on Cliff.

"I said next question," Cliff responds definitively.

Jasper stands and makes his way over to the table and sits. "No, I'd like to know as well, Cliff."

Jasper and Cliff hold each other in a stare, fueling the intensity with the unspoken challenge to crack first. It's too early into this trip for them to be fighting, and a headache builds between my brows.

Cliff doesn't pull his eyes away from Jasper as he speaks to Prudence. "I said. Next. Question."

Prudence is undeterred as she turns her body toward Jasper. "Jazzy P … Should I call you by your stage name or would you prefer I call you Jasper? Why don't you tell me about your experience at the Grammys in '96."

Her question melts Jasper slightly at the use of his stage name in an official interview and he does crack first by rotating toward her and away from Cliff as he responds. "Whichever you prefer, doll. And to answer your question, it was the best night of my life as well. We performed our single, *A Way*, and it was our best performance to date …"

Prudence is nodding, "I've watched videos of it. It was incredible." Cliff scoffs at her praise.

Jasper ignores him as he keeps his focus on Prudence. "Thank you. Later on, we won the Grammy for best song. I was on the highest high. But following the awards, Cliff decided he didn't want to celebrate with us. I guess he can tell you where he went for the four days we didn't hear from him," he glares at Cliff before continuing. "Shortly after, Gnasher was no more." He turns his attention away from Cliff, who is gritting his teeth so hard, the tension in his jaw is obvious.

"That sounds like a wild ride as an artist," Prudence starts, "Can you tell me—"

"What's the story behind your name?" Cliff's voice cuts her off, and we're all thrown off guard by the sudden topic change, even though this is common for Cliff.

She cocks her head and furrows her brow in confusion, letting her eyes scan Cliff's face. Possibly searching for the hint of a joke, but he remains stoic and waiting for her answer.

I almost miss it, but a brief flicker of bewilderment flashes across her face. She composes herself and jumps back into reporter mode. "I think I'm the one that gets to ask questions here," she says smiling, her red lips making her white teeth another stark contrast.

He nods once and shrugs, unfazed. "Just curious."

She turns toward Jasper, probably knowing she won't get what she wants out of Cliff by asking him directly anymore. "Can you tell me what happened the day Gnasher broke up?"

"Wish I could." Jasper turns toward Clifford and raises a challenging eyebrow.

Cliff doesn't take the bait. "So, were your parents Beatles fans?"

Prudence adjusts her expectations quickly because this doesn't throw her off at all. "What did you do while the rest of the band celebrated, Cliff?" While I am wary of her tactics, I'm starting to realize she's exceptional at her job.

He rips the glasses off his face. "Were you even born when my song won a grammy?" I don't miss the fact he referred to it as his song, and neither does Jasper because I catch the red color rising on his face.

"If it was the best night of your life, why did you decide to quit?" she retaliates, ignoring his rhetorical questions.

"Number one. Best song. I was on top. You know what they say about quitting and being on top." He waves his hand nonchalantly with his chopped-up words.

Jasper sneers, stands, and walks to the back of the bus behind the curtain. Darrell hesitates as he halfway stands, clearly wondering if he should follow him. He does after a few seconds of contemplation by pushing himself all the way to standing and stumbling with the movement of the bus behind the curtain. I completely forgot about Travis until he stands and walks to the back as well without a word, shaking his head in what appears to be disappointment with Cliff's behavior.

"Interesting," Prudence says, pulling my attention back to her.

Cliff takes off his glasses and folds them on the table. "Interesting that I won a Grammy?"

"Interesting that instead of continuing toward possibly winning more, you basically … disappeared. You haven't won a Grammy since. Care to elaborate?" Her pen moves across her notebook, but she keeps her eyes on Cliff.

Cliff taps a finger on the table twice before responding, "No."

She nods. "So what spurred this decision to go back on tour?"

"The chicks," sarcasm oozing through his words and sealing up any tiny crack she may have thought she was chipping away at.

I bring my fist to my mouth and clear my throat, mostly to break the tether holding them in deep focus on each other, and also to cut Cliff off before he continues into his malicious spiral.

He's speeding toward offensive and hurtful, and I do not want Prudence in the path of his disrespect. I'm not exactly sure why I don't want that, and I shake my head, trying to make my thoughts notch into the correct spots. She's distracting me. I settle on the idea that I don't want Prudence to record Cliff's anger. Protecting Cliff is my main focus right now. Or at least, it should be.

I'm lost in my swirling thoughts when I realize now she's staring right at me. I can't look away, so I stare back at her. She opens her mouth to say something and I lean in toward her body, as if I'm too far away to hear her next words. She recoils slightly. *Down boy,* Cliff's previous words echo in my head.

I cut off whatever she was about to say. "I think that's enough for now."

Her blue eyes widen and her brows scrunch together. How can someone appear so mad and so striking at the same time? Jesus Christ, she pisses me off. I clearly didn't get enough sleep last night, and my dick-for-brains is controlling me right now.

Cliff chuckles and makes a shooing motion to Prudence. "Move."

She turns to him, her brows deepening even further. "Excuse me?" I can hear how offended she is in her tone of voice.

"Sorry, excuse me," Cliff's voice is indifferent and unapologetic.

She rolls her eyes and slides out of the booth seat to let him out. He walks past her, and she stands with her arms crossed watching him disappear behind the red curtain. She turns toward me and her glare stabs me. Instead of saying anything since I can't entirely trust myself right now, I choose to glare back at her. The bus makes a somewhat jerky motion, and she loses her balance. Before I realize what I'm doing, I reach out to stabilize her, but she doesn't notice. She places her hand on the table, then straightens back up.

"If you think you're going to be able to ice me out, you're wrong." She refolds her arms across her chest.

Before I can respond, Cliff returns holding his acoustic guitar: a cheap, classical Yamaha with nylon strings he uses for practicing his finger technique. Prudence eyes it like she's considering asking him about it since it's somewhat abnormal for a rock star to have such a low-end instrument. He sits back into his seat, not acknowledging either of us, and props his feet on the table. He starts strumming and humming to himself as if the two of us do not exist. Which is fair, considering we are still in a staring contest pretending he doesn't exist, either.

Keeping her eyes locked on mine, she slithers back into her seat and glances at her device still recording. She stays still, considering something, but tucks the thought away and her face returns to her previous determination.

Over the guitar notes, she pulls out her verbal crowbar once again. "Writing something new, Clifford?"

"You can call me Cliff." He picks the strings without faltering.

"Not unless you call me Prue."

A small smile spreads across his lips and he starts nodding in time with his music. "Touché."

"They were Beatles fans," she says suddenly, her posture raising slightly.

Something in him softens, and his smile spreads upwards toward his cheeks. He pauses his fingers as he raises his gaze up to her. He adjusts his fingers up the neck and starts to play something lighter. He plays a few bars, humming along, and after a few beats, she hums in unison with him.

I'm confused as I don't recognize the song at first, and assume it's a Gnasher song. That is until their humming begins to harmonize tighter, his low and hers perfectly pitched up. He's playing *Dear Prudence*, by The Beatles.

I turn my head between them both, feeling like I fell into an episode of *The Twilight Zone*. They're completely locked into each other as they both sing the words. They both adjust their pitch, their singing locking in like puzzle pieces and her voice perfectly fits into his as if they've been singing together their entire lives.

I've heard Cliff sing before, obviously, but not like this. It's softer. Their voices raise slightly as they continue to harmonize. The curtain shifts open from the corner of my eye. Travis and Jasper walk back out together. Jasper's eyes hold something I can't quite discern, and the slight smile on his face looks like pride.

As they finish the song, Prudence smiles shyly as if just now realizing she sang in front of all of us. She has a nice voice, obviously musically inclined along with her talent for writing. Travis and Jasper drop into the couch across the aisle from us. I must not have noticed him come out, because Darrell is also now sitting in one of the chairs at the back. His anxious smile is off-putting.

"You can really sing, Prue," Travis says, holding his drumsticks.

"Thank you." I glance at her phone, something on the screen blinking and numbers continuously changing indicating she's still recording. The intrusive thought that I want to re-listen to what just happened so I can hear her sing again catches me off guard.

Jasper is holding his bass in his lap now, tuning it. There must be some unspoken cue I missed, because all at the same time, Jasper and Cliff jam and Travis starts drumming his sticks on his thighs. They start off fumbling around, but quickly pick up on each other's cues and begin to play *Fuck Me Sober*. This song I recognize, considering I've heard it non-stop for the last year and a half. More specifically, I've had to listen to the three of them practice it over the last eight months.

When they reach the chorus, Cliff starts singing in his signature rasp.

"I don't care if we're over, you can fuck me sober."

They all start laughing as they each add in improvised lyrics.

"Love her, loathe her, Ooo, fuck me sober."

"Red Rover, Red Rover, fuck me sober."

They continue, but their notes and taps start to falter as they break out into raucous laughing. I've never witnessed them coming together this way. I'm not sure if Jasper and Cliff have since the Grammys. Prudence is simply watching, taking it all in, and smiling.

They start to dwindle into random notes and tapping, nodding along to an indiscernible song.

After a few minutes, Prudence breaks their silence between songs. "Let's just talk music."

Cliff strums and nods, "Now you're talking."

A 'whoop' from Travis and a 'yes, ma'am' from Jasper.

I'm wide-eyed and unsure how to take this in. She's single-handedly taken two men who can't be in the same room without filling it with tension and created harmony between them with the thing everyone else has been trying to use to bring them back together: music. She did it in a different way, though, and I can't help how intrigued I am. I'm not sure how she did it in less than a day of knowing them, but I'm not strong enough to hide the open-mouthed expression of shock on my face.

CHAPTER 5

Prudence

The inertia of the moving bus pushes me forward as it slows to a stop at an intersection. I've been lying in my bed—which is more like a little cubby—for the last forty-five minutes. I tried desperately all night to fall asleep, but couldn't get comfortable enough to find real rest, so I've just been laying here, exhausted.

I'd felt mostly positive about my first interview. While I didn't get anything juicy, I was able to tap into them as a band. Besides, I have time to get them to warm up to me. After the impromptu jam session, we fell into a more organic conversation about music. Honestly, it charged me up and made me feel like I could fall back in love with this job I've been having conflicting feelings for lately. These are the types of conversations that help artists consider me as someone they can confide in to eventually open up; but more importantly, these are conversations that I enjoy having. There's nothing like hearing someone talk about the thing they love most in the world. Deep down, we all love to talk about ourselves and the things we're passionate about. And some of us also enjoy how someone lights up when they get to. It's like basking in the sun.

The euphoria was fleeting, unfortunately. After the conversation I had with Felicia after sending her the recording from yesterday, I've been on edge. She called me when we stopped for dinner last night to tell me she didn't love the direction my first interview went. So along with trying to get comfortable on a bus, I also had the replay of her terse voice telling me I didn't meet her expectations swirling around in my head. She told me I could have kept pushing the way I did in the beginning. She said I 'gave up too easily'. I tried to counter this viewpoint by making her aware of the fact that I have more than just a few hours to get information like I normally do, which could possibly produce even better results. Assuring her I'd get the information she wanted made a wash of shameful slime slide over my skin, even with the unenthusiastic 'we'll see' from Felicia.

I'm pulled from my thoughts by the sound of someone trying to walk the aisle of the bus and stumbling as the bus veers to the side. We must be in town at this point and off the highway with the way the bus keeps stopping and turning.

I'm startled when someone thumps their fist against the ceiling of a bunk. "Wake up, baby boy."

That must be Jasper getting Travis up. Travis, who's been snoring this entire time. At least one of us can get some shut-eye. I'm not sure which space pod Macallister is in until someone slinks down from above me. I peek out the tiny sliver my curtain is open and see a suit-clad leg fall in front of it. I roll my eyes because of course he's already dressed in a suit, and of course, his bed is right above mine.

I chose a bottom bunk because I knew if I had to pee in the middle of the night, I would have a ping-pong match inside my head about going or not so as to not wake up the person under me. Better to be ground level. Surprisingly, no one put up a fight when I explained my reasoning. I'm still peering out the tiny sliver as two legs stand in front of me.

I pull my curtain completely open. "Mornin'," I drawl in a fake Southern accent. I look up at his responding scowl. He hates my fucking guts, and for some reason, that fact fills me with satisfaction. I smile and hope it fills him with more indignation. He raises a brow at me, a small smile creeping up his face as I watch his eyes roam over mine. I'm suddenly aware that the last time I looked in a mirror was last night before retiring to a restful night of tossing and turning. I can't even imagine what my face looks like right now.

He walks away and once he's gone, I swing my legs over the side of my bed to get out. Walking up toward the small closet where I haphazardly stored a few of my belongings from my suitcase now sitting in storage at the bottom of the bus, I realize I completely forgot my makeup bag in my rush to grab what I needed. I slam my fist against my thigh.

"You good?" I hear from behind me.

I turn my head over my shoulder at Jasper. My eyes widen, but he seems undisturbed by my appearance. I probably look fine and am overthinking it. I nod and slither my way around the corner to the thankfully open bathroom door. I shut it and squint my eyes in the mirror already covered in tiny flecks of toothpaste. I scrunch my nose, now inspecting the cleanliness of the bathroom more than my own reflection, and making a mental note to grab some basic cleaning supplies when we stop for the day.

In college, I lived with guys, I'm used to it. For two years, I lived in a tiny house with two guy friends and my boyfriend at the time. I swear, men go out of their way to make things messy. I grab a couple of squares of toilet paper and wipe the mirror. It doesn't work very well, so I give up and take in my reflection.

My hair is sticking up in the front, my eyes are still rimmed with yesterday's eyeliner, spread out and smeared around my entire eye, and I'm pretty sure there's a small little patch of dried drool on my chin. So I guess I did fall asleep at one point. I let out a breath of exasperation and clean myself up as much as I can. Luckily, I didn't forget my brush or my other toiletries.

When I'm done washing my face and brushing my hair into a slicked-back ponytail, I push the door open and walk out into the main living area where everyone else sits in varying stages of haphazardness. Macallister appears clean and his suit freshly pressed, as if he woke up in a five-star hotel as opposed to a sardine can the way I feel I did. The rest of the gang looks pretty on par for what living on a bus provides … not much. I can't help but let Macallister's pristine appearance make me self-conscious.

I shake it off and continue. I make a move to sit on the couch but since Macallister is sitting there, I reconsider. Another wave of embarrassment washes over me, making me feel out of place. Precisely as I'm about to resign myself to going back to my personal cubby, the wave of a hand catches my attention. To my left, Travis sits in one of the chairs. It's a recliner-type chair and he's patting his hand against the empty chair next to him. I smile at him gratefully and sit.

With a big sigh, I close my eyes. Waiting for, I don't know what.

"I'm glad you're here," he whispers. I turn my head toward him and smile.

"Why?"

"These boring, old fogeys?" His hand gestures toward Jasper, Macallister, and Darrell sitting on the couches and at the table.

I let out a small chuckle. "You nervous for tonight?"

"Nah. I mean, I'm excited. I've drummed before. But this type of show, at this scale? Never. And I'm drumming for Cosmic Intervention, too …" his words trail off as he watches the passing scenery out the window.

"You're drumming for the opening band as well?"

His head turns back over toward me, and I recognize the reluctance in his eyes. "Off the record," I clarify. I'm used to this as a reporter. Once people catch themselves opening up, even about something inconsequential, they clam up with hesitation.

He takes in a deep breath, and I regard the trust in his expression. "Yeah. They do most of their drums electronically, but wanted the authentic sound live."

I nod. "I haven't listened to Cosmic Intervention much. I mostly know about them because they're so secretive when it comes to the press."

He nods, acknowledging this is well known about them.

"They're great. I like their sound. It's not like Gnasher, but it is at the same time." His voice ignites at the opportunity to talk about music; his passion for it obvious.

I nod along as he describes Cosmic Intervention's unique sound, cataloging the words he's saying and formulating response questions out of habit. I stop myself and let a silence build between us. It's not awkward, but comfortable, and I'm truly grateful for him. He's someone I can see being an actual friend while on this adventure.

"I'm glad you're here, too," I smile, reciprocating his earlier sentiment.

"Don't let them get to you. They're grumps, but they grow on you," he peers over his shoulder and I watch his eyes land on each of them. When his eyes reach Macallister and Darrell, he winces slightly. "Well, maybe not him."

I'm not sure which "him" he's referring to, and I crane my neck more. Macallister is looking at his phone while Darrell yaps incessantly in his ear. A small vein on the side of Macallister's temple protrudes slightly, and I swear I can see it pulse with his annoyance. The dynamic between him and Darrell makes me chuckle to myself.

Travis's voice cuts into my thoughts. "I read your article."

He doesn't have to clarify for me to know which article he's referring to. I turn toward him. "That was …" I trail off, not knowing how to continue. I straighten up a little and lower my shoulders away from where they were starting to hunch up, giving length to my neck. "That article changed the trajectory of my career. It wasn't easy to write, but nothing I did was considered unethical." Keeping my answers clinical has helped me navigate this topic so far.

He nods, clearly contemplating his response. "In regards to how you found the information or the way you made it public knowledge?"

That's fair. "Torrence knew she was being interviewed by *SubVox* for an article that would eventually get published. When I do a 'Day in the Life' article, the standard practice is to let the artist plan a day's worth of activities for us. It creates a space for organic conversation."

"I think some might think it's unethical you got her drunk."

I nod. I'm not even mad at him for bringing this up. I find myself feeling thankful someone is willing to have an open conversation with me instead of making assumptions or talking behind my back. I appreciate his sincerity and bluntness. "Again, the artist is responsible for planning the day. She got herself drunk. I tried to intervene, which I'm not even supposed to do, by reminding her incessantly we were still on record. I did my due diligence." My words trail off as I internally question myself on the matter. *Did I do my due diligence? Not for the magazine, but for my moral code …*

His voice, again, breaks me out of my inner questioning. "Do you have to write everything they say? The article didn't depict eight hours of conversation, it mostly only depicted the last two. Or so it seemed."

I sigh. "I do have to submit the recording of our conversation and my notes. From there, I'm told what to focus on and what story to tell."

His eyes widen. I'm not usually so open about the practices at *SubVox*, mostly because it fills me with a sense of shame I haven't been able to deconstruct myself; but he's made me feel safe to share with him, and I find a wave of relief having someone here to share with. "Well," he slaps his palms to his thighs before rising up, "If nothing else, it's become a cautionary tale. Artists now know to tread carefully. For the record … er," he chuckles nervously and kneads the back of his neck, "Not for the record, but just one friend sharing an opinion with another, I can tell you're a skilled writer. It's a shame you don't have much control over what you write because you're talented." I don't miss that he referred to me as his friend.

I smile and nod at him gratefully. "Thanks," I say, and mean it.

"I've got to take a piss," he says pointing his thumb behind his back toward the bathroom now unoccupied since Cliff walked out moments ago. His crass words catch me off guard and I bark out a laugh, unable to say anything else. I'm once again reminded of my current position: On a bus with a bunch of men … but more like boys.

I glance out the window when a grunt from the other side of me pulls my attention. I turn and Macallister is standing next to me, looking at me, his hazel eyes intensified by the surrounding whites and his strong jaw still pulsing in what appears as anger. I shift my position in the seat to give him my full attention.

"Interviews need to be scheduled, moving forward." His words sound sharp and authoritative.

I squint my eyes at him and tilt my head slightly. "I'd prefer to call them conversations. And the beauty of being on this bus is—"

"I'm still not entirely sure how you got on this bus, but I realize the advantage you have. And I'm telling you I don't care what your expectation is, but I will make the rules."

"I walked."

"I … uh, excuse me?" He shakes his head, startled.

"You said you weren't sure how I got on this bus. Which is interesting since you literally watched me do it, but I'm happy to refresh your memory. I, along with my exceptionally large suitcase—I know you remember that—walked onto this bus, and then," I throw my hands out to the side and hit him with the jazz hands, "ta-daaaaa! Here I am."

He gawks at me, confusion nestled deep into the creases of his frown. "Smart ass."

A smile creeps up my face. "You think I'm smart?" My tone is teasing, almost antagonizing.

His eyes narrow. "Why are you here?"

His words strike me in my chest and spread like venom in my veins. I'm not sure if it's how strikingly handsome he is, or the abrasive way he speaks to me that makes me nervous, but I am out of my element when trying to converse with him. I'm about to pull myself from the buzzing adrenaline holding my mouth closed to tell him to lay off when I hear a laugh coming up from behind him.

I barely see Darrell, since he stands what I believe to be almost a foot shorter than Macallister, but he peers around his shoulder as he pats Macallister on the back, making him jump slightly from the unexpected contact. "She was summoned by the rock and roll gods to be our poet … our storyteller." I cover my mouth to giggle. I'm not sure I'd consider myself a poet, but I'll take it.

Macallister turns toward Darrell with another horrified expression. I'm ready to watch Macallister crucify him for laying a hand on him. Before he can get any words out, Jasper walks up and removes Darrell's hand, saving his cousin and manager from the wrath of Macallister.

Macallister decides to ignore Darrell and narrows his gaze at Jasper. "You know it's unprofessional to hire a family member, right?" The way he spits this at Jasper makes me wince, afraid of how Jasper will react.

Jasper simply smiles at him, but the upwards turn of his mouth appears more malicious than good natured. "Cute, coming from you …"

I wish I knew Jasper's meaning behind his words, because the flare in Macallister's eyes lets me know he struck a nerve. "First of all …" he clenches his fists, then release them before he finishes, "You know what, never mind."

He turns to a still-oblivious Darrell. "It's your fault she's here," he manages to say through gritted teeth as he points his finger in Darrell's face.

Darrell's eyes widen and he opens his mouth to say something, but no sound comes out.

Macallister tilts his head to the ceiling, sighs, then mumbles something about fucking idiots to himself. He walks through the curtain, and I can hear him banging around once he does. Right then, the bus pulls to a stop and I can hear the sigh of relief from Harvey as he shifts into park and turns off the ignition. I turn to look out the window. We're parked behind a large building I assume is the venue. Another bus pulls right next to us, blocking my view. I look out the darkly tinted windows, wondering if that's Cosmic Intervention's bus. I don't have to wait long for my answer, though.

The loud sound of air releasing indicating the bus door is opening pulls my attention away, and multiple sets of footsteps ascend the stairs. First to enter my view is a tall, blonde woman. She's wearing a white tank top, black leather shorts, and fishnet tights. She's stunning, and I notice the small but striking details of her face: a beauty mark right above her lip, a small hoop ring looping the septum of her nose, bold black eyeliner in a thin cat-eye, and lips painted red. Two men follow behind her. The first has his hand resting on her lower back, which makes me wonder about the relationship between them. He's got shaggy, dirty blond hair that reminds me of the skater/surfer boys I went to school with in the early 2000s. The other is taller with a clean cut, almost black hair styled perfectly. The two men are so opposite it makes me smirk.

"Hellooo," the woman sings.

Her smile is beaming. Her bright white teeth contrasted with the deep red lipstick are almost blinding. Both men's personalities match their aesthetics as the shaggy one waves and smiles jovially, and the other stands straight with a tight expression on his face I sense is his version of a friendly smile.

"And who is this?" Her eyes land on me right away, her cat-like senses finding the foreign member of this group instantly.

"Hi, I'm Prudence Taylor. I'm with *SubVox*," I stand and hold my hand out to her as she approaches.

Her eyes brighten, and the two men exchange a glance. "Prudence," she takes my outstretched hand into hers and envelops it in the smoothest skin I've ever felt. "Lovely to meet you. I'm Roslyn. Boys, introduce yourselves," she gestures behind her and they both immediately step up at her command.

"Hey. Nathan," the shaggy one gives me a friendly handshake and goofy smile.

"Aleric," the other one says with the hint of an accent I can't place as he gives me a more firm handshake and a frown I think might be his face's factory setting.

"Nice to meet you all. You must be the elusive Cosmic Intervention I've been hearing about," I say.

Roslyn raises a suspicious eyebrow at me as she nods slowly to answer my question.

Cliff's voice cuts in from my side. "She's going on tour with us."

Aleric turns his head sharply to him, "To write an article?" His accent comes through even stronger with more words, and I think it's German.

Cliff smiles knowingly and nods slowly. "That's the plan."

Roslyn's green eyes widen even more. "Well, well," she clasps her hands together. "That is exciting." *Interesting response.* Our eyes meet, and hers are filled with trepidation. I keep my face composed and my eye contact soft to hopefully convey she can trust me.

Cliff is strumming his guitar lazily. "Based on all the varied reactions, I guess it is exciting."

Aleric turns to me, running his eyes up and down me as if sizing me up for a fight. Nathan is looking at Roslyn nervously, as if asking her how he should react. Aleric is a Rottweiler, Nathan is a Golden Retriever, and Roslyn is their handler. I am almost positive I see her lay her right palm parallel to the floor and the men instantly retreat slightly. I cover my mouth and fake a cough to hide my small chuckle at this because I can't wipe away the image of her holding them in place with leashes by her side.

"Soundcheck is in forty," Macallister's voice cuts through the thick air, and for once I'm grateful for the sound of his insolence.

With that, everyone around me begins to gather things and stand to make their way off the bus, no doubt to go find food before the events of the evening begin. He walks over and stands in front of me. "I assume you're attending the show."

"That's part of my job," I smirk.

He nods. "You'll need a VIP pass. I didn't have one prepared for you, so we can go to will-call and get you added to the list."

"I'd actually rather be in the crowd." I prefer experiencing music the way fans do. I've been backstage. It was exciting the first time until I realized the music didn't sound the same. There's something about feeling it and hearing it with people who are there because they love it.

He squints back at me, obvious confusion in his eyes. "Oh … kay." When I walk away, he grabs my bicep. Not hard enough to hurt, but firm enough for me to look down at where his skin meets mine in surprise. He releases me immediately and takes a step back.

He clears his throat and looks like he's about to tell me I'm not allowed to stand in the crowd. "You still need a pass," he says instead.

I gawk up at him, eyes wide. "Oh, obviously," my voice comes out choked and unsure.

Darrell walks by and reaches up to squeeze Macallister's shoulder. He closes his eyes and tenses up as soon as he's touched. If Darrell doesn't recognize Macallister's obvious disdain for him, he's an idiot who cannot be saved.

"You coming?" he asks him, and I realize everyone else exited the bus during the exchange between us. I push past both of them to make my way outside, grateful for the deep breath of fresh air I'm able to take in.

Darrell and Macallister step off the bus, and Macallister mutters a "Come with me," as he stalks past me. I look toward Darrell with an eye roll, but follow after him to get my press pass. Not even Macallister's pomposity can diminish the excitement I always feel when walking into a music venue.

I'm standing in my favorite place to stand during a concert: toward the front, but not right up against the stage, right in the middle, surrounded by the fans. Cosmic Intervention was amazing, and I have to admit, I will be promptly downloading their music as soon as I get back onto the bus to continue listening. Roslyn's stage presence was awe-inspiring. She commanded the crowd. She was graceful, but somehow at the same time, so hardcore. She danced the entire time while singing, and she must be in amazing shape because her voice never wavered. It was also fun getting to behold Travis's talent at drumming. He was enthusiastic and lively, with a smile on his face the entire time. His demeanor matched with the rest of the band so well, I wonder while we all wait for Gnasher to take the stage how he'll fit in with Jasper and Cliff's apathy they used to display while performing.

I've watched plenty of videos of Gnasher's performances from the 90s, including the infamous '96 Grammys performance. Back then, Cliff stood at the front with his guitar at the microphone. He didn't move around much and he didn't talk to the crowd much, either. Jasper jumped around more while he played bass, but kept a serious expression on his face. Their original drummer, Constantine had long hair he'd whip around violently as he smashed on his drum kit. He drummed so hard, it was rumored he would go through at least five pairs of drumsticks each show because they'd break constantly. It's pretty common to find drumstick fragments signed in shaky Sharpie on eBay now for more money than anyone should ever spend on a broken piece of wood, but who am I to judge?

"I can't believe I'm here," a younger, and most likely newer, fan say behind me.

"It's been so long …" an older fan reminisces. I turn toward him and smile. He's wearing a faded Gnasher shirt, no doubt originally from the early days.

"Have you seen them perform before?" I lean over and ask him.

His eyes light up. "Oh yes, back in '94. Right here in this exact venue. It was my first concert. I'll never forget it." His eyes marvel at the stage in a dreamy expression. I hope he gets the experience he's hoping for.

Suddenly, the lights dim and the crowd falls into a deafening quiet. Almost no one is speaking, and the stage is so dark, you can't see anyone walking on. I can barely make out two silhouettes facing one another. It must be Cliff and Jasper, and I wish I knew what they were saying to one another. They break apart, one on each side of the stage.

"Evening," Cliff mumbles into the mic, just like he did at the start of every show before.

Travis clicks his sticks together three times, then the lights begin flashing in time with the first notes of *A Way*. It's pounding and electrifying, and the people directly surrounding me dance and feel the electricity. The combination of drums, guitar, bass, and vocals is so dynamic when it hits my ears, I immediately lose myself in it.

I close my eyes and let it wash over me. For a second, I think I can hear the pumping of blood in my veins, but quickly realize it's my entire body buzzing and syncing up with the music. The kick of the drum becomes my heartbeat, the lyrics permeate my skin instead of only entering my ears, and the rhythms float around me almost changing the chemistry of the air and levitating my body. The music blaring from the giant amp speakers is so vigorous I don't know where to look.

I'm so alive, and I have to open my eyes and observe everyone else in this oddly intimate moment we're all sharing. I let myself gaze at the people around me as I dance along with the crowd. We know nothing about each other, and we don't even know each other, but we're sharing this together. I love the collective experience of concerts and live music. I let my eyes scan around. There are couples holding each other, friends singing to each other, and even people so enthralled, they're staring at the stage silent and slack-jawed. I soak up each observation, a small token to hold onto.

I shift my attention from the crowd and follow their line of sight to the stage. Jasper is jumping around the stage, playing bass with the biggest smile spread across his face, lifting his cheeks. There's a small bit of warmth in my chest at the sight. He banters with Cliff a little who actually plays back. Cliff turns his body away from his mic during a solo and plays facing Jasper. They exchange an expression that's heartwarming for reasons I know I don't even understand. Watching them experience being on stage together again fills my head with the numerous angles I could write, but Felicia will never approve. I still let myself get lost in the fantasy as I watch them mouthing words to each other only they can hear.

Cliff comes back to the microphone to continue singing on the far right side of the stage. I wonder where Macallister is, and if he's enjoying this as well. I chuckle to myself wondering if he's standing just off stage, being annoyed by Darrell. He's probably sitting in one of the dressing rooms behind the stage, sulking. The thought makes me smile. I let my worries of him fall back out of my head as I tilt my head, eyes closed, up toward the ceiling and sway my body and limbs in time with the music.

I push my negative thoughts spiraling around him, Felicia, and anything else away, determined to envelop myself in this moment. Cliff rasps into the microphone the closing lyrics,

And I can't imagine earning ... a way.

The crowd erupts into applause, and the older fan from earlier is smiling. I think there's even a hint of moisture pooling in his eyes as Cliff nods once to Jasper, signaling the start of their next song. I thrash around with the other concert-goers as the beat builds, enjoying the music and moving with it. For the first time since taking this assignment, I'm filled with excitement. I am now realizing I get to do this multiple times a week for the next few months. I can put up with anything for that trade-off.

CHAPTER 6
Macallister

I should be watching Cliff, but I can't. He could be smashing a guitar and calling the crowd something modern-day offensive, but I wouldn't know. I don't even know what song they're playing right now, even though I have the set list memorized. No, instead my eyes are fixed on one spot, afraid to even blink.

Prudence is standing in the middle of a rowdy crowd focused on tossing people around like nothing, and it's making me anxious. I'm waiting for someone to knock her the wrong way so I can leap off this stage and grab her. I have no idea why she insisted on standing in the dead center of a riled-up crowd, possibly exacerbated by liquor and other substances, when she could be back here with us, tucked safely behind the stage. Shit, honestly, she'd even be in a better position standing or sitting in the VIP section, which she has complete access to. But no. Instead, she's packed tightly with strangers.

I was able to find her easily right before Cosmic Intervention's set and have been able to keep her in my view because of the bright white top covered in sequins that fit her as tightly as her skin. When the lights rotate around the room, a beam randomly catches one of the tiny flecks, creating a sparkling glint of light cutting across the venue as if she's the disco ball creating the atmosphere. I continue to follow her movements, two emotions fighting each other inside me for dominance. My natural anxiety is causing me to worry for her well-being, while another unspeakable part of me is drawn to her.

I try to pull my eyes away, repeating to myself I keep finding her simply because everyone on this tour is my responsibility. At least, it feels that way and I'm just trying to keep track of her. Which is what I'd do for anyone else. *Sure ... that's it.* As if on reflex, my eyes find their way back to her: still dancing, still smiling, still safe. I let my eyes drift down the parts of her body that are visible. Not to admire the shape, though I can't deny the draw it has on me. More than that, I'm mostly watching how she maneuvers it along with the music, the moments she turns her head or closes her eyes. I've never experienced a show the way she is, and I get lost trying to study it.

"Killer show!" Darrell slaps me on the back harder than necessary, knocking me forward slightly and forcing my eyes to the ground.

I lose sight of her because of this, and the growl in my chest catches me off guard. *She should be up here with me,* I turn to my unintentional adversary, *and Darrell,* I quickly add to my previous intrusive thought. Because she's a professional on this tour and should be back here with us. *Us,* not just me. I realize I never acknowledged Darrell, not like I care, but I nod in response to him anyway, hoping it's enough to appease him but also hint I'm not in the mood for a full-blown conversation. Not like we could, anyway, considering the enormous amount of sound dominating our hearing. I grimace thinking about how I'm probably actively damaging my eardrums, and make a mental note to get some earplugs.

The crowd yells and applauds violently. I sense Cliff's presence next to me as he nonchalantly takes a drink from a plastic water bottle. He slides up right next to me and I can hear the bottle crinkle. I roll my eyes in frustration as I realize the lights have been dimmed so much, I can't see her clearly anymore.

Cliff lifts the bottle and holds it right next to my ear as he crinkles it more, assuming I'm irritated with the noise more than anything else. I keep my eyes straight ahead and he laughs. *They're done already?*

Cliff leans in close to me so his words can be heard over the applause and demand for an encore. "Yikes. Had a feeling about that." He's looking out to the crowd in Prudence's general direction, then right back to me with a small smile and mischievous arch of his eyebrow.

I narrow my gaze, thinking the closer my eyelids come together, the easier it'll be to activate the night vision superpower I don't possess. "Not sure what you mean, but I'm pretty sure you're being summoned for an encore." I do not need him to start picking up on something that does not exist.

His laugh is flippant and he tilts his head. "No shit, Mac. You've got to make them work for it a little." He motions his hands out, and I realize his lips are parted in a grin so big and genuine it makes me do a double take. I've never seen him this happy. I turn my head back out toward the stage.

Jasper and Travis make their way back out to hysterical screaming and cheering. Cliff stays put for another moment longer. I know he's looking at me, but I keep my neck locked in place, my eyes roaming the darkened crowd ready for the lights to illuminate her again. I feel a small squeeze on my shoulder as Cliff walks out of my periphery.

The crowd's chants grow louder for him as he walks out, and the same light that spotlights him illuminates her face enough for me to confirm she's in the same spot she was before. She's waiting for Cliff to speak, as is the entire crowd. He waits so long, the chanting starts to wane. The sea of people collectively leans in closer, waiting for anything, hoping to hear what he's going to say, especially since it's rare for him to speak at all.

"Thank you," he murmurs. "It's been a while. Honestly thought I'd never do this again," his hands come up to grip the microphone and his voice adjusts out of the gravelly mumble to speak clearly. "The reason we're here is because of one song that never even reached the radio when we first wrote it, but you scoundrels dug it up and pushed it up the charts farther than it ever went back in '95."

The audience knows what they're about to play, and the buzz of anticipation is palpable. My gaze stays fixed on Prudence and anyone standing in her vicinity. I watch as the biggest and most heartfelt smile spreads across her face. It's warm and genuine, and it makes my stomach fill with fire. It's unbarred and she doesn't hold back from letting her lips part with excitement, showing off her teeth and emotional intensity. She starts chanting along with the crowd.

Three words, repeated over and over in unison. "Fuck me sober! Fuck me sober!" I wonder what Cliff's reaction is, but now I can't tear my gaze away from her for other reasons making my face heat, no doubt turning red.

Watching her lips form the words "fuck me" over and over is causing my breathing to grow ragged and I know I should look away. I sit in the discomfort instead. The discomfort turns uncomfortable for other reasons, and I adjust my leg to try and moderate the situation in my pants. My teeth are clenched so tightly, I wait to hear the inevitable crack of my molars. I rub my hand down my face and internally berate myself to get a grip.

As the king of anticipation, Cliff lets the crowd continue to chant. I don't have to look at him to know what the sinister, closed-lip smile spreading across his face looks like right now, but I turn to catch a glimpse of it anyway.

I hear the click of Travis's drumsticks. The lights swirl around, causing Prudence's face to become a rainbow with different colors slashing across her skin and illuminating her in time with the music ringing through the venue, much to everyone's relief. Especially my own. I force my eyes to rest at the top of her head, never traveling further south than her eyes since I clearly cannot be professional when I look anywhere else. I'm trying as hard as I can to keep them away from her mouth which I know is singing along to the lyrics. Lyrics making shapes of her lips too unnaturally alluring, like a siren.

As the song comes to a close with the final bang from Travis and Cliff raising his guitar over his head by the neck, the man next to Prudence trips sideways right into her, spilling an undoubtedly alcoholic liquid all over her. I don't have time to think about how this woman is disrupting my life, and interfering with my professionalism, I instinctively move. I'm off the stage, catapulting myself over the barriers and stomping through the crowd, now beginning to disperse at the farewell waves from Travis, Jasper, and even Cliff as they walk off stage.

I'm stomping and pushing my way through, wondering what the fuck I'm doing. When I reach her, she's ... laughing? She holds the shoulder of the guy and as I get closer. My once-determined steps falter at what looks like two friends laughing at an inside joke. I see red again as he places his hand on her shoulder. I stumble up to them, and I can't control the expression on my face from what I've witnessed. I must seem like a snarling wolf.

"You shouldn't touch her." My voice comes out unsure and not as strong as I intended.

He turns his head frantically between us, clearly trying to determine if I know her or not, and she steps in front of me. She has to crane her neck to reach my eyes this close. "He's fine."

"I didn't mean to." The guy tries to assure me, and I let my eyes meet him, realizing he thinks she's mine. But she isn't, so I should lower the intensity.

I keep my eyes on hers as he scampers away with the rest of the crowd, turning to give her a wave. She waves back at him but doesn't move. She just stands there. Her back is to me, and her hair sways lightly as she stands and observes the dispersing crowd.

I stand there, awkwardly as she turns her head back and looks around. "Do you—" My words weaken and I clear my throat to try and strengthen them again. "Do you want to go?" When she turns, I have my thumb pointing behind me at the stage.

She turns her head over her shoulder with a smile. "No." She doesn't elaborate.

"Did you lose something?" I ask.

She shakes her head. "I like to stay until the floor is clear."

"Why?"

Her eyes glitter. "It's one of my favorite parts."

The people around us push past us to make their way toward the door. She occasionally peeks at me over her shoulder, and I'm so confused by her answer that I can only gape at her. I want to ask what she means, but I don't know how.

She must understand the confusion in my eyes because she answers my unspoken question. "Witnessing this, I mean. I love to watch as they leave. Look how happy everyone is," she turns back, and I find myself eyeing the fans leaving. She's not wrong. Everyone is smiling and laughing. Two male friends walk past me side by side, one clapping the other on his back. I think I over-hear them say, "Finally," to each other and I wonder if they were never able to attend a Gnasher concert before, but always wanted to.

I'm left standing with an uncomfortable, and unknown feeling inside me from regarding what appears to be intimate moments. I've never been one for people-watching, the same way I don't tend to go peeking into people's windows.

I'm about to tap her shoulder and encourage her to follow me backstage to get packed up, but I stop, my hand outstretched. I let it fall back to my side before my fingertips reach her. I am antsy, and she must sense it, too, because she turns back to me again. Her eyebrows pinch together and her smile falls.

"What's wrong?" she asks.

Nothing at all. Every single thing. "What?" My voice sounds harsh, even to my own ears, and I can tell my tone catches her off guard.

Her concern dissipates and I watch as her expression morphs into one of annoyance. *Shit.*

"Macallister, you don't have to stand here with me. I'll be on the bus before we have to depart. Besides," she juts out her hip and places her hand on it, "Shouldn't you be managing Cliff, not me?" With that, she turns away again. *God, I hate when she does that. Why do I hate that?*

My frustration grows. I tilt my head up toward the ceiling and pinch the bridge of my nose. Her boldness is causing my brain to have opposing reactions, but I can't think about it right now. So I stand, defeated, and continue to watch her watch everyone else.

She ignores my presence and observes for the next stretch of minutes, taking in everything her senses can. Her body relaxes slightly as if she is absorbing the positive energy around her. I'm fascinated by the way I can recognize her enthrallment with something so minute. She's almost more enthralled with this than the actual concert. My face refashions into something akin to confusion, and when she turns to take me in, she laughs. No doubt, she's laughing at my expression, but for some reason, I can't control my reflex emotions from bubbling to the top.

"Okay," she says, standing in the middle of a completely empty and well-lit venue. The only sounds are coming from the bartenders clinking empty glasses and cleaning behind the bars on the perimeter of the floor.

I don't move, and neither does she. "Was that for your article?" My voice sounds small and unsure, not because I asked a question but because I'm not even sure of the question I'm asking. I hate the way it sounds, but I have clearly lost my control tonight.

"Was what for the article?" Her eyebrow is raised.

I gesture around me, unable to form words.

She giggles, shrugs, and walks toward the stage. She only makes it a few steps before she flips her head around at me and says, "No. That part was just for me." I stand motionless as I watch her disappear backstage.

I currently have only two thoughts. The first is I'm dreading her doing this every single show, which she'll inevitably do. I don't have time to unpack exactly why I'm dreading it because I'm stuck on the second thought I have. The idea that I've completely lost it if I'm even the slightest bit protective of the person who is going to make my job far more difficult than I originally agreed on if she's this observant. Because I have something I'm actively trying to hide.

CHAPTER 7

Prudence

We've been back on the road for hours now, but I can't bring myself to fall asleep. I've been using the light source from my phone to write my thoughts from tonight's show, but it just died and I can't find my damn charger. I'm patting my bed hoping desperately to find it tucked under my covers somewhere when I realize I left it on the table out in the main area. I sigh loudly, but try not to be too loud considering five other people are sleeping within inches of me.

I consider turning in for the night and finishing my task later. Closing my eyes and trying to relax, I can hear a faint sound that hits my ears suspiciously like music. I pull back the curtain keeping my bed a private space and peek out. I don't see anything or anyone, but I strain my ears further. Yep, that's unarguably music coming from the main area beyond the curtain.

I'm too curious to stay where I'm at, plus I do need my phone charger, so I swing my legs out and get out of my little cubby as quietly as I can. I tip-toe to the curtain separating the beds from the main living area and sneak my body out of a tiny crack I force open, closing it behind me. There are no lights on, but the street lights we pass illuminate the space a tiny bit, enough that I can make out the silhouette of someone sitting at the table, their feet propped up and a guitar in their lap. Cliff.

We stare at each other and as my eyes adjust, I can make out his face more clearly. He plays with no acknowledgment of my presence except he's staring a hole into my head. He's playing an electric guitar, but because it's not plugged in, the notes are quiet, only for him to hear. I nod at him and scan the area for my charger. I find the spot where I was positive I'd abandoned it earlier. It's not there.

I tilt my head around the area, keeping my feet rooted to their spot and holding on as the bus drives forward and I try to get my bearings. My eyes land back on Cliff when his faint strumming stops. He's smiling and holding up my charger with one hand. My lips tilt up one side of my face and I raise an eyebrow at him as I quietly pad over to him, holding onto whatever I can so as to keep my balance as I stumble toward the table.

I reach to grab the tangled cord, but he pulls it back slightly just out of my reach and nods his head to the side of him, inviting me to join him. I oblige, thinking if nothing else, this is an opportunity for another conversation with him. More private this time, and not under the imposing ear of his goddamn manager. Or my boss, for that matter, because my phone is dead and I couldn't record anyway.

He begins to pick the strings lightly again as he speaks. "How did you enjoy the show?"

"It was great. Honestly, if I didn't know there's been almost thirty years since you last performed, I'd be surprised."

He grins, almost shyly, and nods along with his tune. "You expected me to choke up there?"

"No. But there wasn't any hesitation. I felt like I stepped back in time. The way you composed yourself, even the way you spoke, was so reminiscent of your prior performances."

He snorts. "You were a fetus, at best, in '96. Videos don't do it justice. Still, you're surprised I remember how after all this time."

He isn't asking, but I answer regardless. "A little. You're right, though, the last time you were on a stage, I wasn't even born yet."

This earns me a bigger smile. "It's like you're trying to make me feel old."

"You *are* old," I deadpan.

We hold the stare for a few seconds, a few more, then almost on cue, we smile at the same time and break out into stifled laughter, trying to keep quiet so as to not wake the others.

"I read your article," he says after we compose ourselves, keeping his voice low.

"Which one?" I ask mischievously, knowing which article he's referring to, but wanting to play it cool for as long as I can before we get into a conversation I know is coming.

He continues on, sidestepping my unnecessary question, knowing I already know. "As a reader, it's definitely interesting. But as an artist, it's hard not to have empathy for her."

I sigh, exhausted from having this conversation. I know I'm about to be more honest with him than I have with anyone else. Maybe out of exhaustion from constantly avoiding it, or maybe because the tone of his voice and softness of his face gives me the reassurance I need that this is a safe space to share.

"I spent about eight hours with her. The first part of our day was spent doing low-key, mundane things. We went to the zoo for goodness sake and mostly talked about the music and movies we felt most nostalgic about. It was pretty boring, but I was excited to write a story about an artist so unpretentious. She was easy to talk to, and throughout our time together, we began to speak like friends. The last hour and a half of our conversation is when she revealed the affair." He stays completely still and lets me continue the waterfall of information falling out of me.

"She suggested going back to her place for drinks. She bragged about this cocktail she made: a Bee's Knees." Cliff nods along, acknowledging silently he knows the gin-based cocktail. I can almost taste it on my tongue again, the sweetness of honey mixed with the tang of lemon, and the burn of gin as it slid down my throat. "She had built a speakeasy in her house with a secret staircase and everything. A big history buff, as I learned in our conversation earlier. She enjoyed learning how to make prohibition-era cocktails." I'm rambling to prevent the inevitable part of this conversation I don't enjoy recounting. The part I haven't wholly let myself dive into. He lets me.

"She made me one, and I think she made herself an even stronger one. Before taking a sip, I warned her she was still on record." I remember watching her bright red nails as she waved me off at my warning. "We continued to talk, and after a couple of cocktails, she started to tell me about her childhood. I'd stopped taking notes at one point, thinking I had the information I needed to write a story."

"But you were still recording," he confirms. I nod, having flashbacks to multiple points during that night when I questioned what I was doing, why I continued to record.

"I honestly could have stopped the conversation, but it felt like our conversation shifted so quickly. I thought she was just talking about getting into the business. I didn't know her story about her rise to fame came with a confession. The words poured out of her so quickly, I didn't know how to stop her." I remember what it was like listening to her talk about meeting the man who would quickly become her manager. She was nineteen. He was thirty-eight and married. Obviously, a scandalous detail, then she casually dropped that she started sleeping with him as he helped her reach a level of fame beyond what she could have imagined, making the secret even more salacious. "I was also drinking, and my resolve was not as strong. I didn't stop her or the recording because my brain wasn't keeping up." My voice breaks as I allow the sting of guilt to pierce my heart.

"Do you usually drink with the people you interview?" It's a fair question.

I look down at my lap and nod. "The artist is responsible for planning our day. So if the artist wants to drink, we drink. I do usually pace myself. At a certain point, it felt like being with a friend—a friend that needed someone to talk to. So I just ..." I'm suddenly at a loss for words. As if what I'd admitted was all I had left inside me.

I decided afterwards to never drink alcohol while conducting an interview. A decision I hadn't told Felicia since her viewpoint is to "do whatever you can to keep them talking."

Cliff stops his strumming and gently sets his guitar beside him. He turns his body to me, and I let out a soft, sad chuckle full of the threat of tears spilling out when I see genuine concern in his face.

"I'm good at my job. I was just doing what I was supposed to do," I sigh, exasperated from the memory getting pulled further upward. "I have to turn in my recording device for review. I knew the story I wanted to write, and it was not the one *SubVox* published. Trust me when I tell you, I almost lost my job fighting to keep her confession a secret."

"Was it worth it?" Another fair question, but one I'm not ready to answer with full honesty. The memory of writing the story overwhelms me: the inky, black betrayal as I typed the words I wanted to keep to myself. Listening to her story, we formed a friendship; but by writing her story I betrayed that friendship. I wrote the article in the latest hours, allowing the darkness to surround me and plague me for three nights as I fought with myself with each stroke of my keyboard. That memory, that truth, causes discomfort with the question Cliff is asking and causes me to keep an honest answer from passing my lips.

Instead, I force a smile and place my hands out gesturing to my surroundings. "I'm here."

He doesn't smile. He doesn't nod. He simply holds my stare in scrutiny which makes me squirm. His eyes hold unspoken questions, forcing me into self-reflection I thought I could push down. *Was it worth it? No.* But I'm not ready to say that out loud. I wasn't ready to face the reality of losing my job, but now I find myself stuck in a situation I want even less.

Finally, he speaks. "While I can appreciate what you're doing, I can't help but worry for you at the same time." *Okay, that was not what I was expecting him to say.*

I quickly compose myself, letting the slight twinge in my chest from his comment settle. "Well, I appreciate that. But you're not my dad so you really shouldn't worry about it."

He barks out a laugh, no doubt at my subtle reference to his age again. My lips turn up. "It appears you have the backbone necessary for this industry, Prudence." He nods his head in approval along with his words, and for some reason, I feel a sense of pride. I'm unsure if it's my own, or if it's radiating from him. The discomfort dissipates, and I'm left only feeling accepted.

"Thank you," I don't know what else to respond with.

He picks up his guitar again and resumes a song I don't recognize. "You should get some sleep."

I stand, grabbing my charger from his outstretched hand, "Thanks, *Dad*. So should you."

He chuckles, more to himself, "Haven't gotten much of that in years."

I make my way back to my bed and lay awake until sleep eventually finds me along with the smallest sliver of daylight. *The life of a rockstar,* I think as I drift off with the early morning sun. *My life for the better part of the next few months.*

CHAPTER 8

Macallister

Two shows down, and about … a billion more to go. The tour route makes no sense. We made our way all the way up to Seattle because of course the first show had to be in the birthplace of grunge. After, we drove back to Portland. We absolutely could not stop there first on our way to Seattle. I've rolled my eyes so many times already.

I'm sitting in the chair at the back of the shared space while the others sit at the table playing fucking truth or dare. I'm trying to focus on my task list, and my work, but I can't help it when my ear tries to stretch to listen in each time I hear Prudence's voice. As I analyze the route drawn out onto a printed map of the United States, courtesy of Harvey, Darrell's voice cuts through my thoughts.

"Oh, come on! You haven't done one dare yet."

I twist to confirm he's speaking to Prudence. It makes me grit my teeth. I look at my map and tune out the rest of the conversation, wanting desperately to get involved now, but holding myself back. Because it's not professional. Right, and playing truth or fucking dare is.

"Cliff, sit down and play." Jasper is the one who insists on playing these tour bus games almost nightly. Surprisingly, no one objects. I guess there isn't much else to do on a bus all day and night. Cliff grumbles something to himself, no doubt calling Jasper a string of crude names, but he still sits eventually and obliges. I've noticed Cliff only does dares, never truth. Prudence only does truth. The rest of the group does a mixture of the two, and I sit out. Not wanting to touch either choice with a ten-foot pole. My leg bounces nervously, the way it does whenever they start playing.

"Mac," multiple voices call my name called simultaneously. I take an irritated, deep breath and simply raise my hand without turning to wave them off.

"Mac, get over here," a singular voice this time, from Cliff.

I turn my head and multiple pairs of eyes are staring back at me expectantly. "I don't play truth or dare," I mutter out.

"Well it's your lucky day, because we decided we aren't playing truth or dare anymore. So get over here." Jasper says before taking a sip from a can of beer.

Apparently, I do have another eye roll left in me. I fold the map up to place into my pocket and walk over to the table where they all scoot and adjust to make room for me. My legs are slightly too long to fit under the table and the booth is packed with all of us sitting around it, so I sit on the edge and let my legs hang out into the walkway. I can't get comfortable, and no matter how many times I rotate my body, a butt cheek is always hanging off the edge. I sigh and accept the half-on, half-off position.

Darrell rubs his hands together in anticipation. "Alright folks, the game is 'Never Have I Ever'." *A new game, great.* "The rules: Each person puts a hand up. We go around the table and say something we've never done. If you have done the thing they say, you have to put a finger down." I swear I can hear Prudence buzzing with the excitement of gaining more information about the players around the table, especially Cliff and Jasper.

My eyes shoot to her. "Off the record," I sneer. Even though I know she isn't recording, I'm still anxious at the idea that she could hold on to a piece of information to bring up later.

While I doubt anything too damning will come out, I can't be too careful, and my eyes drift to Cliff instinctively with a warning glare. *Don't say anything stupid*, it says, but either he doesn't notice me or is ignoring my non-verbal warning. Probably the latter, the asshole.

She raises an eyebrow and her lips pull into a sly smile as the space fills with the sound of chuckles. She shrugs in response, and the way her eyes roll slightly to the side as she does so gives me goosebumps. *Fuck me.* I drop my eyes out of her gaze, and land directly on the V of her shirt revealing a tantalizing line of cleavage that leads to … fuck, *stop*.

I shake my head, as if trying to shake out the thoughts I can't stop my mind from conjuring, and look over to Darrell who is starting to talk us through the game.

"Hands up." Everyone puts a hand up with five fingers splayed out, ready to reveal embarrassing secrets. "Prue, we'll start with you." I glare at Darrell, unsure why Prudence is starting. She's not sitting at the end of the table, an obvious place to start this game. I repress my irrational anger when her voice begins.

"Never have I ever," she pauses as she thinks, "stolen something from a store."

I don't lower a finger, but I glance over to the two idiots next to me who do. Cliff and Jasper snicker, and I'm caught off guard by the glance I am positive I observe pass between them with smiles. It was small, but it was there. That's new. Travis laughs and I turn to him as he puts a finger down. Well-behaved, country boy Travis. We all shoot a look over at him in surprise.

"Okay, I was going to say that's boring as fuck," Jasper starts, "But now I gotta know what the mama's boy stole."

"Oh! That's the other rule I forgot," Darrell interjects before Travis can respond, "If you want someone to explain themselves, you have to take a drink. It's a drinking game. Only one person can share per round."

We all glare in front of us where no drinks sit with the exception of Jasper, then back at Darrell. He makes a gesture for Travis, Cliff, Jasper, and Prudence to scoot out of the bench. He's sitting next to me, and it would make more sense for him to ask me to scoot out since I'm at the end of the table, but he doesn't even turn my way. *Good*, I think, I'm not moving anyway. Travis groans. He's sitting across from me at the other end of the table with his legs splayed out into the walkway as well, and considering we are about the same height and build, he no doubt is sitting as uncomfortably as I am.

He rises. "I've got it. Beers?" We all nod in response. Everyone but Cliff and Prudence, I note. A glance passes between them. I have to stop myself from doing a double-take. *What the hell was that?* My mind starts to race, and heat rises, turning into jealousy. Jealousy? I'll need to unpack that later because now anxiety is beginning to rise as well. Anxiety over the fact that there's something between them I don't understand, which means they've spoken without me. This bus is tiny, how did she get to him without me knowing? I'm propelled to pry, but stop myself. *So much self-control today.*

Travis comes back hugging six cans with both arms regardless. As he places them on the table, everyone's hands reach out to grab one. Jasper makes a show of chugging his can, crushing it, and popping open the new beer with a loud hiss.

He immediately takes a sip, swallows, and says, "I drank, now spill."

Travis has barely had time to lower all the way into his seat and he's already trying to make the worthless adjustments to fit completely into the booth. "When I was five, I asked my mom for a candy bar in the check-out line getting groceries. She said no. So I grabbed it, put it in my pocket, and thought I'd sneak away and eat it later. Well, I forgot. My mom found a melted wad of chocolate in my pocket when she did the laundry," he smiles fondly. "She made me go back to the store and apologize to the manager and pay for the chocolate. I picked weeds for weeks after to pay for it."

"Weeks? To pay for a candy bar? What did you get paid in, pennies?" Jasper is laughing.

Travis shrugs. "That was my punishment."

"Alright, next." Darrell exclaims, clearly wanting to continue collecting secrets like Pokémon cards.

Jasper, sitting next to Prudence, looks up, contemplating his response. "Never have I ever …" he shakes his head, "I've done a lot. Okay … never have I ever … Oh, shit, I have done that," he thinks and I get antsy. I hate playing these games. "Got it. Never have I ever skied."

No one says anything as we all put a finger down unceremoniously. No one caring for him to extrapolate on his mundane factoid, we sit in bored silence until Cliff speaks up because it's his turn next.

"Wow, Jazz. Very cool," his tone is soaked in sarcasm. "Never have I ever played this fucking game."

This is clearly not going the way Darrell intended based on the disappointed frown on his face and slack in his posture. Travis and Prudence put a finger down, and I immediately wonder about when she's played this game before. I take a peek at her hand where only three fingers remain. When I look up at her, she's staring at me. I turn away quickly, knowing she caught me.

Darrell rolls the disappointment off and sits taller as it's his turn. "Never have I ever had sex with two chicks in the same night."

Our faces distort into various shades of "What the fuck?" But he smiles triumphantly. No one puts a finger down. Prudence, Travis, and Darrell glance around, their eyes landing on Cliff expectantly.

He catches on. "I haven't. I've had sex with the same woman twice in one night. But not two different women in one night." He shrugs.

"Okay, this got weird quickly," I grumble. Prudence giggles and my eyes shoot back to hers. She meets my gaze and … my brain short circuits, because she fucking winks at me. The smile on her face stays and it almost makes my lips form into one, too, mirroring her. But my facial muscles freeze and I'm unable to respond to the unexpected gesture.

Her eyes stay on me confidently. With her hand still in the air in front of her, three fingers up, she says, "Your turn."

I shift in my seat, bumping my thigh into Cliff's. "Never have I ever," I pause, berating myself for not thinking of my quip before my turn was up. "Dined and dashed," I land on.

Darrell lowers a finger while glancing around. *You would, you slimy bastard.* Cliff rolls his eyes and put a finger down. Prudence and Travis immediately twist their neck to face him and I know Prudence wants to ask Cliff to elaborate. I literally couldn't give two shits about Darrell skipping out on a dinner bill, but I also cannot have Prudence asking Cliff to tell his story. Shit, isn't there a rule about only asking one person?

Simultaneously, we yell, "Tell me more." "Elaborate." Our voices mingle and become a jumbled mess of words that don't make sense.

Jasper laughs so hard, Cliff has to slap him on the back to keep him from choking. I think he uses the opportunity to slap a little too hard because Cliff's laugh turns slightly maniacal and Jasper shoots daggers at him as he catches his breath.

I watch in slow motion as Darrell opens his mouth, no doubt about to tell us the riveting tale, but Cliff leans forward, opens his mouth, and cuts him off. "It was a dare. I was on a date."

Prudence smiles and takes a sip of her beer. I watch her throat as she swallows, then hear her voice ask, "And?" Her voice drips in sugar and syrup, too sweet for anyone to resist. I would assume we can't ask follow-up questions, but no one cuts in to stop her. I understand why people spill their secrets to her, and I wonder to myself if the sweetness rests on her lips. What it would taste like. I'm transfixed on her mouth, frozen and in acknowledgment that I, like everyone else I'm starting to notice, am pulled under her spell. The spell that has me unable to stop her, but also unable to imagine what her damn lips would taste like if I could run my tongue across them, and …

Cliff's voice interrupts my unwelcome fantasy. "That's it."

"Really?" She inquires, and I go still because she's going to piss him off, egging him on. But something unexpected happens.

Cliff's lips curve upwards, ever so slightly. "That's it for that part of it. But I did send the money, and a hefty tip, the next day." I watch as they hold each other in a brief moment of knowing eye contact. Jealousy and anxiety bubble up inside me again.

At this, she drops it with a wide smile and exaggerated eye roll. I find myself almost wishing she'd continue the witchcraft of her tongue and pull more from him because I can't help the intrigue with how she's melted someone who never responds to prying questions with grace like he is now. I remember the piece of paper I keep folded up and tucked away, and a chill of fear for the information she could get out of him rackets through my body. My emotions are going through a bout of whiplash today.

We turn to Travis and continue the game into the early hours of the morning. Before we part ways to go to our beds, I notice the sun rising in the desert as we enter Nevada. We'll be in Vegas in a few hours, and a sense of dread overtakes me.

I'm the last left at the table, and I gather up the cans of beer taking note of how many empty cans there are left: Two and a half from Travis, three from Jasper, two from Darrell, and one from me. I didn't care a whole lot about people's revealing stories. Except for Prudence, but I was too chicken-shit to ask her to explain. Thankfully, someone else almost always did. Cliff's can is completely untouched. He didn't even crack it open, and I wonder how I missed that.

I never told him he couldn't drink at all on this tour, so I'm intrigued by his self-control. Even more curious, Prudence's can was opened, but there can't be more than a single sip taken from it. No doubt the sip I watched her take. Does she drink? Have I seen her drink before this? A wave of realization crashes over me when I think back to her article. She drank with Torrence. I've even heard her discuss this situation with Travis. She admitted to drinking, but I remember the way her voice was laced with regret. So maybe she doesn't usually drink while she's working.

Now my mind spirals even more. Did she consider playing a game of Never Have I Ever as work? The thought she does makes the letter pop back up into my mind. This is the exact reason having a reporter on a tour bus is a bad idea. Even worse if someone in the band on tour has something to hide, and even though Cliff doesn't know he does, I do.

As I throw away the cans, hardly a party befitting a bus full of rock stars, I can't help but let my mind wander away from the anxiety and settle more on the small tidbits I learned about Prudence tonight.

She's been skiing. Does she like it? She's never been out of the country. Does she want to travel? She's never cheated on a boyfriend but has been cheated on. That revelation bothered me and apparently bothered the rest of the group, too. When asked to elaborate, she gazed off sadly and shrugged before explaining how she caught her college fling sleeping around. The expression on her face filled me with more anger than the actual story. I also didn't miss how she called it a "fling" instead of a relationship and wonder if that term came from her, or from her ex.

She's pretended to like something to impress someone. This was a piece of information Jasper took a drink to get more information about. Though, he wasn't exactly stingy with the drinking part of the game. Her exact words play back in my head as I make my way to my bed. "I spent an entire year and a half pretending to be a Chicago Cubs fan. My boyfriend at the time loved them and loved to talk about the curse and history and all that shit," I remember the way she used her hands to explain herself as if they'd provide more insight.

"So, I tried my best to be invested. I wanted to make him happy. So I 'loved' the Cubs, too," she used actual air quotes and we hung on her every word. "For Christmas, he got me a jersey. It was the first thing I threw out after he decided my best wasn't good enough for him anymore. So fuck the Cubs," she emphasized the curse here, then turned toward Travis with a wince, obviously remembering the Cubs hat he wears frequently, "Sorry, Travis. But fuck pretending to like things I don't. I don't do that shit anymore. For anyone."

At this, Cliff and Jasper raised their can in a toast and took a sip after Jasper proclaimed a loud "Hear, hear!" I must not have noticed Cliff didn't take a drink. I make a mental note to keep an eye on that, and maybe ask him about it later.

Either way, the genuine care and support pouring from around the table as she told her story was palpable. She's a natural storyteller and when I reach my bed, I can't drift off. Instead, I pull out my phone and search for her articles to read her writing. I go through the entire catalog of her writing with *SubVox*, and as I read the words she once typed, I can hear her voice recounting her time with various artists. She asks questions and leads people through conversations so easily. She does it so expertly that most of the time, I don't think people realize she's doing it. I read an article written a year ago and can hear her voice secretly urging the rapper to go into more detail about the robbery gone wrong that inspired his latest single. Her voice rings in my head, but as I roll to my side and settle, I hear her for real. She's breathing, low and deep. She's sleeping soundly below me, and I can hear her.

I lay awake, listening to her breaths, when they get uneven I wonder what she's dreaming about. When there are longer spaces in between breaths, I hold my own waiting for hers. I lay there, and I listen to her breathing, and I grip my hair out of frustration for the conflicting emotions raging through and starting to control me.

CHAPTER 9
Prudence

Gnasher played their first of two shows scheduled in Vegas. Afterward, we all split up to do different things, and I opted to spend more time with Cosmic Intervention. I'm sitting in the noisy casino of the hotel we're staying in while we are here after the first concert with Roslyn and Aleric. I have a gin and tonic in my hand, and I'm watching the people around me as Roslyn talks, her voice a smoky but smooth salve to my tired brain.

"This is only my second time in Vegas. We've never played a show here, but that was so electric, wasn't it, Aleric?" He grunts in response, but his eyes are glued to her, watching her with intent. "The first time I was in Vegas, I was only fourteen. I stopped here on a family road trip to California. I'm from Kansas. But we were going to Santa Cruz. Have you ever been to Santa Cruz?" She doesn't pause for me to answer, but Aleric nods in response. "Oh, the boardwalk there is so perfect. I adored it when I went, but that was years ago. Actually, I've always wanted to go back. And Monterey isn't too far from there. They have the best aquarium. I love aquariums."

It's obvious she's buzzing from the show, filled with adrenaline, and on a high from performing. I don't blame her. When she performs, she floats around with an ethereal quality while singing and dancing. She transfixes the crowd and sucks them into a trance. Myself included. I've been in the business long enough to confidently say they are going to continue to grow in popularity, especially after this tour.

While sonically their music is considered alternative rock, their aesthetic is all glam rock. While performing, they wear a coordinating color. Tonight's color is purple. It's a bright violet repeated in all their outfits, as well as Roslyn's heavy and glamorous eye makeup. She even brought out a feather boa tonight, twirling it around and draping it around the guys as she passed them. The guys usually wear stylish ensembles coordinating with each other. Roslyn's outfits are always covered in sequins, and skin-tight to allow for all the jumping and leaping across the stage.

I enjoy watching her, and I revel in her company after shows because her energy, while upbeat, is somehow soothing. I've always been drawn to artists who genuinely enjoy performing. Hearing them talk about it pulls me into a tranquil pool I seldom want to leave. I nod and listen to her as I examine the amount of glitter covering her eyelids and wondering to myself if it bothers her. It makes my own eyelids itch just observing it.

Nathan walks over to us, holding a glass bottle of beer he takes a swig of as soon as he reaches the table. Roslyn looks up at him with the same sparkling admiration she looks at Aleric with. "Oh, Nathan. Wasn't tonight so much fun?"

He smiles at her warmly and nods, taking another sip. A bubble of worry rises that I'm intruding on something as I observe the three of them revel in their shared joy. I wonder what the dynamic of their threesome is, and how they started playing together. Their personalities are so different and yet complement each other so well. I store that away to analyze later. As their conversation becomes a light buzz in my ear drowned out by continuous bells and songs coming from the various slot machines, I remember something I wanted to do while we were here on the strip.

I cut off their conversation, "Are we near the Cosmopolitan?" I ask, looking between the three of them.

They all gape at me with a range of curious facial expressions, but Aleric speaks up first. "It's down the strip, across the street. Maybe a three-minute walk at most." His German accent catches me off guard whenever he speaks more than two words because it happens so rarely.

Roslyn's face lights up. "Oh! Macallister said he was going to stop there for a drink after the show." I'm annoyed he stole my spot, but Roslyn claps her hands before asking, "Is that why you want to go?"

I know my face screws up into a horrified expression. "No!" I exclaim. "That's not … I just …" I'm flustered and feel guilty of something I didn't even consider. I clear my throat. "No, it's nothing like that."

I push the dread of running into him away. I won't let him ruin my fun while I'm here.

I stand from my seat and grab my bag. "I think I'm going to go. Anyone else interested?" I ask as I rise from my chair, hoping my invitation negates any weird assumption Roslyn is making.

Nathan's hand rises, but Roslyn slaps it down. "I think we'll stay here." Her smile creeps up one side of her face suspiciously. I narrow my eyes at her a fraction hoping she's not trying to set something up, but brush it off.

I give a little wave and walk toward the front door leading out onto the strip, and Roslyn's eyebrows pinch up in concern as she reaches toward me. "Oh, but Aleric can walk you. You shouldn't go by yourself."

I'm about to protest, but Aleric nods once and stands. He gestures for me to walk in front of him. Is this what having a bodyguard is like?

When we get out onto the sidewalk, he steps beside me on the side near the street.

He points up the street. "We can cross the street at the walkway up ahead."

We start to walk, and even though the bustling around us is loud and vibrant, the silence between us is too much for me. "Great show, tonight," I say, raising my voice an octave.

He nods.

"I have to admit, I had only heard a couple of Cosmic Intervention songs before this tour. I've enjoyed your music."

He nods. "Thanks." It's one word, but he fills it with genuine gratitude somehow.

A man of many words. I nudge him playfully with my elbow. "Don't worry. My article isn't about you."

He stops and turns toward me to say something. He must change his mind, and he starts walking again. His towering height allows him to ignore the many people trying to get his attention and give him flyers, pushing calling cards toward him, and asking him if he'd 'like a picture, big boy'.

The way he was about to say something drops a stone of guilt in my gut. It stings, and as we walk, it rumbles around and stirs up the same sadness I've felt since the Torrence article was published. Regardless of how guarded Aleric is, I know he's even more so around me because of what I wrote. That truth burns. It's like I've lost my superpower, and I'm not sure how to get it back.

We continue to walk in silence, and I will away my sadness by observing the bustling commotion around me. The energy in Vegas is unlike anything I've ever experienced anywhere else. I usually love it, and the sights are enough to lighten my mood. I watch Aleric continue to dodge the pedestrians around him, and he is a magnet for the many solicitors we pass. I giggle at how composed he is. It's almost unnatural. He reminds me a lot of Macallister. He glances over at me.

"You, Roslyn, and Nathan are so different but fit so well. How did you all come together?" I ask, internally berating myself for sounding so much like a reporter again and I wince, expecting him to shut me out again.

"Roslyn and Nathan are my best friends."

I'm surprised by his response and his matter-of-fact tone. I got him to answer me, and getting him to crack, even a little, is exhilarating. "How did the three of you meet?" My words come out less composed, mulling around his abrupt but sincere tone.

He stops tersely and turns to me. I also stop and look up at him to wait excitedly for his answer. "We're here," he says. My face falls. I genuinely wanted to know.

I look away from him and up at the building we stand in front of: The Cosmopolitan. Even though I'm disappointed, I quickly determine I can continue to work on Aleric. I'll be with them on this tour for a while.

"Thanks for walking me." I chirp as I skip through the door he's holding open for me.

His voice makes me stop and turn toward him again. "There's a pizzeria upstairs. It's hidden, but it has the best pizza I've ever had. I don't know if they're open this late, but if they are, get a slice." With that, he turns and walks back toward where we came from.

The Cosmopolitan's opulence strikes me immediately. I've never been here, but Jessica told me to visit a bar inside called The Chandelier and get a specific cocktail. I try to orient myself but the flashing lights and music are distracting. I spot a sign directing me to the bar I'm searching for, and walk that way with the flow of traffic.

The bar's elegance and glamor reminds me of my mom, with its purple toned lighting and hanging jewels. I notice two empty high-backed chairs next to each other, turned in slightly for easy conversation, and a small, round table between them. I make my way to a cocktail waitress and ask her if I can sit there, gesturing to one of the velvet chairs. She nods and places a bar napkin on the table.

"I'll be right back to take your order, hun," she says before turning and sauntering away.

I sit and pick up the menu. I let my eyes glance through the words quickly. There's so much happening around me, I can't focus on reading a menu right now. Instead, I put the menu on the table and let my eyes and ears take in my surroundings. I understand why it's called The Chandelier. The bar reaches up multiple levels and looks like it's right in the middle of a giant, glass chandelier. My gaze lingers on the large crystals shimmering subtly in the dimmed light. Its elegance is contrasted by the loud dream-pop playing over the speakers. It's exactly my vibe and I know why Jessica suggested it. I feel a pang when the thought crosses my mind that I'd love to be sitting here with her.

I'm admiring the glittering crystals, so I don't notice when someone approaches and stands next to my chair until they clear their throat. I assume it's the waitress, back to take my order, but when I turn my head I am staring at Macallister. Macallister's crotch, to be exact. I quickly scan my eyes up to his face.

"Hello, sir," I say with a mocking tone he no doubt picks up on.

"What are you doing?"

I consider being a smart-ass, but decide on the truth when I'm not as quick-witted as I usually am. "I'm getting a cocktail."

"Why are you alone?" His voice lowers on the last word. I'm already annoyed and about to lay into him and feel the scrunch of my face formed by my inner thoughts. I'm a grown woman, and I can go to a bar and get a cocktail by myself if I damn well please. *What is with everyone's concern about me being alone tonight?*

Before I can answer him, the cute cocktail waitress saunters up with a little notepad and a skirt short enough to be considered a pair of frilly panties. "What can I get you, sweetie?"

Her smile could melt honey. "Hi, I uh, was wondering if you serve a cocktail called The Verbena? It's not on your menu."

"We do," she says bouncing and I'm not sure how, considering the height of her spike stilettos. "Have you ever had it before?" I shake my head in response.

She jots it on her pad of paper and turns to Macallister, "Another scotch and water, sir?"

He hesitates before answering her, "That would be lovely. Thank you, Lucy."

I raise my eyebrows in question at him as he lowers himself into the identical chair next to mine. "She's wearing a name tag, Prudence," he clarifies without me having to ask how he knows the name of the barely-dressed cocktail waitress in The Cosmopolitan Hotel in Las Vegas.

I shrug. "I don't remember inviting you to join me."

He turns his body toward mine, and his knee brushes against mine when he does. He either doesn't notice, or he pretends not to, but instead tilts his head in a challenge. I'm not sure I'd call the expression on his face a smile with how devious it appears.

I decide to play his game. I don't respond, and instead turn my body toward him so we are sitting face to face.

"May I join you, Prudence?" he asks after a beat of silence.

I roll my eyes upward, acting as if I'm contemplating his question. "I suppose so," I eventually answer as I relax into the cushion of my chair. From the corner of my eye, he settles into his own seat, crossing his leg over his knee. We're turned enough we could still talk to each other, but we don't.

We sit in silence as we wait for dear Lucy to bring our drinks to us. I refuse to break the silence first. *Nope. Not going to be me.*

I can't take it anymore. "So, why are you here alone?"

His eyes narrow, and I'm surprised he can still see out of the tiny slits his eyelids have created. He doesn't answer me, so I let myself go back to letting my gaze wander around. I spot a clear, glass elevator. Once it reaches the first level, the doors open. I watch from the other side as a bride and groom get inside. They're holding hands. The bride is wearing a tea-length white dress and the groom is handsome in a navy blue suit and wide smile. Once the doors close, he places his suit jacket around her shoulders, then pulls her to his lips and kisses her the entire ride up to the top floor.

I can't tear my eyes away. I'm so focused on their romantic passion on display for any stranger to witness, wondering what it would feel like to have someone fully committed to you, and the only thing that breaks me from my trance is the sound of Lucy's voice as she delivers our drinks. "Okay, do you know how to drink this?" she says as she sets it in front of me. I wonder what I got myself into if there's a special way to drink it.

She takes my silence as confirmation that I in fact do not know how to drink it. "So this," she points at a little round garnish impaled by a toothpick, "is what we call the buzz button. Take one sip of your drink, put it in your mouth, and chew it for fifteen seconds. Then take another sip of your drink."

"Uhm, okay?" I say, still unsure of what I just signed up for.

"Don't worry," she giggles. "It's an experience, but not a bad one." With another smile, she saunters away.

I know Macallister is eyeing me as I stare at my drink, afraid to even pick it up. Finally, I grab the glass and take a small sip. Tart and almost sour. It makes my mouth purse reflexively. I place the glass back on the napkin square and grab the toothpick, inspecting the tiny ball on the end before sliding it off the end into my mouth. I chew the bitter-tasting fibers. After about fifteen seconds, my mouth is slightly numb.

Before I can, Macallister grabs the glass and hands it to me with a knowing smirk. I glare at him before grabbing it and taking a sip. The overwhelming sweetness invades my mouth. My eyes widen and I look over to Macallister. He's traded his scowl for a soft smile, as if watching me experience this chemistry experiment brings him genuine satisfaction.

With the liquid in my mouth, I hold the glass up to inspect it before swallowing. "It reminds me of a Warhead. Have you ever had one?" I ask him.

He nods. "Of course. Although, they make them differently now. Not as sour." *He's such a know-it-all sometimes.*

I settle back into my seat but keep my body turned into him. "I haven't had one since I was a child. I remember turning it into a competition with my mom and dad. We would all try to outlast each other before spitting it out. My dad always made it, making the most ridiculous face to get through the sour part, then dramatically sighing with relief when the sweetness hit. I used to try and sneak into the bathroom to wash off the sour coating under the faucet."

He lets out the loudest, most boisterous laugh I've heard from him. "That sounds like something you'd do."

I'm not sure what that is supposed to mean but I chuckle along with him, having a sense that whatever it does mean, it wasn't meant to be malicious. My mind drifts and I look at my feet and fiddle with the empty toothpick.

"Something on your mind?" he asks, noticing the sudden change in my mood.

"Oh, just mourning the significantly decreased amount of malic acid on Warheads. Kids these days will never know the pain they missed out on."

"You mean they'll never know what it's like to cheat their way through one?"

"It wasn't cheating. It was strategy," I argue.

He shakes his head. "Sure."

I place the toothpick back on the table right as he leans in to grab his glass. His knuckles brush against mine as our hands accidentally make buzzing contact. I raise my eyes, wondering what angered expression I'll be met with, but am instead met with a look I'm not sure I understand. Something about it makes me feel exhausted with keeping up the front and want to speak more honestly.

"Truthfully?" I ask, and he nods so I continue. "You said that sounds like something I'd do. Then, I realized …" I take another sip of my drink. "Well, I realized, I've grown accustomed to that." He swallows the sip he just took, and I watch his Adam's apple bob. He contemplates my answer quietly, and I take the opportunity to observe the shape his face takes when he's thinking. I'm sure he thinks I mean since the article, but my mind flashes through every relationship I've been in since high school.

His eyes catch mine. "To people questioning your intentions?" he asks.

"To people assuming the worst of me." I smile sadly as I take another sip and continue to look around, feeling unable to focus on his face any more from the sense of vulnerability I'm not used to feeling. Macallister is quiet and I assume he's done speaking with me. Out of the corner of my eye, he relaxes a little into his chair and he's taking sips from his glass, the ice clinking against the side.

"You're a good person." He says it so quietly, I almost don't catch it.

"Yes, that's why you're so wary of me," I say with a teasing, almost self-deprecating tone.

"I'm wary of your recording device. I know you turn recordings in, and I know you aren't always writing the story you want to, but the one you're told to write based on the direction of your interviews."

I stare at him in disbelief. He's now the second person to have acknowledged that out loud to me, and I'm not sure how to flesh out the emotion it makes me feel, especially coming from him. I also can't help myself from fixating on how he inadvertently admitted he doesn't hate me. Or at least he doesn't think I'm as cagey as I thought he did.

"I don't record *every* thing."

"Are you recording right now?" he asks with a tilt of his head.

"Obviously not."

"Do you record as often as you would have a few weeks ago?" A few weeks ago, the Torrence Gillman article hadn't been written. A few weeks ago I loved my job, and I never questioned it. A few weeks ago … My mind drifts to what this assignment would be like if I had taken it before the Torrence story. Was I deceitful before? Am I deceitful now? Is that why a man has never been able to fully commit to me?

He can't hear my thoughts, but I feel naked. Like he's ripped open my dress from the front, exposing every inch of my body to him and I'm not sure how he got inside to a place I'm unsure of how to get at myself sometimes.

I lower my head when I speak. "No." My answer is so small, but he hears me. I know he hears me because I see his lips curve up right before he takes another sip. I watch the bob in his throat again as he swallows, berating myself for my lack of self-control. I think he notices, too, because his lips continue to curve up the slightest bit more.

He nods. "I've made mistakes in my career. I learned from them. I forged ahead."

My spikes poke out from my back again. "Were your mistakes posted all over the internet?"

"Actually—" he starts, but I don't care to hear his answer.

"And, I'm being asked to do it again. Most people can learn from their mistakes, but here I am," I gesture my hands out. "Destined to repeat it again and again."

"You don't have to work there." I don't like his tone, filled with venom, but also truth.

I tear my eyes away, as difficult as it is. I don't know how to respond yet, so I take another sip of my drink. I sneak a glance at him from the corner of my eye, but when I do, he's looking right at me. He opens his mouth to say something. I turn to face him, eager to hear what he has to say to me and concerned I didn't run my reaction through a filter first.

"How are the drinks?" The energized voice of our cocktail waitress, Lucy, causes him to snap his mouth shut and therefore, hold back what he was going to say.

I curse her in my head, but out loud I say, "Great. Thank you so much."

She nods at me enthusiastically, then turns to Macallister and places her hand on his arm. "By the way, the couple wanted to send their deepest thanks for the bottle."

He shifts uncomfortably. "Oh. My pleasure," he nods to her

curtly. He looks away from her and toward his lap, and I watch, entertained by the way the waitress can't tear her eyes from him regardless of his lack of attention toward her. She lingers for a moment, then walks away swaying her hips more dramatically than before. She sneaks another peek back, no doubt wanting to catch him watching. He's not. He's focused on his pant leg as if it has the secret to life written across it.

"Wow," I breathe out and take another sip of my drink.

He snaps his head up. "What?"

"You can't tell me you didn't notice."

He shrugs and sips from his glass, restoring his nonchalant demeanor. "Notice what?"

I roll my eyes. "Whatever. What was she talking about? Is she talking about the newlywed couple I saw get into the elevator?" I don't know how I know, but I do.

He hesitates, but then he nods once. "Uh, yeah. I told her to keep it anonymous." He says the last part more to himself, and the tone of annoyance makes me want to laugh.

"Why?"

He frowns at me like I just asked him what year this was. "Because. I'm allowed to ask her to keep it anonymous." His body stiffens in defense, and it makes me laugh.

"No. I mean why did you send them a bottle?"

He frowns, as if genuinely confused. "It's their wedding night."

"Do you know them?"

"No."

"You … You plainly decided to send a random couple a bottle of—" I wave my right hand out. "Champagne, I'm assuming?" He nods in confirmation, but his eyes drop as if he's embarrassed. "So, you send people you don't know a bottle of champagne because it's their wedding night? As a random act of kindness?" That's a genuinely nice thing to do, and I struggle to keep the disbelief from my voice as I ask because I haven't seen him do anything nice before this.

He shifts in his seat and rolls his neck, never making eye contact with me. "Yes."

I shake my head. "Geez, I'd like to have you around when I get married." I don't miss the expression his face morphs into at my words and the dark red staining his cheeks. He'd probably rather die than be around when I get married. In my mind, a picture of myself getting married, and the thought of myself wearing a goofy white dress, makes me want to laugh. The thought of Macallister being there makes me laugh until I'm caught off guard by the thought of him being there because I'm getting married to *him*. Nothing like alcohol and staying up late to push intrusive thoughts at you.

He doesn't respond, and I mentally shake myself off until we fall into a surprisingly comfortable silence as we continue to sip our drinks.

I find myself regarding the activity happening around us. My eye catches on a group of men laughing together as they walk past the bar. I'm captivated by a group of five people surrounding a single slot machine, cheering on a guy sitting on the stool in front of the machine, clearly winning. A group of women pose together, embracing each other's waists, while an employee takes a picture for them. I assume they're a bachelorette group because all of them wear black cocktail dresses, except for the one in the middle wearing a dress completely covered in silver sequins and a poofy, white bow made of tulle on her head.

I get so lost watching everyone else, it takes me a while to look back at Macallister. When I do, he's watching me. I give him a questioning raise of my eyebrow. He doesn't respond, but instead stares at me like he's trying to read something in a different language, and I get that naked, exposed sensation back from before. *Why is he looking at me like that?*

I can't take it anymore so I break eye contact first. "Are you a fan?"

He coughs. "What?" He sputters out the words, nearly choking on his scotch.

"A fan of Gnasher. Is that how you got into this gig?" I smile, knowing my original question was a little too open-ended.

He folds his face back as much as he can into a normal, not caught off-guard expression before he nods in understanding. "Not exactly. I like Gnasher alright, but they're not necessarily my favorite band. It's best not to represent an artist you are a big fan of."

I nod. "Makes sense. Have you represented a lot of artists before this?" I'm slipping into interview mode out of habit.

"A few." I want him to reveal who, but I can tell by the hard line his mouth is set in that he probably wouldn't, even if I asked. I still wait a moment in case he wants to divulge, but he glowers back at me, stone-faced, instead.

I lean toward him and ask, "And this was what you always wanted to be when you grew up?"

His demeanor cracks, and he laughs. "I think when I was five, I told my parents I wanted to be a sailor when I grew up."

"Well, what happened?" I throw my hands up exaggeratedly and fix my face into my best impression of someone pretending to be shocked.

"Not the family business," he raises his glass to me before taking a sip. "My dad is a producer. My mom was a performer, and a music reporter like you when she retired from the stage," he uses the glass with hardly any liquid left in it to point toward me.

His mom was a performer and is now a music journalist. Now I'm intrigued. "Really? For what publication?" Would I know her?

"She is the editor-in-chief of *Riff Revolt*." Uh, yeah, I definitely know of her.

My eyes widen. "Your mom is Constance Blackwood?"

He nods and points to himself. "Different last name. Dad is Milton Davis."

His dad is Milton Davis? Davis Records is one of the biggest production companies in the business. How did I not make that connection? I'm ashamed of myself. An experienced reporter always does the right research. I'm still so off balance knowing his mom is the editor-in-chief of *Riff Revolt*, that this reveal nearly knocks me over. I can't even wrap my head around it.

Heat rises up my neck. *Riff Revolt* is another music magazine based out of Los Angeles, and our biggest competitor. Their articles are similar to ours, except they do significantly more reviews of music and we do way more exposé style articles. Felicia wants there to be a clear distinction between the two magazines. She says that's what gives us our competitive edge. Personally, I wish I could review music more, but Felicia wants scandal. *SubVox* reads like a trashy gossip magazine in comparison to *Riff Revolt* with its significantly more technical articles, clearly written for admirers of art and music.

I want that. I want that so bad, it hurts. I let myself sit with this revelation I've kept tucked away, afraid of its truth.

"Where did you go?" His voice cuts me out of the quiet contemplation I had fallen into.

"Hmm?" I turn my body toward him.

"You seemed deep in thought there. Worried about fraternizing with the enemy? Or the son of the enemy?"

I chuckle. "The opposite, actually." I don't give any further explanation, and the way I can tell he's craving one satisfies me to my bones. "I can't believe your dad is Milton Davis."

He groans. "I've contemplated changing my last name."

I turn to him. "Doesn't it help?"

We stare at each other, and I watch the blood drain from his face at my question. I'm not sure why, but instinctively I reach out to him, resting my hand on his forearm in a display of platonic comfort. Instead, once my hand reaches his bare arm, I'm acutely aware of how his sleeves are rolled to a perfect cuff directly below his elbow, showing off the corded vein wrapping upward. My eyes follow the trail to where it disappears under his sleeve.

I snatch my hand back as if I've been burned and my wide eyes meet his. "Uh," I sputter. "I mean it probably helps to have a foot in the door. I didn't mean anything nasty by it."

He doesn't respond, but instead turns his gaze away from me

and brings his empty glass to his lips. Realizing there's no more liquid inside, he pulls it down and fixates on it for a moment, as if he can conjure more scotch. He lowers the glass, places it on the table, and remains slightly hunched over with his arms resting on his legs and hands clasped together. Again, I realize when he does this, the vein protrudes even more.

I use my voice to pull myself from my obvious ogling. "So you grew up around music," not a question. "That sounds cool." I lay my head to rest on the back of my chair. The velvet tickles the nape of my neck, exposed from my hair being pulled up and my current hyper-awareness of my surroundings and nerve endings.

He straightens up again before readjusting and resting in his chair. "Eh. It had its pros and cons. I'm assuming your parents were into music as well?" I lift my head again. I'm shocked he's engaging in such a prolonged conversation.

"I mean, they listened to music. I don't think it meant as much to them as it does to me."

"I can tell." His eyes widen, as if he didn't mean to say that.

"My job give it away?" I laugh sarcastically but have no ill intention behind it.

"Oh. Yeah." I realize that's not what he meant at all. He clears his throat. "Aren't you named after a song, though?"

I shrug. "Maybe? I don't know for sure." He expresses his confusion by scrunching up his face. His face morphs slightly and he looks more angry than confused. I realize I might have fucked up big time with what I've revealed.

I run my hand up and down my exposed arm as if I'm cold. I'm not, but I catch Macallister's eyes watching the motion. "I did ask my mom the meaning of my name once when I had a project about family trees in middle school. She just kind of smiled and said it was a beautiful name, like a song." I shrug to emphasize my confusion, but underneath my blouse, I can feel my core heating up.

"So you lied to Cliff?" His question hangs between us, cutting through the somewhat affable air we'd created between us.

Shit, he's angry. I've been so caught up in the comfortability of our conversation, I lost my composure. I don't even know why I admitted that out loud to him. *Can I blame the drink? I'm blaming the drink.*

I blink back at him. "I needed him to open up."

Shit, not what I was going for. The fibers of my being are tearing from the inside. This is my job, this is what I do. I don't want to feel guilty for that, again. I replay the conversation with Cliff back in my head. I had felt proud in that moment, but now all I feel is sticky, slimy shame dripping over me. I want to take a shower.

"Hmph," he looks at his still-empty glass for a moment. When he looks back up, I prepare myself to see how he shows real, true anger. My bones rattle, and my hands start shaking so hard, I have to clasp them together tightly in my lap. The combination of my guilt and the look on his face is the strongest cocktail I've ever had, and I immediately want to throw it up, get it out of my body where it's settled low in my belly. I've interviewed countless people, but I've never felt this nervous to be speaking with someone before.

His gaze drops to my clasped hands, then back up to my face. His facial expression gives nothing away, but the significantly lighter shade of his usually creamy complexion does. His eyes search for something to hold onto, but he still doesn't say anything. I wipe my clammy palms across the denim of my jeans, and the constant celebratory jingles indicating the strangers around me are winning when I'm clearly at a loss makes my head spin.

He squints at the expensive watch on his wrist, examining it for longer than necessary to read the time. When he looks back up at me, I've already checked the time on my phone and know it's past midnight.

I say it before he can, somehow knowing he was about to scold me for being out late. "Probably time to head back."

He nods and scratches his chin. I focus on the sound of his stubble scratching the skin of his fingers, blocking out the chimes and chatter around us. I press my thighs together and admonish my inability to block out the contradictions pulsing through me, causing so much heat I'm convinced someone is messing with the thermostat.

He raises his hand toward the waiter and without exchanging any words or even making eye contact, he hands over a black credit card. I scramble to reach for my wallet, but he waves me off, irritated by my lack of finesse in paying a bill.

"Thank you," my words come out small and I'm embarrassed by the way they sound. He doesn't notice, or he doesn't care, and he nods once in recognition. He doesn't say another word.

CHAPTER 10

Macallister

I'm lost in my thoughts as we reach the door of our hotel. I don't even realize we've arrived until Prudence veers away from my side, making her way into the still-noisy lobby. My ears ring adjusting to the loud chiming and jingling from the slot machines.

I notice Prudence's steps grow heavier, more determined, and I halt in my tracks watching her practically stomp away. When I call her name, she turns back, and I can barely make out the blue of her eyes because her gaze is so narrowed in an angry grimace.

"What?" she snaps at me, and instead of holding contact with her eyes, my own travel across the curves of her body. She huffs and when my eyes reach her face again, she's scowling at me, impatiently waiting for my response.

My tongue is heavy in my mouth, unable to form the words I don't even have, but her expression grows more annoyed. "Have a good night," I try.

She closes most of the distance between us, and walks up to me with her finger outstretched in my face. "So you think we're friends now?"

I'm shell-shocked and my mouth goes dry. *Friends?* The word tumbles through my head in her voice, and I hate that word. *Have I always hated that word?*

I cross my arms. "Obviously not."

She laughs, but the sound of it lacks any humor or goodwill. "Thanks for the drink, Macallister."

She turns on her heel to walk away, and my eyes are too exhausted from staying open all day to not travel downwards and watch her ass as she sways her hips in pursuit of the elevator.

She's going to be the death of me. Internally, I'm screaming at myself to stop, but I'm also not obeying; and so, I continue to stand, unmoved, until she disappears from my line of vision. A drunk guy calling out to someone named Chelsea across the casino bumps my shoulder in his pursuit to catch up to, who I assume is Chelsea, and it knocks me back into myself.

"Sorry, man," he calls out over his shoulder as he continues on his merry way.

I wave a hand at him in an 'it's fine' gesture, and walk forward. I consider stopping by the bar to order another drink, wanting something chemical to silence my incessant thoughts but decide against it as I continue to walk into the elevator. I press the button to go up, but right before it opens, I notice the sign indicating where the stairwell is located. I hear the ding of the door, but am already on my way to take the long way up.

Even though I want nothing more than to be in my room, I trudge up each step slowly, replaying the last couple of hours in my mind. Did I overreact to her confession? Was that even a confession, or am I digging for any excuse to not trust her? I wanted to tell her I knew I couldn't trust her, but all I could think about was how I felt like I was drowning in the depths of her irises. I wanted to swim forever, using the tiny black dot in the center as my raft. I shake my head in exasperation with myself.

I want to find a way to get her kicked off this assignment, and therefore, off the bus. I also want to do everything in my power to keep her as close to me as I can. I'm giving myself whiplash at this point.

My resolve is about as strong as a wet paper towel, and my mental replay begins to exclusively feature things causing my lips to curve upward at the memories: listening to her talk in an uninhibited way, learning more about her, and picturing her as a child trying to cheat at eating sour candy, but mostly, watching her watch people. She has a way of observing the things and people around her that unnerves me. Does she watch me like that?

It's the one thing I can't stop myself from continuously wondering about as I drag my feet down the hallway like a zombie toward my room. After that first show, it took me by surprise. When I asked her why, if it was for her article, the candid way she smiled and responded it was *just for her* settled in my chest like a golden marble, small but warm. It burned hotter tonight when I watched her do it again. I don't think I've ever observed someone so aware and entranced by their surroundings before. It made the silence between us comfortable in a way I've never experienced with someone else.

I remind myself of the things she did that also pissed me off, unable to latch onto anything concrete. When I walk through the door of my room, I glance at my bag, and I'm reminded of the letter tucked inside. It did piss me off that she manipulated Cliff. Even though it was something small, and insignificant, it's what it represents. Her ability to be so observant leads to her ability to manipulate the people around her. My job is to protect Cliff, and I don't know how to protect him from her. Not fully, anyway.

But am I even truly mad? I can't find the emotion in my body anywhere. I'm lacking anger about as much as I'm lacking the determination to hold onto any resentment for her presence. The realization forces the images of her sitting in the bar, drinking a cocktail, back into my head.

As I splash water on my face and brush my teeth in preparation to hopefully drift off into thoughtless sleep, I remember the blooming warmth in my chest when she learned about my small gesture extended to the newlywed couple. What she doesn't know, and what I was not going to tell her, is that's generally how I've chosen to spend the money in my trust fund. Well, that and dressing well. I don't want my family's money, not anymore, and

I sleep better at night when I can use it on things like that. Things like *that* … because for some reason, I struggle to call it what it is, what Prudence called it: a random act of kindness. I let my memory replay her saying she hopes I'm around when she gets married. The images in my head morphing from her in a white dress next to a faceless man in a tux, to me in a tux holding her hand. I shake my head as if I can joggle the picture away.

"Nope," I say aloud to no one but the confused man staring back at me in the mirror, then make my way toward my bed.

I resign to accepting the fact that I'm honestly too tired to fight my intrusive thoughts, and I write them off with the same excuse. Laying in bed on my back and staring at the ceiling, I close my eyes, but flashes of her won't let my body settle.

I roll to my side, finding the position even more uncomfortable. I roll to my other side, trying to ignore the flow of blood in my body causing discomfort I'm struggling to think away.

I toss around in my bed as my mind flips through stills of her like the View-Master I had as a child. With each click to change the picture, I imagine her eyes, her smile, the way her blouse shifted and exposed the slightest curve of cleavage, and the way she kept crossing and uncrossing her legs. I fight to fixate on anything else, but now my cock is so hard I can't even concentrate on concentrating.

I roll to my back again and heave a sigh of defeat. I'm grateful to be in a hotel room alone tonight as I find my hand gripping myself tightly, trying to force the unwanted hard-on to rest so I can get some as well. Instead, my hand pumps up and down as I remember her looking up toward me. I jerk my hand a little faster as I recall the way her skin flushed as she reluctantly tried her drink and her expression when she tasted the first sip after sucking on the numbing ball. I run my two fingers over the tip, finding a bead of precum and smearing it around the swollen head of my cock, spontaneously being reminded of her mouth, her tongue.

My hips rise slightly as I groan through my teeth. My climax is building as I remember the way her expression changed when she listened to me talk about myself. I've never been regarded like that, and my hand pumps harder and faster as I grip the sheets in my other hand. I scrunch my face, and I curl my toes as I stroke so hard, the buzz rises up my shaft. With my eyes closed, I picture the intent stare of her eyes, staring deep into me. My release drips over my hands and I'm panting into my pillow like a pubescent boy touching himself for the first time.

I keep my hand around my cock as it begins to soften, and I keep my head shoved into my pillow as I think one thought: *You idiot.*

I wake to the sound of my alarm at seven a.m. with a label reminding me to get up and run. I press snooze, then slap my phone onto the bedside table. I wait about a minute, and groan as I roll to get out of bed. I need to run off this besottedness, anyway.

At the gym, I run alone on a treadmill with no music and no TV. I slam my feet with each stride, and grunt as they fall to the moving platform. The stream of sweat coursing out of me and down my body makes an uncomfortable, sticky trail on my skin, but I keep running, letting it continue to slide and drip, focusing on my breath instead of the trails of salty perspiration.

After I shower, I stand at the mirror and stare at my face. I study the way my tan skin stretches across me, and I wonder what her hands would feel like. My cock wakes up, and I'm forced to fuck my hand again before getting dressed and leaving to find Cliff.

It's nine in the morning and I find him sitting alone at a table in the small cafe at the front of our hotel. It's Vegas, so no continental breakfast or complimentary anything. He has a cup of coffee sitting in front of him with the lid off and upright on the table. I don't have to peer in his cup to know he's drinking it black. He probably paid way too much for it, but I doubt his finances are weighing heavy on his mind at this current moment. He doesn't notice me as I approach the table. He doesn't even glance up until I sit in the chair across from him.

His eyes drop as quickly as they rose. "Morning, Mac," he drawls out, his voice still groggy from sleep—or knowing him, lack of sleep. I tried to encourage him to get some medication for his insomnia before the tour, but he only grunted and waved me off.

"Ready for tonight?" I ask, not surprised he's up this early, but disappointed he isn't resting before his second show in a row in the lively city of Las Vegas.

His eyes stay lowered, mesmerized by the tiny bubbles floating on the surface of a sea of caffeine. "You know it," the chuckle he lets out sounds more like exasperation than humor, but I brush it off.

"Great show, last night. Things are looking up." My chipper tone surprises me.

"You mean I'm behaving better than you expected and haven't said anything offensive or incriminating since we left on tour," he says to me but his eyes stay glued to his cup.

I grin. "Something like that."

"Huh," he laughs. "Figures."

"Is this enjoyable to you? Performing again? Touring again?" I ask him, knowing I've lost any semblance of a filter and inhibitions. I would usually never press him like this, but the lack of semen in my body must be the cause. At least, that's what I'm going to blame it on.

His eyes lock into mine, but seem faraway at the same time. "Do you ever think about someone you miss, someone that meant everything to you, and you'll never forget what it felt like to be sharing the same space as them? But then you realize they probably don't even remember you. Probably can't even picture your face, even though theirs is burned into every fiber of your memory so deeply, you can't even sleep without shuddering as your eyes close knowing what you'd see behind them?"

Uh …? Not what I was expecting, especially this soon after the sun rose.

The muscles in my face contract and contort at his uncharacteristic disclosure, but my eyes stay locked into his. "I … I can't say I have …" I trail off, almost as a question to myself. Where the hell did that even come from? Cliff is proving to be more difficult than I anticipated in ways I was not picturing when I signed on to manage the rockstar known for his chaotic behavior back in the day.

He nods solemnly, his eyes back to searching for something in the coffee. "Yeah. I enjoy this. Performing and touring." His tone takes on a robotic quality as he answers my previous line of questioning.

His emotional words startle me. Not so much his actual words as the meaning I know is behind them. I want to prod him further, wondering where my lack of self-control is coming from today when the heat rises at my back. Someone is behind me, and it doesn't take long until that someone opens their mouth and I know who it is.

"You boys are up bright and early." Darrell's voice rings in my ears like two cymbals crashing together.

I don't turn to him. "Good morning, Darrell." Nine is not bright and early, but I doubt Darrell has ever lived a life that has required him to wake up before the sun.

Cliff's head stays lowered, but his eyes rise slightly from the black, caffeinated pool in front of him to meet mine. There's a bit of humor and possibly pride in them. He doesn't say anything back to Darrell, and he doesn't even glance his way.

"Welp. Gonna grab some good 'ol bean water before we get this day rollin'." *I fucking hate this guy.* "Want anything?"

I seize the opportunity to fit in more private words with Cliff. "Yep. Coffee. Black. Large."

He pauses, probably not expecting me to take him up on his offer. "You got it, Mac." I'm not looking at him, but I know he said that while giving finger guns.

Instead, I clear my throat. "Macallister," I correct as he skips away to the front counter.

"Be nice to Darrell," Cliff says aloud before taking a sip from his paper cup.

I chuckle and shake my head. "Do you know why Jasper even hired him? I know he's Jasper's cousin, but—"

"He gets on Jazz's nerves for sure," Cliff cuts me off, "but I think he felt obligated because they're family. He's been trying to get into the business for years. Before we even considered touring or performing together again, he brought Darrell on to help him manage more low-level stuff. Royalties, the occasional appearance, and whatnot. Then, when things started moving, he didn't have the heart to cut him off."

Well, that explains a lot. I didn't care I wasn't representing Jasper or the band as a whole. It's not unheard of for a broken-up band to come back together and have multiple managers from when they were split apart. It can get complicated, but Darrell's lack of knowledge is the biggest burden most of the time.

When Cliff brought me on, he was clear on what he wanted: A smooth transition back into the spotlight with as little gossip as possible. Meaning, he merely wanted to get on stage, play his guitar and sing, then disappear back into the shadows.

Remembering this, my uncaffeinated resolve pushes another question from me. "You said you didn't want any buzz on this tour. What changed your mind about Prudence?"

His expression changes and I don't know how to read it. "I'm not sure," he admits with a shrug of his shoulders. "I guess ... I saw an opportunity to control the narrative while giving someone an opportunity to grow. She belongs in this industry, for sure."

His words don't make a lot of sense to me, and he must understand the confusion on my face. "If she's on the bus, if she's at the shows, I consider that an opportunity for me to manipulate her. Being in the constant presence of a reporter keeps me in check." He shrugs. "But, now I just kind of like her." He shakes his head, laughing to himself.

I'm a bit dumbfounded at how we regard this situation so differently. Where he thinks he can manipulate her, I only see *her* ability to manipulate *him*. "I don't know how much I can control with her here," I admit, vocalizing the fears I've had since she stepped onto the bus a few weeks ago. "*SubVox* is known for being a ruthless publication. Even if she does like you, she is required to turn in all her recordings and is basically told what to write. If something slips while she's recording …"

"There was a point during our first show in Seattle where I decided, fuck it." I wonder what he means. I'm instantly anxious and I need to tell him about the letter I found. *Should I?*

I'm about to tell him we need to talk when a not-as-large-as-I-wanted cup is placed in front of me. "Here ya go, champ!" I pop open the lid and am met with a not-as-black-as-I'd-like liquid encapsulated inside. I can't even muster a thank you for this incredibly offensive gesture.

I take a sip anyway, needing the caffeine to help build back up my indefatigability. I know it isn't Darrell's fault. It's not like he made the coffee. I'm almost about to turn to him and apologize for the insult I didn't even speak out loud when I shudder at the idea of being nice to him. Where did that even come from? I don't know what happened to me last night, but my insides are shifting and I do not like it. At least, I'm not accustomed to it.

"This coffee tastes like shit," I declare to nobody. "Ready?" I turn toward Cliff as I rise from my seat.

"For what?" he whines like a petulant teenager.

"You've got a thing." He doesn't.

Darrell looks between us. "We have a thing?"

I finally turn to him for the first time this morning. He's wearing a baggy, black Gnasher T-shirt circa '94 with the sleeves ripped off and dark wash jeans with a red and black flannel tied around his waist. He always looks like he's trying to cosplay what he thinks the manager of a 90s grunge band would dress like. "No. Cliff has a thing," I clarify.

I catch a flicker in his eyes I don't recognize from him, but it's gone as quickly as it flashed. His usual, goofy expression returns to his face as he spits words out that do not match the expression he wears. "Well, maybe since Cliff is part of a *band*, it should involve the entire band, Mac."

"Macallister. And no, I don't think it should." I am ready for a fight. His words have awakened the nineteen-year-old Mac who was always ready to put a fist in a face. The man, or boy, I haven't woken up in a substantially long time. I need that version of Macallister back, to keep my horny and angry thoughts at bay.

Darrell keeps smiling at me as I grit my teeth. Cliff's hand claps onto my shoulder, visually a friendly gesture, but physically more like a warning.

"I'm ready," Cliff's voice says into my ear, and my vision starts to clear slightly, taking me from a place of only seeing Darrell's face clouded in red, to refocusing back onto our surroundings.

I give Darrell one last squint of my eyes in warning, then turn and continue walking with Cliff.

"You good?" he asks as we step into the elevator.

"I do not know," I admit more freely than I ever have been with him before. I decide having a conversation with Cliff about the letter is not going to happen right now, not when I'm feeling so out of sorts.

He doesn't prod but gives me a nod instead. The elevator doors start to close when I hear a winded "Hold the door!"

Before I can register I recognize the voice that called out, I jut my arm out to push the door ajar and keep it from closing. Prudence scurries in front of the open door, dressed in a matching purple sports bra and leggings. Based on her attire, I'd assume she's coming back from the gym, but she doesn't look like she recently worked out. She's holding a small paper bag and a cup of coffee. She smiles at both of us and whispers a soft greeting as she steps in and turns her back to us, facing the door.

I close my eyes and inhale her scent: dark, tempting, and filled with roses. She smells the way fall smells as it's fading into winter.

I wonder what she smells like in April. Is it the same? I find my thoughts drifting, and I tilt my head to the ceiling to curse myself.

When I open my eyes, I look over and Cliff stares at me, one eyebrow arched high and a smug smile plastered across his face. I can't deny what he witnessed, so I don't bother trying to.

The door opens again with a ding, and Prudence skips off after giving us a "See you later."

"Don't," I warn, once she's out of earshot.

He doesn't say anything but lets the smile plastered on his face serve as his response as we step out together. "I don't have a thing, do I?" he asks.

"Nope." I step out of the elevator and walk toward my room.

CHAPTER 11

Prudence

Bus life is … interesting to say the least. We left on this tour almost a month ago, and I've learned a lot. For instance, everybody will need to use the restroom at the same time. Like they do right now. I watch Cliff impatiently banging on the door to the small, overly compact closet with the singular toilet we all share. Travis's muffled voice comes from the other side.

"I'm so sorry. Hang on. I—" His words cut off abruptly.

"I swear to fucking God, Travis if you don't open this door and let me shit …" Cliff's threat is cut off by Jasper sprinting from behind the curtain toward the same door Cliff is guarding.

He comes to a halt right before running into Cliff. "Sorry, are you waiting?" He points to the closed door with one hand and clutches the other in a tight fist.

"Yes," Cliff grits out. "And I'm next so you better hold it."

"Dude," Jasper looks at him with desperation. "Can I *please* go next?"

"I am literally going to explode right here, right now. No way."

"No, Cliff, you don't understand. I really—"

Cliff holds up his hand, cutting off his words. His voice lowers in volume and increases in intensity. "Jazz, I am about to explode."

Jasper's eyes widen. "Well, same."

From the other side of the door, a gurgled "Please, no," is audible.

I can't tear my eyes away from this scene unfolding, I don't even notice Macallister is sitting next to me now until he taps his pointer finger on the table out of my periphery. He's barely said a word to me since Vegas over a week ago.

What I thought was a pleasant conversation took such a turn, and I honestly haven't made the effort to try again. He mostly speaks to me in grunts and nods. I get the sense he is mad at me, and considering how we left things, I'm almost positive I'm correct. Anytime I directly ask him something, he won't meet my eyes. But once in a while, I'll turn at the right time to make eye contact with him, and every time I do, my skin erupts in goose-bumps. Something shifted during our conversation, at least for me. His stoicism is so unreadable, I wonder if he's not angry with me, but is actually a robot with zero emotion whatsoever.

Anytime I do a recorded interview with Cliff, Macallister is nearby with his ears on high alert, though. A couple of times, he's interrupted after I ask a question he deems unnecessary, and the interjection always makes my body heat up with frustration. Not because I want anything scandalous to fall from Cliff's mostly sealed lips, but because each recording I turn in is followed up by a disappointed reaction from Felicia and I feel like I'm skating on thin ice with her at this point.

I turn my body to face him completely, noticing he's already looking at me. "Worried I'm recording?" I ask, with a tiny hint of malice in my tone.

His eyebrows knit together. "No, that's not ... never mind."

I roll my eyes and turn back to observe the actual shit show near the bathroom as Macallister gets up from the table. Truth-fully, I kind of need to use the restroom, myself, but do not want to get involved in this scenario at all. I can hold it.

I'm watching Jasper do a nervous dance and Cliff clutches the doorframe above the closed bathroom door. "Travis ..." he starts.

We all lurch forward as the bus veers harshly to the side. Both Cliff and Jasper are thrown off balance, and they fall into each other by accident. Holding on to each other's arms for stability, they clear their throats and quickly release their holds. I study the quick glance passing between them. It's so brief and lasts maybe half a second, but I catch it and tuck it away for later.

I go to stand and walk out from behind the table, wanting to get a peek out the window at where we are. I don't notice Macallister has returned until my body is forced forward slightly as the bus pulls to a stop and the abruptness crashes my body toward his. His hand shoots out and wraps around my elbow, stabilizing me. I feel the hair on my arms stand to attention. His hand is warm, but it burns my bare skin like a hot iron. He's holding me, but his grip is barely there at the same time. Enough to catch me from falling, but nothing more. My head involuntarily lowers to see where his hand is. I stare for a moment at the contact before raising my gaze to his eyes also staring at where his fingers are wrapped around me delicately.

His hazel eyes scan up to find mine. His voice cracks, about to speak, when he shuts it quickly and releases my arm. "Sorry," he mumbles instead and turns quickly away from me and faces Cliff and Jasper. I stand in shock for a moment as my brain can only focus on the sensation of coldness in the shape of where his hand was.

He clears his throat, causing Cliff and Jasper to turn their heads toward him. "I told Harvey what's going on. We're at a rest stop," he announces.

Cliff and Jasper nearly sprint off the bus. Darrell appears from nowhere clutching his stomach and running after them. They all whoosh past me, my previous fixation dissipating with the motion. A small giggle escapes me as I watch them. Once they're off the bus, Macallister stands with his back still to me.

I keep the smile on my face, noticing he didn't follow. "I take it you didn't eat any meat from the questionable street vendor they all stopped at outside the show last night, either?" I say to his back.

He turns slowly and the smallest hint of a smile creeps across his face. "I almost did, but I'm glad I didn't."

In all honesty, the aroma coming from the sizzling gyros had made my mouth water so much, I'm shocked I didn't cave and get one like Travis, Jasper, Darrell, and Cliff did. I find myself grateful for the voice inside my head telling me that eating something heavy at one in the morning was a terrible idea.

"You think that's the culprit?" I ask when he doesn't move.

He nods, "I'd bet money on it."

Just then, Travis stumbles out of the bathroom hugging his middle. His face is pale and appears almost green. His eyes are barely open, but the small sliver appears bloodshot and glassy.

"You should lay down," I say, but he's already walking through the curtain. Without turning back toward me, he waves a hand in a 'Yeah, I got it' gesture.

I turn back to Macallister. He's standing perfectly still, his brow furrowed and any trace of a smile gone from his lips and his eyes cast toward his feet.

I start walking down the aisle toward the door, wanting to seize the opportunity to walk around for a bit when he asks, "Did you eat any?" His voice is laced with concern I'm not sure I understand completely.

"Oh, no. I just want to walk around," I say over my shoulder.

He nods in response and walks behind the curtain.

The fresh air is a welcome relief. You don't realize how stuffy a bus can get until you can walk around outside for a bit. We've stopped at a rest stop barely off the highway. I have no idea exactly where we are, but I know we are headed toward Arizona from LA. The rest stop sits atop a large, grassy area surrounded by nothing else. I make a few laps around the building enjoying the morning air that isn't too hot yet when Cliff emerges and stomps back toward the bus.

I'm about to follow him when I decide to take advantage of the restroom before we continue driving.

As I walk in, Jasper walks out. "You okay?" I ask tentatively.

He chuckles. "Better."

"No more street gyros for you," I say and continue walking, but his voice stops me.

"Are you okay?"

I stop and turn back to him. With a smile, I confess, "I didn't have one."

"That's not what I meant," he deadpans and my smile falls.

"I'm okay," my voice comes out small from the surprise of his question.

He shrugs. "Just checking. Let me know if you need anything," he says the last part as he starts walking back toward the bus.

I walk to the bathroom but stand in the stall for a full minute contemplating that brief interaction. Did I do something? Do I not seem okay? I rattle my brain trying to determine what prompted the concern from him, because surely he wasn't *just* asking. I shake it off and after I pee and wash my hands, I make my way back to the bus.

I smile at Harvey, sitting in the driver's seat. "We staying here for a while?"

He hums. "Probably for a bit. Can't stay too long or we'll be off schedule, but I want to give them time in case—"

His words are cut off by the sound of Travis stomping his way down the tight bus corridor and straight out the door.

He chuckles and it makes his air ride seat bounce slightly. "Well, in case of that."

I place my hand on his shoulder briefly before I walk back into the main living area. It's empty. Everyone must have gone back to their beds to get some rest. I wonder if there's any medicine on the bus, specifically some Pepto-Bismol. I assume not.

I turn back toward Harvey. "Hey, Harv? If we have the time after leaving, do you think you could find a convenience store?"

He nods. "Yes, ma'am."

We leave after Travis returns and no one else emerges from the back of the bus. Harvey stops at a 7-Eleven, and I run inside gathering two bottles of Pepto-Bismol, a bottle of Advil, a few Gatorades, and some ginger ale.

Once we get back onto the road, I decide I'll take advantage of the quiet time. I pull out my laptop to get some work done but I end up staring at a blank screen with my cursor blinking at me expectantly for a long while before I give up. I heave out a sigh as I close the top of my computer and stand to look out at the passing scenery.

We're still on the highway, so I can't focus on anything with it all blurring past the window, but I try anyway, giving myself a bit of a headache in the process. I close my eyes, shake my head a bit, and fall back onto my seat. I lay my head onto the table, trying to will away the motion sickness resonating right behind my eyes and groan. A soft chuckle startles me, and when my head snaps up toward the noise, Cliff stands at the door of the bathroom.

"You alright?" he asks me.

"Oh, I'm fine. I didn't eat anything from the cart."

He raises an eyebrow. "I know. That's not what I meant." *What is it with people asking me if I'm okay today if they're not referring to the gyro-poops making their way around this tiny, enclosed space?*

He must read my stunned silence exactly. "Sorry," he holds an innocent hand up. "I wasn't trying to pry. You seem … frustrated with something. Is it something on that computer of yours?"

I know my cheeks are turning pink and I wonder to myself if I'm self-centered. "Oh, yeah. It's …" I pause not knowing if this is appropriate to bring up with him. "It's this story," I decide professionalism be damned right now because it does feel kind of relieving to talk to someone about this.

He nods. "Not getting what you wanted out of us, I assume?"

I shake my head and look at my hands where my fingers are intertwined in my lap. "More like not what Felicia wanted out of you." I snap my head back up at a realization. "I'm so sorry, you probably need to use the bathroom. I'm really okay. I put some Pepto-Bismol in there, by the way, if you need it."

His responding smile is gentle and comforting. "I do, thank you. But just so you know, I've read your articles. You're a good writer, even when you're told what to write. It would be cool to read what you write when it comes completely from you."

I'm stunned into silence, which isn't a big deal since he immediately retreats to the bathroom without leaving enough time for me to respond anyway. I sit silently for a beat or two before I'm struck with a burst of inspiration. I open my laptop back up and create a new document. I'm so engrossed in what I start drafting, I don't even notice when Cliff comes out of the bathroom and disappears back behind the curtain.

"Truth or dare? And don't be fucking boring." Jasper has a bottle of ginger ale in one hand and his other hand rests on his thigh. After about five hours, the guys have started to trickle back into the main area and someone proposed playing a game. We've been playing Tour Bus Truth or Dare, lovingly named by Travis, for about two hours at this point, and there's no end in sight.

When I woke up this morning, I had planned to set-up another interview since Felicia has been blowing up my phone. But after the street gyro aftermath, and how I spent my few hours alone drafting a completely new story angle, it never felt right to ask.

Macallister narrows his eyes at Jasper and takes a sip from a beer. "Truth."

We all groan, disappointed because Jasper is the best at giving dares and we've all been waiting for when he can finally get Macallister, who is the only one drinking tonight. Or at least, the only one drinking alcohol.

Jasper rolls his eyes, then asks noncommittally, "What's something we don't know about you?"

As far as truths go, that is pretty open-ended. Fairly, we're all running out of questions to ask Macallister he'd be willing to answer.

He genuinely ponders the question. "I collect sea shanty vinyls."

Our heads swivel, eyes wide with a cocktail of confusion and shock. Each of us on the verge of asking him to explain further, but the surprise has a tight grip on our vocal cords.

I clear the bewilderment from my throat with a small cough. "Sea shanties?"

It's all I can manage, but Macallister turns and his eyes dig directly into mine. "Don't knock it till you try it."

The slight smile lifting his face with his words makes warmth spread across my skin. He hasn't given me the slightest bit of benevolence since Vegas, but this small gesture warms me. The briefly passing moment between us catches me off guard. I shake it off, but find my thoughts hazed over as Macallister dares Travis to recite a poem from memory. I barely catch the end of *Invictus* and then it's Travis's turn to ask someone. He picks me. I pick truth.

"Alright," he taps his fingers together. "What's your favorite Disney movie?"

I laugh at the innocence of his question, and the vibration in my chest pulls me out of my stupor. "The Lion King," I say.

"Animal lover?" Darrell guesses.

"Shakespeare lover," I respond. When the varying facial expressions tell me what I said made zero sense to them, I continue. "It's Hamlet."

I peer around to gauge the response. Jasper is deep in thought as if replaying the entire movie back in his memory. Cliff's lips turn up slightly, right before he takes another shot of hot pink bismuth subsalicylate. Darrell still appears confused with deep wrinkles indenting his forehead which is not surprising, but it's Macallister's expression that reminds me of driving over a speed bump too fast the way it jolts my body upwards from the shock. His mouth is slightly open, his eyebrows drawn, and his head tilts to the side slightly. He's unabashedly staring at me, and a familiar feeling I felt in Vegas of being stripped naked creeps back.

I cast my eyes downward, unable to stay locked into his gaze anymore. I focus on breathing when I realize it's my turn. I look up and the others sit quietly waiting on me.

"Okay, Darrell. Truth or dare?"

"Uh, let's go with …" Darrell pauses for a dramatic effect no one finds entertaining. "Truth," he declares.

"Okay," I think for a moment, finding the lingering awkward air has diminished my filter a bit. "How'd you get into this business?"

Cliff's eyes widen, along with a smile showing his teeth. Rare. Jasper crosses his arms and looks at Darrell with an unreadable expression, waiting for his answer.

"Well, I …" he trails off, obviously disappointed in the question but also uncomfortable with the answer. I find myself craving his answer, and my professional candor kicks in. I lean into him, showing him my attention. I push my eyebrows upward in an empathetic, active-listening facial expression.

It must work. "Well, Jazzy P here, helped me realize my love of music." Jasper scoffs quietly. "Always been a fan of the band," Darrell turns his face and smiles so brightly at Jasper, it gives me second-hand embarrassment when the gesture isn't returned. It's obvious Darrell is a fan, considering the large collection of vintage Gnasher T-shirts he owns. I swear he has had a different one every day and has yet to repeat.

"My aunt needed him out of her basement," Jasper deadpans.

There's a short break of silence before the sound of various forms of laughter. I keep my poise. After years of practice, I can keep my face from portraying my inner thoughts. He laughs along nervously. I almost feel bad for him. Darrell has been the outcast on this tour so far. I thought that would be me, but surprisingly, everyone wholly acts like I belong here. Everyone except Macallister, but I don't care. I really don't. *Sure you don't*, I think to myself.

"Okie dokie, Jazz! Truth or dare?"

Jasper sits slightly bent over a pillow he's pressing to his middle. "Dare," he grumbles.

"I dare you to ..." Darrell takes a deep breath. "I dare you to open a window," he says. I notice that the queasy look on his face mirrors the same screwed-up expression on Jasper's face.

Jasper barks out a laugh and stands. "You got it." He pulls the window open above us, letting in the fresh air.

Darrell breathes a sigh of relief for the fresh air clearing out the stuffy atmosphere we've all been sitting in. Cliff takes another sip of his Gatorade, and raises up to pass the medicine bottle to Jasper as he sits back down, whose eyes widen in surprised at the offering. He doesn't reach for it right away, and Cliff gestures the bottle between Jasper and Darrell, indicating they should both take some.

Jasper eyes it first, but eventually grabs it and unscrews the cap. He hovers the opening above his mouth, pouring the liquid into his mouth before passing it to Darrell and whispering "Thanks," in Cliff's direction.

Jasper swallows, nods to Cliff in gratitude, then turns to Macallister. "'Kay, Mac, truth or dare?"

I know Macallister has turned his eyes on me as he answers because I can feel the heat he's pulling up my body to my face. "Dare."

Again, the reactions following are varying degrees of surprise.

"This just got interesting," Travis whispers to himself.

Jasper smiles, and the sinister gleam in his eye concerns me. When he opens his mouth, I lose my breath. "Sing a sea shanty."

Jasper smiles as he and Macallister enter into a third-grade-style staring contest. Something shifts in Macallister's expression, and I half expect him to start singing "What shall we do with a drunken sailor" while dancing a jig.

He doesn't, though. Instead, he takes a long pull from his beer can, closes his eyes, takes a breath, and begins to sing in a deep baritone I never expected to come from him. We gape at him, awestruck, as he croons about loving a woman named Sally. The sound washes over me in a way I've never experienced before, and I find myself unable to fully interpret why. I can't tear my eyes away from him.

"When I came home, she was married to a tailor ..."

When he opens his eyes indicating the end of his song, there's a sharp sting connecting the back of my throat to my eyes.

He looks right at me when he finishes for some reason, then chuckles. He's about to speak when Cliff starts slowly clapping. Jasper and Travis join in as the pace of clapping increases. Darrell turns his head back and forth before relenting and joining in on the clapping with a wide smile on his face. I can't move, like my muscles are thick glue, sticking to my bones and transforming me into a statue. Macallister's eyes keep drifting back to me in my immobile state. I lift my hands as much as I can and clap lightly, in shock at what he just did.

"Well, wow, Mac. We might need to bring you out on stage one night," Cliff teases.

"You do and you're dead," Macallister retorts, falling back into his more familiar persona.

Chuckles rise up and Jasper pats Macallister on the shoulder. "That was damn good," I think I hear him whisper.

Later on, after a few more rounds of truth or dare, and some shuffling of seats due to people getting up for drinks or the bathroom, I'm seated right next to Macallister. Due to the tight space we share, my thigh is pressed up against his. I haven't been able to shake his performance, which I want to admit is silly. I look over to him and find he's already looking back at me, his eyes a little glassy from the beer. While the rest of the table jokes and talks loudly, I ask in a whisper, "Why sea shanties?"

He opens his mouth, about to answer, when he's interrupted by Jasper slapping the table.

We both turn back to the group and Darrell's mouth is gaping wide.

"What happened?" Macallister's voice asks next to me.

"Uh ... Darrell asked Cliff truth or dare, and he chose Truth," Travis says, breaking through the strained silence.

I gasp, surprised he's opting to tell a truth. He probably doesn't imagine Darrell can compose a question that will dig too deeply into his well-protected fortress of secrets.

Darrell is bouncing with excitement. "Oh, wow! Okay ... What's your biggest regret?" For Darrell, this is a deep question, and I hold my breath waiting for how Cliff is going to answer.

Cliff's eyes narrow, and I almost wish I were recording. *No, you don't*, the angel on my shoulder confirms. No. I actually don't, and the realization knocks into me the same way a tether ball would after missing your hit. I doubt Cliff will say anything too major. He might not even answer at all. I look over and Macallister's focus is burning a hole into the side of Cliff's head. Macallister must notice me because his head snaps in my direction.

His face is turning red and he looks almost panicked. I gesture that I don't have it, knowing exactly why his eyes have turned suspicious on me. I never wanted to reveal Torrence's secret, and I only spent a few hours with her. I realize with my reaction to the impending answer coming from Cliff that I'm starting to feel somewhat protective of him, and everyone else on this bus, for that matter.

My eyes burn as I mentally play a split-second montage of what would happen if I blew up these people's lives. My heart beats harder, and I'm concerned everyone can hear it. Before I can full-on panic, Cliff takes a deep breath that pulls me out of the shame spiral I'm falling into for something I haven't even done yet.

"You think I'm going to say breaking up the band, don't you?" That was obviously rhetorical since he didn't pause long enough for Darrell to respond. "I don't regret that. My biggest regret is when I lost the love of my life. I regret it every day."

No one moves. I don't think anyone even breathes. This is not only the deepest Cliff has gotten, but *any* of us has gotten. I can feel the air change as the entire dynamic on this bus shifts from where it once was. Now we're playing Truth—capital T—or dare. My face contorts instinctually. The searing facial expression Macallister is giving me makes my heart drop. He probably thinks I wish I had my recorder. In reality, I'm genuinely grateful I don't. I don't even look toward him to confirm this time.

CHAPTER 12

Macallister

What Cliff just said makes my blood go cold. The only thing keeping me from completely freezing over is the heat radiating from how close Prudence is sitting next to me. *Prudence.* I look to her, and out of reflex look for her phone. For a split second, I expect the phone in her hand, the speaker pointed at Cliff and screen lit up. When I look over, she's sitting in the same paralyzed silence everyone else is, no phone in hand, no recording happening, and I'm instantly sobered.

Cliff's confession brought the letter up to the forefront of my mind, but I realize I'm not sure what that has to do with Prudence. I've been so wary of her pulling something from Cliff, but I know he only said it because he feels comfortable enough to do so. This is the second time he's said something so emotionally raw and vulnerable. He doesn't know about the letter I found, and I've been projecting a lot of anxiety in the form of resentment toward someone who I know doesn't deserve it.

But it's my job, I remind myself. Prudence is a reporter, and I know the end goal is to get information out of them, specifically Cliff, on why Gnasher broke up. My job is to help protect Cliff, but I'm finding I don't even know how to do that anymore when he's oblivious to the thing keeping me up at night. I especially don't know what to do when she's pressed against me, and I can't find it in me to have any contempt toward her presence anymore even though I know I should.

My head throbs from the mental gymnastics and I massage my temples to relieve the tension.

Cliff, unfazed by the disbelief and shock painted on our faces, stands with a smile. "I think that's enough truth or dare for tonight," he chuckles to himself as he makes his way to the bathroom.

Everyone comes back into themselves to varying degrees. Glances pass around the table to the soundtrack of nervous chuckles. I feel Prudence take a deep breath next to me.

I turn my head and she smiles reluctantly. "So, uh ... you going to answer my question?"

Her eyes shine up at me, and I swear they're a brighter blue when she looks at me. They shift into almost aquamarine when they lock into mine. I forget she asked me a question until her expression changes from curiosity into embarrassment. That's when I remember before Cliff dropped a huge bombshell on us, she asked why I collect sea shanties.

I clear my throat and turn my body to face hers, feeling the alcohol I've consumed buzz in my veins again, making my resolve a little weaker than usual. "The men on my mother's side were sailors. My grandfather, and his father, and so on. I grew up around them my entire childhood. Hence why I wanted to be a sailor as a child." I keep the volume in my voice down, to keep this between us. Not because it's a secret, but because I enjoy sharing something with only her, even in a group of other people. I imagine myself reaching out and playing with the tendril of hair splayed across her shoulder, but the sobering realization that she's pulled me under her spell, gotten me to open up, pushes the fantasy from my head.

I notice the creases in her forehead soften as I talk, so I fall right back down the rabbit hole and continue, more concerned with the hope I can fully iron them out. "When I moved out and went to college, there was a record store near campus. It was deserted most of the time. Vinyls weren't as trendy yet. I would spend time in there to be alone." I remember myself flipping through the stacks of vinyl records mindlessly for hours as puffs of stale air wafted up my nose from the crinkled cardboard. All were old, and most were in less-than-ideal condition, and each had the powerful scent of slow business and lack of hands rifling through them on a regular basis. I had no intention to buy anything, until I came across one I couldn't leave the store without.

"I'd spotted a sea shanty vinyl. It reminded me of my grandfather and being home. So I bought it. It was the first record I ever bought. I didn't even get a record player for years after. I just started … collecting them. Anytime I found one, I bought it." I shake my head and chuckle to myself remembering the way it felt like my chest had cracked open at the sight of it, and how I have that same sensation sharing this with her, even though I know I should feel more apprehensive to unwrap pieces of myself to her.

"And you listen to them?" she asks, her blue eyes reflecting genuine interest in my answer and I don't sense a hint of any judgment.

I nod, "Sometimes I do, when I need a burst of nostalgia. But I also know a few sea shanties from hearing my grandfather sing them."

She smiles and her eyes crinkle in wonderment at my honest confession. My chest fills with warmth I haven't ever felt before, except the last time she showed interest in hearing me talk about myself. I'm so wrapped up in her and our private conversation that feels as intoxicating as it did in Vegas, I've tuned out the voices around us starting to rise until I no longer can.

Jasper abruptly stands and exclaims, "Take it back!"

I look up, realizing Cliff had returned to the table at some point during our conversation. He holds his guitar upright like he's about to start playing a song, but was interrupted. His face is a bright shade of red and his crinkled brow indicates his own rising anger. He's gripping the neck of the instrument and staring at Jasper unblinking. Darrell sits with his mouth hanging open and Travis looks truly concerned. *What the hell did we miss?*

I am trying to understand what's happening when I look over to Prudence, her eyes wide and scanning between the two men with almost visible steam rising from them. I can't read her emotions in this moment, but she looks uncomfortable. I scan my eyes down and she's holding the edge of the booth, tapping her fingertips almost impatiently.

As if she can feel my eyes on her, she abruptly stands. Hardly anyone notices her walking toward the back of the bus through the curtain. *Maybe to get her phone so she can record this.* I hate the way I can't stop the thought from forming, even after what we just shared. I clench my teeth, wondering what the hell they're arguing about.

This was bound to happen, I know, but a stray bead of sweat still makes its way down my forehead as Jasper opens his mouth.

Cliff cuts him off before he can speak. "Why are you mad?" While physically, he looks like he's heating up, his tone remains even.

Jasper scoffs. "Because you said we were …" he trails off, looking at his hands searching for his next words. "Say it again. I want to hear you say it again."

Cliff shrugs and opens his mouth to respond, but Jasper cuts him off, not allowing him to do the thing he's just requested. "Sellouts. You said we were sellouts, Cliff!" He's screaming now.

"We were." Cliff's tone stays level, and I'm shocked, considering the outbursts of anger he used to have.

"We were NOT! And even if we were, who fucking cares, Cliff? We were doing what we loved, and what we said we wanted to do. We were happy. I was happy." He starts heaving, obviously trying to catch his breath, and I'm dumbfounded so much could have transpired while I wasn't paying attention.

I look toward the curtain expecting Prudence to walk back through at any moment, but she doesn't. I know I should feel concerned that she'll capture this and send it to her boss. But I can't deny I'm purely concerned for *her* after witnessing how antsy she was before getting up.

"I wasn't happy." The level of Cliff's voice at this point is admirable. He has barely wavered and his volume is the same as when he dared me to sing.

"Yes, you were. You were until you got it in your head there was something better out there. You were until she—"

"Don't." Cliff's word booms as he stands abruptly, now allowing his tone to match his physical appearance.

Just then, my body leans forward when the bus comes to a stop. Looking at my watch, it's only about five minutes past eleven o'clock at night. It's late, but Harvey must have heard the commotion in here and grown concerned. Jasper and Cliff both have to grasp what is around them to keep their balance, but as soon as the bus comes to a complete stop, Jasper makes a beeline for the door. He stomps down the stairs and pushes his way outside.

I narrow my eyes at Cliff, and he glares back. "Don't start. Not right now." It's a warning. One I'll take for the immediate moment, but I fully intend to bring it back up later. He storms off out the same door, but once he gets outside, I'm certain he plans to walk in the opposite direction as Jasper.

Travis and Darrell sit with different expressions conveying the same confusion. Darrell's mouth hangs open like he's hoping something flies inside. Travis is staring blankly beyond my shoulder. I know his eyes are physically fixed on something, but he doesn't actually see. He's not trying to gaze into something, but pull his mind's gaze out of something, instead.

"What the hell happened?" I ask tentatively.

Darrell, mouth still agape, turns his head back and forth in slow motion. Travis stares for half of a second, then snaps back into himself with a quick shake of his head.

His eyes adjust toward me shakily as if reaching for an anchor.

"Cliff started talking about a song he's writing and Jasper asked to hear it."

"He said no," I say, not ask because I know.

"No, he didn't say no. Not exactly," Travis's eyes find mine. Okay, I guess I *don't* know.

"Then …" my voice trails off as I gesture at Travis to continue.

"He looked at Jasper and said, 'It's called *She's Better.*' I think Jasper … well, I don't really know, actually. Anyway, it escalated from there."

I stare at him waiting for more, but after about seven point five seconds, I realize that's it. I let my gaze fall, understanding this is something very much between them no one else is privy to. I shudder knowing there's probably another secret I have to hide. Or is it the same secret, possibly? Did Cliff get into a situation with someone close to Jasper? Will this ruin the tour?

I start to question my next move. Do I chase after one of them? Or do I go check on Prudence? Prudence, who ran away and might be staying directly behind the curtain with her phone capturing the confrontation that just transpired. Prudence, who is on this bus to get to the bottom of what the dynamic between two grown men with some serious shit in their past is. Something I'm desperately trying to hide so this comeback can be successful. My chest constricts a little bit with the strain of my incessant thoughts coupled with my anxiety over the situation when I notice the red curtain shift. She's standing in the open slit in the blood-red cloth.

Our eyes meet and my grimace falls. The way her face is drained of color and crumpled in worry lines is humbling, and I'm immediately sorry for those thoughts, for the story I just wrote that I now believe is false. I keep my eyes on hers as they widen when my gaze doesn't falter in the slightest. When so many seconds pass, I'm unsure how long I've been standing stagnant.

She takes a step further out from behind the curtain, toward me. "Is everything …" her voice fades off as she turns her gaze around at those of us remaining on the bus, unequivocally taking note of who isn't here. Her head lowers, then raises back up to my ever-present gaze, locked into where her eyes line up perfectly with mine again, "Okay?" she asks.

I scan her face, intrigued by what must be going through her head at this moment. For someone who I've watched read others with concerning accuracy, I'm realizing she isn't one to wear her emotions on her face. She definitely isn't right now.

I almost pull my typical tactic, which is to be an absolute dick. Tell her to mind her own business and send her back on her way. Because I shouldn't be leaning into whatever she's causing me to feel, even if I'm simply trying to write it off as curiosity. I can't stand the thought of speaking to her harshly when she already seems so vulnerable and unsure, mostly because I've never seen her this way before.

I let my hands drop to my sides from their crossed position. "I don't know." My answer floats out in a whisper, and I don't know if her ear caught it.

I forget anyone else was even there anymore until Darrell's usually annoying voice speaks out. "Should we go get them? Or something? Where are we, anyway?"

My face heats, and my muscles tense as I turn at him. "They need air." The last thing they need is Darrell's lack of charisma, particularly in an already explosive situation.

At the same time, of course we need to go fucking get them. But frankly, I cannot move from this position, standing in front of Prudence as I discern why her usually strong armor is missing.

Still, I turn away from her and toward Darrell. "On second thought," I say, actively trying to soften my face. "You should go after Jasper. I'll go after Cliff."

He tilts his head at me, probably shocked by my gentler than normal demeanor, then utters, "Alright."

He stands and slowly walks off the bus, apparently carried on a river of molasses with how fast he doesn't go.

I turn back to Prudence and she stands still, rooted in the same spot. "Can I get you something?" I take a step toward her. I notice my hand is outstretched as if intending to reach out and cup her face, hold it close to mine. I'm overcome by the sudden craving to be close enough I can taste her breath. But I catch myself, and pull my hand back to my side, flexing my fingers as I do so. I don't even know why that was my first reflex, considering I don't ever hold anyone close to me, physically or emotionally.

She shakes her head in short little turns but holds her eyes to mine. *Stay with me.* I wonder if her head is flip-flopping between unwanted and unexpected thoughts, but someone clears their throat loudly next to me. *Oh yeah*, Travis is still here.

He stands and as he walks, his blond head passes me by. He stops directly in front of Prudence and places his hand on her shoulder.

"You okay?" I can't fault him for worrying about her, but I also can't help the bubble of jealousy that rises in me.

She nods. I can't see his facial expression, but I get the impression he doesn't believe her because I see her mouth the words "I am," before smiling at him.

It must be enough to satisfy him because he walks past her and disappears behind the red curtain. When he's gone, she drops into a chair and sighs heavily. I've never heard her sound so dejected and a piece of me cracks a little on the inside at the sound, still left wondering what she's feeling.

"Are you okay? Can I—" her eyes move over to meet mine and it almost knocks the breath from my lungs, "fix it?" I whisper, crouching next to her, not recognizing the congenial, almost compassionate, resonance of my words.

With her head up toward mine, we're close enough that if I pushed in a tiny inch, our mouths would brush. As if that would happen, but I can't help but notice her eyes are … fixed on my mouth? *God damnit.* Her eyes slink back up to meet mine quickly, but I can't deny what I already saw.

Her brows scrunch in confusion at my question, but she heaves a sigh. "Oh, yeah." I tilt my head, urging her to elaborate how. "I mean, no. Sorry. I just got out of a pretty shitty relationship ..." *Fuck me, I will fucking kill that guy.* Heedlessly, I feel the desire to ask for this guy's name and address and ... I shake my head slightly to rid myself of the ridiculousness of my reaction.

I nod faintly letting her know she can continue.

"It was—" she searches for her words, and I notice something in her tone shift as if she's trying to remember lines from a script, "triggering, to hear them yell so loudly at each other." She shakes her head and takes another deep breath to steady herself, and I put my hand on her shoulder, pushing past the alarms in my head usually stopping me from touching her. She instantly softens under me, and I imagine making her entire body soften. Of laying my body across hers, showering her with kisses as her entire being melts below me. I could make her forget this guy. I could make her forget everything. *The fuck? Focus, you ass.*

"I'm okay," she takes a deep breath in and pats my hand. "I'm really okay. Thanks." Her voice firms up and it's like watching her armor click back into place around her body.

There's something else right behind her eyes, a glimmer of something she isn't telling me. I feel betrayed by it, especially after the story I shared with her earlier tonight. I don't believe she's okay either, especially considering the answer she gave me is not the entire truth of the situation, but I want to respect her; and right now, without saying it explicitly, she's telling me she needs space.

Despite the awkward pat she gave my hand, I give her shoulder a reassuring squeeze and my throat closes up at the thought of leaving her as I walk away. I'm unable to say anything and I rub at my chest as I step off the bus to find Cliff.

CHAPTER 13

Prudence

I'm shaken by everything that's happened in the last hour, but more specifically, I'm shaken by Macallister. I know he thought I was going to bring out my phone and start recording, documenting the fight between Cliff and Jasper. I'm sure everyone did. Rightfully so, if I'm being honest with myself, and it's hard not to be as I sit on the darkened bus. I'm a reporter, living on a tour bus with two of the most infamous rock stars in history. It's well known they have a history. It's not well-known why they broke up, but the information is so desired, I'm crazy for not recording. I missed a huge opportunity.

If I were a liar, I would say I didn't even think about it. Truth is, I felt an instinct to jump up and grab the device the instant I heard Jasper's tone inch up in volume. The entire exchange would have been like gold in Felicia's hands. She would have done anything to get that information, get the front-row ticket to the long-awaited crack in the already fractured window peering in on Gnasher's downfall. If she knew what happened and what I did not do, I'd probably be applying for unemployment.

If my first instinct was to grab my phone, my second happened only a second afterward and was a much stronger instinct: *Protect them.* Why? I do not fucking know. They are basically my meal ticket. If I were able to uncover the source of their problems, the reason they broke up ... I'd be a household name. I'm not saying that out of arrogance or even narcissism, but simply from fact. I've been in this business long enough to know what makes the clocks tick and bells chime. I know how to write an intriguing story, and I also know the story I was sent on this trip to uncover.

But I cannot. I won't, and I'm having a hard time deciding what to do about it. Which is why I ran off at first. I didn't want to sit there, witness something that would be considered journalism gold, and not do anything to collect the information my boss would praise me for. I didn't want the guilt. Plausible deniability. But then, Jasper and Cliff started to go at it. The sound of Jasper's voice rising to the point of yelling ... something about it took me back to every single relationship I've ever been in. It reminded me of every guy I've allowed to treat me like crap and yell at me without remorse. I needed time to breathe. But I'm still shaking from the adrenaline.

I'm stunned when I gaze up at Macallister, his face screwed up and appearing like the precursor to murder, and he opens his mouth. I brace myself. Instead of screaming, or accusing me, he simply asks, "Can I fix it?"

I'm shocked, and I struggle to even form a complete thought inside my head. Even with the exchange we had right before the fight, where he opened up to me willingly and I watched something between us shift and change, I awaited the irritation to slip back into place. But it hasn't. My jumbled thoughts continue to get cut off by my infatuation with the person showing genuine concern at this moment. I'm shocked by the way his eyes anchor into mine, reassuring me he isn't angry in the slightest. I'm sure of it.

And for some reason, I get close to the edge of an emotional waterfall I have yet to un-dam. It's been clogged up and I haven't had time to even consider moving the logs from their safeholds. But then I do. I remove one when I mention my previous relationship. I don't make it plural out loud, because I'm already revealing something so intimate, but also easier than telling him the initial reason I ran off. I can't be completely honest with him, though, because if I tell him I'm not only shaken up from the volume and my underlying concern for how this will continue to play out, but from the back-and-forth tug in me to do my job and guard the secrets of people I only just met, I'm being too vulnerable.

His face tenses and his jaw spasms. I'm in utter shock at myself for even having this thought, but the way his face contorts right now, I think he'd kill someone for me. I have to be misreading everything in my heightened emotional state. *Stop being delusional*, I scold myself. The multiple mistakes I've made previously, believing someone liked me enough to truly invest in a monogamous relationship with me rise up. I promised myself I wouldn't make that mistake again.

When I tell him I'm okay, non-verbally urging him to go, he looks physically pained to walk off. His facial expression is so visceral, there's a prick tugging at the back of my eyes, and empathy shoots through my veins, making me instantly agonize over a decision I helped to make. But I also need to decompress. I'm still doing mental gymnastics telling myself I did the right thing by suppressing the initial instinct to record what transpired between Cliff and Jasper.

I lay my head back and sigh deeply when the distinct rustling of fabric comes from the curtain opening again.

I don't open my eyes, knowing it's Travis and knowing what he's wondering. "He went to get Cliff."

"Hmm," the sound radiates up from his throat.

"Yeah, so, hopefully, they'll be back soon and we can keep rollin'." It sounds silly, my words dripping in glittery gunk. I know I'm dreading when they come back, because I can't help but wonder how it will change the dynamic.

"Prue, do you feel safe here?"

My eyes shoot open, and I jolt straight up, finding him staring back at me in earnest. "Yes." I say loudly, then utter, "Why?" less confidently.

"You deserve to feel safe in this situation, and I'd never thought about that until literally twenty minutes ago." His eyebrows pinch together with concern.

I study his face, finding the complete truth in his eyes. "I do feel safe. Their fight was ... triggering in a way, but I am okay." *Two ways, really. But I don't say that.*

"I'm not talking about the argument between Cliff and Jasper, and why you ran."

I search his eyes with mine, probing for him to continue, but he doesn't. "Macallister?" I relent, assuming whatever transpired between the two of us was as aberrant as I interpreted it to be.

He nods once with his eyes still trained on me, but keeps his lips pressed tightly into a taut line.

"If I said yes, would you believe me?" I'm worried he won't because I'm so accustomed to the people around me not believing me.

"Should I?"

I keep my eyes on his, hoping I portray the most sincerity I can in my emotionally heightened state. "Yes. I think if I regard anyone as an ally, it's you. From the moment I stepped on this bus, you've been the most welcoming, accommodating, and considerate from the get-go. So if I'm going to be completely honest with anyone, it's going to be with the person I trust." I nod in his direction, indicating I'm talking about him.

"I appreciate that. I don't take it lightly." I believe him.

"Then trust me when I say, I realize what just transpired was a bit bizarre. I'm not sure I completely understand it myself. Actually, I know I don't. And I won't lie and say I'm not confused, but I know for a fact I've also never felt safer than I do on this bus." It's a slight exaggeration, but also the truth at the same time.

He stands watching me for a long time. My perception of time might be warped by this point, though. His face softens from stiff and concerned, to empathetic and understanding. His head lowers toward his feet and he nods. He's clearly unconcerned about Cliff and Jasper returning, so I decide to pull from our trust bank and cut away my concern. Or at least I let it sway my logic a bit and this eases some of the anxiety I've stored in my shoulders over the last thirty minutes or so.

I've been concerned Cliff and Jasper won't be able to mend what just broke between them when I realize what happened was just pressure on a fracture formed a long time ago. I'm not sure this crack was unavoidable.

"I think there's a gas station out there. Do you need anything?" Travis's question jerks me from the whirlpool of thoughts starting to make me dizzy, and I'm grateful to be pulled out.

"I'm okay," I respond, and he gives me a halfhearted smile before walking down the aisle and off the bus.

I sit and stare for a moment thinking I could actually go for a candy bar. I'm about to follow him and go get one, but then I decide I need to get some sleep. I stand and walk through the curtain to climb into my bed. Into my pod, where I can at least have the illusion of being alone.

CHAPTER 14
Macallister

I'm pacing around the dark parking lot of a strip mall where barely any lights exist, aside from the glow of the 24-hour gas station. I turn my head back toward the bus and Travis steps out onto the pavement, his hands shoved into his pockets, and makes his way toward the beacon in the dark promising snacks and sugary drinks. I consider turning back to the bus now knowing Prudence is alone, but remember space is what she needs right now.

Travis glances around, probably trying to find one of us, and spots me. He hesitates in his movements before he eventually decides to walk toward me. When he's within reasonable speaking distance, he asks, "Find him yet?" I know he's talking about Cliff, but I haven't seen Jasper or Darrell, either, so I shake my head.

I gesture toward the bus. "She okay?"

He raises his eyebrow at me. "She is."

I nod.

I watch as he rolls his eyes, clearly having decided to just spit out what he was mulling around in his head. "You know ... you treat Prue like the enemy sometimes. Glaring at her, especially when it involves her job. Being short with her when you speak to her. But sometimes ..." his eyes dart around as if searching for what he's going to say next. "Sometimes you look at her and speak to her like she's yours."

That's perceptive. Or is it? Is Travis perceptive, or are we all admittedly trying to share an incredibly tight space that it's impossible to hide anywhere from anyone? I suspect a little bit of both, but more of the latter, and realize I'm being unprofessional. His concern also fills me with jealousy. Why does he care so much?

"She is not." I can't even say the word mine, especially when it pertains to Prudence, so I don't, hoping Travis understands my meaning.

"Alright. Well, then let her do her job."

I grit my teeth. "How am I not letting her do her job?" Before I can let him respond, I let the real question I want answered cut him off. "Why do you care, Travis? Do you have a thing for Prudence?" It would make sense. They're right around the same age. I'm only older than her by, what I guess is about 5 years or so, but Travis and her are most likely separated by only a year or two at most.

He tilts his head at me and frowns. "Not in the way I think you might. I do care about her, Mac, but as a friend. I don't want her to get hurt."

I let my facial muscles I didn't realize I was holding so tight relax a little. "I don't either," I say it more under my breath, but he hears me anyway.

"Don't play games with her. Don't take advantage of her while she's vulnerable."

"What is that supposed to mean? I'm not pursuing her, Travis."

His responding facial expression tells me he believes other-wise. "Okay."

He doesn't wait for me to respond, but instead turns on his heel and walks away. I mentally slap my forehead, knowing he was referring to the comment about her not being the enemy.

Closing my eyes, I take a deep breath and remember I'm out here for a reason. I survey the space around me, stretching my sight as far as I can in the dark to find Cliff. I don't find him. I don't even spot Darrell or Jasper. It's dark as hell out here, though.

I start walking around at a faster, more purposeful pace. I peer into the windows of the convenience store attached to the gas station. I count the tops of three heads: Travis, Jasper, and Darrell. *Great. Check them off the list.*

I continue forward in search of Cliff, knowing he wouldn't be in there with them. As I'm walking quickly past the alley between stores, someone coughs. I look down, and there sits Cliff. Right between the jewelry store and the running shoe outlet. *A rock and a hard place*, I think.

His figure sitting alone with his back against one wall, his legs bent up, startles me. I stand and stare at him until he cranes his neck up at me and smiles. "What's going on?" I say louder than I intended.

"I wrote a song."

He shrugs his shoulders, and it makes my face automatically screw upwards so tight my muscles pull. "Uh, that's great, Cliff. And why did that cause Jasper to start screaming at you and run off the bus?"

"He's ..." Cliff studies his hands, watching his fingers intertwining in a nervous habit I've watched him form as of late. "He's just angry still about what happened. I think he'd like the song if he'd just let me play it for him ..." his words trail off, and he sounds like a child.

I nod once. "Okay. Well, if there's something you're needing me to hide, you better tell me right the fuck now." My face heats, and my fists clench so tightly I know I would find half-moon shapes taking shape in my skin if I looked at my palms. The idea of trying to keep another secret grows up like a pine tree in my chest, poking and prickling me from the inside.

He shakes his head. "No, it's nothing like that. We just used to be really close. And now ..." He shrugs a little again. "We're not," he finishes in a whisper.

"Cliff, I —"

He abruptly cuts off my words with a quick raise of his hand and his words tumbling on top of mine. "This is nothing you need to concern yourself with, Mac." The tone of his voice shifts into something harsher, more assertive. "I've been behaving. I've been following directions. I've been properly diluting myself." He looks up at me, his eyes immediately finding mine. "I've been doing every single thing you've told me to do."

"I didn't tell you to write songs." I don't know why this is how I respond. He isn't wrong. Truthfully, he showed a lot of restraint when Jasper was coming at him. Restraint I didn't know he had that much of. But it's too late to scoop the words back into my mouth, so they hang in the air between us.

"Huh," he laughs humorlessly to himself. "You know what, Mac?" He finds my eyes with his own. Even though it's dark, I can still make out the blue. "You're so right. You got me there." He points a finger at me, pulsing it repeatedly in the direction of my chest.

His action brings more anger up to the surface, and I can't stop the next words from coming out. "You trying to get another Grammy, Cliff?" I spit, unsure where this pent-up anger is boiling from. My comment is way out of line, and I know that, but I can't stop myself.

He jumps up to his feet with an agility I cannot comprehend fast enough. "I don't want a fucking Grammy, Mac. I already won a Grammy, in case you forgot."

"Oh, I didn't," I raise my voice sarcastically. "You won't let anyone forget." My defense strengthens and I recognize the adrenaline pumping through me, fueling my responses, is coming from the stress of the secret of his I'm keeping. The secret he doesn't even know about to acknowledge. I feel so sorry for him, but at the same time, my spikes grow sharper. I do feel sorry for him, but I'm also angry with him.

"Well, good. Just so you remember who you work for." He turns to walk away from me and takes two steps before stopping and turning his head over his shoulder at me. "You know what, Mac? You're scared."

I squint my eyes back at him. "What?" I have no idea what he's talking about or why it pertains to this situation in the slightest.

He walks up to face me, our noses getting dangerously close. "You're. Fucking. Scared. Scared for me to fail. Scared for the responsibility I come with. And mostly, you're scared as shit to admit to yourself the feelings you have for Prudence." He's fuming. But now, so am I.

I suck in a breath, trying to compose myself, but feeling more like I swallowed a fly. "You hired me to help you rebuild your image. I'd like to say you hired me because that's what I'm accomplished at, but you and I both know I was your last resort. You hired me to help you keep yourself more contained to not fly off the handle and say things you can't take back. I know what I signed up for, and I still sign up for it willingly." I take a breath in, and he lets me, knowing I have more to say to him. "Now as for Prudence, I'll only say this, and then we can drop it ..." I pause as I make sure his eyes are locked into mine. "I am not ashamed of anything, because there is nothing, and even if there was, this is my job."

His eyes widen. "Mac, you can ..."

I cut him off. "I absolutely cannot. It is not professional, and it is not what someone like her deserves. I'm not taking away her security or her ability to be a professional while on this bus, writing her story." Travis's words come back to me. *Let her do her job.*

He shakes his head a little, his eyelids going slack with empathy. "You're so wrong. Haven't you been listening to me? You poor fool."

That's all he says before he starts walking back toward the bus, and I follow after him. When we get back on, I'm surprised that everyone sits around the table. Even Prudence sits, with her head down and her cheeks so beautifully pink. I quickly avert my eyes with an internal reminder to reel it in.

Cliff sits right next to Jasper. I stand looking between everyone except Prudence, unsure of how we can dissipate the energy, thick with negativity from before.

Darrell pulls on my arm. "Sit down, Mac."

"Macallister," I correct, but in a much softer tone than I normally do, as I lower in the seat. I don't know why I even bother anymore. I turn to him and force a smile in a silent apology.

Travis knocks his knuckle on the table three times. "Alright, Darrell. Truth or dare?"

The silence that stretches after his question only lasts a brief moment before small, anxious chuckles escape everyone's lips in various tones.

"I think we've had enough truths for the night," Darrell uncharacteristically says.

We all silently agree to continue playing truth or dare. Honestly, it's just a game of dares as no one is in the mood for any more deep conversations. It does take a few more rounds, but we fall back into the same place of joy we were in before all hell broke loose.

Jasper is dared to dance like a leprechaun while singing *Come On Eileen*, and he gives a genuinely hilarious performance. The sound of our laughter and resulting gasping from catching our breath fills the space on the bus and dissipates any lingering harshness.

When Jasper is done with his dramatics and sits again to the dwindling laughter, he knocks his knuckle on the table. Once. Twice. Then lifts his head. "Cliff, truth or dare?"

Cliff's expression falls into unreadable neutrality. "Dare," he says, no waver in his voice.

"Play your song." I realize I'm holding my breath after no one says a thing. No one even moves for what must be a full minute. Cliff turns to Travis, sitting at the end of the table.

"Can you hand Sheila to me?" He says, gesturing out a finger pointed at his worn, acoustic guitar leaning up against the kitchenette I didn't realize had a name. I decide to brush-off the fact that it's just something else I have to learn about him.

Travis grabs it, his face in an expression of confusion and anticipation. Handing it to him, he settles back into his seat and twiddles his thumbs. I'm watching anxiety overtake his body as his smile drops and I swear I can see the bead of sweat forming at his hairline. I wonder if anyone else is holding their breath the way I am.

Prudence sits stone-faced staring at Cliff. It's hard for me to stop my thoughts from assuming she's trying to commit the situation to memory to recount later while writing. That's when I see her reach into her pocket and my heart rate spikes. I'm too shocked to even do anything as she pulls her phone out. The back of my neck prickles and heats, and I watch her hold down the side button and the screen flashes with the prompt to power down the device completely. I'm stunned when, without hesitation, she slides her finger across the screen and it goes completely black. Without a glance toward me, she places her phone back into her pocket.

I allow my eyes to linger on her and understand with my entire being she's genuinely invested in the outcome because she cares. She has no interest in a story full of gossip, but in the relationships, her observations of interaction. She's letting her entire heart leap out and mine beats a little harder in defense of it. I want to shield her from the hurt of living with your heart so outside your body any element can affect it. She looks over toward me, finding me staring back at her into her blue, now somewhat glassy, eyes. I should divert my attention, or at least pretend to, but I concede my resolve is shot for the rest of the night. I'll try to be stronger tomorrow.

I hear her small intake of breath right before Cliff strums his first note, a loud A. He begins to pluck a bunch of notes strung together in a melody I immediately recognize is in three-four tempo, making it sound a lot like a waltz. I'm torn at who I want to focus on more: Cliff to see his reaction to being in this vulnerable state, or Prudence for the exact same reason, but of a different catalyst.

I hear Cliff's voice, but I hold my eyes to the side of her face, observing. Her cheeks push upwards, causing the skin around her eyes to crease. They blush slightly and quiver a bit. Her lip pulls downward, but still resembles happiness in a contradictory way. Her chin, dimpled and trembling slightly, has a curve so perfect, I want to trace it with my thumb.

A single tear escapes her eye and slides down her cheek as Cliff rasps out his song.

Anyone?

I'll take anyone.

Pruned the thorns from my side are they

Wires or vines?

CHAPTER 15

Prudence

Cliff finishes on the last note and raises his head back up to signal he's done. We sit in quiet contemplation, and I can't help my mind from swirling. Travis is tapping his thighs as if already writing the drum part mentally.

After a moment, Jasper nods. "Can we play around with it? You and I?"

He's so hopeful, it takes forty years off his face. Travis turns his gaze between Cliff and Jasper, and the look of feeling left out fills me with so much sadness, I almost jump to his defense irrationally.

"Yeah, all three of us can." Cliff doesn't look directly at him but tilts his head toward Travis. As I watch this unfold, I'm almost nauseous from the roller coaster of emotions I'm currently riding on. The grin spreading across Travis's face soothes my previous concern like a balm on the chapped part of my heart, healing what happened earlier tonight. Or at least, starting to soothe it.

Just like that, we move on. At least everyone else does. As we play a few more rounds of truth or dare, I'm fighting to pay attention. I don't want to be alone right now, but I also can't stop myself from dissecting everything that's happened in the last few hours. The fight, the unspoken resolution between Cliff and

Jasper, and then Cliff's song. With a title like *She's Better* and Jasper's resulting reaction to hearing the title, I expected Cliff to reveal something salacious. I really thought I was about to hear why Gnasher broke up, and that realization is what caused me to press the power button on my phone. Mostly from the need to give myself an alibi, albeit a weak one. The closer I get to uncovering Gnasher's decades-old secret, the farther I want to scoot away.

The song wasn't about the band at all, though, and it wasn't about an affair ... it was just about Cliff. It was hard to listen to, and I couldn't even control the tears I felt falling down my cheeks at some point, because the lyrics were so raw, about depression and loneliness. It was such a far cry from the Cliff I'd researched in preparation for this tour. While I didn't have a lot of time, of course I watched videos and read as much as I could before stepping foot onto this bus. Cliff in the 90s was ... rude, to put it mildly. Multiple videos captured his outbursts, cursing out interviews when asked a question he didn't like, saying off-handed and vulgar things when presenting at award shows clearly not on an approved script. I even found articles and documents of all the hotels he's blacklisted from, for life. I actually found those articles after being on the bus for about a week, and it made me chuckle a little wondering how fun that must have been for Macallister when planning out this tour.

It was a far cry from the Cliff I'd researched, but not from the Cliff I've gotten to know personally. I look over to him, strumming his guitar quietly and watching everyone take turns giving each other lazy dares. A never-ending circle of yawns begins, and everyone starts to retreat to the back for sleep. When I finally rouse my muscles to stand and go to bed myself, Cliff and Macallister are the only ones left sitting at the table.

"Goodnight, Prudence." I turn to Cliff and his smile is almost sympathetic.

I nod to him with a smile, then turn my attention to Macallister and give him the same. He doesn't say anything, and he barely even raises his eyes to mine. I wonder if he saw me pull my phone out earlier.

"I didn't—" I start, but his head snaps up.

"I know." His tone is harsh, but in a reassuring way. Like he wants to make sure I heard him, not like he's angry.

I turn and walk behind the curtain.

As I'm laying in my bed, the events of this one day pile as high as three days, like listening to an audiobook sped up three times to get through it faster. I sigh and let my eyes drift closed. As soon as I do, there's a loud buzz. I reach over and grab my phone. My stomach drops. I've been completely sucked into this lifestyle of touring and living on a bus, I've completely forgotten to check in with Jessica and my mom. I did text Jessica after Vegas to let her know I tried the drink, and we texted a little back and forth, but nothing too in-depth.

Her name lights up my screen now, and I hold my breath as I press to open her message. It's so late, or early depending on how you look at it, and I'm worried something is wrong.

> Sup bitch

I cover my mouth to stifle a little giggle. My fingers fly across my screen, typing my response.

> I'm sorry I've been out of touch

I skip the small talk. Jessica and I have been friends for so long and we are so in sync, there's no need for pleasantries.

> Dude you're on a tour bus living like a rockstar.
> Don't worry about it! Just want to make sure
> you're alive

> I'm alive

> I'm actually loving this

3 a.m. Prue is an honest Prue

Lol

I'm on a tour bus, so I have an excuse. But what are you doing up?

Don't laugh

No guarantee

I have a sunrise hike

Eew you hate hiking

And mornings

Wait …

With who?!?!?

If I tell you her name, I might jinx it

Secret for secret?

I use our old childhood tactic to get the other to talk. If you share a secret, the other has to as well. My heart warms for my best friend as I type back and forth with her. I miss her.

You first

Ugh

I think I'm falling for someone

I haven't even admitted this to myself, so typing out those

words to her takes me longer than it normally would. I hold my breath as the tiny dots indicating her typing a response pop up, disappear, pop up, and disappear again. Either she's writing a novel, or she's at a loss for words.

I drop my hand, still holding my phone by my side, and close my eyes while I wait for her to respond. My palm buzzes with her response and I raise my phone back up to my face to read what she said.

> Her name is Inez. Spill.

I chuckle a little as I draft a response. I start typing, and I let the early morning haze fill my head as I let my completely unfiltered response come out before I can change my mind or regret saying anything.

> His name is Macallister. He's Cliff's manager. He hates my guts. At least I thought he did. He's so hot and cold, but more than anything, he's intense. Sometimes he'll look at me and I swear his eyes dig tiny and revealing holes into me. He makes me vulnerable, but comfortable at the same time. He doesn't trust me because of what I'm here to do, but I find myself wanting him to trust me. I have barely been recording, and I know Felicia is frustrated with my lack of recordings and lack of information

I hit send and immediately start typing again.

But that's the thing. It's not even just him. I don't want another Torrence situation. But I also am growing close to these people. It might be the fact that I'm stuck on this tiny bus with them most of the time, but it's been a long time since I felt this sense of camaraderie. It's crazy. They fight, then they make up. They argue, then act like nothing happened. They simply move on, and instead of creating chasms, it brings them closer. I'm watching Jasper and Cliff's relationship mend. I'm watching them accept Travis in, even though he's a lot younger. I'm experiencing something I didn't anticipate. There's a story worth telling, but I know Felicia doesn't care about it

And I'm experiencing this with him. With his eyes on me, waiting for me to expose something. In reality, all I want to do is bask in this feeling. It's like a haze

Hmm sounds cool. Goodnight

I laugh out loud, knowing Jessica is giving me grief about how much I wrote in comparison to her four-word secret. I'm worried the loud sound I let slip out might have woken someone up. I clap my hand over my mouth and stretch my ear. I don't hear anything, so I assume I'm okay. I feel the buzz of my phone against my palm.

Prue, that's a lot to unpack. First thing first, enjoy yourself. Felicia can suck it. You'll write the story that needs to be told, and you'll do a killer job at it. So let yourself bask in it. It sounds like you're meant to be there and meant to be a part of this

I read her message and three dots pop up at the bottom of my screen. I don't respond, and instead stare at the bubble waiting for more words to appear.

> Now, as for Macallister … I say lean into it. I know how you are. So if he's giving you a look that heats up your loins, he probably meant it to. Stop second-guessing yourself. That's how you've ended up with assholes like Jake. You deserve an orgasm from someone who doesn't call you names and hold you emotionally hostage

She's not wrong.

> Thank you. I needed that. I miss you

> I miss you, too. But Prue, don't let him drag you along. If you want a label, you need to be brave enough to demand one this time

Her words cut through my heart to one of my deepest insecurities. She knows the struggles I've had, mainly men using me and never providing me what I crave: an actual commitment. I don't type anything back, but another message from her comes through, lighting my screen back up.

> Prue, I'm excited for you. Get some sleep. And just know you deserve whatever makes you happy

I adore her.

> Text me later about your date :)

> I will. Love you

I type back I love her before I plug my phone in and tuck it away. I curl on my side, fixing my eyes growing heavy with sleep on the curtain. I can't help but wonder if Macallister is asleep above me. I'm not sure how long it takes me to drift off.

———

When I wake up the next morning after only a few hours of sleep, I know the bus is currently parked because of the lack of movement. I rub my eyes and reach for my phone to check the time: It's 8:49 a.m., which means I got approximately four hours of sleep. I turn in my bed, letting my legs out as I open the curtain. Some curtains are opened and some remain closed. Someone is snoring softly, so I sneak out into the main area of the bus in search of caffeine.

Darrell is sitting at the table with a paper cup of coffee. Noticing a logo on the side of the cup makes a small bubble of anger rise up. So we stopped for coffee, but no one woke me up.

I shake off the irrational irritation caused by lack of sleep and notice Darrell's face. He seems hypnotized because his eyes don't even lift from the black plastic top on his coffee until I clear my throat a little.

"Oh, morning," he says, lacking his usual peppiness.

"Rough night?" I ask, mentally pulling up a replay of last night. I don't remember him getting drunk. I actually don't remember him drinking at all. Though, without alcohol, last night was rough for all of us.

"Well, I don't know." His gaze lowers back down. "Tired. I guess."

I look around, noticing Darrell is the only one sitting out here. "Where is everyone?"

He nods his head toward the curtain. "Travis is still sleeping. Cliff, Jasper, Mac, and everyone from Cosmic's bus is out there."

I peek out the window. "Are we … at the Grand Canyon?"

He nods. "Cliff wanted to stop."

I walk toward the door to go outside. I turn slightly back in Darrell's direction. He's still sitting and staring. I wonder for a moment if last night shook him up. Assuming that's what his demeanor is attributed to, a wash of empathy for him overpowers me. He usually annoys me, but right now he appears so human. Even with his recently touched-up leopard spots.

"You sure you're okay?" I say over my shoulder.

He nods, but says, "I think so."

"Well, I'm here," I say instinctually the way you'd tell your annoying baby brother you're there for him, even if he drives you crazy most of the time. I mean it in the same way, too.

"Thanks," he raises his head and meets my eyes as if to inspect the sincerity in my consolation.

I nod and turn to get off the bus. My feet hit the ground, and I can hear my stomach begging for sustenance. I should have grabbed a granola bar or something on my way out, but I force my feet forward wanting to explore more and take advantage of the fresh air.

When I step out onto the rocky terrain, a blonde head approaches me from the side. I turn to see Roslyn's smiling face and smile back at her.

She walks up to me and stops by my side. "You missed the sunrise."

"Have we been here that long?"

She giggles. "We have. You all pulled in a little less than an hour ago." It makes sense that our unplanned stop last night set us back.

"I guess I forgot your bus didn't stop last night."

She turns and eyes Gnasher's bus parked next to Cosmic Intervention's. "Must be interesting living so closely with the two of them."

I know she's referring to Cliff and Jasper, and I nod in confirmation. "Interesting is one way to put it." I turn and see her concerned expression.

She contemplates my words and I'm almost worried she's going to ask for a play-by-play of what happened last night.

That's what Jessica would do. My skin buzzes with anxiety at the anticipation of having to rehash everything.

Instead, she shakes her head and smiles, seemingly to herself before making eye contact with me again. "Music really has a way of tearing people apart or bringing them together."

It's a somewhat cryptic thing to say, but very on brand for Roslyn, and I should have known better than to expect anything else. "You say that like you have experience." She just smiles in response and continues to admire the landscape.

I haven't pushed for an interview with Cosmic Intervention. As much as I've thought about it, there is enough on my plate at the moment and I'm not going to even mention it to Felicia again. She'd push for it the same way she's pushing me now. I rub my temples because just the thought of it is giving me a headache. Or maybe that's the lack of caffeine.

"I do," she says with zero hesitation in her voice.

Before I can say anything in response or ask her for more, she flashes me her white teeth in a smile, pivots on her heel as graceful as a trained ballet dancer, and walks away. I stand in shock for a moment before deciding to walk around myself and stretch out my muscles, sore from lack of sleep. As I'm walking, I can hear Cliff and Macallister speaking, but I don't make out what they're saying. I turn to walk toward where they stand together. They both hear me approach, and their expressions puzzle me. Cliff slides his sunglasses on. Macallister stares at me in disbelief as if I shouldn't be here.

I've disrupted an important conversation and I immediately retreat. When I turn to walk away, Macallister calls out to me, "Prudence." Hearing my name from his mouth makes me halt instantly.

I turn, and he's holding a paper cup and a banana. Seeing his coffee brings awareness to the dull throb starting to make itself known at the base of my skull.

He reaches me and holds out the cup toward me. I marvel at it, wondering what it means.

"I got you a cup of coffee. I tried keeping it hot for you, but I'm afraid it's probably just warm at this point," his eyes don't meet mine, as if he's ashamed he does not possess the power to keep coffee hot. What is hot, is me. Thinking about the fact he not only got me coffee, but he let me sleep and waited for me to wake up. I couldn't care less what temperature the liquid is.

I reach out and grab it. My fingers brush up against his as he transfers the cup from his hand to mine. He holds my gaze for only a moment before stepping back quickly.

"I also got you this," he extends his other hand holding the banana toward me.

I don't take this immediately, and instead, gape at his hand like he's holding a dirty diaper out to me.

I scrunch my nose, not wanting to be rude, but unable to hide my reaction to what he picked out for me to eat. "You got me a … banana?"

CHAPTER 16

Macallister

"I … is that …?" *Shit.* Why the fuck did I get her a banana? "I thought you might be hungry?" I don't know what else to say. In truth, I'm still exhausted, getting hardly any sleep after the events of last night. I contemplated over and over this morning on whether or not getting her something would be considered professional.

She stares at the banana in my hand as if it's a bomb about to detonate. "Bananas are the potatoes of fruit."

I shift my feet, uncomfortable in my astonishment as the reality of what she said washes over me. She shakes her head a little.

I can't stop the small laugh puffing out from between my lips. "What?" I ask, even though nothing has ever made more sense to me. "Bananas are …"

"The potatoes of fruit, yeah," she finishes for me.

"Did you come up with that while high in the shower?" I ask, trying not to picture her in the shower.

She places her hands on her hips. "Tell me I'm wrong."

I can't. "Well, I apologize. So you … hate potatoes?" I don't know what else to say.

"No. I mean, it was super nice of you to grab me a small banana. I just don't want it. And no, I love potatoes."

I turn the fruit over in my hand and examine it. "Small?" It's not huge, by any means, but I'm confounded at why she felt the need to criticize its size.

She giggles. "Oh come on, that's small."

I raise my eyebrow at her. "I think I'd call this average." I hold up the banana to give her a better view of how large, or not large, it is.

"Yeah, I'll bet you would. Most men feel the need to stick up for," she clears her throat, "the size of their banana. Out of embarrassment."

My face flares at her innuendo. The flame blazing fills me with a boldness I shouldn't exhibit right now, but don't do anything to stop myself. "I don't refer to it as a 'banana,' but trust me when I tell you, Prudence, I am not embarrassed about the size of my cock." I can't believe I said that. That was not professional in the slightest.

I walk away before I can examine her reaction too closely. I know the perfect bloom of pink undoubtably spreading across her cheeks would bring me to my knees. I walk a few paces before I hear the crunch of gravel behind me.

"Hey!" she calls as she jogs over to me. "You can't say stuff like that to me."

Fuck, why did I do that? I know that was reckless of me. I know I promised myself I'd be more professional, but she's the one who brought it up. I cannot continue to run on fumes anymore. I need to sleep because I have no self-control. Did I jeopardize my career? Worse, did I jeopardize *her* career?

She reaches me and stands with her arms crossed in front of me. The motion is so cute, it's hard for me to not smile right now. But I'm quickly sobered by the fact that she's probably about to scream at me about sexual harassment, and rightfully so.

I put my hands in front of me. "Prudence, I'm so sorry. You're right, I shouldn't—"

She cuts me off before I can finish with a loud huff. "It confuses me."

Now I'm the confused one, and I don't respond. I am trying to gather my thoughts and a response based on what she just said.

Her face grows red, with anger or embarrassment, I'm not sure. "You can't say stuff like that to me," she says under her breath, and I'm positive she said it more to herself than to me.

"You're right," I confirm, having nothing else to say back.

She starts gesturing with her hands along with her words, now flowing out in a stream of consciousness. "One minute, you're mad at me. Or you're looking at me like I'm a toddler about to do the thing you told me not to do. You don't want me on this tour, and you've made that very clear. But then, you say something about your," she gestures toward my crotch without letting her eyes fall. "Or sometimes, you get this look in your eye," she says the last part much quieter and her mind seems to drift further in thought.

I start to respond but she cuts me off again. "Whatever. What is this?" Judging by the way she's moving her hands back and forth in the space separating us, she means us, and that's when the reality I've been dancing around crashes over me: There is no us. At least, there shouldn't be an us.

I know that. There can't be an us, as much as I fantasize about it. I shouldn't fantasize about it anymore. I shouldn't picture her sitting in my lap when we play truth or dare. I shouldn't imagine myself whispering into her ear, secrets only we know. I shouldn't picture her eyes when I close my own, using them as an anchor of comfort. And I certainly cannot keep treating her like this. She deserves better than this back and forth, hot and cold I've given her since Vegas. I'm trying to stay neutral, and I'm doing a terrible job of it.

"We're nothing, Prudence." The words burn my tongue like hot acid. They're technically true, but I am also somehow flooded with the overwhelming shame that accompanies a lie.

She blinks back at me. "Right," she breathes out as she walks past me toward the bus. I watch her walk away, glued to my spot. I was supposed to walk away first, but like she always does, she stunned me speechless and I'm left here standing in my own brand of shock and confusion.

I take in the average-sized banana in my hand, twisting it to examine it further. "The potato of fruit," I whisper to myself as I replay her words in my head. Why the actual fuck is that the smartest dumb thing I've ever heard? Why am I standing in the middle of the Grand Canyon, caressing a banana and chuckling to myself? If I walked past myself, I'd be concerned. I *am* concerned.

When I walk back onto the bus, everyone has dispersed. Darrell is sitting at the table, holding a paper cup of coffee between his two hands and staring at the black lid on top. It's a little creepy, so I let my eyes roam until I spot Travis sitting in the back, reclined on a chair with his baseball hat over his face. Jasper opens the curtain, looks at Travis, smacks his foot, and says, "You good?"

Travis barely responds, but simply grunts from under his hat. "Want a banana?" I ask him.

At this, he pulls the hat from his face and sits up abruptly. "Oh, hell yeah!"

I hold the banana out to him and laugh at his enthusiasm for an average-sized banana. He immediately slumps back down and peels his new treasure.

Jasper goes to sit on a couch, and I notice Darrell sits unmoved from his previous position. He is staring so intently at his cup of coffee, I wonder if the meaning of life is written on the lid.

"Darrell," Jasper calls to him.

His head pops up, but he doesn't respond verbally.

Jasper tilts his head a little and scrunches an eye.

Darrell nods once.

I wonder briefly if I intruded on something, even though all I witnessed was a completely wordless conversation.

"Darrell?" This time, my voice calls his name in an invitation.

His head raises up, slower this time, and his eyes meet mine. "Yeah?" His voice is reluctant.

"Are you okay?" I ask what Jasper's body language already conveyed, so I don't know if I'm expecting a different answer or just stupid.

"I—I've been better."

I asked, so I shouldn't be stunned. But I am. I am tied into this. I can't walk away now. *How are you? Oh shitty? That sucks, bye now.*

"What's up?" This line of questioning is unnatural on my tongue. So I channel Prudence, leaning toward him, letting him know I care about his answer.

"Do you even like me?" *Shit.* I want to use a vacuum to suck back up the last minute and a half.

Instead, I stare at him wide-eyed, not knowing how to answer.

He shakes his head and looks back down at his cup. "Yeah, I get it."

Jasper gets up and sits next to him, clapping him once on the back. "Darrell, shut up. Did you get any sleep last night?"

Darrell peers over at Jasper with a half-hearted smile and shakes his head indicating he did not.

Jasper smiles back at him and nods once. "Thought not."

"I didn't." For some reason, I'm still channeling Prudence so much so that honesty has started to leak out of me without my control. Jasper and Darrell both widen their eyes at me. "I didn't like you, I mean. You're unorganized, inexperienced, and you get hair dye all over the bathroom when you touch up your ..." I point my finger at his head. "Hair spot things." Jasper chuckles into his fist. "But I like you now. And all this work managing these assholes is hard. So it's nice to only have to worry about one."

He gawks at me before he finally smiles. "Thanks, Mac." I don't even correct him this time.

Jasper claps his hands together. "Well, Kumbaya. Anyone want some shrooms before we start moving again?"

My eyes narrow and cut to Jasper. "Shrooms?" The tone in my voice rises.

"Yes, lover boy. Shrooms. Like the … uh …" he starts snapping his fingers in mockery of me. "Oh, uh … Drugs." His eyes find mine on the last word.

I keep my tone even. "Jasper, you have an image to uphold."

"No. You're not my manager, remember? You're Cliff's. So you don't need to waste your time worrying about my image." He points a finger at his chest. His tone is light, but his words piss me off nonetheless.

I scoff. "Jasper, everything I do is for the better of all of you. You're a band. His image is your image."

He closes his eyes and shrugs exaggeratedly. "Hmm."

That's it? Hmm? Is he goading me right now, or is he serious?

I'm about to open my mouth when Cliff walks up behind me. I know this because his hand is on my shoulder. The familiar grip when he's trying to bring me back to center.

"Don't worry, I'm not going to do shrooms," his voice says in my ear.

I turn with a narrowed gaze but step out of his reach. "Really?"

Cliff raises an eyebrow as his lips turn up.

I shake my head at him. "Are there drugs on this bus right now?"

There's a giggle from behind the red curtain cracked with a line of light, along with a perfectly peach fingertip with the nail painted black. I know she's there, right behind the curtain. I want to fling it open and catch her. I want to behold the surprised glimmer in her eye at thinking she was being sneaky, and in reality, she's horribly unsubtle. I want to scowl at her with mock disappointment. I want the corner of her mouth to hitch up before breaking out into the contagious smile that reaches her eyes, causing the blue to reflect a gold shimmer that pulls me so deeply in, I'd rather drown than even attempt swimming back up.

I face the curtain, willing her to push it open again, wanting her to catch me. I'm a fool. I told her we were nothing, and yet I'm standing here willing her to constantly be in my line of sight. I've completely forgotten about the topic of my anger already evaporating from my body.

I'm broken from my trance by Cliff's voice. "Mac." It's a question, a command, and a comforting gesture all at the same time. My eyes scrape away from the curtain to find his raised eyebrow.

My face morphs back into a complete scowl, mostly out of embarrassment from getting caught once again, and I put a finger up toward his face. "No drugs."

Jasper chuckles to himself. "You can have some," he teases me.

I take a deep breath in. "We're rockstars," Cliff says with a shrug.

"No, you were rockstars. Now, you're—"

"Don't you dare say old," Jasper spits.

"I wasn't going to." I earnestly wasn't.

"Well, we are kind of old," Cliff admits, and it sounds like it's a confession he's making more to himself than anyone else. "We're also rockstars. We're also …"

"Heading to Tucson." Travis's voice calls as he dances out of the bathroom. He must have gotten up at some point during this conversation and I didn't even register it. As if the banana brought him back to life, he starts shimmying his shoulders with his fists balled up in the most ridiculous dance.

Jasper starts laughing, and even Cliff lets Travis's attempt to break up the tension wash over him as his lips turn upwards.

The high-pitched, feminine laugh from behind the curtain stops my heart momentarily. Travis reaches over, and pulls the curtain free, revealing a giggling Prudence covering her mouth. Everyone else turns to her and bursts out laughing. I feel my mouth creep up in a smile despite the tension pressing through my muscles.

A hand gently grips my shoulder. "There are no drugs on this bus, Mac."

I turn and am face to face with Cliff. "None?"

He shakes his head, and Jasper stands out of the corner of my eye. "None," he confirms. "Just like riling you up sometimes."

Normally, I'd be irate at this, but something inside me melts, and I think it's partially from the sound of the laugh coming from her. I shake my head at him and sit at the table as the bus drives forward again.

CHAPTER 17

Prudence

I wasn't trying to be discreet. I know Macallister saw me standing behind the curtain, and I know exactly what he thought: I was trying to record the fight between Cliff, Jasper, and him. For the record, I wasn't. I heard some commotion, and curiosity got the best of me, so I pushed up against the curtain to listen. I know I'm on a tour bus with a rock band probably notorious for doing drugs back in the day, but for some reason, I was still caught off guard to hear there are drugs on the bus right now. I was even more surprised to hear the confession that, in reality, there *aren't* any drugs on the bus, but Jasper said it only for the purpose of getting a reaction from Macallister.

I honestly have not undergone the level of partying I expected to on this tour. Drinking, sure. Some rowdy behavior, especially after shows when there's still adrenaline coursing through them or during truth or dare. But even thinking through that, I find myself laughing. Are these guys the lamest rockstars in history, or do I have a warped sense of what goes on during a tour?

I'd be lying if I said I wasn't relieved I'm not living in a scene from a movie where the rowdy rockstars get blackout drunk or high and destroy hotel rooms. But did I expect that to happen? Yeah, I did.

Jasper pats the seat next to him. "Sit, Prue. Let's chat."

My eyes widen. *Does he mean …?*

"Aren't we due for another one of your interviews?" Yep, he does mean what I thought.

I wait for protest from Cliff, or Macallister, but am met with silence. Instinctually, I want to go get my notepad and phone. I have a great memory, but if we're being honest, I haven't been recording as much as I should and I'm way overdue to send something to Felicia. A fact she pointed out to me curtly in a text written in all caps earlier.

"Let me—" I point toward our beds, then skirt away quickly to grab my stuff.

When I return, no one has moved. I sit next to Jasper. Macallister's eyes are pinned on me the entire time. I realize it's causing my muscles to seize up, almost in protest. I'm uncomfortable and I'm sure that's obvious to everyone else. I take in a deep breath through my nose discreetly, then remind myself of who I am when I open my mouth slightly to release the air.

I let my muscles release the tension and I will my body into a casual composure as I turn to Jasper, hitting the record button and saying, "Whatcha wanna talk about, Jazzy P?"

He tilts his head back and laughs. "You're the reporter," he teases me, and out of the corner of my eye I see Cliff sit down across from us.

I hate that he turned this back on me. I am more aware of my words because the recording app is on and I don't need Felicia getting mad I'm not pushing for more or asking more prying questions. I decide to forget about it completely, and just have a conversation the way I normally would.

"Actually, let's talk about *Fuck Me Sober*. We haven't yet, and I'm pretty sure none of us would be here right now if it wasn't for that song." I point the end of my pen toward him.

He closes his eyes and nods. "Kids and their internet these days." When *Fuck Me Sober* went viral, it went so viral, it bumped it onto the Billboard Hot 100. All the way to number one for a solid two weeks. It's almost unheard of for an older song to do that besides *All I Want for Christmas* by Mariah Carey yearly in December, especially a song that never charted when it was first released.

"What was it like hearing your song, which never even got radio play before, was on the Billboard Hot 100?" I swivel my head slightly between both him and Cliff to indicate my question is for both of them. Macallister sits on the other side of Cliff.

"I'm not on the Tok thing ..." Jasper says hesitantly.

"Tik Tok?" I ask for clarification.

He waves his hand. "Yeah, whatever. So I didn't even hear about it for a few days."

"I called him," Cliff interjects.

"You did," Jasper nods.

"What did he say?" I raise my voice in enthusiasm for the story I'm about to hear, and excitement that both Jasper and Cliff are participating.

"Well, it was the first time I'd heard from him in ... years." Jasper's voice trails off slightly on the last word. He stares off.

Cliff fixates on Jasper's reaction without speaking. I want to ask what I'd normally ask in an interview which is 'Why?' But something stops me, and I'm unsure of how to react to that something sitting directly behind my ribs.

Instead, I pivot the conversation to bring us back into a safe space. "I've been wondering what it's about."

Cliff rolls his eyes. "I don't fucking know. Jazz wrote that shit, so I'll let him take this one."

The light that previously faded from Jasper's eyes returns, and he practically vibrates at the opportunity to tell me. "You ever get so high that you end up with someone in your bed? And you fuck, obviously, but it's so mind-blowing, your climax hits you so hard, you're sober again?"

I blink at him. "Have I ... uh ... no, Jazzy P, I can't say I have had that experience before."

I hear a chuckle, and I assume it's Cliff. But when I turn

around, I realize it's Macallister. His laugh is soft, but his eyes burn.

"And what the hell are you laughing at, Mac?" Jasper asks with mocking accusation, turning his attention toward Macallister.

He crosses his arms and sits back, pressing against the back of the seat. "Some of us can do that without drugs, bud."

A low swoop of my stomach fills my belly with molten lava. The thought of Macallister in bed with someone fills me with so many rushing thoughts and images, along with conflicting emotions. Conflicting because when I picture it, I don't want to picture it with anyone but me. Heat rises up my neck.

Cliff starts laughing and slaps his knee as if he can't hold it in anymore. "Jazz, shut the fuck up. You wrote that song about the love of your life."

Jasper shoots Cliff a glare that screams, *Oh come on!* Before falling into a fit of laughter himself. "Alright, alright. I wrote it about the love of my life."

They both nod and simultaneously talk over each other.

"Kimberly."

"Michelle."

They both tilt their heads as if choreographed with the same closed-mouth smiles, holding for a brief moment before bursting into loud, uninhibited laughter so heartfelt it can only be the laughter shared between two old friends with an inside joke.

Jasper turns back to me after the sounds of their joy subside. "I think Cliff is right. It was probably Sarah."

I smile, and press on, loving how this conversation is going so far already. "I looked it up, and *Fuck Me Sober* never even reached the charts when it was released. Mostly because it wasn't a single. It was a crowd favorite at shows, but nothing compared to what it is now. What does that feel like?"

"Fucking rad." Jasper nods. "It brought us back." His tone is almost wistful, all hints of joking pushed away again.

I eye Cliff, hoping for him to jump into this conversation. "Scared me a little, frankly," he follows.

"Scared you?" I ask.

"I thought we'd keep falling, further into oblivion and out of the spotlight. I didn't think we'd be catapulted back up into it. Especially without even trying." He taps his fingers absentmindedly on the table in front of him.

"Would you consider it a good thing or a bad thing?" His tone makes it sound like a bad thing, and this tugs at the unknown parts of Cliff haunting me.

He shrugs. "Neither? It's just life. Unexpected things happen and I don't have a lot of time to wonder what if. I'm too busy wondering about other things ..." His words trail off.

"Constantine loved playing that song live," Jasper's voice cuts through Cliff's unspoken words.

Cliff finds Jasper's eyes, in a soft understanding, and they both nod, remembering their friend and former bandmate.

"I know this is a sensitive topic ..." I start.

"Not really," Cliff says. "I miss Constantine. He was a great drummer. He was also funny as hell. He would sometimes wear this T-shirt he wrote 'No One Cares About the Drummer' across in black Sharpie. Made us all laugh." Travis's shoulders shake with a laugh at the playful jab at drummers.

Jasper shakes his head. "He was a great friend. And he was amazing on the drums." He nods at Cliff. "You broke his heart."

"Don't even try to pin what happened on me," Cliff's words come out sharp, and it's as if the temperature rises slightly. My fingers tingle with tiny prickles from the possibility of causing another rift between the two of them.

My eyes find Macallister's eyes. I expect a stone cold expression piercing my phone, the screen showing the moving clock of recording, the green light blinking, capturing the information spilling from Cliff and Jasper. Instead, his eyebrows are pinched together slightly in a concerned expression, and he's looking right back at me. It makes my skin break out in goosebumps. I'm almost shivering under his noticeably protective gaze and preparing myself for a full-on fight to break out between Cliff and Jasper.

Instead, Jasper drops his head and his voice comes out low and controlled. "I would never say that. He fell into his habits all on his own. But—" he peers up, "he deserves to be celebrated for the things he did right."

I turn toward Cliff, and the previously tightened muscles of his face have softened slightly. "You're right." He turns his eyes on me. "Constantine loved performing *Fuck Me Sober* because he always did a drum solo right in the middle of it."

Jasper starts nodding enthusiastically. "He would actually change it up. It was never the same solo, so every show, each crowd got something special, a souvenir only for them."

We sit in silence, no doubt each of us holding space for Constantine's memory. "We should bring that back, to honor his memory," Cliff says after a moment.

He turns toward Travis. "You in?"

His words sound like an apology disguised as a proposition. An apology for never fully pulling him into the band. He asked Travis if he was in because he knew Travis has the talent. Travis gives a small nod. "Hell yeah, I'm up for it."

"Nice." Jasper exclaims, now filled with excitement. "Let's start it in Colorado so we can practice it a few times."

"I always admired Constantine as a drummer," Travis cuts back in, and we all turn to face him. "He was someone I watched a lot when I was learning. His technique was unmatched."

Underneath his statement, he's trying to express people do care about the drummer. My heart cracks a little bit for him.

"Is that why you wanted to join this?" I gesture my hands out.

He chuckles. "I wanted to join this because there's nothing like playing live music with a band. I would probably have taken any opportunity given to me. I got lucky it was the opportunity of a lifetime." I love the way his optimism cuts through any sadness. I love the way he still talks like there's nothing else he'd rather do than go on tour with a band with so much baggage and history, the air is thick with it.

"We're lucky to have a performer like you with us, now. *Your* skill and *your* technique is unmatched." I'm somewhat startled by Cliff's raw emotion. I've spent this tour watching an iceberg melt slowly. I also can't help the spark this conversation is lighting within me. There's a much deeper, much better story here than the one I was originally assigned to I now feel desperate to lean into, and I can't help but think back to the draft I started.

Travis nods. "I know." A small smirk spreads across his lips. "I'll still do my best to do Constantine's memory justice."

We continue to talk, not getting into anything too deep, and a sense of belonging I've never fully felt before wraps around me like a blanket. I didn't grow up in a big family. It was my mom, my dad, and I. Then, it was just my mom and I. We didn't have much to argue about. I haven't seen a lot of conflict between people, and likewise, I've rarely learned how to resolve it. I have this assumption that when people get so mad at each other that they yell or say hurtful things, it can't end well. I know this seed was planted and watered by the many men that have simply just called it quits with me instead of trying to work anything out. And yet, being on this bus, I've realized when families argue, it *can* end well. It can end with a smile, with laughter, and with understanding. Bonds can mend.

At some point, I forget I'm still recording. I also don't notice the text from Felicia until much later.

Haven't had a recording in a while. Send ASAP!

CHAPTER 18

Macallister

We have one more show in Arizona and a show in Salt Lake City before we get to Colorado. I am so anxious to get to Colorado because we've opted to get hotel rooms again. We do this when we have more than one show in an area. So not often, and at this point, long overdue. Luckily the beds on the bus are decently comfortable, for being a mattress on a vehicle, but I am craving the alone time. We literally sleep on top of each other, the beds being stacked two levels high, and there's nowhere to go besides your bed and the common area. So, we are together constantly.

I sit at the table having my coffee. We talked for hours yesterday, then had a show, and I'm honestly still so wired from it all, the caffeine isn't as necessary. That's what I'm adjusting to the most on this bus. Not the proximity and space issues. Not the singular bathroom. Not Darrell's personality. Not Cliff's constant strumming. Not Jasper's contagious laughter. Not Travis's incessant tapping on every single surface. And not even Prudence, and her intoxicating scent, sharp blue eyes, or incandescent beauty. What I'm struggling to wrap myself around is how these tiny things can crawl up my skin, and become part of my being and my source of energy.

Growing up, I didn't have the closeness in other families. My dad worked constantly. He barely stopped to eat. My mom was around and spent time with me. But when a unit is operating at two-thirds capacity, the other third missing leaves its toll on the others. The absence will always be noticed. She was all I had, and forming closeness with others has never been easy. That's why when I look around at these people I genuinely care about, the emotions surrounding that phenomenon are conflicting.

Darrell's voice cuts through my thoughts and pulls me from the strange bittersweet tug of reminiscing. "Can we make a special stop?"

I'm about to tell him we cannot make another stop, when Jasper says, "Sure" without even glancing up from his newspaper, and Darrell wastes no time rushing to the front of the bus where Harvey sits driving. I'm about to ask him who the fuck reads physical newspapers anymore when I pause to examine the giant picture on the front page. It's a black-and-white photo of Gnasher on stage. The photo is taken from somewhere behind the crowd, so you can see the back of hundreds of heads, along with a body lifted in the middle of the crowd surfing across outstretched hands, with Gnasher on stage in the distance. I squint a little and notice this is not a recent picture.

I strain my eyes even more and try to read the date printed in the smallest possible print above the picture. Jasper holds the paper so the top is folded slightly and he reads intently. I can't take it anymore and am about to ask him if that is an old copy of a newspaper when my question is answered without uttering a single syllable.

"Jazz, why are you reading an old article about us from almost thirty years ago?" Cliff is standing, bracing himself on the counter of the kitchenette as the inertia from the moving bus threatens to push him off balance.

Jasper scans the paper, crinkling it in his grip and he shifts his gaze from right to left. "A fan gave it to me last night after the show. Did you know we played in Arizona almost exactly to the day twenty-nine years ago? Same city, different venue, but …" he shakes his head. "Wild, huh."

Cliff frowns. "In '96?"

Jasper still doesn't lower the paper. "Your math sucks. It was in '95. Right after we released *A Way*."

"Hmm," Cliff sounds bothered by this information.

Jasper reads the paper for another few seconds, then folds it and places it in front of him. The curtain opens and Prudence steps out. I can't pull my eyes from her as she busies herself in the kitchenette behind Cliff's looming presence. She walks over, and the obnoxious voice in my head I can't quiet starts pleading she sits next to me, even if it's simply from a lack of options.

"Ever seen one of these, reporter Prue?" Jasper holds up the folded paper and waves it at her.

She rolls her eyes, but the smile on her lips says she doesn't mind the teasing. She slides into a seat next to Jasper and picks up the paper. Her eyes scan it briefly, then she leans into Jasper as she points to the printed words. "Your old-man eyes can read this small print?"

"I use a magnifying glass. The ones with the little light. Very useful," he quips back.

I watch the comfortable back-and-forth banter she has with Jasper, and I can't help the smile spreading across my face from how quick-witted she is. Before I can mask it, I'm caught.

"Yes?" Cliff asks in a low voice, directed only at me.

I look at him for a beat before I decide to completely ignore him and take a sip from my coffee instead.

Darrell walks back out and takes a seat on the other side of Jasper. "Just spoke to Harv. We're all set for The Thing tomorrow."

Prudence bursts out laughing, and I'm so confused about what is happening. "What … thing?" I ask.

Prudence starts laughing even harder and Darrell smiles wide, his solemn attitude from yesterday a distant memory of the past. "*The* Thing. It's where we're stopping."

Special stop, right. "It's a place … called The Thing?"

Prudence's laugh grows, and the sound of it is so intoxicating, it almost pulls me from my annoyance with Darrell. "It's ... a ..." she's trying to gasp and catch her breath, but her body is so riddled with laughter, she can't.

"It's a gas station with a museum in it," Travis says in an even tone. "You haven't seen the billboards? We drive by one every five seconds."

"Well, that's obviously an exaggeration," I mutter under my breath. "And why are we stopping there?" I've turned my attention to Darrell, struggling not to keep every ounce of it on Prudence.

"We have to."

"We have to?"

He nods. "Yeah."

"Because?"

"Because the billboard says so," Cliff says, pulling his guitar onto his lap.

"Yep!" Darrell's nods grow bigger along with his smile.

My eyes find Prudence, who's slowly starting to giggle less and breathe more. "Have you been to this ... Thing?" I turn my eyes toward her and ask, now desperate to know why she's laughing so hard. Tears form in her eyes, and I can honestly say I'm so conflicted by the image. They glisten and her face is so beautifully flushed from laughing. While I would rather die than see her cry, these are a different kind of tears and I want to see her filled with this much joy over and over again.

She nods. "I have."

I want more. "And?"

"And it's a sca—"

Darrell cuts her off by putting his hands over his ears and loudly proclaiming, "DON'T RUIN IT!"

This makes her fall into a fit of laughter again. This *Thing* is obviously a tourist trap, and I can't even be annoyed because I love watching this side of her so much.

Jasper shakes his head at his cousin and Cliff chuckles to

himself as he strums on his guitar. Prudence goes to wipe away a tear from the corner of her eye, and her eyes latch onto mine. I know I should look away, but I don't.

"Is Harvey going to let the other bus know?" I ask.

"Just did it," Harvey hollers from up front.

I'm finding the typical tension in my shoulders at a change in plans isn't gone completely, but also doesn't hold my muscles as tight as it once did. I continue looking toward the woman I'm suspecting holds the key to why.

I hate how Prudence insists on standing in the middle of the crowd for every single show. It gives me so much anxiety. I stand where I always do, directly off to the side of the stage where I scan the crowd until I find her. Thankfully, she isn't hard to spot.

I watch her interactions and follow her movements. She dances along to the music and she doesn't look like a reporter at all. She's wearing tight, black jeans ripped at the knees and a flowy sheer blouse with buttons. It's white and almost transparent, a black bra visible underneath. I can't help my eyes latching on when the flashing lights illuminate her for the briefest second. She blends in as a fan enjoying the show. And I am a fan of her.

I keep my eyes pinned on her, desperate to watch her. Unable to pull my eyes away for fear of her safety, but also selfishly because I've grown addicted to watching her get lost in the music. Watching her when she drops her inhibitions and bathes in the music is so intoxicating I'm dizzy.

She sways seductively during Cosmic Intervention's set, and when her head is tilted perfectly in the light, I notice she's singing along to the lyrics. I wonder if she was a fan before coming on tour, or if she's learned these songs from coming to the shows night after night and immersing herself completely into the experience of each crowd. The latter is most likely true, and it makes my heart ache more.

I keep her in my sight but also make a point to scan the people directly around her. She's magnetic, visually, and at each show I watch men and women alike light up around her. They admire her in a way that makes my skin crawl because I know it can't be the same way I do.

I admire her physically, of course, but I also admire her tenacity. It riles me up because it's what makes her reckless. It's what got her to agree to go on tour with people she doesn't know. It's what makes her think she can stand alone in a crowd of people at a concert without risk. It's why she found herself at a bar in Vegas completely by herself. It's what led her to write the article exposing Torrence Gillman's secret affair.

She wrote an article that completely obliterated someone's career. She revealed secrets that caused an uproar so intense, someone had to disappear completely from the scene. No one has heard from or seen Torrence Gillman since the story broke. The only report is a second-hand statement confirming she is done with music for now and needed to get out of the spotlight. Prudence wrote the article, and when I saw her walking onto the bus, knowing she wrote it, a blanket of dread fell over me, tucking me in. I thought I was fucked.

And boy, was I right, but not in the way I thought. My breath quickens as my eyes scan as quickly as possible around her. She's dancing and singing alone in a crowd, and she has no idea what she does to me. Her shirt is unbuttoned quite far and I imagine right at the intersection of her bra. The part I imagine having a clasp in the front, instead of the back. Where I would love to snap apart, completely letting her breasts fall in front of me with a bounce. Where I'd watch the small gasp forcing her lips open in the shape of an O, right before the arch of her brows as she realized I was about to devour her.

I watch the curve of her cleavage pop out of her shirt when she moves her body a certain way, tugging the buttons sideways and pulling apart the unbuttoned part at the top. I picture myself running my fingertip over the curve and letting my eyes feast on the quick spread of goosebumps across her flesh. What I imagine would be the softest flesh I've ever felt or tasted. Because when I ran my tongue over her, her bright pink nipple would peak up, and her hips would tilt forward just so. I know, without a doubt, my cock would be so rock hard, I'd be itching to stroke myself into a little bit of relief.

Her hips are swaying along with the music and I can almost feel my hands gripping the delicate curve of bone and skin. Where I'd press my fingertips until the skin around them turns white. I can imagine the sound she'd make, the whimper, and from that alone would know she's wet and throbbing.

She keeps her movements in time with the music so perfectly. Her lips moving along to the words, and I can almost hear the crying plea she'd sing, begging for me to help her with her release. And while the sound of her begging me would be so pretty, I know I'd cave almost immediately for her. Wanting to give her whatever she needs, which is my fingertip sliding across her clit. Her clit, so hard and so slick from her arousal, it makes me moan.

I take a small step to the side and discreetly adjust myself. I can't take my eyes off her because I'll lose her in the sea of people, but I also can't keep gawking at her. My body is acting up and I'm transported to my teenage body letting it, letting myself slip into such erotic delusions nowhere near the professionalism I was recently berating myself about. I take a long pull from the plastic water bottle I didn't realize I was gripping tightly, and swallow it down along with my fantasy.

Right before Gnasher steps on stage, the lights go out. I hate this part of the show because the crowd is invisible from up here. I wish she'd stand backstage with the rest of us. The lights come on, illuminating the stage with three spotlights: one on Travis holding his sticks up in the air, one on Jasper smiling with his fingers poised over his bass, and one on the final microphone with no one behind it. The crowd begins to cheer loudly and Cliff walks out onto stage, unhurried, as if he's browsing the aisle of a drugstore.

His guitar hangs from his frame and he steps up to the microphone. "Evening," he drawls, right before Travis hits his sticks together three times and they start playing *A Way* together. The lights oscillate around the venue space and I can find Prudence again.

I watch her sing along with Cliff to the lyrics.

> She comes, she goes.
> We ebb, we flow.
> Well she's right behind me yearning
> While my cigarette is burning … away.

She's dancing. She's safe. Those are the only two thoughts I let myself focus on for the remainder of the show. That is until I remember a moment when she first got onto the bus and told Travis she was 'unavailable'.

CHAPTER 19
Prudence

After the show, we play a short round of truth or dare trying to dissipate our adrenaline, before passing out. Cliff, Macallister, and I didn't even make it to our beds before falling asleep completely. I woke up, my face on the table and a small amount of drool oozing out of my mouth. I lifted my head and saw Cliff passed out, his arms crossed across his chest, in one of the recliner chairs at the back of the bus. Macallister lays sprawled out on the couch across from me.

I sit up and wipe my mouth as I continue to take in my surroundings. I'm so discombobulated at first and my heart knocks against my chest quicker. A quick flash skirts across my brain wondering why I'm not in my bed, in my apartment. I quickly remember I'm not in LA. I'm somewhere in Arizona, speeding down the highway on a tour bus with five men I've grown close to in different ways. Cliff and Jasper have provided the kind of company I haven't had since my dad: Older, male, with a love for music and a quick sense of humor so dry, it puts the desert to shame. Travis, who feels like an older brother, even though I'm pretty sure we established I'm a few months older than him. He comforts me and teases me in a way that only comes from closeness. Against all odds, even Darrell, a goofball I honestly started off less enthused with, but now I'm accustomed to his quirkiness. Dare I say, I appreciate that oddball who invited me and also happened to be the first to welcome me on the bus.

Then there is Macallister. I let my eyes settle on his sleeping form. I remember the first time I saw him. His face scrunched up in anger, but so handsome at the same time. For a moment, I thought I was flipping through a menswear catalog instead of standing in front of a person I suspected despising my existence. His jaw was clenched so tightly, it pulled his cheek slightly upwards. I study his face in the low light and know the exact shade of light caramel his skin is. In the sun, it has golden flecks I've studied so frequently, I can imagine them right now. His eyes are hazel and unlike any color I've ever been able to find in a box of crayons. If hazel was a spectrum, graded on a scale, his would fall right between the middle and green. The brown is mostly only present around the edges, and it's the most striking brown I've ever seen, almost metallic copper.

I watch his eyelids flutter, making his eyelashes dance only slightly, and I imagine the bold irises staring back at me when I catch them at just the right time. I wonder what he dreams about. Because the last few nights, I've dreamed of him. I can't stop visualizing his face when I close my eyes. This is the first time I've opened my eyes from imagining him in my sleep, to be met with his actual form. His face, his body, his eyes, even closed, are there in front of me. His chest rises and falls and I imagine myself laying against him and feeling the movement against my body.

He scrunches his face a little before his eyelids separate slowly revealing the whites of his eyes as he surveys the area, then finds me. I'm frozen still as his eyes pierce mine. He holds my stare and I hold his, afraid to move. We are locked in for what feels like an hour but couldn't be longer than a moment. His eyes study my mouth before meeting mine again.

I can't help the small curve of my lips, and I break our eye contact when I flutter my gaze downwards in embarrassment.

"You okay, baby?" His voice sounds groggy. I'm shocked into

silence at first, wondering if he is speaking to me; but with his eyes undeniably in my direction, I know he is. I wonder if he meant to say what he said, call me what he did. Regardless, his words stir up heat inside me and I can't help it when my lips curve upwards.

I lift my eyes, and I'm fully smiling now. "Yes. I'm okay."

"You should go to bed."

"*You* should go to bed," I tease.

He smiles, and if there were light, I know I'd see a blush across his cheeks. "Yeah," he breathes.

I want to get up and curl into him. The intrusive thought freaks me out so much, red, hot shame washes over my body. I hope the light is dim enough he can't see.

"Hey," he says, forcing me to flit my eyes upwards again on instinct alone because my want is at a level zero.

"What?" I ask, my voice sounding so small.

"Can I ... Are you .... What did you mean?" He sputters, and I almost wonder if he's still asleep.

"What?" I ask again.

"What did you mean? When you told Travis you were unavailable?" His voice is still groggy from unrestful sleep.

I suck in a breath, searching for air because all of mine got sucked out of me with his words. "Wha ..."

"Do you have a boyfriend? Please tell me it's not the Cubs guy."

I blink at him, lost in a loud cacophony of my thoughts. I open my mouth, but words don't come out.

"I know you said you broke up with him. And you told me you just got out of a relationship, but ... It's ...." His head swivels frantically around as if realizing where he is. "I'm sorry. Don't ... don't answer. I'm sorry." I'm pretty sure now he *was* half asleep and is now realizing the words he's spoken aloud to me.

But I don't care. And, if I'm being honest, I don't hate the direction of this conversation. For some reason, I find myself wanting it to continue.

I shake my head. "I'm not with him. We broke up years ago. And my boyfriend …" I take a deep breath and become slightly confused at this middle-school-level conversation we're having. "I don't have a boyfriend." *Technically, I've never had a boyfriend because no one ever wants to claim me as their girlfriend.*

"Right," he coughs and his eyes browse around unable to find a definitive target.

"I said it more as a joke." This conversation could end, but I keep pushing because again, I find myself not wanting it to.

"You're available?" he asks, his eyes finding mine.

He's never been this vulnerable with me, and my stomach aches. "I am." I don't know why I say it so definitively, especially since I haven't considered myself available. Not necessarily. Not after Jake. But I do if he's the one asking. *I'm available for you*, I want to say.

"Can I …" He considers his next question and I hold my breath waiting for what I think he might ask me. "Can I help you to your bed?" He says each word like he's picked each one carefully. I know he isn't asking to go to bed with me. He's simply asking if he can be the one to make sure I make it to bed. Safely. He's taking care of me. And while it isn't the question I thought he was getting at, it's just as satisfying for some reason. Better, even.

"Yes." I let my smile spread wide across my face, the dark and quietness surrounding us protecting my unabashed response.

We both slowly get up out of our uncomfortable dozing positions. We stand facing each other for only a moment before I tilt my head toward the floor and turn to walk toward the curtain. His hand is warm as it presses to my lower back, guiding me through. I glance over at Cliff before we pass through, and I'm pretty sure I catch a small smile on his lips, even though his eyes stay closed.

We get to the back of the bus where it's even darker and I can hear the others sleeping. Someone snoring softly, others simply breathing heavier, deeper, the way you do when you dream. We stand in front of my cubby and he tilts his head subtly and leans in just a touch. I lick my lips in anticipation because I think he's about to kiss me, and I'm going to let him if he does.

I remember his voice calling me baby less than three minutes ago and sparks shoot up my body like little fireworks. *I wouldn't only let him kiss me*. I hope he does because I really want him to. His eyes lower to my mouth again, and this time it's unmistakable his eyes are on my lips. They part instinctively and his throat bobs with restrained hunger.

"Macallister," I whisper so softly in an attempt to not wake anyone.

He swallows and leans toward me another fraction of an inch. The loud clearing of a throat shoves us out of this moment. I step backward and his eyes widen. I'm not sure what we thought was going to happen. He quickly nods at me and mouths "goodnight" before gracefully crawling up into the cubby above mine.

I stand in shock, taking a deep breath, before I crawl into my own space. As soon as my head hits the pillow, my eyes droop closed. I wait for sleep to overtake me, but it takes longer than I thought it would. Behind my eyelids, I replay the last five minutes. I analyze the expression in his eyes, and his body language, and wonder if I misinterpreted something. I don't think I did, and the thought follows me into my dreams.

I'm startled awake by the sound of the person above me jumping from his bed, loudly. The person I know is Macallister. My eyes crack open and my smile spreads. I'm fully smiling from ear to ear, my teeth showing, because I know no one can see me and I have to physically express all my emotions right now, before crawling out of my bed.

I don't know what I'm giddy for, exactly, but it's not for what I'm met with when I walk through the curtain. Macallister is in the kitchenette grabbing a bottle of water out of the fridge, and when I come through, he peeks over his shoulder at me, immediately turns away, and freezes in place. He stays there for a couple of seconds before standing up, facing away from me, and walking briskly to sit next to Darrell. Darrell, of all people! I immediately feel silly, and the shame drips from the top of my head through my entire body to my toes. I misinterpreted something last night, that much is obvious. The realization slams into me harder and is worse than getting picked last for teams in gym class. I'm so confused, and now I'm mad at my confusion.

I sit in one of the lounge chairs next to Travis with a huff. He turns his head, assessing me with his eyes. He tilts his head slightly and gives me a questioning smile. I nod once, and look away, hoping it's enough to pacify him and make him believe I'm actually okay when I am certainly not. His smile morphs into a frown with a touch of concern wrinkled on his forehead. I don't make eye contact with him. I can't right now.

When the bus comes to a stop, I get up and speed past everyone off the bus. I forgot we were stopping at The fucking *Thing* until now. I march off the bus toward the front. I pull the door open and step inside. I grab my hair and tilt my head upward, trying to take in a deep breath. I hear the door swing open behind me and an almost breathless, "Prudence," in Macallister's voice.

I turn my head slightly to confirm it's him and then, desperate to get away from him as quickly as possible, step up to a red-haired, freckled-faced teenager at the counter. "Hi," I glance frantically around at the signage. "Aha," I exclaim, pointing to a placard on the front counter. "One ticket, please." One ticket to the museum I know is a scam, but a reasonable place to escape to right now.

The kid mumbles something incoherent while ringing me into the cash register and printing me a ticket after I frantically shove my plastic credit card toward him. I'm directed on where to walk to enter the museum, and as I'm walking away, I point my finger at Macallister and say, "Don't follow me," because I know that's exactly what he's going to do.

His face screws up in an expression I can't pinpoint as anger or desperation. The delusional girl from the early hours of this morning would guess desperation or desire. And based on his behavior the last fifteen minutes, I'd guess she'd be wrong, so I'm going to say it's anger. I think I almost hear him growl behind me. The sound pulls two different emotions from me, but I quickly push them down. I need some space to collect my thoughts.

I keep walking, though, and I take my sweet time walking through a room filled with models of dinosaurs and aliens, feigning interest in each over-the-top write up on the wall depicting the possibility of aliens and their possible interactions in human history. I even walk past a stunned Darrell, gazing word-lessly at an alien sitting in a Rolls Royce. I feel the smallest bit of warmth knowing he's enjoying this as much as he wanted to, and I don't interrupt him.

I meander so long, I lose track of how long I've been back here with the oohs and ahhs from passing tourists. By the time I reach the exit door leading me back to the photo op of an alien riding a giant T-Rex, I take a deep breath bracing myself for the return to reality. I peer around reluctantly making sure Macallister isn't hanging around. When I can confirm he isn't, I tentatively meander through the store. It's a typical convenience store filled with snacks and odd souvenirs. But it's also the gift shop for the museum, so it's filled to the brim with alien T-shirts, stuffed toys, hats, bags, coasters … literally anything and everything you can print an image of an alien, a dinosaur, or both on.

I get lost browsing through some '90s-esque alien charm neck-laces when I look at my watch. My eyes bulge as I realize we've been here for almost two hours. My head snaps back up and moves around the store frantically, trying to find one of the guys. I look mostly for Travis, him being six-foot-four, but can't find his dirty blond hair, or his stupid Cubs hat. I drop the necklace I was holding in my hand and race through the front door. The sun is a startlingly bright contrast to the inside and I have to squint with my hand shielding my eyes.

When they adjust, I realize I can't find the bus.

I can't find the bus, because it's no longer here.

CHAPTER 20
Macallister

I've been lying in my bed since she looked me in the eye and told me not to follow her. That was almost four hours ago. I've laid in the same position, on my back with my arms crossed and staring right up at the ceiling. My jaw hurts from clenching it so hard, but I am so frustrated with her I can't think straight.

She startled me. I don't understand what happened last night. Were we about to kiss? I think I was about to kiss her, but was she about to kiss me? I use my pinky finger to scratch the skin of my arm harshly. I asked her about a boyfriend. The thought makes me want to slap my face. *Am I the biggest fucking idiot or what?* I think I was half asleep, but the questions and comments that came from me were honest. As I lay here, I miss the way her lips parted, just so, when I leaned in closer to her …

But she said she didn't. She doesn't have a boyfriend and I think she was about to kiss me. So I woke up this morning a little bit shaken. I felt embarrassed of the way I let myself give into my desires, once again. If I'm honest, though, I'm exhausted trying to fight what I feel. I'm unsure what to do. I'm unsure what I can do. This isn't professional, for one. What does that even look like in our situation? On a fucking bus, for Christ's sake. I've also got this fucking letter looming over my head constantly. I still don't know what to do about it, and I know I need to talk to Cliff, but fuck, what do I say?

I can't get this out of my head. I can't get her out of my head. My head is a mess. I'm so drawn to her, I can't even control it anymore. I'm tapping my fingers when I realize something isn't right. I vault from my bed and fling the red curtain open. Travis is sleeping in a lounge chair, and Darrell and Jasper are sitting at the table playing cards. Cliff is on the couch with his guitar, but where the fuck is Prudence?

"Where the fuck is Prudence?" I ask.

Each head turns toward me. "Check her bed?" I think Travis's voice says. I turn quickly and fling open the curtain to her bed underneath mine. It's empty.

"She's not in there. Where. The fuck. Is Prudence?" My head is swiveling around frantically. No one moves. I run up to the driver's seat, bracing my hands along the side of the bus so I don't fall.

"Harvey, where the fuck is Prudence?" He doesn't turn to me, but stares out the windshield wide-eyed and terrified.

It's at this moment, I realize what I'm scared to admit: we left her at The Thing over an hour ago. "Go. Back." I grit out, trying to think of what the fuck to do right now. I pull out my phone and dial her number. It rings in my ear, but I can also hear the vibration of a phone on a mattress … no doubt her phone is sitting on top of her bed.

"Fuck. She doesn't have her fucking phone." I'm screaming so loud I can't hear anything. Or maybe that's the adrenaline. I'm not even sure.

Harvey doesn't miss a beat as he picks up his walkie. "Harv to Bruce."

He holds the little black device, waiting. The scrape of the other walkie plays over the speaker, followed by a "Sup."

"We need to turn back and head to The Thing. Prudence is there."

He doesn't respond. There's no crackle, there's nothing.

Then, finally, "No she ain't."

I snatch the walkie-talkie from his hand and press the button. "What do you mean no she isn't."

"She ain't at The Thing," I hear a small giggle in the background.

I look over to Harvey and hold up the walkie. "Who is this? Who the fuck is this?" I have no idea who Bruce is.

"Bruce. He drives Cosmic Intervention's bus."

The ringing in my ears dissipates, and I hold the speaker back up to my mouth. "Is she safe?"

He answers immediately, but I quickly realize it's her speaking this time. "Yes, *baby*, I'm safe. See you in Salt Lake City."

I press the button with unnecessary force. "No, we will stop. Bruce, you will catch up to us and stop. Prudence, you will get back onto this bus. With me." I snarl.

Harvey doesn't argue at all, he nods and pulls the bus into a truck stop off the highway and grabs the walkie-talkie from me to give Bruce the location. I stand right next to Harvey for over half an hour, waiting and staring out the windshield. I have my arms crossed and I'm standing directly in front of the door waiting for the moment it can swing open and I can hold her.

CHAPTER 21
Prudence

I can hear Roslyn giggling behind me. I turn and walk back toward their main living area, which is laid out almost identically to our bus. Our bus. *When did it become my bus, too?*

I plop onto the couch next to her. Aleric and Nathan sit across from us at the table talking animatedly and drawing diagrams or something on a piece of paper. I watch them for a few seconds when I sense someone's eyes on me.

I turn and Roslyn is smiling. "I take it that was Macallister?" Her voice drips with sugar-coated implication.

I turn to her, and I'm not even the slightest bit frustrated. If nothing else, I'm grateful for her right now. I needed another female to talk to, and I didn't realize that until now. I nod.

"He likes you." She says it so matter of factly, her sweet voice vocalizing it makes it true.

I shrug up one shoulder. "I thought he might ..." I let my words trail off.

Out of the corner of my eye, Nathan and Aleric's heads pop up in tandem. "No, he does," Nathan's voice says and Aleric's nod agrees.

I start laughing at their synchronicity. "Okay ..." I say, sounding unsure.

"No, he does," Roslyn cuts back in and I turn back over to face her. "He watches you at every show."

He what?

I open my mouth to ask but find I'm unable to form words. So instead, I tilt my head in question.

She nods again. "He watches you dance in the crowd at every single show." I heard her the first time, but hearing her confirm for a second time makes her words truly sink in.

We sit in silence for a few minutes and I let the information she's told me simmer. I'm starting to wonder if I didn't misinterpret him last night, but instead, I misinterpreted him this morning. What happened between us, or almost happened rather, might have spooked him. Macallister is concerned with being professional. He's never said those words aloud, but I know in the way he carries himself, conducts himself with others, and speaks. I know he takes his job seriously. Did I jeopardize that with the loss of my filter and inhibitions last night?

Roslyn cuts off my thoughts. "Do you like him?"

I turn to her and feel engulfed in the warmth radiating from her. "I think I do." It comes out as a whisper because it's a confession I've barely had time to acknowledge for myself.

Her eyes soften, not with pity, but with genuine care. I realize now I want Roslyn on my side. I want Roslyn as my friend. She has this way of pulling you into her orbit, so much so that you want to stay there.

My head falls from the overwhelming press of embarrassment as if my thoughts are written across my face, and when I do, I feel a warm touch on my arm. I know it's her hand, and we sit in a comfortable silence.

We continue to drive, to pull closer to the bus I know has stopped and is waiting for me. "This is a little ridiculous," I mutter, mostly to myself, but aloud nonetheless.

"Yeah," Aleric agrees with me, followed by the light slap across his arm from Nathan and "tsk" from Roslyn.

"I think it's sweet," she says, partially to me, but also partially to Aleric as a way to scold him.

"No, it is ridiculous. I was sent here to write a story about why Gnasher broke up, but now I'm sitting here on a bus with Cosmic Intervention taking me to another bus with people I didn't know over a month ago, but now consider some of my closest friends and a man I might be falling for on it, and I'm …" I look up at her wide eyes, realizing I'm rambling. I laugh.

"Maybe this is exactly where you're meant to be right now."

I nod. "Well, maybe you're right. It's better than where I was right before I got onto that damn bus."

She tilts her head to the side. "You don't like your job?" I'm not sure how she's able to discern so much information from so little, but I'm not strong enough to fight the perception she isn't wrong about. Instead, I just shrug.

We sit in silence before I meet her eyes. "Do you trust me?" I think the thing I felt was lost after the Torrence Gillman article was trust. Trust from the people around me, scared to mutter the smallest hint of a secret, for fear it would get published for all the world to read. It's not the only reason I've started to resent my job, but it is a big part of the why.

"Do you want me to be honest?" she asks.

My stomach sinks, but I truthfully reply with a nod of my head.

"No. I do not." I understand her answer, but it hurts. "But …" she continues, and the knife she shoved in starts to pull out slightly. "But I like you. And trust is something built between people who like each other first."

Her eyes shine with her answer, and the wound I thought she'd created disappears completely. Her answer is so genuine, so raw, it makes my chest constrict as my heart grows a tiny bit bigger, making room for her.

"I like you, too," I whisper.

She smiles and my body leans forward a little as the bus pulls to a stop. I stand, looking out the window, and we've pulled off to the side of the road at a rest stop. Up ahead is Gnasher's bus. Barely after stopping, the dust swirls up from Macallister stomping toward the door of the bus.

CHAPTER 22

Macallister

As soon as the bus pulls up, I run down the stairs through the open door out onto the dirt road. I march up to Cosmic Intervention's bus as it barely comes to a stop. I rap my knuckles on the door and it swings open. Marching up the stairs, I hear a brief, "Well, hello there," from who I assume is Bruce, but I don't bother to say anything back.

She's standing and facing away from me, looking out the window. When I take a step toward her, she turns to me, wide-eyed. I don't have time to glance toward Roslyn, but I know her eyes are on me and her face is split into a grin.

I reach my hand out, wanting to grab Prudence by the arm, but instead leaving my hand out, fingers splayed, an invitation for her to grasp it. She does.

I walk back up the front of the bus, down the stairs, and out the door, her following behind me.

"Macallister, stop," she practically yells.

I stop walking and I turn my body, but I don't let go of her hand. I use it to tug her closer to me. When she's close enough, I grab her with my other hand at the nape of her neck, pulling her in even closer. When we're only millimeters apart, my breath tangling with her breath, I whisper into her mouth, "I don't think

I can stop anymore." Before pulling her in and crashing our lips together.

I hold her tighter and push my tongue into her mouth where she willingly pulls me in deeper. I shiver as her hands drag up my sides, gripping me through my shirt as her tongue brushes against mine so softly it sends jolts through my body.

I am the one to break the kiss because I know we are so far off schedule and need to get to the next show in Salt Lake City in record time now, due to my demand that we stop. Otherwise, I'd hold her here for hours and do this.

I do have enough time to ask, "Is this okay?"

Her eyes search mine. "Yeah," she says in a whisper.

Without responding, I slide my hand down her arm and back into her hand where I intertwine our fingers and pull her gently behind me again toward the bus. The same bus I didn't want her to get on in the first place. So much can change in a matter of weeks.

Now that's out of the way, I feel like I can breathe again. That is, until a small whisper behind me says, "Wow," and all the air from my lungs is sucked back out.

CHAPTER 23

Prudence

"Wow," I whisper behind his back from the overwhelming shock I can't keep bottled inside after that kiss. My brain can't even process any of the questions I know I should fixate on, like the most important one: what does this mean? What are we? I brush off the desire to know, wanting to bask in this feeling a little longer.

I follow him back up the steps inside our bus. I'm grateful for the cool blast of air conditioning that hits me as I walk up. Everyone sits ramrod straight staring at us with wide eyes.

I brace myself for questions about us holding hands, about Macallister growling into the walkie-talkie and racing to grab me out of the other bus. But no one says anything about any of that at all. Instead, they look back at me with varying expressions all conveying the same thing: relief.

I'm taken aback by this. I don't know what I expected exactly, but when I realized I'd been abandoned and didn't have my phone, the only thing I could think was I need to figure this out now. I didn't think anyone would be too concerned. I had the passing thought maybe they'd be excited to get rid of me, the reporter there to uncover all their dirty secrets. That they'd probably keep driving and hope they got far enough away and I'd be out of the tour.

The way all their eyes shine back at me tells me otherwise, though, and I'm not sure I've felt this much emotion from so many people at once before. Someone breathes a sigh of relief, and I guess it's Darrell based on the dramatic nature of the sound accompanied by the drastic way his shoulders fall and he lets his body hit the chair like he's finally able to relax. Jasper's eyes are slightly glassy, and he looks like he's trying to smile but can't quite muster it from a build-up of worry starting to dissipate slowly from him with each slow breath he takes.

Travis gets up and walks over to me, ignoring Macallister, and pulls me into a tight, bear hug. "Holy shit, Prue," he breathes in my ear before holding me by the shoulders at arm's length. "Don't do that again."

I study his face, admiring the genuine expression and I suddenly realize I care about him as much as I can tell he cares about me. "Well, then don't leave without me again," I tease and the smile spreading across his face makes me laugh.

I hear Harvey's voice whisper behind me, "I'm so sorry, Prue."

I turn and give him an accepting smile. I know this was no one's fault. I'm not blaming myself, but I also know forgetting my phone was a big mistake, and trying to hide in the museum was immature. I can't forget the huge stone of fear I felt drop in my belly when I realized they left. I was so relieved when I saw Bruce walk out. He told me later on the bus he was "stuck in the bathroom," so that's a fun thought, but I'm thankful regardless.

Roslyn, Aleric, and Nathan acted as if there was nothing amiss with me walking on the bus. Roslyn even made me a cup of tea. Considering the fact that we are in Arizona in the middle of summer, I didn't need a hot cup of tea, but I accepted the gesture. It was actually nice to sit and talk with her since we rarely get to interact besides the quick pleasantries as we cross paths.

As we sat together and talked about nothing in particular, I heard the loud message crackling over Bruce's walkie-talkie. Even through the static, I knew who it was talking over the speaker.

I glance toward the back of the bus and Cliff has settled back into his lounge chair with his guitar. He's wearing his sunglasses as always, so I can't know for sure he's looking at me, but with his face turned toward mine, I assume he is. He starts strumming and I watch him for a moment, wondering if he's going to say anything when the sound gets louder.

After a few notes, I realize he's playing "Dear Prudence" like he did during our first interview.

He starts singing low but picks up the volume as other voices join in, just like the last time. By the third verse, everyone is singing along to the words. No one is focused on sounding impressive, or even in tune, they're all letting their voices flow freely, and it's the most beautiful sound.

I start giggling and singing along with them. I even hear Harvey's voice singing loudly as the bus navigates back onto the highway. Macallister picks my hand back up into his and leads me to sit on the couch with him. We all continue to sing along and finish the song together in loud, exuberant excitement.

Later, when I get up and walk to the back to get my phone, Cliff gently clutches my wrist and I turn to him. I tilt my head down, expecting him to say something, but he doesn't. His glasses are off now, and his dark blue eyes scan me over. They're filled with so much concern, I'm overwhelmed with appreciation for him even though he hasn't said a word.

He takes a deep breath and meets my eyes. "We won't let anything else happen to you. I promise. I won't let anything else happen to you. I'm so sorry."

I can hear the emotion starting to clog the back of his throat and am surprised when I find my voice comes out gravelly from containing tears pushing against my eyelids. "I know," I whisper, because it's all I can manage.

I look over my shoulder and Macallister's eyes blaze. He's staring at me, not in an angry way I realize, but in a possessive way. I give him a soft and reassuring smile as I pull the curtain open and go to my bed to find my phone. I crawl into my little space and lie down.

The screen lights up with four notifications: One missed call from Macallister, a text from Jessica, an email from Felicia, and a voicemail from my mom. *Shit.* I've sent her updates here and there to let her know I'm alive and well, but not as often as I'd promised. I internally berate myself as I stare at the notification but am unable to press the button to hear her voice just yet.

I hear footsteps, and then the curtain of my cubby opens. Macallister is crouched, his legs spread and bent in a way that makes my eyes linger a little longer. But the way his face twists and scrunches guts me. He looks distraught, like he could cry. He opens his mouth and closes it several times, as if trying to form words, but physically unable to push them out into the space between us.

"What is it?" I ask a single question holding more than one meaning.

His eyes move back up to mine and the hazel beacons I've grown to admire and seek out hold so much emotion which is unusual for him. "Are you okay?"

I nod. "I am."

"I'm not," he admits in a whisper.

"What do you mean?"

"I was terrified. I was laying in my bed, so conflicted about you, replaying the moment you turned around and told me not to follow you," he winces.

"I'm sorry." I blurt out.

He shakes his head. "No, you don't need to be. You needed space, but I just," he forces a breath out before continuing. "I laid there letting myself stew, and the entire time you were left behind. When I realized you weren't on the bus, I ..." his words trail off, but I think I know what he was about to say.

I roll onto my side and reach for his hand. I don't know why it's so instinctual, almost reflexive, but it feels like I've done this a million times: comforted him with my touch. And I know it is a comfort to him because his eyelids fall closed and he lowers his forehead to the top of my hand. I realize his touch is as much a comfort to me, too.

"Macallister, I'm okay. Even if Bruce hadn't been there, I would have been okay. I can't lie, I'm definitely grateful his bowels decided to act up," he lifts his head slightly and the mix of disgust and confusion wrinkling his face makes me laugh. "But regardless, I would have been okay. I'm used to taking care of myself."

He lifts his head completely, nodding. "I get that." His eyes are cast downwards at where my hand still rests on his forearm. "I think I'd like to take care of you for a while so you don't have to anymore."

My heart rate picks up and I can barely manage the "okay" I breathe in response.

CHAPTER 24

Macallister

I can barely hear her, but I heard enough. I climb into her bed next to her and she moves over to make room for me. There's not much to give in these tiny bunks, but she still makes the effort. When I'm lying on my side facing her, I reach out to brush her face. Her skin is so soft underneath my fingertips, and I draw indiscernible shapes on her cheek, watching as her lashes flutter. I suck in a breath, and my body warms watching her respond to my touch.

"Prudence."

"Hmm?" It comes out sounding more like a moan and the sound feels like honey dripping into my ear.

"Baby," I try again, this time more awake than I've ever been.

"Mmm." Now she does moan, and I can't help when I wrap my hand around the nape of her neck. My fingers are met with the cold clasp of her dainty silver chain necklace. It's such a contrast to the warm skin on her neck. I pull her toward me and we're so close, her lips just barely rest against mine in a feather-light brush. She doesn't pull away but instead leans in closer to completely close the gap between us.

Before she can, with my hand on her neck I pull her head away from me slightly. "Can I kiss you?"

Her eyes open, and the blue of her irises hypnotizes me. She doesn't answer verbally, but instead crashes our lips together. I slide my fingers upwards, tangling in her dark locks and gripping her to me. My other hand, previously trapped underneath my side, reaches up and holds her cheek.

She moans into my mouth as I run my thumb across her soft skin with one hand and massage the back of her head with the other. Her tongue coyly plays with mine, and I continue to reach inside of her.

As if an alarm went off in her head, she pulls back and searches my face, no doubt digging for a sense of remorse or regret. She isn't a mirror, so I'm not sure exactly what she sees, but I hope it's what burns inside of me. I want more of her, and I'm done denying it any longer. Especially after the realization she wasn't on the bus. I'm not strong enough anymore, and I press the reservations I've been battling down deep in a place I hope they don't resurface.

Her disbelief relaxes, only slightly. "What does this mean?"

"For once in my life, I don't want to worry about the logistics. I feel strongly about you, Prudence, and I have since you walked onto this bus."

She snorts. "Trust me, I know. You hated me."

"I never hated you," I correct. "I was wary of you, and obviously for good reason, but not for the reason I expected. I expected you to come on this tour and implode an already delicate situation. Instead, you imploded my heart, and I've never experienced something like this before." I gesture between us.

We lay in silence, and I inhale deeply because her scent has surrounded me. I want to inject it into my veins.

"Truth or dare?" she says, and the question catches me off guard and makes me laugh.

I look back at her, assessing what she wants me to say because I want to give her exactly that right now. "Truth."

Her eyes widen with some surprise, and she contemplates what she wants to ask me to reveal about myself. "Why are you so guarded?"

I ruminate on her question, almost regretting my willingness to be so open when I'm so exposed right now.

I take a deep breath. "I'm worried about my image, how people perceive me." It's true, but she's a little confused, so I continue to explain. "When I was nineteen, I asked my dad for a job. I knew I wanted to work in this industry, but I didn't want to have to work for it. He gave me one. On my second day, I was accused of being a nepo-baby." I remember the rage bubbling inside me at those words of disgust spit at me by a man who had been working for my father for years.

"That's not very nice," Prudence says, most likely from a lack of anything else to respond with.

I shake my head slightly. "It was true, though. It was the hard dose of reality I needed." I smirk, remembering that wasn't my reaction in the moment. Instead, I threw my fist into the guy's nose and was technically fired. "I decided I didn't want to have anything I hadn't earned. I think that overwhelming pressure has started to affect my … demeanor."

She giggles. "I like knowing things about you. For the record, I like your demeanor." She lowers her voice on the last word in a mocking, but playful tone. Her confession warms me, and we continue to lay together not speaking.

"Truth or dare?" I say, breaking the silence that's stretched too far between us and I'm craving the sound of her voice.

"Dare," she says.

"Tell me something I don't know about you. Something only for me."

A half-suppressed laugh falls out of her mouth. "That sounds like a truth."

I raise an eyebrow. "I dare you to choose truth, then."

She rewards me with one of her whole-hearted laughs and a defiant eye roll, making my pants fit a little bit tighter. "Something about myself?"

"Please," when it comes to her, begging is not beneath me.

She considers me for a moment as she ponders the request,

and I watch her smile fall into a serious line. "I never knew my real dad. The man who raised me, my stepdad, married my mom when I was nine."

I wasn't expecting this kind of confession, and I can't help my physical reaction. I run my hand along her bare arm, finding the skinny strap of her tank top has fallen down her shoulder. Instead of responding yet, my fingers play with the strip of fabric before moving it back over her shoulder. I let my fingers linger there as I watch the trail of goosebumps forming along her arm. The light is dim in here, but the smallest glow of daylight outside illuminates our space, and therefore the freckles on her shoulder. My fingers draw lines, connecting them.

She's watching my hand, and when I stop, her eyes meet mine. "What are you thinking?" she asks.

"That I want to hold you. Can I hold you?"

She smiles up at me before turning and pressing her back to my front. I pull her in even tighter and wrap my arm around her. Her hands grip my arm protectively fixed across her chest.

"You're safe," I whisper into her hair, inhaling the light scent of roses. I'm saying it more to reassure myself.

She settles into me, and at one point, I can hear her breathing become long and even. I hold her while she sleeps, safely in my arms. I can't help when my mind wanders to the same question she asked me, *What does this mean?*

I push it away because right now, I don't want to care about what it means. Right now, I want her to rest, and I want to hold her close to me while she does.

CHAPTER 25

Prudence

I don't know why I told him. Well, I do know why I told him, but I'm not entirely ready to admit it to myself. He said something *just for him*, and it's the first thing I thought of that I haven't shared during the many conversations and games of truth or dare we've played.

His arms are wrapped around me, and I'm not sure how long I was asleep, but I know it was for long enough, he ended up falling asleep, too. I can hear low murmurs from beyond the curtain, and part of me can't help but wonder if they're discussing us being back here together in the middle of the day.

I reach for my phone and look at the screen. It's not the middle of the day like I thought, but it's almost seven in the evening. My notifications are still there, glaring back at me and reminding me of the things I've been ignoring. Not things, people.

Macallister's breaths cause a steady rise and fall of his chest against my back as I open the text message from Jessica first.

Bitch. Update me

I stifle my laughter, not wanting to wake up the sleeping man with his arm still thrown across my middle, holding me to him even in his unconscious state.

> Do you remember the gas station in Arizona we stopped at on our road trip after we graduated?

Uh ... not exactly what I meant, but I think so. The one we got matching alien shirts at?

> That's the one. We went and I kinda got left behind ... Don't worry, I'm fine and back on the bus now. Macallister had a FIT!

You just put me through so many emotions. I will need that story later. For now, let's focus on the fit

> Basically, I hitched a ride on Cosmic Intervention's bus. When Macallister found out, he made the bus stop and pull over until I could catch up with them. He stomped in, dragged me back on our bus, and kissed me ... a lot

Hell yeah, he did! Okay, so ... now what?

> Jess, I don't know ...

Prue, stop overthinking it. I know you're trying to tiptoe a line right now and you're overly cautious about being professional. But you're on a fucking tour bus with a rock band. I think it's fine if you are hooking up with someone. If anything, you're being prude only hooking up with ONE someone.

> We aren't hooking up

> I mean, we haven't hooked up

Not yet

I read her message and focus on the heat radiating from Macallister's body. It sinks into me, and it's so comforting, I push back into him a little further.

This is crazy

For someone who works in the entertainment industry and hangs out with rock stars all day, your definition of crazy is a little skewed

How's the story coming?

Ugh

So I assume you don't yet know why Gnasher broke up, LOL

I don't know if I even want to know anymore

Because you don't want another repeat of what happened after your last story?

I mean, I obviously don't. But not necessarily for myself. I don't want to hurt anyone

Babe, you'll figure it out. I'm here for you

Macallister stirs behind me, so I let Jess know I'll call her later.

I pause for a moment, expecting him to say something. Instead, his head nuzzles into the back of my neck and his breathing returns to long, even inhales and exhales. I open the email from Felicia and read it. She received the recordings I sent her and she's less than pleased with the quality of the material. Phrases like "Not juicy enough" and "Ask better questions" stand out to me. She doesn't sound mad as much as disappointed.

I type a quick and concise response, assuring her I'm trying to build a relationship with them first so they can open up comfortably and give me the information freely, even though I know the deeper connection I make with them, the less I want to expose anything. Based on our conversations, I know something happened that is still raw for both of them, regardless of how many years ago it happened. Cliff and Jasper have tension between them pulled tight by their history. However, they also have the air around them of wanting to reconcile, and if I came in between that, I don't know how I could live with it.

"Mmm," I feel more than hear Macallister hum into my neck. His lips find the clasp of my necklace at the base of my neck and press a kiss into it. The cold of the metal is a searing contrast to my warm skin and his warm lips. He's so vulnerable in this position in a way I've never seen him. I rotate my body around, his arms still wrapped around my middle. I'm facing him and his eyes are still closed, but the small smile on his face tells me he's awake.

"We fell asleep for a while," I whisper.

"Needed it," he responds in a gravelly voice filled with sleep.

"Me or you?"

His eyelids part slowly. "Apparently both of us."

I smile in response to him, and his small smirk spreads into a wider grin. I decide to stop worrying so much about trying to define this and trying to work around imaginary complications I keep forming in my head.

"Will you stand with me at tomorrow's show?" he asks.

"In the crowd or backstage?" I ask.

He takes a deep breath and closes his eyes. "I hate that you stand in the crowd. It stresses me out."

"Why?" I ask with a laugh.

His eyes open and find mine immediately. "I worry about you. I watch you the entire time."

I remember what Roslyn told me. I didn't think she was lying, but hearing him confirm it causes a swooping sensation in my stomach.

"We can stand backstage." I haven't experienced one of these shows backstage yet. It might be interesting to get a different perspective.

"We can stand in the crowd, together," he offers up on a sigh. "I know you love it."

I do. And his acknowledgment of it makes me smile. Label be damned right now. I'm not used to someone compromising for me or recognizing the things that bring me joy. I want to tell him, but I don't know how. So instead, I stretch my neck a little to reach his mouth and press my lips to his.

"Can you help me?" I'm struggling to yank my suitcase from the under-bus compartment, but it's huge and frankly, stuck.

"Uh …" Darrell's quivering uncertainty makes me turn to face him head-on. I turn and am met with the reason for his hesitation. He stands in front of me with a halved potato covered in black hair dye, a towel stained with bleach around his neck, and goopy globs stamped all over his freshly bleached head.

"Is it a touch-up day already?" I ask, unenthused.

He nods and saunters back into the bus. I'm not even sure why he was out here, but I roll my eyes and go back to yanking and failing to release my bag.

"Need help?" the deep and confident voice says from behind me. I turn and Macallister stands close to my back and peers down at me with an amused expression on his face.

"Nah," I flick my hand in a downward wave. "I've got this."

He knows I'm joking and chuckles before moving his body in front of mine, forcing me to step a little to the side to give him room. He pulls a couple of times, adjusts some of the luggage on top, and yanks my bag free as if it were no problem at all.

He sets it on the pavement in front of me but doesn't move. "Gonna watch me pick out my underwear?" I ask with a smirk.

His eyes widen slightly, but not with surprise as much as excitement. "I am now."

I roll my eyes and unzip my bag. I obviously forgot I packed it like a sardine tin, didn't secure anything, and it's been on a moving bus. Therefore, the contents have shifted, and when I unzip the top half, some of my things tumble out.

"Shit," I curse under my breath, reaching to pick things up.

Macallister bends to do the same and help me, but I notice he grabs only one thing and slowly rolls back up to a standing position. I continue gathering my clothing and stand. Random articles of clothing spilling from my hold, I realize what he's clutching in his hands.

He's not looking at me, but instead turning the black, satin bag around and smiling at it. I reach for it, but some of my captured items fall out of my hold. I scramble in an attempt to catch the falling items and hear his laugh above me.

I muster the best scowl I can at him.

"What's this, Prudence?" His voice sounds even deeper but runs smoothly through my ears. It's like a sip of the most expensive whiskey, and it takes everything in me not to let the sound of it throw me off.

I reach again and grab it from him, but he pulls it back. He waves it, taunting me.

I shake my head and give up, resigning to grabbing what I need from my so neat and so organized array of chaos.

I hear the unmistakable sound of the slow pull of ribbons and slide of fabric. He takes a peek into the bag and his smile grows even wider. "Prudence, is this a vibrator?"

"No." I love messing with him, and I'm honestly starting to grow aroused at this game we're playing now.

"Mhmm," he hums, reaching inside the bag and starting to pull out the toy my best friend deemed a necessity when she gave it to me. *Damnit, Jessica.*

I reach out my hand, clutched around a handful of panties, and prevent him from pulling it out further. "Don't do that. I'm already exposed enough holding my intimates out in broad daylight." I've started stuffing them into my pockets, not wanting to walk back onto the bus holding my underwear, no matter how comfortable I've grown with everyone on the bus. I've already dropped a few pairs on the ground.

He grins. "Have you used this?"

I glance downward and notice the shape in his pants starting to press against the inside of his zipper. I'm trying to be sexy and playful, but this flusters me and makes my head fuzzy and thoughts jumbled.

"Uh, I ..." I peer back up at his eyes. "Obviously not," I whisper even though no one else is around.

"Why did you bring it, Prudence?" The way he keeps using my name like that is making my insides heat up.

Wanting to give the illusion of aloofness, I shrug.

He inspects it, rolling the bagged toy around in his hands, twisting it around as if he'll notice something other than the fabric in his hands. He runs his index finger up the length of it, and it shouldn't be so erotic, but it sends a wave of goosebumps across my arms imagining the same finger sliding up parts of me.

He taps it against his palm once. Twice. Then turns on his heel to walk back into the bus.

"Macallister," I yell after him.

He turns over his shoulder smiling, then walks away.

"Macallister," I try, louder.

His shoulders shake with laughter as he ignores me and keeps walking without a pause in his steps.

I tilt my head to the sky, the mixed parts of annoyance and arousal battling inside me for dominance. I let out a laugh on a breath I didn't realize I was holding, and bend to scoop up the dropped panties.

When I walk back onto the bus, Macallister sits at the table next to Cliff. I rapidly roam my eyes over the space but don't spy the satin bag anywhere. Jasper sits on the couch, tuning his bass. Travis reclines in one of the chairs in the back with his hat over his face, most likely trying to get in a nap. Darrell hums to himself in the bathroom while he touches up his leopard hair. But I don't see the bag. I do see Macallister's smirk, however, and when my eyes find him, he tilts his head at me in a silent challenge. I'm certainly not going to ask him where it is in front of the others, and knowing the back of the bus is clear, it's my only opportunity to go stuff my clean panties away.

I narrow my eyes at him and walk toward the back. The bus doors shut and I quicken my steps before the inevitable lurch that will surely throw me off balance as it has a million times.

"Something uh … fell out of your pocket," Cliff says right as I'm about to reach the curtain.

My face turns red, and I don't even have enough time to grab my dropped unmentionable because Travis leans out of his chair and reaches for it. Before I can say anything, and before he even realizes what he's holding, I notice the bright red thong in his hand. I reach anxiously for it, and right as I grab it, he realizes what it was he was holding and his entire face turns the same shade as the lacy pair I spent way too much money on.

His eyes are wide as they meet mine, but before he's about to utter the apology I know is on the tip of his tongue, the bus starts moving. I'm unable to balance myself, so the inertia pushes me forward into the curtain and out the other side where I fall, bracing myself with my hands.

I hear multiple voices exclaim a variety of "shit"s and "fuck"s, and when the curtain swings open, I know it's probably Macallister. His arms wrap around my middle and pull me up to stand. He holds me there for a moment, and I don't even need to turn around for confirmation.

"Are you okay?" he breathes in my ear.

I nod.

He turns me around, holding me steady with his arms, but now facing him so he can inspect me for injury.

"Where is it?" I ask.

His face shifts from concern to mischief with a devious grin when he confirms I'm truly okay. "It's safe."

That's all he says before he lets me go and walks back out to the table. I shove my panties away and walk back out. I fall onto the couch next to Jasper, directly across from Macallister where I sit and stare at him for the remainder of the drive to Salt Lake City. He stares back, and we each go back and forth trying to keep our faces straight and contain the giggles trying to force their way out.

CHAPTER 26
Macallister

The show in Salt Lake City went well until the cold stone of anxiety dropped into my stomach. I don't know what it was that reminded me of the letter, but I realized as the set was shifting from Cosmic Intervention to Gnasher I didn't know where I'd placed the letter last. I'd been stashing it in various places, like an idiot that wants to lose it. I didn't think Prudence noticed my mood shift until she stood on her tiptoes to whisper in my ear right before the encore "Are you okay?"

All I could do was force a smile and a nod, which I don't think she bought due to the distinct shape her eyebrow arched into at my response. She didn't pry further, though. Everyone was so exhausted after the show, Prudence included, so we all fell into bed quickly after boarding. Well, everyone *else* did. I pretended to fall asleep, but quickly and quietly got up to search for the letter. It was exactly where I thought it might be: tucked into its envelope and nestled in my duffel bag between neatly folded shirts and pants.

I had allowed myself to spiral for no reason. Well, not for no reason. Because I knew the real anxiety looming over me wasn't where the letter was, but what the hell I was going to do about it. The same burden that's plagued me since I found it.

We checked into our hotel a few miles away from the venue in Colorado and I've been anxiously pacing around my room for the last twenty minutes gripping the piece of stationery that's been the heaviest weight since I found it a few months ago. I've gone back and forth with approaching Cliff about this letter. When I think I can, I don't. When I don't, it grows heavier and my shoulders are sore from the metaphorical weight.

I reread the words, letting each one sink in. I stop pacing and grip the paper at eye-level, not reading anymore, but giving my eyes something to focus on while a realization washes over me: I've never even tried researching into this to confirm the validity of it. Isn't that my job? Why would I tell Cliff something that would completely alter his life if I don't even know it's true? Something about that soothes a bit of my worry. *Maybe this was just a scam.*

A soft knock pulls me out of my thoughts. I shove the letter in the bottom of my bag before going to the door to open it. When I pull it ajar, Prudence is standing in the doorway. I let my eyes scan up her body to take her in completely. She's wearing a pair of black shorts frayed on the edges and a bright red tank top. The shorts are short enough to drive me insane and her tank top is cut low enough to actually kill me. Her black hair flows easily down over her shoulders and her lips are glossed instead of painted red. They're so pouty and kissable as they always are. They pucker slightly with a sly grin.

I meet her eyes and I swear the brightness of the blue in them makes me take a small step back.

Once again, she cuts off my train of thought. "Hi." She says it softly but confidently.

"Hi," I respond as I move to let her in.

She cocks her head to the side briefly and regards me with a raise of her eyebrow before slowly walking past me. When she does, I can smell her signature scent of roses. The scent goes in through my nostrils and wisps through my brain, erasing any previous worry I had about the letter before she came over.

I follow behind her as she walks into my room. I watch her walk toward my bed, and I have the overwhelming desire to pick her up and throw her onto the mattress. The curve of her backside and the way she swishes it from side to side when she walks doesn't help. She turns and catches the angle of my gaze. Instead of scolding me, she rewards me with the widest, most gorgeous smile.

"Yes?" I gesture my hands out, feigning innocence.

"You can do more than look."

Well, fucking Christ, that's not at all what I expected. My mouth gapes, unable to form words.

She giggles. "We're finally alone. No pressure, though." She sits delicately on the edge of my bed, crossing her legs at the ankles.

My feet move below me quickly and I see my speed confirmed in her wide-eyed reaction. When I reach her at the bed, I push her backward. I thrust myself toward her, my arms finding their way right along her sides and my hands finding the mattress in tandem with her back. The back I intend to make arch up in pleasure as she loses all control of herself and her body reacts involuntarily.

She isn't laughing anymore, but staring up at me, her blue eyes burning and begging. I still need to hear her say it, though. "Prudence, is this okay?" My voice sounds husky, even to my own ears, thick with lust but soft with genuine concern for her and her well-being, her happiness. The realization consumes me, and I'm no longer in my body but up on the ceiling watching us. Because I've never felt this way for anyone. And the few times I've been able to touch her skin with my own have absolutely stitched parts of her being into me.

Her eyes flit back and forth, searching mine. For what, I don't know. I'm watching her trying to understand this completely when I already have. *I'll wait for you*, I think, meaning it wholeheartedly because she deserves nothing less. She deserves more, but at this current point in time, I know no other way to show it.

"Prudence ... Baby?" My voice cracks on my last word and I don't even have it in me to feel embarrassed about it.

She reaches a hand up to my face and strokes her thumb across my cheek. "I need you to trust I won't do anything I don't want to. I need you to trust me when I say I want this. Because I do. I want you."

Her words soak into the skin of my chest, dripping into the cavity pumping the blood through my veins. I'm utterly and completely gone for this woman. I'm so gone for her, I'd happily wait multiple lifetimes for her to catch up with me.

I lower my face to hers, my lips toward hers, and find my eyelids fluttering closed the closer we come. Her lips tickle mine for only a moment before I push into her, forcing our lips together. She meets me with enthusiasm by pushing her breasts up into my chest so I can glide my hand into the space between her back and the mattress, and hold her as close to me as possible. Her arms both go around my neck, and one of her hands finds its way to the back of my head, tangling through my hair in a way that makes my balls draw in tight.

My cock grows thick and pushes into her leg. She can feel it, too, because she moans into my mouth and wraps her leg around my waist to pull me closer.

"Mmm, you like that, baby?" I ask her, desperate to hear her say it.

"Yes," she pants, continuing to run her fingers across my scalp with harder strokes.

"I'll bet you're already wet for me. I'll bet your clit is just as hard as this cock."

She makes an indiscernible sound into my mouth and I eat it like the sweetest treat that I worked hard for.

"Can I feel? Can I feel how wet your pussy is for me?"

"I need you to," she breathes.

I trail my hand down her body, over her tank top, and realize she's not wearing a bra by the way I can feel her nipple pebble up through the ribbed fabric. I press my palm, moving it around in a circle over the top and her moan comes from deep in her throat this time.

"You're aching for me."

"I have been," she's full-on panting now and her fingers are gripping onto me like I'm about to start bucking like a horse. I might.

"Me, too," I say as I bring my hand to the top of her shorts. I run my finger along the top seam.

"Yes," she says as I push it lower, finding her warm center. I hold my palm against her and slowly undulate it around in circles on her center over the roughness of delicate lace.

"Prudence, do you want me to touch you here?" I push my palm into her, aroused by how wet I can feel she already is.

"Yes, please," she says pushing herself up into my hand giving more pressure around her clit, and no doubt giving her the most torturous relief.

I slip my hand into her panties and run my finger gently up her slit. "Baby, I want to feel your pussy. I want to pump my finger into you and feel how wet you are for me."

"Yes," she breathes as I do just that. I start slow, letting her adjust to the length of my finger, and letting myself bask in the tightness of her walls surrounding my digit.

I push further inside her, hearing her hiss as I stretch her. "And I'm going to find the spot I've been dreaming about. Because I have to reach the place, deep inside you that makes you drip down my hand."

"Oh, my god," she pants as I run my finger along her walls, finding her g-spot almost instantly as if there's a magnet in my fingertip attracted to the one inside her pussy.

"You can call me whatever you want. I'm going to make you come now."

She opens her mouth but words don't come out as I use my finger to stroke an orgasm from her. My thumb lays on her clit, skimming the surface back and forth in gentle swipes. My middle finger brushes against the spot that's rendering her speechless. I take my ring finger, and I slide it around at her entrance, collecting her arousal from there. I push it inside, right up next to my other finger, and her pussy begins to pulse as I allow her to adjust to the fullness of having both my fingers inside her.

She takes both hands and clenches them around the back of my neck. "Macallister, I'm gonna—" she takes another breath. "I think I'm about to—" She pants a few times and tries again, "I … right there. I …"

"Shh," I press my lips to hers, letting her know she doesn't need to focus on telling me because I can feel it coming. Then, pulling up slightly to say, "I know baby, I can feel you clenching. Come for me, baby. Can you do that? Can you come for me?"

She yelps and pushes her pelvis up into my hand. Her legs tremble slightly, and I gently stoke her pulsing pussy as she rides out her release.

"Holy shit," she says when her breathing begins to slow a little bit.

"I'm not done with you," I say with a smile pressed into her lips before I get up from my bed to rifle around in my bag. I pull out the object, and I notice the recognition on her face.

I hold up the black, satin bag containing the vibrator she brought with her and I was lucky enough to have fallen at my feet. "I've been wanting to use this."

"Oh, I …" she gasps as I quickly reposition myself over her. I slink down her body, spreading kisses across her still-clothed torso. I lift myself up and pull her shirt with me, trying to force it over her head, needing to see all of her. She lifts her arms and wiggles around so I can get the shirt completely off. When I do, I realize my previous suspicion is incorrect. She *is* wearing a bra, if you can call it that. Two sheer, white triangles lay over her breasts. A floral lace overlay placed so strategically, it hides her nipples. I pull out the toy and turn the vibration to a slow, steady pulse.

I press it to where I know her nipple waits for me and watch her mouth fall open in silent pleasure. I roll it across the fabric, back and forth across the sensitive peak before slowly sliding it to the other side and repeating the same care on the other soft pink bud I know lies beneath the fabric. Her eyes are closed, and she's panting slow, deep breaths as she tries to hold on to the tiny bit of composure she has left.

I growl and use my free hand to pull her bra up and over, too. Her breasts fall when I yank them up slightly with the bra and release them. They're gorgeous, and I can't resist letting my face fall in between them. I brush my nose across her clavicle and relax into the warmth of her breasts against my face. I come up for air and she's smiling at me and panting. I want to stare into her blue eyes all day but decide I have to taste her first.

I kiss lower, reaching the top of her shorts. I maneuver the metal button and hastily slide the zipper down. I'm on my hands, stretching upwards over her to grab the shorts and pull them down when a knock bangs on my door.

I freeze over her and glance toward the door. She's reaching upwards to cover herself and gaping up at me with wide eyes. We both hold our breath for a moment, and I realize the vibration is still buzzing in my hand against my palm. I quickly maneuver the device so it's turned off.

"Who is it?" she whispers.

"I don't know," I answer her honestly.

We wait for a second knock, which does sound shortly after. "What," I yell out, desperate for whoever is on the other side to get fucking lost.

"Mac, Cliff needs you." I immediately recognize Darrell's voice from the other side of the door.

Prudence's eyes lower slightly, and she nods at me with understanding in her gaze.

"Just a second," I grind out loud enough for Darrell to hear.

I hear his footsteps fade, and Prudence is already wiggling out from under me to collect her clothing.

"Hey," I say placing my hand on the side of her face.

She stops, startled by my gesture, and looks up at me questioningly. "Yeah?"

"I'm still interested in picking this back up."

"Okay," she says in a clearly unsure tone.

I lock her eyes into mine and bring our faces closer, under-standing she needs this reassurance, and I can give it to her. "I am. I will. Don't doubt me."

She looks up at me, the lines of anxiety relaxing and releasing her from the doubt I want to rid her of as soon as I can. "Okay," she repeats in a significantly more positive tone while nodding.

I press my forehead to hers. "Don't doubt me," I whisper before climbing off to get dressed quickly and discover what's going on with Cliff. His timing is impeccable, as always.

"So tell me again," I mumble to a pacing Cliff outside the hotel while pinching the bridge of my nose in frustration.

"Mac," he presses his fingers to his head, "I feel like a fucking phony, man."

I look at the ground, not at him, and I start shaking my head back and forth. "Well, Cliff, I think you and I know that's not true." It holds zero sympathy, but I can't find it in me right now. Not after what he interrupted.

He's grabbing his hair with one hand while he walks back and forth, not even acknowledging my answer as if he didn't even hear it. He's so stuck in his own head right now, he prob-ably didn't. "And that thing with Prudence. Freaked me out, man, and I don't really understand why. I just … I don't know. I can't."

"We're not canceling the Red Rocks show, Cliff, so suck it up."

His head shoots toward me now, his longer brown hair spin-ning around him with the inertia of how quickly he spun to look at me. "Excuse me?"

"Cliff, we can't do this tonight. Prudence is fine. I made sure of that. I will continue to make sure of that. And you are Clifford Lee, lead singer and guitarist for Gnasher, a Grammy-winning band. So if you think I give a shit you're not feeling 'up to it' tonight, you'd be very wrong."

He blinks back at me a few times, his face completely neutral. He throws his head back, cackling the loudest guffaw straight to the sky. "Oh, Mac, you dumb shit."

"Alright, Cliff," I say, rising to stand, ready to get back to the woman waiting in my room as quickly as possible.

I make an attempt to walk away when he pulls me back around by the shoulder, not violently, but somewhat forcefully. "Mac, shut up. Look at me. You're a dumb shit because I can't believe it took you this long with Prudence. You're right. I'm acting like a baby, and I have no reason to. I hired you for a reason," he slaps his hand on my back. "And it's because I knew you'd keep my ass in line when I needed it, and you'd bring me back down to earth when I started to stray a little far."

"And how'd you know that?" It's a genuine question considering I know he didn't have many options when he hired me and always assumed it was more out of necessity.

He smirks. "Because of who your old man is. Having to deal with a dad like yours … well, it's got to count for something." He leans his head sideways slightly, almost winking at me. I don't know what to say back, so I don't say anything at all. I nod, truly contemplating his words, and for the first time feeling like I'm valued for my own merit.

"This show is a big deal. I'd never dream of cancelling. It's just nerves."

I let his confession sink in. "Was this a problem back in the day?"

"No," he admits to his feet instead of my face. "And don't say 'back in the day' like I'm an old man."

I chuckle. "You got it, old man."

"We never played Red Rocks." His voice sounds far off and nostalgic.

"I know."

He nods, gazing past me. "I always wanted to."

"I know," I repeat, not knowing what else to say.

"Thank you," he says, shifting his eyes back to mine. "For getting it booked. For getting all of it booked. I know Darrell didn't do any of that shit." His appreciation, and pride in me eases all the frustration I felt previously toward him.

"No, he didn't really do much at all," I say, but then am awash with a realization that makes me instantly warm slightly to Darrell. "He did get Prudence, though."

Cliff gives me a knowing smile tinged with a sadness I can't place and nods once. "He did do that."

"Which I don't know if I should still hate him for or thank him for."

"Why would you hate him for it?"

"I am in way over my head," I admit out loud for the first time.

"Love does that," he whispers.

I don't correct him, because all I can wonder is *do I love her*? "Someone get away?" I ask, wondering where all his cryptic comments on lost love come from, but fearing the answer.

He contemplates me quietly, and I'm positive he won't answer. Or he'll give another response heavily fogged over in secrecy.

I'm shocked when I notice the shimmer of moisture in his eyes threatening to spill over. "Mac, that's why I left."

He says it in such a low whisper, accompanied by the unmistakable quiver that can only come from the poke of genuine emotion trying to cut its way out. Even through this, I heard his words loud and clear and I don't know how to process them. He's never admitted to anything or any reason why he split up Gnasher all those years ago. He did just now, though. And he admitted it to me, of all people.

I suck in a breath. "Over a girl?"

"A woman. *The* woman," he corrects.

I realize I'd make the same correction about Prudence, and the thought scares me because it's accompanied by words I'm not strong enough to say or even admit are sitting on my tongue. I mentally put myself in the position to lose Prudence, and I don't even have to ask myself if it would cause me to completely upend my life, quit everything, and seclude myself, because I already know the answer.

I take a deep breath. "I don't want to lose her." I'm shocked I'm letting my composure crumble with him when usually I'm the one rebuilding him after he cracks.

He throws his arms out slightly before bringing them to the sides of his legs in a slap. "Then don't be fucking stupid." He walks past me toward the hotel but grasps my shoulder when he gets right next to me. "Gotta get ready," he says before walking away and leaving me alone with thoughts swirling so rapidly, it makes me dizzy.

CHAPTER 27
Prudence

I've never attended a show here, and honestly, I don't think I'll be the same now that I have. I can't believe the way this venue makes music come alive. I don't even know where to focus because, while the stage is an obvious choice, I'm surrounded by the giant majesty of red sculptures that tower perfectly like they were strategically placed by a god who knew the exact position for them to complement the acoustics of live music.

I'm so lost in the dynamic sound of electric guitar, drum beats, and perfectly gruff vocals, I forget about Macallister. But only for a brief moment. When I twist toward him, he's already looking at me. His body is turned into mine and his head is tilted slightly. He's not hiding his stare, and a small smile creeps across his face when I notice him.

I smile back and let my eyes wander over him. He's wearing fitted, dark-wash jeans that probably cost as much as the designer slacks he usually wears. They fit him so perfectly, I'm positive they were specially made. Or at the least, tailored to him. He has a white V-neck T-shirt tucked in only in a small spot of his waistband. He doesn't wear T-shirts a lot, but I think he should start wearing them more often. His arms are toned, his biceps bulging slightly and his forearms corded with veins. I get the desire to run my fingers along his arms and am elated with the realization that I can. So I do.

His eyes fill with heat as they watch me reach out to him and tickle my fingertips up his forearms. I follow the path of his veins, watching him watch me, and a prickle of arousal settles in my core at the way his eyelids fall slightly with unmistakable desire. I slide my fingers to his wrist, then lower to the small hill curving up from the side of his palm. His fingers twitch slightly from the tickle and he pulls up slightly, intertwining my fingers with his.

He marvels at our hands locked together for a moment before he pulls his gaze back up to mine. The music is loud, and we'd have to lean in even closer to speak out loud to each other, but we don't need that right now. So we don't. We regard each other and I realize he's just another view competing for my attention. I can't lie to myself, locked into his stare is the only view I want right now.

"Thank you," I mouth to him, knowing my whisper didn't carry to his ears.

He cocks his head to the side and leans close to my ear. "For what, baby?"

There's a tingling heat washing over me from how endearing he is, and how quickly I've warmed to it. "Standing in the crowd with me."

He pulls back and smiles at me for a moment, before tugging me close again and notching his mouth at my ear. "I've wanted to do this, hold your hand during this, since the first time I saw you in the crowd at that first show."

An electric shock shoots straight down my arm at his words. I want to respond, but my tongue is heavy as lead in my mouth as my mind drifts to earlier.

He smiles and his shoulders shake from a chuckle before he turns to face the stage, sliding his hand up around my shoulder and pulling me into him easily.

I lay my head against his arm, and close my eyelids for a

moment. Taking a moment to breathe along with him and focus on the heat of his body pressing into the side of me.

Cliff addresses the crowd for the first time, stepping up to the mic and saying, "So, uh, this is my first time playing Red Rocks." Screams go up from the crowd as he pauses. "And, uh, I've always wanted to play here." More screaming, jumping the octave slightly. "I'm really grateful to be here, but I feel like I have to acknowledge someone who isn't here tonight."

The crowd cheers, but the volume is lower, indicating they know exactly who he is talking about. "Yeah, Constantine … he always wanted to play here, too. He deserved to play here." The cheering continues, but again, as if someone turned the volume dial down. "I know he's lookin' down on us, from … I don't know, wherever. Or maybe he's looking up from, uh …" laughter erupts from the crowd at the obvious innuendo. "But anyway, even though he can't be here to play the drums for us," he turns his body to the side, gesturing his arm out to Travis. "We have the wonderful and incredibly talented, Travis Pickett"

Screams erupt at full volume again. As people are jumping and clapping, I watch the giant screen displaying Cliff holding his hand out to a blushing Travis.

He nods. "Yeah, and in honor of Constantine, Travis is going to give us an original drum solo tonight."

The crowd erupts even louder, and a shy grin spreads across Travis's face to complement what I assume are still bright red cheeks. A flash of a camera bulb from the front of the stage grabs my attention. The photographer studies her camera screen for a brief moment to admire the capture she got, and she smiles. I watch her, wondering what's going through her head.

I look up again right as Cliff counts off the band and begins *Fuck Me Sober*.

He bobs his head in time with the drum beats, and his hands play a completely different rhythm. He steps up to the microphone and begins to sing.

High, I'm just a touch too high.
But you look so fly,
Cross my heart and die …

Macallister watches me. He wraps his arm around my waist and pulls me to stand in front of him. I rotate my hips in time with the music and his hands press into my sides in time with the melody. I lay my head back against his shoulder as he lets me grind against him.

I grind my ass a little deeper when the hard press of his growing erection through his pants presses to the back of me. His moan reverberates through his chest and it makes me pull my hands to find him at my waist. I curl my fingers into the spaces between his and rock my head back and forth a little bit.

The heat from his breath hits my ear as he bends his head. "Baby, you trying to kill me right now?"

I giggle and his arms tighten around my middle. "I think you're actually trying to kill me right now. You are, and I think I'm going to let you."

My insides warm and I know I moan at his words even though I can't hear it over the loud thump of bass and drums. I need to stop. We need to stop. I turn my head around and everyone's focus is on the stage. No one's eyes are on me. It's too dark and everyone else is completely entranced by Cliff, Jasper, and Travis. No one is even aware of what I'm doing. In reality, we aren't doing anything, but it's what's happening inside of me making me question if it's wrong. Not wrong, but dirty. I like dirty, and no one I've been with has allowed me to fully enjoy that.

I roll around in his arms to face him straight on. His eyes find mine, his arms wrapped around me, and he smiles. I squint from immediate confusion. *Why me?* I know he hated me when I walked onto the bus, right? At a minimum, he was wary of me and even feared what I had the power to do. Right now, he's looking at me like he'd run away with the circus if I asked nice enough. I'm so sucked in, I almost forget myself for a moment, forget why I'm here, forget how I know him, forget what will happen when we leave Colorado.

My eyes dart back and forth across his face, the questions starting to materialize with the lines on my face. A small crease forms between his brow and he leans closer, sliding his hands up to cup my face.

His eyes fill with concern as he leans close enough for me to hear his words. "What are you thinking about?"

"Why me?" I ask, my voice breaking and cracking with the threat of emotions fueled by salt water.

He regards me for a moment, searching my eyes with his and tracing patterns into my skin with his eyes. "You are ..." he cuts off, taking a breath and continuing to run his eyes across my face and back.

He leans further so his lips are at my ear. "You are remarkable. And you bring me to a place I've never been. I am completely outside myself, and I know I should be terrified, but I'm not. I'm free-falling, but I can't help the smile pressed into my face. You ..." he stops and I think I almost stop breathing. "You have completely ingrained yourself into my being. I can't get enough of you. I need all of you."

I can't tear my eyes from his, completely unaware of anything else going on. "I need you," I whisper, hardly able to find my voice.

"Let me take you?"

"Please," it's on half a breath as he pulls me through the crowd toward an exit. He's pulling out his phone and pressing things into it as he guides me swiftly to the incline of stairs.

"Where are we going?"

"Your bed," he says, then stops. "Actually, my bed. Because I will be the one taking care of you tonight. My bed," he says over his shoulder before continuing to walk.

I nod, letting him pull me along as the crowd erupts into even louder cheering as Travis begins his drum solo. My core heats at his words and actions alongside the soundtrack of raw talent reverberating through the air. I admire the way his bicep bulges slightly from his tight grip around my hand. I can't pull my eyes away and my legs get weak at my arousal. His steps falter at the slowed pace of my own, and right before descending a set of stairs, he turns and picks me up and lays me over his shoulder. He brings his hand to my ass. "My sweet girl," he rumbles as his hand lands a playful smack to my backside.

He walks briskly down the steps but is still able to keep me steady. And even though I'm thrown across his back, I'm clenching my thighs together with how turned on I am. My clit is starting to engorge and is rubbing against his shoulder muscle popping out with each step he takes. I'm desperate for him and I grip the bottom of his T-shirt as I moan into my fist.

He slaps my ass again causing one of my feet to pop up. He caresses the spot he smacked with a gentle touch, and goose-bumps rise up my thighs. He must notice, too, because his moan vibrates from his chest against my legs. The arm not wrapped around my legs shifts and goes into his pocket. No doubt to figure out a way for us to get back to the hotel since we would not be waiting to ride over on the bus.

This tension between us has been pulling for what feels like forever, and I'm grateful we have our hotel rooms tonight. Even though I'm positive we will only need one and mine will go to waste.

When we walk to the VIP parking lot where the bus is parked, a black SUV pulls up. This happens upside-down of course, because I'm still draped over his shoulder. He maneuvers me gently back over and places my feet on the ground, leaving his hands on my body for a moment to make sure I'm steady. His eyes darken with need and anticipation, his pupils taking over the hazel irises. He opens the back door of the SUV and gestures for me to get in. I do, and he shuts the door and quickly makes his way to the seat behind the driver where he gets in.

As soon as he's in the car he reaches toward me and I scooch myself a little closer to him. He wraps his arm around me pulls me all the way into the side of his body and holds me there, drawing circles on my thigh with his thumb.

He says words to the Uber driver, but I can't even focus on what he said because I'm so focused on his face, his jaw, his neck. I reach out a fingertip and glide it down his neck muscles gently. He shudders under my touch and he turns his face to mine. We stay locked in a stare with each other, neither one of us daring to break the hold with words or movement. I watch his eyes drink me in the same way mine do to him.

I watch him, my arousal turning so hot I have to clench my thighs together again. I cross my ankles and press my legs tight. I don't want to be able to feel my legs anymore after he's done with me. I don't want anything but the tingling heat from where his hands touch me. I wonder if my expression communicates how needy I am for him.

I'm almost sure it does because of the sly smirk and tilt of his face.

I'm obviously lost in the embrace of his eyes, holding me, locking me in, so much so that I don't realize when we pull to a stop.

I don't register what happens between him opening my car door and my back hitting the mattress, but I know there's a lot of kissing because my lips are delightfully sore from going back and forth with his. I know if I looked in a mirror, they'd be swollen and darkened. My fingers tangle in his hair and massage his scalp while he grinds into my hips and grips me tightly. He starts tugging off my clothes, and I arch into him, pressing my core into his erection as hard as I can, loving the small relief it brings me. He's pulled my shirt over my head and his hand wraps up around the small of my back, holding me into position.

"Macallister," I whisper, close to his ear. "I want you."

He grunts a yes into my ear right before he drags his mouth to my neck. Kissing, sucking, and completely obliterating my conscious train of thought. I have three words dancing along the tastebuds on my tongue, and I want to spit them out, but keep them trapped inside, dancing still while my insides light up.

I reach around his neck and pull his mouth closer to me, pressing him into my skin as forcefully as I can. His mouth glides up in kisses right under my ear. "You want me?" I moan a confirmation. "Want this cock?" He growls deeper and my hips buck up into his.

"Yes, I do," I manage to say after a deep moan.

He holds himself up over my body. His eyes dig into me like no one ever has before. I'm on fire under his examination, and I notice my hands creeping up my body to cover myself. I reach them up to wrap around my chest, and his hand intercepts mine. He grabs my wrists, and pulls them up over my head, clamping his hands around them holding me in place.

"Don't," he breathes out. "You're so beautiful."

My eyes grow wide and the tips of my fingers tingle. "I am?" I force through a shaky and disbelieving whisper. I've had plenty of men tell me I'm hot, and even more men just grunt their approval like a caveman at the sight of me. But this … this is new. So new, my soul doesn't know how to accept it. I haven't asked him what we are, what this means, but his words wash over me and reassure me this is different than it has been with anyone else before.

He doesn't respond, but instead smiles at me before dropping his face into the skin of my belly, kissing me in no straight line up my body. When he reaches my breast, I ache for him to suck my nipple into his mouth. But instead, like he knew it would torture me, he kisses right near the erect bud on the soft flesh of my breast. I let out a frustrated groan as he works his way up.

When he reaches my neck, he glides his tongue up in the direction toward my ear. The wet lick is hot and it leaves behind tiny sparks of electricity. He reaches my ear and puffs a few breaths across it. The contrast makes me shiver.

His hand cups my breast. "You're *so* fucking beautiful, Prudence." He takes a breath before looking directly into my eyes with a mischievous grin. "I want to destroy you."

His words verbally stroke me, and my clit throbs between my thighs pressed together so tightly now it's making my muscles quiver. He lowers his face to force our lips back together. He uses his tongue to maneuver mine around, and we breathe into each other's mouths with desperate anticipation.

He pulls back and his tongue peeks back out to glide across his lower lip before he says, "Your mouth tastes like candy."

I grin at him, right before I say, "Why don't you kiss a little lower and tell me how my pussy tastes, like you were supposed to earlier."

His eyes widen, but a flame flares in the center of them. "Fuu-uuck," he breathes and moves his body down quickly, and this time, in a direct line to quickly reach where I need him most.

He unbuttons my pants in record time and yanks them down my legs, wrapping a hand around the back of each knee to help my legs slide out of each pant leg more easily. Once he's tossed the pants to the side, he turns back to me. His eyes drop to the small triangle of black lace. He presses his nose and mouth into the lace of my panties, rocking his head side to side slightly.

I grab the string of my thong to pull it down, but his head jerks back and his hands come to mine, stopping me.

"Mine," he says.

CHAPTER 28

Macallister

When she reaches for the sides of her black, lacy panties, an overwhelming territorial instinct surges through my body.

"Mine." I grab her wrists and pin them above her head. She obeys, holding them over her head without further instruction.

"Good girl," I purr as I slowly guide the, what I now fully see is a thong, down her thighs. As I'm about to push it to her ankles and guide her feet out of it, a thought wracks me.

"You're staying here tonight, right?" I ask, already shrinking slightly at the thought of her leaving this bed at some point before the sun rises. I want to wake up wrapped around her.

She tilts her head to meet my eyes and confusion overtakes her face. "Do you want me to?"

Her question flies through my chest like a dagger, and the pooling blood begins to choke me from the fatal wound. "Prudence, that's all I want."

The mischievous smile spreading across her face heals me from the inside, out. "The only thing?" I know her question is meant as playful coaxing, but the way she says it causes my cock to thicken even more. She wants me to continue, and I will. But I wish I could continue to look her in the eyes and tell her the truth.

Because yes, it is all I want, so desperately it's going to devour me. But I need to taste her right now, as she asked.

I hunch between her thighs, holding them open and lowering my head methodically and slowly lining it up with her center. Her legs quiver in my grasp with the need to press together, the need for friction. I take my finger and brush it up against her pussy. Running my finger all the way up her slit, I collect the evidence of her arousal, her desire. I pull my finger back in tandem with the sound of her moan.

"Is this for me?" I ask, raising my finger and peeking at her, trying to find her eyes through the me-sized gap in her thighs.

Her eyes snap to mine, and she brings herself upward on her forearms to get in my eye line better. We meet, her blue piercing my hazel.

I raise an eyebrow in further interrogation, and I hear her take in a sharp breath. "What?" she breathes on her exhale.

"Is this," I hold up my finger slightly higher to indicate what I'm talking about, even though I know she knows. "For me? Because," I stick my slick finger into my mouth and hold it on my tongue before releasing it from my lips with a pop. "You are soaked. And delicious."

Her eyes widen and her mouth is parted like she wants to speak words, but her tongue has forgotten the exact choreography to do so. I smile back at her in response before dipping my head down and using my tongue to swipe the exact same spot my finger did. I do it once. Then again, but harder, and her answering moan is my answer. I plunge my tongue deep inside her and her body arches up, curving her spine.

I push my finger against her clit, just slightly, which forces a guttural moan to come from deep in her chest. I keep my eyes open, watching every brilliant movement. I push my ears to strain more, catching every incredible sound. The sounds she makes have me in awe.

I find a rhythm she likes, her pussy clenching around my tongue. I take my tongue out, sliding it up to her throbbing nub, while I move my finger with slight pressure before it slips right into her tight, wet pussy. Her walls instantly squeeze around me and it makes my cock twitch against the mattress.

It hurts. It hurts so bad. I'm so hard, I can't even help myself from slowly grinding my hips into the bed to get the slightest bit of release from the friction. It's not enough and only makes my dick throb harder. I let out a pathetic groan into her wetness, and she responds with a beautiful cry that almost sounds like my name.

I close my eyes and push my face further into her heat and her pussy walls spasm all over my finger. I groan into her, my tongue slowing from how turned on I am from her coming on my face.

"That's it, baby," I pant into her pelvis. "Come for me." She's grinding her hips as she pushes her back upwards.

I continue to stroke her, slowing slightly while I let her ride out her release. Her climax drips down my finger as I pull out, and I admire her, almost lost in wonderment. Before I realize it, her hands have wrapped around my wrist and she's guiding my hand, finger still outstretched from my fist, up. She opens her mouth and guides my finger in, pulling her lips closed around it and sucking slowly.

"You taste what you did, baby?" I ask, in amazement at how I got so lucky. Lucky to be here, with her right now.

She keeps her lips closed tight around my finger, giving it the equivalent of an incredible blow job, as she hums in agreement.

I pull my finger out, begrudgingly, with a loud popping sound from her swollen, pink lips. I stare at them a moment before pressing my lips to them. Warmth radiates from her and as we glide our tongues together, it pulls more from all over her body. I hold her head in my hands, and I ravage her mouth the way I've wanted to for weeks. I taste candy again on my tongue, now mixed with the intoxicating taste of her climax. It reminds me of the first time I ever ate the candy Pop Rocks. Tiny sparks of electricity ignite across my tongue, lighting up my tastebuds in a new way. I never want to go back.

We pull apart when we both start gasping for air. We're panting together, but staring at each other intently. Her eyes glance down, and I know what her gaze is locked in on.

"Do you want this?" I ask guiding my palm down my straining cock, needing her to let me know. Hoping she knows I'd do anything for her, even wait.

She gazes up at me and places both of her hands on my cheeks, holding my face in line with hers. "I do. I want this," she says, nodding her head on the pillowy mattress beneath her.

I rise from the bed, and her startled eyes follow me. When I reach into my bag for a condom and start walking back, her eyelids grow heavy again in understanding. I kneel between her legs, staring at her, as I open the packet and start to roll the condom on my shaft. When it's halfway on, she reaches up and rolls it the rest of the way. Her hand on my cock sends a shudder through my body, and I have to close my eyes and concentrate to compose myself.

When the condom is on, I line my cock up, right with her entrance, holding it there for a moment. I keep her eyes locked into mine and hold the tip of my aching hardness against her wetness. When I push it inwards, unable to keep my eyes from drifting to watch myself enter her, she lets out a deep moan and closes her eyes.

"Oh, Prudence," I say, almost unable to breathe with how perfectly she wraps around me. "You feel," I take a breath and tilt my head back in ecstasy, "so good."

She grabs my shoulders and pushes her hips up into mine. "So do you," she says, and I can't believe how amazing it feels for her to push herself onto me, completely to the hilt.

I pump in and out of her, finding her spots. Knowing when I tilt a certain way or go a certain speed, her moans get deeper. Or when I lick the pad of my thumb and glide it across her clit, she pushes her head deeper into the pillow and opens her mouth on an endless exhale. She's beautiful, and I feel like I'm watching her experience everything in slow motion.

I grasp her hips with my hands, holding her down while I continue to thrust into her. Her hands wrap around my wrists, and she locks her gaze into mine. "I'm going to come," she whispers, as if out of breath.

My speed picks up slightly and I push my face into her neck, kissing and sucking. I'm trying to grasp for any extra moment, because I'm close and I can't imagine the separation. I lick a spot where her neck meets her clavicle, and she places her hands to my back. I can feel her nails dig into my skin as she grips tightly and whimpers in my ear.

Her panting synchronizes, and I find the rhythm that sings to me she's there. I push in as deep as I can and her body seizes around mine. Her muscles go tight, just before her legs shake out the tension. I hold her trembling body and bask in the beauty of watching her come. Knowing she found her release, and I'm the one that helped her do it, is life-altering. It brings me to my own release, which I let out with a groan and a tilt of my head up at the ceiling.

When I look back at her, I know I'm unable to hide the love from my eyes, and I have no idea how I've fallen this far.

"You're stunning," I say, and her eyelids flutter open and she gives me one of her smiles that reaches all the way to her eyes.

CHAPTER 29

Prudence

I'm wrapped up in Macallister. His legs are interwoven with mine and his arm is draped heavily across my middle holding me to the bed and holding me to him. His other arm is snaked under my neck, belted around my chest gripping my shoulder. He's holding me like he's terrified someone will come grab me from him. Even though no one is, with the way his arms are holding me, no one would be able to even if they tried. His chest rises and falls against my back. It's slow and deep, so I know he's still asleep.

I have no idea what time it is or how much sleep we've gotten —or haven't gotten, for that matter. We went back and forth between little cat naps and waking each other up for more. More touching, kissing, biting. More licking, panting, moaning. Just … more. And I'm still not satiated. I scootch and shimmy myself backward, further into him. I'm completely pressed into him, but I convince myself if I try hard enough, I'll completely melt into him and his warmth.

It's not that I'm cold. Or maybe I didn't realize I was cold until I felt his heat. I let it completely encapsulate me, wrapping around me like an invisible blanket, one I didn't know I was looking for. I shudder slightly, as if I've been living completely frozen and he's thawing me out to my bones. Right now, he feels like my everything. I push down the creeping sensation from the rising thought continuing to plague me. *Am I his?*

I blink around and let my eyes adjust to the darkness of the room while I settle deeper into his hold. I face the window draped completely with a blackout curtain wondering what time it is, but feeling too heavy to move and find a clock. It could still be dark outside, and I wouldn't have any idea. Twelve hours could have passed, or only two hours could have passed. I wouldn't be shocked at either. That's how up in space I am.

He buries his face in my neck, pressing his nose deeper into the skin blending into my scalp where my hair begins. My eyes flutter closed at his conscious attention. I brace myself for more. I want it. I'm completely worn out and I don't even know if I can have an orgasm again, but I want to try. I let out a little moan and his motions turn more aggressive. His hands explore the front of my body, his fingertips tickling across my bare skin and his palm sliding up to find what he wants.

One of his hands grips and releases my breast. Grip. Release. Grip. Release. I roll my hips backward into what I can quickly determine is an actively growing and already stiff erection. It slides slightly up the length up my back as it hardens further, the tip of his cock already wet with precum. He moves his hand over so he can grip my nipple between his thumb and pointer finger. He grips it with a slight amount of pressure and rolls it between the pads of his fingers.

The texture of his hands feels amazing on my skin. I love his hands. The way they're slightly calloused on the tips like he secretly plays guitar in his spare time. It's only on a couple of the fingers, and they're so minimal, you'd miss them if you weren't paying attention. But I pay attention. I shiver at the texture change when he takes his middle finger and circles it around my throbbing clit.

"Ohhh," I let out a deep sigh at the brush of contact.

"Oh, baby," he whispers into my ear from behind. "Your clit is so hard. Do you like when I touch it?"

"Oh, yes. Yes, I needed it," I grit, entering into a primal state I've only ever gotten to with him.

"Mmm," he moans into my ear and the sound of it sends shivers through my body.

"Macallister, please," I pant, focusing on the need for slightly more pressure and to feel something inside of me. Not something, but him.

He knows exactly what my body is asking for because he responds with exactly that. His finger slips inside me and we can both hear how wet I am. The spread of red, hot shame washes over me. Right before it can completely take over my nerves, he guides his lips back up to my ear breathing a little bit.

Two puffs of breath hit my ear before his deep voice, sounding like it was dragged through gravel, says, "I love how wet you get for me." I'm instantly charged with his praise. I'll replay the sound of his voice saying those exact words for the rest of my life. The memory will be the star of any fantasy I have from this day on.

My hips tug and buck against him. He glides his arm from my breast to wrap me across my hips, holding me still.

I'm in shock when he reaches that place, deep inside, and strokes back and forth. I grunt and buck my hips back, but he's holding me in place, forcing the pleasure to radiate through my body. I'm grateful for him doing so because it feels more amazing than anything I've felt before.

"That's right baby, you're such a good girl coming all over my finger," he says as he slips a second finger into my wetness and my body begins to shiver at the overwhelming pleasure. "Fingers," he clarifies just in case I missed what happened. Like I could with the way he stretches me.

I keep thinking, after each orgasm, I'll probably never come like that again. But then I do, and not just like that, but better. How can that be possible? Does pleasure have infinite growth?

I'm panting and bent over, pulsing around his fingers and

riding the wave of my climax. He pulls out of me when I start breathing slower. He uses both his hands to turn me to face him.

"I …" I watch him literally lose his words. His eyes flit back and forth between mine, searching for something. My brow scrunches in confusion, and maybe a little in fear.

His expression crumples. "No, Prudence. I—" he pauses, "I like you." His last three words sound somewhat resigned.

I blink back up at him and my facial muscles relax a little. "I like you, too." The word sounds flat and tastes wrong in my mouth, but I can't start getting into the four-letter word that changes things. Changes *every* thing. Not that I have a lot of personal experience with that word, but still, I have no business expecting it from him anyway.

We stare at each other for a moment before we're both startled by the loud knock coming from the door. Macallister turns toward the door as if he'll be able to see through it. He waits for a moment, and another knock comes. "Yeah?" he yells at whoever is on the other side.

"Mac, we've got sound-check in forty-five. I wanted to debrief last night with you. I know you're mad, man, but listen … that was a big deal. Last night was … a big deal, okay?" Cliff. If the sound-check is in forty-five minutes, that means it's two fifteen in the afternoon. No wonder I'm starving.

Macallister snaps his head to me, blinking in the universal sign for *What the fuck is he talking about*? I shrug my shoulders, giving him a silent response.

He turns his head back over his shoulder. "Cliff, I need—." He rolls his body away from me, my body already complaining at the loss of his warmth. "Give me a sec."

He starts racing through the room looking around frantically and snatching random articles of clothing. He has to peer around when he eventually needs his shoes. He tilts his head back to the ceiling before sprinting into the bathroom. He turns on the sink for a second then starts to aggressively brush his teeth. He spits, stomps out, puts his shoes on, and stands.

He's looking directly at me, and it's like time has stopped for him as much as it has for me because he's just *looking* at me. He releases the tension in his body slightly.

I smile at him and nod a little before I whisper-scream and mouth the words, "It's okay." I have to get ready, too, and forty-five minutes is already going to be pushing it considering I want to take a shower.

I scamper up, taking the sheet with me to cover up, and hop around gathering my clothes. He's still standing there, and a grin spreads across his face. I hop over to him, smiling, and plant a kiss on his lips. It's a simple peck, a smack on the lips without tongue, but something about the comfort in it is more intimate for some reason.

"I'll see you at the show, pretty girl." My stomach bottoms out and I know I'm grinning like an absolute fool.

He presses another kiss into my lips and turns to leave. I hop into the bathroom so Cliff won't spot me when he opens the door.

When he closes the door and they walk away, Cliff's voice carries down the hall, and I hear him say, "Finally, man."

CHAPTER 30

Macallister

I can't believe I almost told her I loved her. The scrunching of her face made me think she might be scared I would. And she'd be justified, because I have no business telling her I love her, or trying to drag her into my crazy life. So I said I liked her to gauge her reaction. She softened, but I also recognized something still frozen inside her. I can't help but hold on to the possibility that it was a tiny shred of hope I *would* say love instead of like.

How does this work after the tour? Can this even work for the remainder of the tour? I'm usually more pragmatic than this. I usually think things through before jumping in, but Prudence has pulled me in so deep, I've lost the ability when it comes to her.

I'm pulled from my mental spiral when Cliff gives my arm a playful punch. I turn and glare at him. I'm not going to deny or confirm his suspicions. Instead, I raise an eyebrow at him before turning my head and continuing to walk forward. He lets out a small chuckle and I shake my head.

"Cliff, what's going on?" I ask, not trying to hide that I have no idea what it is he thinks I'm mad at. I don't have the energy to try and pretend. I left all of it back in my room with the most beautiful woman I've ever had the pleasure of almost saying I love you to. I internally cringe and decide I can continue to unpack that later.

He walks with purpose, but turns his head to me at the same time. "What do you mean what's going on?"

"I am assuming you didn't notice I wasn't on the bus last night? I left the show early, Cliff. Prudence and I both did."

"At what point?" he asks, hesitantly.

I squint my eyes, trying to remember what part of the setlist they were at when Prudence and I snuck away when I remember getting to hear Travis wrap up his drum solo before throwing her into the car that picked us up. "*Fuck Me Sober.*"

Cliff stops walking and I turn to him, his eyes wide. "Well, shit."

"Cliff …" I say in warning. He better tell me what the fuck is going on because the anxiety starting to fill my body is pushing out every last joyful feeling Prudence filled it up with earlier.

"Here," he says, stopping at a hotel room door I assume is his. Instead of pulling out a key, though, he knocks twice.

Jasper opens the door, his hair disheveled and wearing a bathrobe.

He rubs his fingers along the sharp scruff on his face, and I can hear the scrape against his fingertips. "Still no word?" He asks, his head turning back and forth between both of us.

"No word about what?" The temperature of my blood is starting to rise.

They both ignore me. "Not yet," Cliff says.

Jasper pulls the door open a little wider signaling we're both invited inside.

I walk in and Darrell sits on the edge of Jasper's unmade bed shaking his head. He looks up when we walk in and stands. He must realize it's unnecessary for him to do so and sits with his hands on his knees.

"Someone better fill me in. Now," I boom. I can hear the slight shake of my voice, but hope no one else can.

Jasper gestures to a chair. "Sit."

I do so reluctantly, not fully relaxing into the chair, but hanging off the edge in anticipation of what is about to come out of their mouths.

Jasper and Cliff remain standing and goggle at each other. There's a small hint of humor in their smiles. "What?" I yell.

They all turn to me and confusion splashes across Darrell's face. I don't have the patience to explain to him I wasn't there last night after a certain point. It appears no one was concerned we weren't on the bus and that thought fills me with anger, especially after what happened only days ago in Arizona.

"So last night was amazing," Jasper starts.

"Best show, yet," Cliff agrees, and I know he means ever, not just on this tour. Red Rocks is a venue he's dreamed about his entire life. Had he not called it quits right after the Grammys all those years ago, there's no doubt they would have played there sooner.

"Great, glad you all enjoyed yourselves. Now what is the fucking problem?" I'm getting sick of the energy it's taking to pull this information from them.

Jasper and Cliff share another look, and apparently, a silent conversation, because Cliff finally turns to me ready to spill the entire story. "The crowd called an encore, and we kinda kept playing. Instead of the typical three-song encore, we—"

Jasper cuts him off. "We brought Cosmic back up and we jammed."

"How late?" I ask, knowing this isn't necessarily the point of the story.

Jasper laughs. "We played an extra hour." Cliff scowls at him in a way that calls bullshit. "Or two ... ish?" He throws his hands out and smiles wide like a toddler asking for forgiveness.

I nod. "Okay ..." my voice drags uncertainly, still waiting for the information they thought I was already mad about. I know they're tiptoeing around this. Delicately dropping petals of information, and it's honestly making me more frustrated. "If the venue wasn't concerned about it, I'm not either. So cut to the chase."

Cliff clasps his hands together. "Afterwards, we went back to the bus, still riding the high of the show, and started drinking." *Here it comes.* "A lot." I glance at the three of them, all sporting dark bags under their eyes. Darrell clutches his stomach, and now I'm afraid he's going to projectile vomit right onto me. I lean back instinctively. So they're hungover, whatever. I'd normally be more strict about this, considering a big part of my job is to help Cliff maintain his image. He's not an alcoholic, but he stepped back into this scene out of hiding, and since no one had seen him in years, their last memory was how he left.

Cliff continues. "We also invited others onto the bus to celebrate with us." I notice how he uses the word 'celebrate' instead of 'party.'

"Who?" Now I'm concerned.

"Not many," Jasper cuts in. "A photographer, an older fan I recognized from back in the day, and one of the security guards."

"A fucking security guard? From the venue?" That might be the stupidest thing I've ever heard.

"Don't worry," Darrell says in a shaky voice, "He's cool." I squint at him, wondering if there's more to Darrell piping up for him, but brush it off in pursuit of more important information.

I motion with my hand for them to continue because I know they aren't done with this confession. "Travis might have … left with the photographer at some point." *Interesting.* "And we haven't heard from him since …"

I rub my hands down my thighs. "Our drummer is missing." It's not a question, but a confirmation. I want to laugh, considering it's a common stereotype that drummers always go missing and are perpetually late. However, this is uncommon for Travis.

They all nod. "Your sound check is in—" I look at my naked wrist, realizing I can't see what time it is because in my hurry to get dressed and leave, my wristwatch was the last thing on my mind.

Darrell saves me from having to reach into my pocket for my phone when he says, "Twenty minutes."

"We have to fucking go," I say jumping up. I, unlike musicians, hate being late.

There's a small knock on the door. We all gander at each other hoping it's Travis, but knowing the light rasp was too delicate to be from the muscular, six-foot-four-inch drummer.

Jasper opens the door. Whoever is on the other side giggles then says, "Are you wearing that to the show?" It's Prudence.

I turn my head and she steps into the room, clearly studying all of us.

"Everything okay?" she asks with concern in her voice after examining each of us all and no doubt reading the varying expressions on our faces.

Darrell, Cliff, and Jasper look anywhere but at her. I stare at her, and she finds my persistent gaze and holds onto it like an anchor. *I can be your anchor*, I think, almost wishing I'd said it out loud to her regardless of our audience.

Instead, I say, "Travis is missing."

A sneaky smile spreads across her face. "No, he isn't. He's waiting for us at the venue."

The reactions around the room are all different. Darrell's eyes widen and move toward Jasper. Jasper puts his hands in his pockets and shakes his head, quietly chuckling to himself.

Cliff crosses his arms. "How do you know?"

She holds up her phone. "He texted asking where we are."

I hear Jasper disappear into the bathroom with the click of the door. Cliff and Darrell sit in silence. I rise from the chair and walk over to Prudence, placing my back toward them.

I grab her gently by the shoulders. "You okay?"

Her eyebrows form a frown, but the smile on her lips stays. "Yes?"

"Okay," I whisper back and turn toward them again. "Get your asses on the bus," I say to them.

I turn and place my hand on her lower back, guiding her out of the room. As we walk by the bathroom door, it opens and Jasper steps out fully dressed.

He claps his hands together. "Round two. Let's do this."

CHAPTER 31

Prudence

Night two at Red Rocks was less eventful than night one, or at least from what I've heard. Macallister and I stayed for the entire show this time, even though I wanted so badly to pull him away multiple times. We stood off-stage instead of in the crowd, which was my decision, but I didn't miss the breath of relief I heard from Macallister when I told him.

Standing by the bus as everyone filtered back in, I reminisced on the experience tonight. We'd stood out of sight from the crowd, and I realized how amazing it was to watch a show so closely. The acoustics were still amazing, but it did sound different from that vantage point. As if the music hit my ears from the opposite direction. I continue to replay the night, and my skin begins to buzz when I remember the way Macallister's warm arm wrapped around my middle from behind me, pulling me closer to him like he is right now.

I giggle. "Hi," I breathe.

"Hey," he leans down and whispers into my ear. I notice he lingers there for a moment. "Your hair smells nice."

I turn around and face him. "What do you want?" I ask, playfully with an eyebrow raised.

He looks back at me earnestly, clearly missing the teasing in my tone. "You," he says so honestly that the words sink into my chest cavity and shatter inside. The shards sprinkle around, warming me as they nestle in tiny cracks and crevices I didn't know existed.

He puts a finger under my chin and lifts my gaze to his. "What are you thinking?"

I let out some air, realizing I'd been holding my breath. "This is not something I could have ever expected when I took this assignment." Saying the word 'assignment' throws me slightly off-kilter, remembering I'm technically working right now.

His face falls and he takes a small step backward. I notice the loss of heat right away, and even though it's not particularly chilly outside, my body responds with a shiver.

He runs a hand over his chin and jaw. "I'm not ..." he searches inside for the words he's trying to say. "I don't ..." he tries again, but then shakes his head and lets out a humorless laugh through his nose.

"I didn't mean it in a bad way," I reassure him. But maybe I'm reassuring myself because deep down, I don't know what I'm expecting. I've been so wrapped up in him, in us, since Jessica gave me the permission I didn't need as an adult to let myself explore this thing happening between us.

"Do you feel like I've taken advantage of you?" he asks, his eyes filling with concern and moisture.

"No," I practically shout, reaching toward him. He doesn't back up this time, and my hand lands on his chest. The hard swell of his pectoral muscle momentarily sidetracks me.

My palm vibrates from the rumble of a chuckle. "My eyes are up here," he says, low and deep.

"I'll show you mine if you show me yours," the playful tone is back in my voice, but this time he picks up on it.

"I'll take you up on that," he coos at me and I almost get lost in him when I'm startled by Travis' voice from behind me.

"Has anyone seen Victoria?"

I don't turn around, but keep my eyes on Macallister as they widen and I mouth, *who the fuck is Victoria?*

He smiles and shakes his head a little.

"Hey," Travis places his hand on my shoulder. I turn toward him. "Have you seen Victoria?"

I pause, debating whether or not to tell him the truth, which is that I don't know who Victoria is.

He keeps his hand on my shoulder but keeps his eyes down, his face an expression of defeat as he shakes his head. "Shit." He says it in a whisper, meant for himself. I grow concerned now.

I turn my body completely, pulling away from Macallister's hold. "Who is Victoria?"

When he looks up at me, his eyes glimmer from either adoration or tears. A sad smile spreads across his devastated face. "She's the photographer."

I think back to the night before, which quite honestly, feels like a million years ago at this point, and remember watching the tall woman moving back and forth at the front of the stage snapping pictures. I recall the way she looked at her camera screen smiling every few clicks to admire her photos.

"Do you know her?" I ask, trying to put the pieces together.

He nods. "We met last night." He turns his head around, breaking our eye contact, no doubt continuing to catch a glance of her just in case she's wandering around.

"I haven't seen her since last night," I say. While I wasn't in the crowd, I know I glanced toward the front pit of the stage and didn't notice her there. I did notice a couple of new photographers. I know as a reporter, you usually only get a ticket to one show and you're lucky to get that sometimes. "She most likely didn't get a press pass for the second night."

"No, I gave her a ticket. She was going to sit in the crowd and … watch," his voice trails off and is broken as he turns his head around, still searching.

"Well, she wouldn't be here if she had a general admission ticket," I hear Macallister say from behind me.

Travis snaps his head to make eye contact with him. "I looked everywhere else."

"Can you text her or call her?" I offer.

His eyes lower. "I can't believe I'm saying this, but ..." he shakes his head.

"You don't have her number?" I ask.

The slight change from frantic to harsh realization is so apparent in his eyes, I don't need the verbal confirmation.

He starts walking away, his shoulders slumped and his feet dragging like a pubescent boy getting turned down at prom. My heart hurts for him, and I know I have to pull him aside at some point tomorrow to talk to him. We've formed a bond on this tour. Enough so that I know when he is upset, he needs some time to decompress. Afterward, he needs someone to talk to.

Harvey peeks his head out of the open bus door. "Alright, if we want to stay on schedule, we need to get moving."

I turn back around and Macallister looks at me. "Ready?" he asks.

I nod and walk up onto the tour bus with his hand resting on my lower back. I nodded, but now as I'm walking up the steps, I'm not so sure I am ready. Ready for what, exactly? Ready to walk onto this bus like the last few days didn't happen? Or am I walking onto this bus in a completely different position than I was in before? The questions I can't help from swirling around my head pop back up. What exactly are we to each other? What do I want us to be?

I mindlessly walk toward the back of the bus, passing Cliff sitting at the table. His feet propped up and his guitar on his lap. Everyone else must have made it back to their beds or haven't gotten on the bus yet because no one else is around. When we walk past him, I smile and nod awkwardly, not knowing what else to do.

He runs his pick across the strings as he chuckles. "Sleep tight," he calls to our backs in an exaggerated and teasing tone. I hate it. It almost feels weird, like my dad watching me take a boy to my room. I'm not sure if Macallister makes a face or flips him off behind my back, but Cliff laughs so I know he did something.

When we get to the back, I pull out my bag and search around for a pair of pajamas and my cosmetic bag. I am out of sorts not knowing what is about to happen, and I turn around trying to get my bearings. Do we just go to sleep in our separate beds? That probably makes the most sense, but a part of me is devastated by the idea. Because I have no grasp on how I'm supposed to act right now, I grab my stuff and walk quickly to the bathroom to wash my face and change, not saying a single word to him as I pass through the curtain.

When I emerge a few minutes later, I don't see him. He must be asleep. I walk over to my bunk, a small wash of relief that I have an answer, but sad it isn't the one I wanted, regardless. I pull the curtain open, and his cracks slightly.

"Come here, baby," he whispers, and I melt from the sound of his voice and what he's saying.

I put my stuff away and climb up into his bunk. He tucks me under his covers, kisses me on the cheek, and tells me he'll be right back. He returns only a few minutes later, smelling faintly of soap. I snuggle into the crook of his armpit, resting my hand on his chest. I look up through my lashes and a small smile overtakes his lips. He rubs the hand wrapped around me up and down my arm.

I want to say something, but I don't know what to say. So I lay there, and drift off as he draws shapes across my skin and I daydream they're in the shape of little hearts.

It's been three days since Red Rocks. There's another two-day stop in Austin we are on our way to now. We stopped yesterday in New Mexico for a show. Everything is normal. Nothing is the same. I've had my head completely up in the clouds, but always on the edge of falling. It feels like this can't last. But I want it to.

I've slept with Macallister every night since we left Colorado and no one has batted an eye. Since my bed is on the bottom, we've slept in mine more often than his. He's held my hand any chance he gets, and no one takes a second glance at our intertwined fingers. He acts like he's been holding onto me his entire life, and I'm in a constant state of worry for when he lets go. It feels inevitable since he doesn't define our relationship with a word, and I still haven't asked.

But I relish every time I feel his grip. Any other man that held my hand felt insignificant. Their fingers woven between mine loosely so they could let go, which they always did hastily. Macallister holds my hand like he can't let go.

I'm sitting with the entire group around the table and Felicia's last email is burning through the phone in my pocket as a constant reminder. She didn't outright say my job was on the line, but the meaning was tucked between the words of disappointment. I'm bouncing my leg anxiously when Macallister's warm hand rests atop my thigh. I look around frantically and Macallister catches my gaze, finally able to hook me to him. Concern fills his expression.

"You okay?" he whispers as everyone around us talks.

I nod, but I know it's unconvincing. I don't know what to do because I'm on the brink of losing my job, or worse, losing this man and these people who have wiggled themselves into my heart in such a short amount of time.

He scrunches his eyebrows up, a question sitting on the tip of his tongue, but gets cut off by Jasper. "Mac, Prue … you in?"

We both look toward him confused, considering we didn't hear anything he said before.

"Truth or dare?"

I nod, and Macallister rolls his eyes but also nods reluctantly.

Jasper rubs his hands together maniacally. "Perfect. Prue … truth or dare?"

I gawk at him, contemplating my options as he stares back at me waiting. "Truth," I say, thinking for sure they're about to ask me about Macallister.

"What's been the worst part about being on tour with us?" I stop nervously twiddling my thumbs because that is not what I was expecting at all.

"Oh, uh …" I look at everyone sitting around the table, about to say *nothing*. His question pulls my attention back to the snowball of anxiety growing bigger with each email Felicia sends me causing constant chills up my back. *I'm not doing what I'm supposed to be doing*, I almost say.

"When you all got food poisoning," I say instead.

Everyone laughs and waits for me to ask. "Darrell, truth or dare?"

He tilts his head, and I can tell he's surprised I'm calling him out. "Truth."

"Did something happen between you and that security guard from Red Rocks?" I saw a security guard wink at him after the show in Colorado, and even though it was dark, I could see the blush spreading across Darrell's face when he did.

"I … uh …" I almost feel bad for putting him on the spot. Any other time we've played, it's all in good fun. Right when I think I might have crossed a line, he starts laughing. "Kinda …" he says bashfully.

The bus goes silent for a moment before we all start laughing. Not in a teasing way, but in a well-intentioned way that causes him to join in with us.

He turns to Travis, and I know what's happening before I can stop it. "Travis, truth or dare?"

Travis lifts his head slowly, making eye contact with him from across the table. "I know what you want. Truth."

"What hap—"

Before Darrell can finish asking, Travis cuts him off. "I don't know. Friday night was amazing. I woke up in her bed, and we spent more time together, I gave her a ticket for Saturday night's show because she didn't have another press pass. I didn't see or hear from her again. She just … didn't show up." My ears catch the slight break in his voice.

"And you didn't get her number," Macallister confirms.

Travis nods. "Don't start, I already know."

I'd asked Travis yesterday if he was okay and if he wanted to talk. He's been forlorn since we left Colorado on Saturday night. I started to worry when he told me he didn't. I'm shocked he just shared what he did.

We all look solemnly at him, but Cliff's voice breaks through the silence. "Don't give up."

That's all he says. Travis and him make eye contact briefly, Travis nods, then he turns to the rest of us. "I don't think I want to play anymore," and walks to the back of the bus.

"Why did you tell him that?" Jasper is searing at Cliff after the curtain closes and Travis disappears completely.

Cliff turns to him. "You know why I told him that."

I think everyone, including me, is considerably confused now.

"Travis is a grown man, Cliff."

"So was I."

"Who's going next?" Darrell asks, no doubt to break the tension. He's nervously drumming his fingers on the table. I squint, watching him, wondering if he is actually confused, or if he knows something.

Macallister shifts slightly out of the corner of my eye. I turn to see his furrowed brow and clenched jaw as if he's holding it together as tightly as he can. He clearly knows something. Maybe *I'm* the only confused one, now, and I hate the feeling of being on the outside.

My instincts kick in, and before I know it, I hear myself ask, "Care to share with the rest of us?"

Cliff frowns, his gaze shifting from me over to Macallister and Darrell in a confused, but slightly accusatory expression. "Nothing to share."

I can almost hear the echo of Felicia's voice in my head telling me to *keep trying, work your magic!* But it instantly gives me the ick.

I'm trying to read the situation, and my gut is telling me this is something I should continue to pry open like an oyster sealed tightly protecting its pearl. But my gut is also telling me that if I harvest this pearl of information, I could end up really hurting someone.

My phone buzzes in my pocket, and I pull it out. Holding the screen up while Macallister watches, I read the text message from Felicia. Her ears must have been burning.

> You haven't sent a recording in a while.

I want to throw up, and my body is tormented by jitters at the thought of losing my job. I've been living in this bubble for so long, I keep forgetting I even have a job.

On instinct, or maybe out of fear, I blurt out, "We haven't interviewed in a while. Maybe now is a good time." I regret the words and the way I said them as they came out of my mouth. Macallister scoots slightly away from me.

"Maybe," Cliff challenges me, and the piercing glare on Macallister's face directed at Cliff stings.

"Maybe not right now," Macallister tries as I start pulling up the recording app on my phone.

He turns to me, and we engage in a silent conversation. *Tell me what I am to you.* He looks a little hurt, but I almost resent the expression. I've always only been on this bus for a job. I think I forgot. I think he did, too. My loyalties are torn, and I miss the contact of having his body even an inch closer than he is now. I'm holding my phone, my thumb hovering over the record button and my hands tremble.

"Hit record, Prudence." I turn my head. Cliff stares ahead with a neutral expression on his face. I can't say the same for anyone else's face.

I press the button. "Tell me more about why you're so invested in this topic."

"What topic?" Cliff asks, feigning innocence and tilting his head slightly with his lips set in a straight, firm line. He knows I'm hesitant to bring Travis's personal situation into this.

"You speak as if something happened to you. Was that something a catalyst for Gnasher's break up?"

"Why are you doing this?" Macallister whispers from beside me.

I turn so our eyes meet. *What are they hiding?* The tug pulls me to react defensively. "It's my job."

I turn back to Cliff, but he's staring at Macallister, studying his face as if he's searching for something. "Mac," it sounds like a warning.

"Cliff, stop. Prudence, this should be a scheduled thing," Macallister says, keeping his eyes pinned anywhere but on me. His tone has shifted into the Macallister I knew before: before he kissed me, before he touched me, before he wiggled his way into my heart.

"Why did Gnasher break up?" I ask, more forcefully.

"Because Cliff called it quits," Jasper says, matter of factly.

"Let me rephrase. Why did you call it quits, Cliff?" This is beginning to spiral out of control.

"Is that why you're on this bus?" Cliff asks me.

"Oh, boy," Darrell drops his head into his hands and Jasper's face morphs into confusion.

"This is enough," Macallister's voice booms.

"I called it quits because I was depressed and tired," Cliff charges forward, his voice picking up in speed and volume.

"And did you get back together because you feel like that's something you've been able to resolve?" I'm so in reporter mode, I barely recognize myself anymore. Or at least the person I've been over the last couple of months. Even my voice sounds different to my ears, like when you hear your friend at their job using their customer service voice. This isn't me.

"No," Cliff grits out. "It'll never be resolved, and I don't want him to make the same mistake I did." Him, meaning Travis, but I don't push for him to clarify. This should be more than enough to satisfy Felicia. I feel so dirty.

My energy is drained from this mysterious but concise exchange, and I fall back into myself when I comprehend the torn expression on Cliff's face. I don't want to hurt him. I don't want to hurt any of them. I decide right then as I press the stop button to turn off the recording, I am going to have to be strategic with this more than I ever have before. I am realizing now the people at this table all have something they don't want me to know. The reporter in me wants to find out. But the me that's felt found and safe wants to help protect what should belong to them. The same way I should have with Torrence.

I stand and go to walk to my bed. I need sleep.

I turn my head over my shoulder toward Cliff and Macallister before I disappear behind the curtain. "Sorry," I mutter as I quickly make way toward my bed before they can respond.

My thoughts start swirling around my head like loose pieces of paper I can't catch to tuck neatly away into a filing cabinet of sanity. I curl into a ball and press my fists up under my chin. I take a few deep breaths as I will myself to fall asleep. The last thing I remember hearing is the sound of Macallister climbing into his bed above me.

CHAPTER 32

Macallister

I didn't climb into bed with her last night because I didn't know if she'd want me to. If I'm being completely honest with myself right now, I don't think I wanted to. I didn't know how to process the outburst that occurred. She hasn't conducted an interview, let alone such a persistent interview, in a while. The way she whispered "sorry" before retreating to her bed broke me because I know she meant it. I've watched her feel torn by this job without realizing it until now.

Of course, I didn't forget why she was here. She's never said it out loud to me, but I knew she was on this bus to get to the bottom of why Gnasher broke up. Knowing the contents of that damn letter and hearing the way Cliff and Jasper speak to each other sometimes, I'm beginning to put the pieces together. I don't know exactly what happened when Cliff called it quits back in '96 but I think I'm on the right track, especially after the emotionally raw conversation we had in Colorado. He confirmed to me his reasoning was about a woman, and that truth makes telling him what I know even more important. I need confirmation. Especially before I bring the information in the letter to Cliff.

I had already decided to do more research. To get more information. But with the excitement of the Red Rocks show, that plan got put on the back burner. Well, it can't anymore.

The bus finally arrived in Austin. We arrived early in the morning and had all day to kill before the show. When we have time like this, we've usually done some sightseeing or meandered around the city.

I assume that's what everyone else will do today, even with the tension from last night. I have a specific mission, though, and I want to be alone while I do this. I make sure the letter is tucked safely into my bag, along with my laptop. I can hear footsteps and low murmurs at the front of the bus. When I charge out, Cliff, Jasper, Darrell, and Travis sit together at the table. I don't see Prudence. She probably already took off to do something with Roslyn.

"Got errands," I say over my shoulder with a hand up as I walk briskly down the steps and out the door before anyone, especially Cliff, can stop me or ask what I'm doing.

I walk to a cafe down the road and order a black coffee. I find a table tucked into the corner where I can hopefully have some privacy, and I sit. After taking a sip, willing it to help me through this task, I pull out the letter and open my laptop.

I start typing things in as I reread the words on the page. The name and return address from the sender lead me to a variety of things. I found out the last name on the envelope is a maiden name. So, she's been married since sending it. Shouldn't shock me since she sent this letter almost thirty years ago. After some quick web searches, I find her married name and it sends chills up my spine. I take a deep breath and a sip of coffee. It burns my throat as I swallow the liquid past the lump in my throat. That's a common last name, right?

I continue searching, which leads me to an obituary for a man who passed away years ago from cancer. I shake my head, hoping it'll knock out the intrusive thoughts continuing to creep inside my brain. My memories teleport me back to laying in bed with

Prudence, playing our own game of truth or dare. I open the obituary and read through it.

The last line sinks like a stone in my belly, and I want to throw up: His memory lives on through his wife, Sylvie, and his daughter, Prudence.

Fuck. *Fuck*.

I knew something felt off as soon as I saw the last name, Taylor because it's her last name. Taylor may be a common last name, but something tells me the combination of Prudence and Taylor isn't that common. She's never told me her parents' names, but I'm pretty sure I know them now. I read the last sentence multiple times, wondering if I missed something about a sibling. Prudence never mentioned a brother or sister, but I keep hoping maybe that was an oversight. But I know it isn't. Because I know when Gnasher broke up, and I know how old Prudence is. It's never seemed relevant until now as all the pieces fall into place so rapidly, I can barely catch my breath.

I can't look at this anymore, so I slam my laptop shut more forcefully than necessary. Pinching the bridge of my nose, I close my eyes and all I envision behind my eyelids is her. The conversation that happened the night before is washed away. I desperately want to get back to her, but I also don't know how to face her right now. While I am almost positive I've found something completely life-altering, I also can't deny that reading her dad's obituary without her is intrusive.

I need to talk to Cliff, but I don't know how to.

I don't even know the first thing I'm going to say to him.

"So, you should read this," I say, sliding the letter toward him, realizing I didn't land on the smoothest intro.

Cliff raises an eyebrow at me as he pulls the letter out of the envelope. I think he thinks whatever is happening is somewhat comical because he even gives me a small smile and chuckles as he lowers his eyes to the paper. After he reads the first few words, though, his smile drops. I can tell he's rereading it for the third or fourth time when he eventually looks back up, his eyes frantic and filled with sorrow and panic at the same time.

I reach out and wrap my hand around his wrist to try and ground him. "Cliff, you need to take a deep breath." His face has started turning pale from his lack of oxygen.

He nods, taking a few deep breaths in his nose and out his mouth. "Mac, what is this?" He holds up the piece of paper clutched tightly in his grip.

I know he means why I have it and where I got it. "It was in your box of fan mail I went through."

"When?" he bristles, and I know he's realizing I've known a little longer than he'd prefer.

"Before the tour," I put a hand up, stopping him from interrupting me. "Cliff, I was doing my job. I wasn't going to keep this from you forever, but I needed to make sure this was even true. My job was to help keep your reputation clean on tour. That's what you said, and that's what I did. That's what I tried to do at least." I say my last words more to myself than to him.

I watch him take in each of my words, allowing them to massage out some of the tension in his face. He nods and grunts what I am going to read as a confirmation I can continue. Which is great, but also horrible. Because if he thinks what I just told him is the biggest bombshell, he's about to have an even harder time filling his lungs.

"Cliff, it's a girl. The baby … Sylvie had a girl. And named her … Prudence."

He blinks at me, not registering what I've said for a few seconds. He studies his hands resting on the letter on the table in front of him. He locks in for a second, two seconds, three seconds before raising his head to mine. When he does, his eyes go wider than I've ever seen and his throat bobs like he's choking on the air in front of him.

I frown at him, but immediately feel the presence coming up behind me. I know before she speaks that Prudence is behind me.

"Why are you talking about my mom?" Her voice is so thick with suspicion that bile burns its way up my throat.

I rise from the booth and turn to reach for her but she steps backward, pulling herself out of my reach. She squints her eyes at me and turns her head slightly.

"Macallister," she warns. "Tell me," she says this in a whisper, just for me. For the me she's felt hold her. The me she's falling for, I can feel it. The me that wants all of this to be a dream, in which I wake up. *Right now. Please?*

"Baby," she holds up a finger cutting me off, and I know what she's demanding. "Prudence," I correct, hating the loss of the name that makes her mine from my lips.

Cliff stands and pushes me aside. "Mac, I think … I think I need to do this."

I look at him, fully understanding the words from his mouth, but despising that they are true. This has nothing to do with me. I have no part in this whatsoever. I lower my gaze and nod. I turn to walk off the bus when she grabs my arm. Her blue eyes shine with misery and it squeezes my heart.

She tightens her fingers around me. "No, please," her words break off and her voice takes on a shake. "Stay with me. I'm so scared." What I detect in her eyes is understanding, but immobilizing fear from what it is she understands.

I turn my body so I'm next to her and I start pushing her gently to guide her to sit. She obeys and Cliff follows suit by sitting across from her. He slides the paper to her wordlessly. She picks it up, her eyes growing with recognition as she glides her eyes back and forth to pick up the words. She reaches the bottom but doesn't lower the piece of paper.

Cliff knocks his knuckle twice on the table and clears his throat.

She keeps the letter held above her face. "I don't think I fully understand."

"Is your mother named Sylvie?" He cuts right to it.

"Yes," she says, the letter still held up.

"Does that look like her handwriting?"

"It does," she says, hand holding steady but voice shaking.

"Then, it would appear that ..."

She lowers the letter, along with her eyes. She takes one big breath before raising her eyes to meet his for the first time. I'm so proud of her. I am so in awe, watching her face this. She's so strong.

She turns to me, and says, "Actually, I think you should leave."

CHAPTER 33

Prudence

Macallister's eyes grow wide at my request. If I'm being completely honest, I'm having a hard time going back and forth on whether or not I want him here. I'm terrified right now, and he's my biggest comfort. At the same time, I think he kept this from me which makes me angry and feel betrayed by him. It makes me question whether I know him the way I thought I might, and this situation deserves to be more private.

He nods, then stands and leaves. I keep my head turned toward him as his footsteps hit each stair and the bus door opens and shuts again.

I turn to Cliff whose eyes are glued to me in concerned confusion. "You're my father," I say.

He nods once. "I think that's what this is implying." He gestures toward the letter.

"How?" I ask on a breath, knowing how. Somehow, I know it's the truth as I scan his face and notice the things I have always acknowledged in myself, but have never been able to recognize in my mother, specifically, my overpowering love of music.

His eyes scan mine as I watch them grow heavy with moisture and emotion. "Prudence, I'm not sure how to divulge all this to you, especially if you are in fact, my daughter. Which, I cannot lie,

I don't have many doubts about. Your mother was an honest woman."

I am taken aback by his obvious compliment toward my mom, a woman he hasn't seen in almost thirty years and is claiming she had his child. I'm flattered on my mom's behalf, but I'm also so confused.

"What do you mean?" I ask.

He takes a big breath in, holds it for a few counts, then lets it go. "I met Sylvie right after the Grammys in '96. I was at a bar alone instead of the parties with Jazz and Constantine, and she was there." I reflexively scrunch my face, trying to picture my mom in a bar. He laughs, as if reading my thoughts. "She was out of place, for sure. Friend's birthday, or something like that. Anyway, she didn't even recognize me at first."

I chuckle. "That sounds like Mom."

"She told me she thought she might have heard one of my songs on the radio at one point." He chuckles and shakes his head. "Honestly, though, it was so refreshing to meet someone who didn't care who I was. I know that's such a cliché rockstar line, but it's a cliché for a reason."

"That makes sense," I say as I twist my fingers together out of anxiety. No, not anxiety. Fear? I'm not sure if that's the right way to describe it, either. What is someone supposed to feel when the largest bombshell has been dropped onto their lives?

"She was beautiful. And funny and smart. We talked for a while, about so many different things, I couldn't even remember any of it if I tried. But I can still remember the way I felt during our conversation." His lips tip up in a smile as he glances off to the side, replaying the memory of when he met my mom. "We ended up back at her place at some point, fell into bed, and I didn't leave her bed for three days."

I must have a shocked expression on my face, because he laughs harder now and shakes his head before saying, "Sorry. I'm sorry. She was wonderful. I had never connected with someone so strongly. I still haven't. She made me realize a lot of things about myself. Some good, some bad. But all things I needed to be aware of. And that changed the entire trajectory of my life. Which I guess means you," he gestures his hands out to me. "You changed the entire trajectory of my life." His voice cracks on the last sentiment. He huffs a laugh as he looks at the table, shaking his head in disbelief and understanding at the same time.

I hate it, but there's something I can't help but ask him. "Why … why didn't you …" I don't even know how to ask it. How do you ask a man why he abandoned you? A sob makes its way up my throat, and I want to stop it, so I hold it there. I hold it in and it gags me.

His eyebrows scrunch together in concern and he leans toward me. "I didn't know, Prudence. I didn't know about you until today. At least, I didn't know you in the way I do now. The way that attaches you to me."

I look into the blue eyes that I can now see match mine. That explains where I got the blue from since no one on my mom's side of the family has blue eyes, and I never knew this other side. I stare at him and know he's telling me the truth. That almost devastates me even more. He's nothing like my dad, the dad who raised me. They have nothing in common, in build, personality, or mannerisms … but something about him is as familiar and the revelation crashes into me. It rains down sadness and grief, along with belonging and closure. I hate the way it scoops into my guts and swirls around like a serrated spoon.

"I had a good childhood," I don't know why, but I need to reassure him.

He sniffles a little and scratches his eye. "I'm glad." He turns his head and makes eye contact with me. "I still wish I had been there for it, though. And I'm sorry I wasn't."

I nod, my mouth scratchy and my throat too tight to form words.

"Is there anything you want to ask me?" His question comes out unsure, like he doesn't know what to say anymore and that's the first thing he could think of. Fortunately, I do.

I clear my throat. "Is she the reason why?" He tilts his head in confusion, so I clarify. "The reason why you left Gnasher."

He holds my gaze, then drops his eyes to the table again and nods. "Yes and no," he says, still nodding his head. "But the short answer is yes."

"What's the long answer?" I can't help myself, and even though I'm not asking this as a reporter, I can't help the habits emerging.

He holds nothing back, knowing there's no recording capturing his words. "Not being recognized felt so refreshing, I decided to continue talking to her. Not being treated like a celebrity made me stay. The way she spoke, the way she opened up to me … it was so genuine. She'd have said this to anyone. But not actually anyone. She'd say it to who she felt safe with. And that was me. Not Clifford Lee, lead singer of Gnasher and Grammy winner … just me."

His eyes lift to mine, and I nod in understanding. "I was depressed. I'm still depressed, but less so. When we kept hitting the charts, and our songs were played on the radio, and we won awards, it stopped being about the music. It was notoriety and celebrity, which felt amazing, but only for about fifteen minutes. I started feeling horrible and lonely. I didn't feel lonely when I talked to Sylvie."

"What happened?" I ask, feeling a little dirty for pulling this from him like a thread on a spool, but also not having the self-restraint not to because I truly want to know the answer so badly, and now I know he's my father, I feel like I deserve to know.

He sighed. "It was never meant to be anything permanent. There was an unspoken agreement that at some point, I'd have to leave. We were in the middle of a tour and award season, and I had commitments to fulfill. We parted ways, and that was it. I headed back out. It was miserable. *I* was miserable. I thought for a minute my time with her was restorative. I'd return ready to continue with my spark again like you do returning to work after a relaxing vacation." I kind of hate how he's referring to my mom as a vacation, but his mouth parts like he's going to continue without a verbal push from me this time, so I keep my mouth shut and compose my face in a neutral expression.

He taps his pointer finger on the table loudly in a quick rhythm for four beats. "But she wasn't a vacation. She was everything, and then that was that." He shakes his head. "I've never lost the memory of those nights we spent together, and I never will. She never left my mind. And when I walked up to Jazz that day in the studio and told him I was done, all I could see in my mind was her smile. I could barely hear Jazz's response as I walked out the door because all I could hear in my mind was her telling me she was proud of me."

"She's better …" I whisper to myself, remembering the song he played for us all those weeks ago and putting pieces together.

He nods once. "When I left … I wasn't in the best headspace. Jazz tried to get me to stay because we had something good going, according to him. My last words to him before I left were, 'She's better.' That stung, and saying that to him is another regret I have."

"You never tried to find her? If you felt so strongly, why wouldn't you look for her? Especially after breaking up the band because she was better." I'm torn, listening to this man speak about her in a way that pulls my insides apart a little bit. He harbors intensely strong feelings about my mom, but he never went to find her? He feels the way about her that I feel about Macallister, but when I'd rip the world apart for him, he did nothing? I shudder from my own passion and impulsive thoughts scaring me shitless.

His eyes are searching mine, back and forth, as they fill with moisture pushing the boundary of his eyelids so much I'm genuinely intrigued by what the capacity is before it spills down his cheek, a physical representation of what he didn't do. "I didn't think she'd want that. I certainly didn't think she deserved it, either. I thought so highly of your mom and I thought she deserved way better than anything I could provide her. I was going to, but then I realized she'd be better off without me. Fame and complete loss of privacy? She didn't need that. She was the sun, and I knew Hollywood would extinguish that as fast as it could. That was why I loved her. Going to find her felt selfish." He's taken aback by the use of that word in light of recent information. His eyes widen slightly and his head jerks back a tiny bit.

"I wish you'd been a little selfish," I say, astounded at the immense amount of selflessness that's so grand, it's not such a positive thing anymore.

He nods a little, his eyes back on the table. "I wish that, too, now." He takes in a deep breath and lets it out slowly. "Did he take care of her?"

I scrunch my face in momentary confusion before I snap straighter. "My dad?"

He winces slightly but nods. "Yeah. Did he make her happy? Did he take care of her? Of you?"

I shiver. "Yeah, he did. He was a wonderful man. We miss him a lot. He's been gone for a while, now."

"She never got remarried?" he asks, his tone lifting slightly.

I shake my head. "No. She's never even dated since him."

I sense the buzz of thoughts going on in his head, but pull myself back into the realization that this is my mom he's thinking about. I push myself up and take a deep breath in as I do. When I'm standing, my hands on the table, my back slightly crouched, I just stare at him.

He looks fearful of what I'm going to say. "Thank you for being honest with me."

I hold his gaze for a moment longer, then push up to fully standing and turn to walk off the bus, needing some fresh air.

"Prudence," he calls right as I'm about to descend the stairs.

I turn to him. "Yeah?"

"We listened to 'Dear Prudence' by The Beatles probably a hundred times together over those few days. We loved it. Sometimes, I'd play it for her on my guitar, and she'd sing along with me. I told her it was my favorite song. It still is my favorite song."

I look at him for a moment, my eyes burning from the threat of tears. I'm going to ask him if that's why he refused to call me Prue when I suggested the nickname, but I can't. I know, anyway. I shake my head and chuckle out the emotions in my body. I descend the staircase and I can hear Cliff pick up his guitar and play the first few chords of the song I am now certain I'm named after.

CHAPTER 34
Macallister

I'm pacing in front of the bus door when it opens and she pushes her way through. A heavy breath leaves me and dissipates into the thick air between us. She makes eye contact with me before stepping off the last stair. Instinctively, I hold out my hands, hoping she'll reach back out and let me catch her.

She does, and another breath of relief leaves me. I step a little forward as she steps down, and I pull her into me. Her eyebrows curl together in worry. I want to press my thumb down the center of her forehead to release the tension. I hate the emotions wrinkling her face, because they make the hurt inside her visible, and I can't stand it.

She breaks eye contact and a small sob comes from up her throat. "I think I have to go home."

She doesn't raise her eyes to me, even when I brush my finger under her chin to pull her face back up to mine. Her lip quivers as she keeps her gaze cast down.

Please don't leave me. "What do you need right now?" I'd do anything.

She raises her blue eyes. She stops right before reaching perfect eye contact. "I need to go home. I need to talk to my mom, and I don't want to do this over the phone."

My heart shatters at her words and the truth in them. She shouldn't have to. "I'll get you a ticket."

"No, I can get one, it's—"

"Please? I want to." I hope she hears the sincerity in my voice.

Her eyes flick up to mine. They're stunning. "Did you know?"

The harshness in her tone makes me snap to attention after partially melting from her gorgeous stare. "I—" I'm not sure where to start with this story, but she deserves to know.

Her eyes scan back and forth between mine. Gliding across the bridge of my nose and making it harder to find the stillness in the blue.

"I knew Cliff had a child he most likely did not know about. I also had a hunch the love affair was partially, if not completely, the reason he left the band."

She searches my eyes with her own. "And about me?"

I take a deep breath. "That I found out this morning. Right after I found out, I ran to tell Cliff."

She takes a step back from me and my heart tries to lurch toward hers. "Would you have told me?"

I'm not sure what the correct answer here is; because on one hand, if I told her first that would have been me staying honest with her, but also betraying Cliff in a way. If I told Cliff first, I wouldn't be putting her first, and that devastates me because I'm realizing now, looking at her, she means more to me than I can put into words.

I nod once, then turn my head to the side in a half shake, before pulling my head back up to face her straight on. "Cliff is my client." She winces at my words, my heart stops for a beat before picking up irregular rhythms. "But you … you are, what I believe might be the love of my life." Her eyes widen, and her mouth begins to form the most beautiful pink circle.

I continue, needing to be honest with her before she walks away. "I'm pretty sure I've loved you since Vegas, Prudence. And I can tell you for certain, I am a completely different man than I was before that night. I view things with more compassion, more wonder. You've continued to open me up in a way I wouldn't know how to sew back up." I have my hands splayed out to my sides and I shake my head, completely surrendering to her.

"So if you want me to be honest, the answer is no. I wouldn't have told you. Because of the respect I hold for Cliff and his right to speak with his child first. But also because of the respect and adoration I have for you, and the fact that you deserve to hear that from your own father. That doesn't involve me. But your happiness, your well-being, that involves me. I want to be involved in maintaining it forever."

She sucks in a breath and puts a hand up as she takes a step back. "But what am I?" She says it so softly, I barely catch her words. I'm not sure what she means, and I reach out to her.

She puts her hand up and takes another step away from me.

I went too far. *Shit.* I lost track of my words, and I am searching for a way to shovel them back into my mouth because I've probably fucked this up. I'm a complete idiot, and I am so vulnerable standing right here confessing my feelings to someone I'm not sure is going to reciprocate those feelings. I take my own step back and shake my head. *Shit, shit, shit.* Now, I am the one who needs to get out of here.

"Prudence, I'm so sorry," I say quietly. I continue taking steps backward, now growing faster in pace wishing I could just disappear instead. "I am so sorry. Please, go home. Disregard … just disregard what I've said. I didn't mean to—" I turn and walk briskly away from her.

She stays silent behind me and it pulls at my insides. It feels like betrayal, not turning toward her. It's taking all my strength to hold me back. But I do it. I continue to walk further away.

A single tear spills out as I do, and I wipe it away quickly, the wet path it created so foreign, it makes me sick to my stomach.

I can't believe I let myself fall and land here.

CHAPTER 35

Prudence

It's been exactly twenty-four hours since I watched him walk away from me as fast as he possibly could. His steps never faltered, and his body never wavered. For a minute, even after he disappeared from view, I stood there willing him to turn back around. Hoping I could manifest the vision of his frame, walking back into view.

He never did. And I'd never felt so alone.

I replay, not only the memory but the emotions, on a loop while I sit in the crowded terminal of the airport. Mechanical and rehearsed voices come over the speaker with updates periodically, but they're never strong enough to interrupt the reel playing in my head, causing my body to fluctuate all ranges of temperature and tenseness at the same time. I keep crossing and uncrossing my ankle over my knee in an attempt to rattle the shakiness out of my limbs but with no such luck.

He said he loved me, but did he mean he wants me? No one has ever told me they loved me, and I wonder why that still wasn't enough for me. What more do I want? I know what I want, and it's for him to say I'm his, for him to fully commit to me. I buy an overpriced bottle of Advil when the pounding in my head is too much to bear.

When I lay my head back, resting uncomfortably on the edge of my metal chair, a robotic and under-caffeinated female voice says over the loudspeaker that my flight is boarding. So I lift my head and I stand up, steadying myself for a moment when I am fully erect. I drag my feet toward the line of people forming.

I zombie-walk onto the plane, find my seat, and fall into the dark blue and slightly scratchy abyss. Once I click my seatbelt together, I lay my head to the side and doze off. I keep myself conscious enough to prevent drool, so I get just enough sleep to feel even less awake, to the point my eyes are almost glued shut and I'm fighting to keep them open.

When I find myself on my mother's doorstep hours later, I pause. I don't need to ring the doorbell. This is my home. I don't live here anymore, but it's always been my home. I'm struck with how not waiting and barging in makes me pause. I feel like I don't know her anymore because of one piece of information I've found out. But she's still my mom. I remind myself she's still the mom I've always known, but with some extra information now.

I stand there long enough that eventually, I raise my hand to pound my knuckles into it, causing a knock I hope radiates enough because I'm not sure I have the strength for one more. I stand for a moment, making a half-turn to possibly escape, and continue licking my wounds until I can muster up the courage to face her; but I hear the click of the knob and before I know it, my mom is standing in her doorway wearing her robe, gawking at me like she has no idea why I'd be here, standing on her doorstep, ringing her doorbell at eight p.m.

"Hi, Mom," I breathe.

"Honey?" She tilts her head at me slightly and gives a cautious smile. "What's going on?"

"Can I …" I point toward the slightly open door, asking for the invitation to go inside.

She pushes her hip on the door, making the crack wider, and moving to the side so I can walk in. Her eyes follow me as I cross in front of her. She closes the door and follows me into her sitting room where she has two wing-back chairs, back toward a large window at the front of her house.

We both lower into seated positions, both poised delicately at the edge, the threat of an uncomfortable conversation ahead. At least I know exactly what it's about, because her eyebrows are pinched tight like she's terrified of the billion possibilities that could come out of my mouth.

"Mom, do you know Clifford Lee?" My voice sounds like someone else, even to myself.

Her eyes widen. "I … yes, I mean, I did—" her eyes glance around, searching the ground for salvation she won't find. She's trying to avoid this.

"Mom, is Clifford Lee my father?" My tone wavers slightly at the last word, but she hears me loud and clear.

Her eyes raise to find mine and we lock into a staring contest for at least five seconds before she clears her throat slightly and leans forward toward me. "He is." She nods once with her raspy words.

I put my forehead into my hands, wondering how I could experience this twice. Wouldn't the first time negate that? This isn't news, but it's also the first time I've heard it. Life-changing news is like that, I guess.

I raise my head, snapping my neck and finding her eye contact again. "Mom, why wouldn't you tell me?"

She stares at me in consideration, her head tilting, but her gaze staying right on me. "Sweetheart, how could I?" she breathes.

I know she's right, but she continues. "I wrote to him, and I never heard back, so I—" She shakes her head. "It's not like I could turn on the TV, point him out and tell you 'That's your daddy, but he doesn't want us.' He never responded, and I knew he was in a delicate state. Then I heard about the break-up, and I assumed it was all too much for him."

The realization brings a sob up my throat and she moves into my chair, pulling me to her. She holds me, stroking my hair, pressing her kiss to the side of my head, and wrapping her hold around me.

"Mom, that's where I was." The hand running through my hair stops and her chin dips slightly. "I was on tour with Gnasher. With Clifford Lee," I say.

She places a hand on her chest in a held breath. I sit up out of her arms and grab her shoulders. She raises her head, tears in her eyes. "Why didn't you tell me?"

"Mom, I didn't think it would mean anything to you. We never talk about music. We never talk about my job much at all."

Her eyes search mine, dropping tears down her cheeks as she does so. "Oh, Prudence. I'm so sorry." She looks down and shakes her head. "I'm so sorry. What could I have done differently?"

My heart breaks watching this, especially after watching Cliff's reaction, and the conversation with Macallister. I feel so low, and I'm not sure I could go much lower.

"Mom," I whisper. "There's nothing you could have done differently. You're right. Cliff never got your letter, by the way. Or, at least he didn't read it until yesterday." I can't believe that was only yesterday. It feels like a million years ago.

She uses her hands to wipe away her tears and shake away the emotion clogging her insides. "He didn't?" she shakes her head, on the verge of saying more, but is unable to.

She lets out a built-up, nervous laugh, and pulls her face to her concerned mom-look again. "Can I ask how he is?"

Her question catches me off guard, and I rear back slightly, raising an eyebrow. "Uhm …"

She giggles. "Prudence, how is he? How is Cliff?" Her tone is playful, and even though she still has tears tracking her cheeks, she's smiling now.

I chuckle and shake my head. "You are not Parent Trapping me."

She laughs, and I pull her back into a hug we both need, letting the thick emotions rest in the air around us.

Afterward, we continue to talk about everything, and the night is filled with tears and apologies, forgiveness and love. I tell her all about the tour and end up telling her about Macallister. When I do, my tears start again.

After recounting my time on tour to her, leaving out the parts I can't bring myself to say out loud to my mom, she sits in contemplative silence. "Do you love him, too?"

I sigh. "Yes. But I'm also hurt and confused. Why would he say all that, then walk away?"

She tilts her head to the side. "Honey, did you say anything back?"

I search the memory from his perspective, wondering if I said or did something. "I tried to, I was a little speechless. He also never said what I was to him."

"Honey, he said he loved you."

I stare back at her. "Yeah, but—"

"I've watched you be treated badly by men who didn't want to commit to you. I understand. Him confessing his love, though, probably means he's committed to you."

I feel kind of stupid because she's right. "He walked away, though."

"I don't think he necessarily *wanted* to walk away."

I squint, trying to discern her meaning. "But he did—"

"Probably because he thought what he said was too much for you. I don't think someone could bare his soul, and then walk away because he changed his mind. I think he walked away *for* you, not *from* you."

Her words bring up memories of Cliff's song, *She's Better*, again. The lyrics depict heartbreak, and the loneliness that followed as a result. I understand why when Jasper heard the title, he was defensive, but after he listened to the lyrics, he softened.

I roll that around in my head, scrunching my brows together as if it will help me understand my own situation better. I'm not sure I do. Not fully, anyway. "Maybe," I say quietly, now feeling unable to continue this conversation.

She places a hand on my arm. "Honey, if there's any advice I can give you in this specific situation, it's to not give up so quickly."

I tilt my head in question and she's smiling, but it's filled with sadness and regret. I understand what she's saying now, and the revelation is gut-wrenching.

***

My body is exhausted, but when I try to fall asleep, my head feels too busy. I can't stop thinking about everything: Cliff and my mom, Macallister's confession and how I somehow misinterpreted it possibly, and also, a story I have no idea how to write now, let alone continue.

I toss and turn a couple of times before giving up. Sitting up in my childhood bed, I reach for my phone and text Jessica. I haven't told her anything, which feels like a betrayal to our friendship in some way. Maybe talking to her will help my mind settle. I start typing out a text when I give up and press the button to call her instead, wanting to hear her voice.

She answers on the second ring. "Hey, babes."

Hearing her on the other side soothes me and I realize not only do I not want to have this conversation over text, but the phone isn't enough either. "Can you come over?" Jessica moved back in with her parents for the time being to help them, which means she's less than five minutes from my mom's house.

"Uhh. Aren't you in Colorado? Or Texas, or something?"

I sigh. "It's a long story, but no. I'm at my mom's."

I barely finish my sentence before she says, "Be right over" and hangs up.

Less than twenty minutes later, we're sitting on my bedroom floor with a bag of Doritos and two cans of Coke between us.

She takes a long pull from her drink and pops a chip with a loud crunch. "Alright, spill."

I tell her everything. Spilling the dirty details from the last couple of weeks, watching her eyes widen and hearing her small gasps with each revelation. Her mouth falls completely open when I go into detail about Cliff and that he's my father.

"Prue," she breathes. "You know I'm no good with words. All I can say is holy shit."

"Yeah," I chuckle. "Trust me, I *am* usually good with words, and that's about all I have to say about it."

"When are you going back?"

I take a quick sip of the soda I've neglected due to the constant talking I've done over the last half hour. "What do you mean?"

She shovels a stack of chips into her mouth. While Jessica isn't necessarily what I'd call polite, she doesn't talk with her mouth full of food. Instead, she gives me a look that says enough with her eyes narrowed and brows pinched together.

I expel a breath I'd been holding and toss my hands. "Go back to what, exactly? I don't even know if I want to continue this story. I know I've blown up someone's life before, but I'm certainly not interested in doing it to anyone else, let alone myself."

She's still chewing, so she tilts her head to the side and her eyelids lower slightly with the expression of calling bull shit.

"Jessica, what the fuck am I supposed to write? Clifford Lee broke up the band in 1996 due to his obsession with a woman named Sylvie, who surprisingly, had his love child he never knew about until now." I'm speaking in a 1940s reporter voice, which makes her smile a little but doesn't completely wipe off the knowing expression from her face.

She claps her hands together, brushing off the crumbs. "Prue, that's not what I mean. Fuck Felicia, and fuck *SubVox*. You hate that job, and you know it. I know you've hated your job since the Torrence drama. But you have to go back. Cliff's your dad. And what about Macallister? You love him."

I never said that to her, but I decide trying to fight her on what I know is true isn't worth it. "Yeah, but—"

"But nothing," she cuts me off. "Okay, Prudence, time for some tough love."

I shake my head and a small smile creeps onto my face. "But I don't want tough love," I say in a smaller voice, half kidding, but half serious. My heart already hurts right now.

"No, too bad," she shakes her head. "What kind of friend would I be if I didn't hold you accountable?"

She doesn't wait for my answer. "I know why you're scared, and it's valid, but it's also shit, and I'm not going to let it hold you back from something I know could actually be good for you. Macallister didn't just tell you he loves you, but he *showed* you he loves you."

I scrunch my face at her, silently goading her to continue to explain her point. "Prue, Jake was a dick and we can all agree on that. He was a dick for more reasons than just the fact that he never called you his girlfriend, though." She's not wrong.

"I could sit here and go through the list of guys that have fucked you up equally as bad, or even worse, but we'd be here all night." *Ouch*. "So I'm not going to. But what I will do is sit on the floor of your childhood bedroom with you for as long as it takes to get you to admit to yourself you're scared, but that isn't worth giving up on something like what Macallister is offering."

"And what is he offering?" I pipe up, but wince knowing she'll be quick with a comeback I most likely won't be able to deny.

She smiles. "He's offering himself, Prue. If what you told me is exactly how things went down, and I suspect it is knowing you have the memory of an elephant and can recount a story like your life depends on it, then you're missing the most important part. He said you've changed him, and in ways he appreciates. He *appreciates* you. He's taken care of you from day one, with or without you knowing it at the time. And it sounds like he's so madly in love with you he's willing to walk away if that's what you want."

Her words settle in my chest where the ache I've felt the last day and a half sits. I nod, unable to speak out loud, and I feel a stray tear roll down my cheek. She lets me sit in silence contemplating what she just said.

I feel her hand on my knee after a while, and when I look up at her, she has a tear rolling down her own face. "You're right," I choke.

"Of course I am," she sputters.

We laugh, but then reality settles on my shoulders. "I don't know what to do," I admit.

She picks up her phone to check the time. "Well, for right now, you should sleep. You look like hell, and I think some rest will do you some good. Let's figure out the next step in the morning. With mimosas or something."

I smile at her before leaning over the almost empty bag of Doritos to give her a hug.

She rubs her hand up and down my back. "Let yourself be happy, no matter how weird the situation looks from the outside. You weren't meant to live a normal life anyway."

I chuckle as I pull back and let my eyes scan her face with a watery smile. "Thanks."

She shakes her head. "Alright, let's get in bed."

So we do. She climbs into my bed with me and I fall into the deep sleep I desperately needed, feeling so grateful for my best friend.

CHAPTER 36

Macallister

I'm standing behind the stage at the show in Austin. I know Gnasher is playing. I even know they're on the crowd favorite, *Fuck Me Sober* even though I can't hear anything over the buzz in my ears that's been there since I turned my body away from Prudence and walked in the other direction. It was as if I was plugged into her, and once I turned and moved my body too far, we disconnected and it's been static since.

My eyes search the crowd out of habit and linger on the spot I know she'd be. The image of the middle-aged gentleman in cargo shorts and hair dyed blue long enough ago it looks more like chlorine damage begins to soften and blur away. In its place, I see Prudence dancing along to the music, observing the people around her, and allowing the notes to course through her body.

She isn't there, though. I tried to call her, but she didn't answer. She didn't respond to the text I sent either, letting her know Felicia called Darrell looking for her and her submission of the last week's worth of recordings. A week's worth of recordings I know contains a somewhat heated conversation that happened only days ago with somewhat juicy information. Or at least the start of some juicy information I know Felicia is foaming at the mouth for. Prudence never turned it in and something about that gives me hope. I didn't try again, though, knowing if she wanted to answer or reply, she would have.

I had asked Darrell about her. Since he was the one who coordinated Prudence's presence on the bus, I assumed he had some insight. "What did Felicia say when she reached out to you about this assignment?"

If I said I didn't think there was a possibility this entire thing was orchestrated somehow, I'd be lying. It seemed too coincidental. Although, how coincidental is it to meet the love of your life so randomly because the two of you were placed in the same place at the same time? I have an overwhelming suspicion the universe is constantly working with purpose, and that covers me like a comforting fear. It gives it an explanation, but not an explanation that makes any sense.

I remember the way Darrell looked down, shaking his head. "She was … well, she had a strong personality. I dunno. She said she had this great opportunity, it would benefit the band, blah, blah, blah. I thought, well, great! Who wouldn't want that? And so I said yes. I told Jazz about it and he …" his voice trailed off, and I remember Jasper's support from the beginning.

"He, what?" I felt desperate for his answer, needing it to confirm the possibility someone knew, and did this on purpose.

"He had a long talk with me about why the situation I'd found us in was bad management and how I needed to avoid things like this in the future. He told me he'd cover for me by supporting it, but he explained how I'd put the band in a possibly dangerous situation with the way *SubVox* records their interviews and spreads them, especially after the Torrence Gillman thing was released. He'd known," he shrugged his shoulders upwards. "He knew, I guess, and I felt … not great about it."

His admission shocked me. The admission that approving Prudence was a mistake. Not only a mistake but a mistake Jasper tried to help him cover up and pass off as intentional, a positive thing even. So, Jasper's intentions to have Prudence on this bus are clear to me now: To help his cousin succeed and move forward to gain footing in this business. The blaring conflict of interest in this situation with them being related is overpowered by my respect for Jasper's willpower and loyalty.

So it wasn't Jasper, but that leaves Felicia. It also leaves Prudence's mother in a way. While I know holding suspicion against her is, in a lot of ways, inappropriate and not loyal, I can't help but add her to the list of suspects just on knowledge alone. She might have told family, possibly her late husband, but there's something in me still doubting that. She's seemed to have kept this tight-lipped, so much so that it's severely affecting my client now. Not solely my client, but my friend. There wasn't even a breadcrumb to this revelation, and I honestly feel horrible for Cliff. I know he is searching for Prudence as much as I am, if not more. I know her absence is felt by everyone.

After she walked off the bus, Cliff disintegrated. I've never seen him so out of character. When the rest of the group returned to the bus, he was a sobbing mess at the table with his head in his hands. They all froze at the sound of his wails. Jasper walked over to him first and placed a hand on his shoulder, but bracing for Cliff to fling his arms back in defense. He didn't, though. He let Jasper's touch soothe him enough that the hysterical crying lowered into quiet sobs.

He raised his head to Jasper, and clearing his throat as much as he could, he choked between tears streaming down his face, "I have a daughter. I had a daughter with Sylvie. It's Prudence."

Jasper's head snapped to mine instantly, piercing me with a scowl. "You knew about this?"

I held my hands up in surrender, and to show I was as unarmed as I could possibly be. "I knew about the child. I didn't know the child was Prudence until this morning." My voice sounded foreign to me, from the lack of her breath mixing into my air anymore.

Travis stood with a hand over his mouth and his eyes wide, searching back and forth between all of us. Darrell stood there with his hands at his sides, an unreadable expression on his face because it was so straight and neutral, almost in defeat.

"Where is she?" I heard Travis's voice reach out.

I shrugged. "She went home to her mom. She said she needed to talk to her."

Cliff's eyes found mine. I'm sure I'm nothing more than a blurry mess to him with the amount of moisture still pooled in his eyes. "She left?" The way his voice broke tore a new hole in me.

I nodded, not able to form a verbal confirmation.

He laid his head back on the table and didn't talk for the next twenty-four hours besides the soundcheck and show. He didn't sit with his feet propped on the table and guitar in his lap. He didn't wear his sunglasses to hide away. He wore every expression on his face for all of us to witness. I couldn't tell if he was more upset about Prudence, or hearing about Sylvie, but I suspected a combination of both was true. So, as I stand here, searching the crowd, he's in my peripheral vision, doing the exact same. Scanning the mass of people, searching for the straight, black hair that shines like a night sky, and bright blue eyes that sparkle in a way only the clearest ocean water does right as the sun rises in the morning. Skin so creamy, stretched over a frame so perfectly curved, I can't help but imagine my hands sliding down the contour. I may never have her again.

I think we're done, but I don't understand how we can be done when we barely even started. My hands are so empty. My heart ... well, my heart doesn't even feel like it's in my chest anymore. It's wherever she is.

CHAPTER 37

Prudence

The tapping of Felicia's fingernail against her desk makes me want to crawl out of my skin. Over a mimosa or two, Jessica helped me come up with a plan I felt confident with. I felt a fire under me I haven't felt in a long time. This morning, I made my way over to the *SubVox* office. I didn't use the company credit card to fund my flight back. My reasons were personal and it was my choice to come back without approval. However, I am going to ask my boss for a few things before I agree to go back.

Without diving into the revelation that Cliff is my biological father, I told her an abridged version of events. When I was finished, she sat there quietly, tapping her green painted fingernail against the white marble table she perches behind.

I stare back at her, wishing I knew what to say, but coming up empty. She must understand my panic because she ceases the tapping, raises her hand, and shakes her head. "Prue, you're going back, right?"

I look at my hands, then back up at her. "I am ..." her smile returns, pushing up her Botox-filled cheeks. "But," I add and her scowl reappears., "I have some things I need to discuss with you about this story."

She leans forward with the rising smile again, raising her

eyebrows in the universal conspiratorial dance. "Yes," she urges me.

I force my eyes to raise to hers, exuding confidence even if it's a farce. "Felicia, I would like to discuss how we submit this story. And honestly, all stories moving forward."

Her face contorts again. Not angry, not even disappointed, but purely confused. She nods reluctantly at me to continue.

"I am not comfortable with submitting recordings to you weekly and being told the story to write anymore."

Her head snaps to attention. "Prue, that's how we do—"

I cut her off before she can continue to feed me the same speech I've heard her feed to me and others over the years. "No, it's not how I'm willing to do things anymore. I want to be able to find the story. I want to create a mixture of music, storytelling, and descriptions of what it's like to be in the crowd during their shows. Maybe even go into what it's like to be on tour with a band. I want to write something I think would bring others joy while they read because it's taking them on a journey, even if they can't go on it in person."

She blinks at me, and her face relaxes into a completely neutral expression. "I'm not sure if I can approve that."

"Felicia," I raise my voice, not in a yell but in an excited tone. "You are the Editor-in-chief. You are the only person that can approve that." I am smiling at her, hoping she realizes the power she holds to make a difference for *SubVox* and its journalists.

She shakes her head at me. "No, Prudence. I mean I don't think I can because I don't want to."

My face falls in tandem with my shoulders. I'm stunned.

"I don't understand," I say, even though I do understand. I think I just need to hear her say it again.

"I am not going to do that. I still need recordings weekly that I will review meticulously and choose what story gets written. That's how we do it at *SubVox*. That's how we get the stories we want. You didn't have a problem with that before."

I blink at her, thinking briefly I might respond. I decide not to, though. Instead, I stand, raising my body completely from the chair steadily. When I am fully erect, I hold her eye contact for a full count of five seconds, which isn't long unless you're having a stare-down. I crook the side of my mouth up slightly and put my hand out toward her.

She just frowns at my outstretched hand for a beat, but raises herself so she can lean over the desk and grasp my hand, confusion written across her face. I pump it once. "Thanks for everything, Felicia."

I drop the envelope containing a letter of resignation I wrote before coming over here. While I had hoped I wouldn't need it, something inside me told me I would. I hook my purse over my shoulder and walk out of her office. The click of my heels on the tiled floor to the elevator ring so deeply in my ear, as if they're dictating the pumping of my heart. All I can think is, *what did I do?* But my heart is pumping so strong, it's holding me upright and making my muscles scream, *Hell yeah, you quit!*

When I get out onto the sidewalk, I stop. Making a point to turn around and look up at the building I just exited, most likely for the last time. I didn't even go back to my desk to gather anything because I never left anything personal enough for me to want to take. This place was never a home. It was never *my* home, at least. It was my house for a little while. But now, I needed to find my home.

———

As I strut away from the office, I dial a number and raise my phone to my ear. I listen to the ringing while I wait for him to answer.

"Prue?" his voice says over the speaker pressed to my ear.

"Hey, Darrell, I have a favor to ask."

I can hear him moving around, and I wonder where he's at. Is he on the bus? Is Macallister nearby?

I don't hear a response and assume he's nodding and forgetting I can't see him. "I just quit at *SubVox*." I give him a moment to process before I continue, which he does with a small intake of breath. "I don't want anyone taking this story, though. I think there's an actual story here, and I want to be able to write it."

Again, more silence where I picture him nodding before he speaks. "Prue, none of us want anyone but you to write the story."

"But I need to know what your contract says, because right now, Felicia can take all the recordings I've already turned in and write the story herself if she wants. We need to read how the contract is worded because if it contains my name, I think there's something we can do."

I hear him moving around again, hear the familiar sound of maneuvering your body around a tight space, and I know he's on the bus. I want so badly to ask him if Macallister is there, but I don't. I open my mouth, holding the words there, but never pushing them forward into the space between my mouth and the mic of my phone.

He's called. He's texted. And I've … ghosted him. I hate when his name pops up on my screen because I know it's another olive branch I'm throwing to the ground. I don't think he's responsible for what happened, and I do genuinely understand his reasoning for why he told Cliff before me. I simply feel like I need to be in a different position before I speak to him again. I need to get my footing underneath me before I go waltzing back up to him, falling into open arms I know will be there when I'm ready.

At least, I hope they're still there when I'm ready. I should respond. But I don't know how.

"Okay, I've got it pulled up on my screen," he says. "Where should I look? This one is a doozy." I hear the nervous chuckle at having to rake through legal jargon.

"Scroll down," I say, pulling my words out as I scan the contract I have in my hands. The only one I could find was an old agreement with another celebrity whose time I stole to record and regurgitate a story about. I finally find it. "Find section IV."

"Okay, I'm there," he says tentatively.

"Read it aloud to me."

"Reporter Prudence Taylor will be in charge of conducting and recording interviews. She will live on the bus throughout the length of the tour with [Gnasher], or until deemed necessary. She will record conversations and turn in said recordings to *SubVox* offices for review. Her supervisor will then relay information back to [Reporter listed above] to write the story. Prudence Taylor is the only reporter on this assignment."

I breathe a sigh of relief. "That's amazing. Darrell, I need you to follow my next instructions very closely."

"Okay, Prue." So I tell him. I tell him the words he needs to say, and how to say them. We set up a plan. Our plan. After I hang up with him, I make another important phone call. One I need to do for myself, and one I absolutely have to do before talking to Macallister again. It terrifies me, but excites me at the same time. When I hang up again, my somewhat broken heart swells with love for these people who have nestled their way into my chest, shown me so much love, and pushed me to take initiative for myself, even when it's hard.

CHAPTER 38

Macallister

Darrell walks onto the bus holding his phone to his ear. "Maybe?" his voice wavers with uncertainty.

He listens, nods once, then opens his mouth to respond. The voice on the other end grows louder, though, cutting off his ability to respond. He snaps his mouth shut and nods another time.

I glare at him and when he finally makes eye contact with me, I mouth, "What's up?"

He shakes his head while trying to form a response. "No, I ... I guess not, but ... That's not really fair." He looks to me, his eyes wide and fearful.

I stand and walk over to him. The voice on the other end is still screaming fairly loudly, and I can now hear the voice is female. I hold my hand out to him, nonverbally telling him to give it to me so I can take care of it. This sounds like business and I am even more positive I'm right because of the fear I can hear in his voice trying to convey confidence but failing miserably. If it's business, I can take this from him. Even if it has to do with Jasper specifically, because we're a team now.

He covers the mic, clearly unaware all mobile phones have a mute feature. "Mac, I don't know if you can help me with this. She entrusted me, and I know she just doesn't want you to worry," he whispers and the sharpness of his hushed voice stabs into my gut like a knife. *She doesn't want you to worry.* She, meaning Prudence.

"Darrell, what's going on?" I whisper back, clenching my jaw and narrowing my gaze instinctually.

He shakes his head. "Felicia wants to write the story herself. I told her the recordings she has are null and void because the terms of the contract were broken, just like Prudence told me to. Now, she's throwing a bunch of legal jargon my way I don't understand. She probably knows that and is saying a bunch of nonsense to freak me out."

I snatch the phone from him, irate and instantly comprehending the situation. "If Prudence doesn't write the article, no one writes the article," I growl into Darrell's phone.

"Who is this?" the woman on the other end sneers like a snake slithering into my ear.

"Macallister Davis. Clifford Lee's manager and Darrell's partner. Anything he signed, I've signed by connection, so you can talk to me now."

"Not how it works, Macallister." Her voice slips through and it makes me cringe.

"If Prudence doesn't write the article, no one writes the article. You run that story and she wasn't involved, you can guarantee we will sue you for breach of contract. Unfortunately, that wouldn't be a great situation for you because the evidence is incredibly clear and I have no problem smearing the name of a trashy music magazine that can't even hold enough integrity to comply and behave through the terms and conditions laid out *by them* from the get-go."

She sucks in an annoyed breath and releases it in defeat.

"That clear?" I force, wanting to get off the phone with this woman immediately.

"Clear," she says, defeated.

I hang up, forgoing a goodbye, and hand Darrell back the phone.

Making eye contact with him as I do, I grind out the question, "What. The. Fuck?"

"Prue called me and asked for my help," his voice shakes, and I know he thinks I'm upset with him. I'm not, but I can't help the emotions filling my body knowing this is about Prudence.

"Is she okay?" I think my words will come out more forceful and strong, but instead, these fall from my mouth steeped in despair.

He nods rapidly and puts a hand on my shoulder. I don't even make a move to flick him off. I let him. I close my eyes as I let out a breath so deeply it forces my head downwards.

"Darrell, I need you to explain."

When he finishes telling me how Prudence quit *SubVox* but wants to still write this story the way it's meant to be told, my chest grows hot and I have to literally clutch it from the love I have for her and the woman she is. Whether she wants me or not, I respect her so much.

Darrell nods. "I signed the contract so I needed to be the one to call Felicia. But I really messed up." He's transitioned into shaking his head now.

I pat him on his bicep, and the out-of-character affection from me is probably what caused him to snap his head up. "You did great. You're doing a good job, Darrell," I reassure him.

His eyes shine and I'm starting to get uncomfortable now, so I nod once and say, "Yep," before continuing to walk past him through the curtain.

I'm not entirely sure what that was, but I'm not fighting it anymore. I'm different, and I can't deny the reason why.

Does this mean she is coming back? It's all I can think about, and if I'm honest, I've given myself a headache over the last two hours tossing this question around, letting it bump off the sides of my brain like a tennis ball. She hasn't reached out to me, though, and she hasn't responded to any of my attempts to reach out to her. So even if she does come back, it doesn't necessarily mean she's coming back to me.

I'm lying in my bed, rolling my phone in my palm to give my nervous hands something to do, and a vibration tickles my palm before the ring reach my ears. I turn it over frantically, hoping her name flashes on my screen.

Mom.

My mom is calling? Why? I stare at her contact picture as it appears on my screen along with the option to answer her call or send her to voicemail. I contemplate the option on the left, colored red, for only a half second before I tap my fingertip over the green.

"Hello?" I say, and I realize how tentative my voice sounds. I haven't spoken to her in so long and my guilt flares.

"Mac?" she asks. The only other person that calls me that. Well, at least until recently.

"Yeah, hi, Mom."

"You doin' okay?" She can hear she isn't talking to the same Macallister she did last. Which, to be fair, was a while since I've been bad about keeping in touch. Another thing to add to my list of things I want to change.

"I'm fine. Tired," I lie. I'm restless. "Tour is a lot. What's up?"

I can tell by her pause she isn't satisfied with my answer, but I think I'm still safe from her pressing me on it. "Alright. Well, I'm sending a reporter out to cover the tour with Gnasher."

Uhm, what?

"What do you mean what?" she says. *Oops, I must have said that out loud.*

"The story got transferred over to *Riff Revolt*. The reporter will meet you in Dallas. That's where you'll be next, right?"

We're en route now. We have two shows in Dallas, so we are getting to a hotel tonight and staying until Monday when we'll take off toward Kansas City.

I take a deep breath. "How? We have a reporter on the story already."

"You did. With *SubVox*. From what I hear, you broke off the relationship with the editor-in-chief." *The editor-in-chief from hell,* I think as the anger from my conversation with Felicia bubbles up again.

I circle my temples in frustration. "Yeah. But how did a transfer of the story get approved?"

"Not everything has to go through you to get approved." Her tone suggests she's saying this playfully, with the tone of love, but also as a minor warning in the tone of accountability. And honestly, therefore love.

I hold my eyes closed and take a deep breath. *Guess this means she's not coming back.*

I hope I did say that one in my head and not out loud again. I breathe a small sigh of relief when she says, "You there, Mac?" Her tone is much softer, concerned.

"Yeah," I breathe. I feel almost silly for having hope this would work out.

"Okay. Well, I love you. Good luck on the rest of the tour. Let me know if anything pops up with the new reporter." We don't say 'love' a lot in my family. At least, between me, my mom, and my dad. But she'll pull it out once in a while, put herself in the discomfort, when she knows it's needed and I am filled with so much appreciation for her right now.

"I love you, too," I say, hoping my tone sounds as sincere as I mean it. "And thanks, I will."

After hanging up, I lay in my bed until the familiar gravitational pull indicates the bus has stopped and we've reached the hotel. I waste no time grabbing what I need and rushing off the bus into the privacy of my room where I lay on top of the bed feeling my heart shattering. When I at last drift off after hours of being conscious and in torment, I think about how she isn't coming back, and now a new reporter is coming onto the bus.

CHAPTER 39

Prudence

I'm sitting in an Uber taking me to the hotel I know the guys are staying at. I wanted so badly to call Macallister, but after I ignored him for so long, I'm not sure where we stand anymore. I'll know when I can talk to him, and right now, that's all I want to do. While I'm nervous about the direction our conversation might take, I know it's a conversation worth having in person.

After leaving Felicia's office and talking with Darrell, I made a phone call to the HR department at *Riff Revolt*. I was able to get on the line with someone far up enough to listen to my pitch and push me up even higher to the one I really needed to speak with.

Constance, Macallister's mother, was pleasant to talk to for unexpected reasons. She's very no-nonsense. After listening to my pitch, she only asked three follow-up questions.

"Isn't that the tour my son is managing?"

"Yes," I said, trying to keep my voice strong and confident.

"What makes you think you have what it takes to write for *Riff Revolt*?" *Okay, that sounded a little cliché.*

I found it hard not to chuckle at first from how much it felt like I was in an early-2000s rom-com. "Well, as a writer, I respect what the publication stands for. I've written a lot of exposé pieces that hardly ever mention the music or the art. I'm sure you know how *SubVox* operates, and know that as a reporter there, I was always instructed and told what to write. I know I can write quality pieces digging into the music and the artists as musicians. Because that's what people want to read, and it's what I want to write."

"What's your angle for this story?"

I took a deep breath in. "It's a reunion tour, right? It's also the reunion of two friends. Two friends who are incredibly talented, but broken. It doesn't matter why they broke up. What matters is why they came back together. What matters is the music keeping them tied together, and hopefully, music yet to be written binding them to each other forever."

She apparently liked this answer, because now I'm on my way to my new assignment: A story written by me. By *me*, completely. A story I can be proud of, for once, and a story I already started drafting back in the desert.

The driver pulls the car up to the front of the hotel. I thank him and get out to retrieve my suitcase from the trunk and go inside. I pull it behind me and wonder why I didn't think to condense it before heading back out. I know it's because it was the last thing on my mind and laugh to myself when I imagine having to shove it back into the already tight storage space at the bottom of the bus.

I check in at the front desk with an enthusiastic brunette woman. She's got such a big, red smile plastered on her face, it makes me involuntarily laugh when I step up to her counter.

I give her my information and she grins even larger, which I'm shocked is even possible, and hands me a tiny paper folder with two plastic keycards stuffed inside. I'm in such a hurry, I yell a rushed, "Thanks," over my shoulder as I'm walking away toward the elevator. It's clear glass like the one at The Cosmopolitan in Las Vegas. It makes me remember the first real conversation I had with Macallister. It reminds me of when he later said he'd been in love with me since that night. My stomach flips, hoping he'll still have those feelings toward me now.

I step inside and press the number five, my heart pounding. The elevator rises at a glacial pace, but I don't mind the extra time to breathe in through my nose and out through my mouth while I watch the lobby below me grow smaller as I rise, the heads of people appearing as small flecks dancing around each other.

The loud ding indicates I've reached my floor, but I'm looking down examining the keys, flipping the plastic over between my fingers, because I forgot my room number already when the doors slide open. Someone gasps from the other side. I raise my eyes to notice Cliff and Macallister standing in front of me.

My feet are frozen to the floor, but I know I need to get out before the doors close again. I grab the handle of my suitcase and drag it behind me as I awkwardly step off. They both separate more dramatically than they need to, making space for me and even more space for the bag. Macallister's eyes flit to my suitcase before he reaches to grab it from me. I step out and the three of us face each other.

I'm surprised when Macallister speaks first. "What are you doing here?" He's still holding my suitcase up, and as if he realizes he doesn't need to anymore, he sets it on the ground next to him.

"I—" I don't know where to start. The one-million times I rehearsed conversations in my head with both Macallister and Cliff didn't help me because I didn't envision talking to them together.

Cliff glances between the two of us and realizes this. "I'm going to—" he clearly wasn't going anywhere as he struggles to think of an excuse and he's pointing his finger in no particular direction. "Well, I'll let you two talk," he settles on the truth and drops his hand.

Walking closer to me, he places a hand on my shoulder and I can feel his uncertainty in how physical he can be with me. I smile gently at him, communicating it's okay. "Mom says hi," I whisper to him, and I'm not sure why. His eyes get glassy, though, and I don't regret it.

He nods and presses the button for the elevator. When the doors open, he doesn't step inside. Instead he turns back to me.

He places both hands gently on my shoulders. "Next time, please say goodbye to me before you leave. Please." His voice cracks on the last word, and I know he's holding back tears. *He was worried about me?*

A lump forms in my throat, and I nod. "You got it, Pop."

His eyes sparkle back at mine and I can't quite evaluate his expression right now, or my eyes will lose the fight to hold back the moisture pooling behind them.

He winks at me, then turns back to the elevator, but the doors have closed so he presses the button again. The door dings open almost immediately. He walks forward this time, and keeping his head lowered, he presses a button and raises his head barely enough to give me the faintest hint of a smile before the doors completely close.

When I turn back to Macallister, I'm transfixed by his face. The muscles in his jaw twitch. I brace myself against his anger, thinking he's about to yell at me now Cliff is gone. I keep staring at the bump of muscle moving in his cheek, when I realize it's not from anger. When I move my gaze up to reach his eyes, I realize he's actually holding back tears. He's clenching so hard to keep the moisture from spilling out. The only reason I know this for certain is because his resolve finally fails, the clenching no longer strong enough. I watch as one tear makes a trail from the corner of his eye down his cheek.

It falls off the cliff of his chin, and he clears his throat, bringing my attention back up to meet his eyes.

"Do you have a room?" he says, obviously aware enough to not want to conduct this conversation in the hallway.

I nod. "526," I raise my key card as I say it.

He nods and picks my suitcase back up, opting to carry it instead of dragging it on the rollers. It makes me smile and reminds me of when I first got onto the bus.

We walk down the hallway to my room and enter. My stomach flips, still not knowing his feelings toward me regardless of the warmth I felt as soon as I saw him.

CHAPTER 40

Macallister

We step into her room, and I'm not sure what expression is painted on my face. I know I haven't been able to take my eyes off of her. I set her suitcase down and I want to reach for her. I don't know how she'd take that, though, so I lock my muscles into place, treating her like a skittish animal that could bolt at any moment. Although, *I'm* the one who walked away from *her* the last time. The realization sobers me, and I know deep down that was the one and only time I'll ever be able to do that.

My face must reflect my inner turmoil because she scrunches up her expression in concern.

"You didn't answer my question," I say bluntly, unable to say anything else.

She quirks an eyebrow, so I gesture at her suitcase, finding my vocal cords unable to work right now. She must recognize the various emotions and thoughts racing through my head in such a short span of time because she giggles and reaches for my hand. I push mine out and grab hers instead, and when I do, my eyes immediately fall to her hand resting in mine. I'm not gripping her tightly, but my fingers hold onto hers to make sure she doesn't slip away again. I run my thumb along the top of her knuckles, trying to memorize the ridges like my favorite mountainscape.

I get lost in touching her, when I look back up at her, her eyes are wide, watching mine. "Sorry," I mumble as I loosen my grip to release her hand.

She turns her wrist around so her fingers grip around mine, keeping us locked together, and she tugs a little. "Let's sit."

I follow her to the inside of her room. There's a king-sized bed, a green armchair, a small desk against the wall with one chair, and a mini fridge with one of those machines that make fake coffee that doesn't even pretend to taste good. We settle on the edge of the bed, close to each other, but not touching. I know because it's all I can focus on and it's killing me.

She takes a breath and starts. "I'm here because I represent *Riff Revolt* as a freelance reporter writing the story about Gnasher's reunion tour." She lets her breath out and a small, tentative, smile quirks her lips upward slightly.

I blink at her, so caught off guard by her formality it's taking me longer to process her words. *I was right.*

She tilts her head to try and catch my eyes that have wandered. "Right about what?"

I need to learn to stop thinking things out loud like a lunatic. "My mom called me to tell me she was sending a reporter to finish the story. I had helped Darrell talk to Felicia, so I just thought … it was someone new. But I had the crossing thought, which was honestly more of a juvenile glimmer of hope for something I knew would be too good to be true. But then I had the thought again after seeing you here and I berated myself not to." I release a shaky exhale starting to form into a laugh.

"You wouldn't let yourself hope?" Her question is valid, even if it is out of the blue.

"I … no. I wouldn't," I say, shaking my head.

"Do you still want me?" She bends her head again to try and meet my eyes, and I immediately hate myself for making her work so hard for it, for the attention she deserves right now as she's speaking to me.

I snap up to meet her gaze dead-on. "Prudence, I want you

more than I've ever wanted anything. I honestly think I need you. I know I could live without you. I'm not that big of a fool, even though I feel like one. I know I'd live, but I also know I'd never be okay again. I've spent the last handful of weeks, that I honestly don't know the actual count of because you've sucked me into a total whirlpool, learning about you," I reach out and run my thumb down her cheek while I cup her face. "Knowing you have a birthmark on your shoulder. It's small and it looks like a small circle with squiggly lines, like God's hand was shaking when he drew it on your body. I know you're strong. You're so strong, talented, and capable. And I'm watching you realize that, too." Tears line the bottom of her eyes, threatening to spill out. "I know you hate bananas, but you love potatoes, and I'm the only one who knows why that's weird."

She chuckles at this and her tears spill down her cheeks, creating the most beautiful glimmer of moisture down the skin toward her neck. Beautiful, because I know she isn't sad.

I reach out and wipe one away, her eyes reaching mine again. "I know that, even though you're strong, you're willing to show me your vulnerable side and I'll never take that for granted for a single day."

Her eyes scan back and forth across mine. "I love you, Macallister. I was so scared you didn't love me anymore."

I shake my head. "No, baby. Not gonna happen. I'm here. For as long as you want me to be."

I wrap my arms around her and we fall back together onto the bed. Her entire front is pressed to mine, and we gaze at each other for a second before she closes her eyes and nuzzles her head into my chest.

"Say it again," I whisper into the top of her head.

She pauses. "I love you?"

"Mmm," I moan because those words are the cooling salve I need on the burn I've been suffering since I last saw her.

"I love you, Macallister." I'll never get sick of hearing her tell me.

"I love you, too."

"Am I your girlfriend?" she asks me as I let my eyes flutter closed.

I feel the involuntary smile spread wide. "Do you want to be my girlfriend?"

I feel her shimmy in a little closer to my body and squeeze my sides a little tighter as she does. "I do."

I can't help my rising chuckle from how juvenile this conversation feels. "Will you be my girlfriend, Prudence?"

"Yes, please."

My smile is so locked into place, I wonder if it'll ever fade. It's perfect. She's perfect. We are perfect.

CHAPTER 41

Prudence

"So, I like your mom," I say after we've stared at each other for too long, but neither of us can stop.

Macallister laughs, and I know from the breathy sound he's releasing tension he'd been holding onto. "Why didn't you tell me you wanted to write for *Riff Revolt*? I would have—"

I put my hand up to his lips, stopping him. "That is why."

He lets his eyes drop toward the fingers I have pressed gently to his mouth and his lips curve upwards under my touch.

"I wanted to do this myself. On my merit. Not because I'm sleeping with the boss's son."

He opens his mouth and before I can remove my fingers to let him speak, he catches my pointer finger in his mouth and sucks to pull it deeper in where he draws his tongue across my skin. It makes me shiver. I want to let him continue, surprised at how good it feels and how it sends bolts of electricity south, but I also want to continue our conversation before we get too lost in the sheets.

I pull my finger out, with plenty of imitation resistance from him, and he smiles. "You're not just sleeping with him, you're his girlfriend." Warmth spreads across my body at his words, and his smile falters a little, giving him a more serious expression. "I understand your reasoning, though, and I've always admired your drive to make your own way. Can I ask you something?"

I nod, "Of course."

"Why do you want to continue writing this story after everything that's been revealed?"

He has a point, and I'm not entirely shocked by his question. "I'm not writing the same story I thought I'd be writing when I started this."

"Oh?" He beckons me to explain further, and the small sliver of Cliff's manager peeks through, still trying to protect his client.

"For me, I wasn't ever really fascinated with why Gnasher broke up, but more with how they came back together. Watching how they're repairing a deep friendship that was broken for so long with music has been one of the best parts of this tour."

He nods, taking my words in. "I think that's the story that deserves to get written. For you, for Cliff and Jasper, and the fans."

"It is." I'm stunned by an overwhelming sense of pride, something I haven't felt for a long time in my writing career.

"That's something else I love about you." He reaches over and tucks a strand of my hair behind my ear.

"I wish I could go back and do the same thing for Torrence," I say, letting the tiniest hint of melancholy seep into my words.

"Maybe you can," he says, and he pulls me to him, pressing his lips to mine before I can respond.

I melt into him. He uses his teeth to gently tug my bottom lip and it forces a moan from me. He coaxes my lips apart with his tongue and I let him taste me. I run my fingers up the back of his neck, holding the back of his head as if I could push his kiss further into me. His hands hold onto the hem of my shirt, sliding underneath my body and it lights my skin on fire.

When he reaches the underwire of my bra, he grunts in frustration. I break our kiss, and his facial expression makes me want to laugh. I do giggle a little as I sit up. He rotates his body to give me room, and when I grasp for the hem of my shirt to raise it over my head, he is even more gracious in giving me space to do that. He's impatient though, and ends up grasping my shirt and pulling it off of me himself.

With a mischievous smile, he also reaches to unhook the front clasp of my bra, which he does in record time. My breasts fall out and his eyes are glued to them.

He raises his eyes to mine, and it looks almost painful for him to do so. "I'm hungry for you," he says right before he pushes me back, my fall cushioned by the mattress.

He presses one more heated kiss to my lips before trailing kisses to my neck, lightly nibbling and sucking along the way. When he reaches my collarbone, his tongue replaces his lips and he uses it to draw pictures of passion on my skin toward the erect peaks of my nipples. My body is buzzing and aching for him. I'm so desperate for him to take me into his mouth when he finally does wrap his lips around the pink bud, I cry out in relief.

I can hear him hum his approval as he sucks and swirls his tongue around, causing my hips to buck upwards. Having his mouth on me brings a hyper-awareness to the sensitivity between my legs, now starting to throb and protest at the lack of attention. As if he can sense it, he slithers down my body, kissing and licking along the way, to the apex of my thighs. Over my jeans, he presses his palm right where I need him to and it sends a shock-wave through me. I let out a groan in response.

He holds his palm to me, pressing with the right amount of pressure on my pubic bone, and moves his hand gently, but with precision, grinding the seam of my jeans right across my clit. My muscles tense up in the best way and release like melting butter. I am not even cognizant of the noises I'm making anymore, because my ears are buzzing with the pleasure coursing through my body.

When I can't take it anymore and will not wait any longer to have his skin pressing into mine, I reach and fumble with the button on my jeans. I put my hands at the top of the waistline, and push and crumple them down my thighs. He reaches up, taking over the action for me, and grabs the sides to pull in one swipe getting the pants to my knees. He leans down and presses a kiss to the bone of my hip, naked and jutting out with the string of my thong across it. He runs his tongue on the string back and forth once, twice, before tugging it with his teeth.

I can't take my eyes off him as he does this, and it's a scene so salacious, I should blush and turn away. But I can't tear my eyes from his, and the overwhelming pull fuels my fire even further, I can feel how aroused I am. I rub my thighs together, searching for any sort of relief, but am left severely disappointed.

I close my eyes, push my head against the mattress, arching my neck slightly, and groan. His fingers grab my thong and he wastes no time pulling it the rest of the way with my pants before he pushes my thighs apart roughly and dives his head toward me. His tongue reaches my center faster than I can comprehend, and I can't help the way my spine curves at the euphoria of having him eat me the way I've craved since the last time we were in bed together.

He uses his tongue to trace patterns and words I can't fully discern because I'm too windblown from the wet and warm sensation. I press my hands onto his head, twirling my fingers into the short tresses there. I wonder if I'm forcing my fingers too roughly in my massaging of his scalp, but he lifts off of me just barely to say, "Fuck, don't stop. That feels so good."

He's so close to my center, having only pulled off enough to speak, his breath hits my most sensitive parts and I shiver as the lightning bolts shoot through me. "You don't stop," I whisper as I grab his head again and pull him back into me, where he devours me.

The tension builds, and the muscles low in my belly tense up, knowing what's coming. I grip the sheets on the bed, grasping a little corner of the fabric and pressing my nails so hard on my palm, they sink into the tiny divots I've created. "Oh," I say, wanting to warn him. "I'm ..." I can't even make out words, but he knows.

His licks grow more rapid before he uses his mouth to suck

my clit completely. "Yes," I yelp, having an explosion detonate my insides. My legs shake and I tilt my head down to make eye contact with him. Two hazel eyes, that are currently so dark they're going for black. I've never looked someone in the eye while I came, but I can't tear my gaze away from him now.

My breathing comes out in short pants as I ride my orgasm like the longest wave. "I love you," I manage to breathe out, and the words envelop him with more want and hunger. His eyes are predatory as he pulls his mouth away from me. Using his hands he walks up my body until we're face to face again. His hardness notches into where he just licked and sucked like I was his favorite piece of candy.

"Fuck," he breathes out. "I need you."

I nod my head enthusiastically, letting him know I need him, too. When he rises from the bed, I know he's going to grab a condom. I encircle his wrist with my fingers and he looks at me, questioning.

"I'm on birth control," I say, "And I've been tested recently. I'm clean."

His eyes grow darker from his pupils dilating at my words. "I'm clean, too. I haven't been with anyone in a while."

I shake my head. "I haven't either. And I don't want to be with anyone else."

He reaches between us, brushing my clit purposefully once, then grabbing his hard cock and running it across my center. He uses the head to spread around my arousal, then glides it up so easily to draw a circle around my clit.

"Oh, Jesus," I say on a breath as I close my eyes.

"It's Macallister, baby," he says before notching himself at my opening and pushing into me with one hard thrust. He pushes to the hilt, and the soft skin of his balls rests right against my ass. "I like it when you say my name."

"Macallister," I breathe again, gripping his back.

He pumps into me, deep. He is so far back, I'm already about to come again. He hits me right where I need him, and he reaches between us again to swipe his thumb across my clit. It drags enough to cause the explosion of sensitivity I need. I open my eyes and watch as he takes his thumb he swiped across me and places it into his mouth, sucking it. Removing it with a smile, he skates the saliva-covered fingertip across me, and I can't physically keep my eyes open. Stars explode behind my eyelids.

I moan so loudly, I'm worried someone in the next room will hear. He pumps once more before releasing a primal sound. His dick pulses inside me, and I know he's coming. I was so close, but fuck I don't even care. It still felt so good.

He stills for a moment, no doubt emptying into me. He pulls himself free, and when I think he's about to rise from the bed, he stays in place over me. "Your pussy feels too good, baby. But I'm not done fucking you."

I take a breath and continue to stare up at him, my clit starting to beg for more from his words. He brushes his hand down my body, still sensitive to the touch, and I immediately arch into him.

"I love how responsive you are to me," he coos.

I place my hand over his, guiding it to my center, still throbbing for his attention but now dripping with his spend. He takes his finger and slides it down my slit, barely grazing where I need him most.

"I love how wet you get," his praise is like winning the grandest achievement.

He takes his finger and lazily tours the entirety of my pussy except for the inside, spreading my arousal and his around. My clit hurts now from how hard it is, and when he smears his cum-covered fingertip across it, I moan. He takes a finger and presses it inside me. My walls immediately clench around him. The sound it pulls from his throat is so intoxicating, I want to record it and listen to it every morning when I wake up.

He pumps in and out of me, curling his finger against my frontal wall and strokes against the spot that will have me coming quickly as long as he doesn't stop. He adds a second finger, covering more surface area of that spot and when his thumb

presses my swollen nub. The sensation makes me yelp in pleasure. He presses his other hand on my belly and the commotion it
sends through me is almost blinding.

He sweeps his finger against me twice more before my walls
tighten and pull around him. "That's right, baby. Come around
my fingers. I love to feel your pussy come for me and watch the
flush of your face."

I arch into him, but he continues to pull from me. "Your pussy
is too good, Prudence. You're such a good girl for making me
come so quickly. Now it's your turn." He bends to suck on me one
last time while I ride out this pleasure.

My legs are shaking and I'm about to pull him off of me when
he stops. He holds his hand in me for a moment longer before
pulling his fingers from me. He leans down and kisses me on the
cheek before he leaves the bed. I'm wondering where he went to
when I feel a warm, soft wetness against me. Macallister is
cleaning me off with a warm washcloth. He's swiping the
terrycloth across my skin so gently and with such care, I can't
fully comprehend the motion. I lay still, letting my eyes fall closed
as I bask in the attention. I don't think I could move right now,
anyway.

No one has ever done that for me. I keep thinking about the
way he continued to pleasure me, even though he was done. I
think about the way he's cleaning me now, taking care of me. He
finishes and comes back into the bed where he pulls me into his
chest and holds me to him. I'm so overwhelmed with happiness
and satisfaction, I don't even realize it when I drift off to sleep in
his arms.

CHAPTER 42
Macallister

I hold her while I listen to her breathing, not wanting to move. When it's time to leave for soundcheck, I know I have to. I gently wake Prudence. We peel ourselves away from each other and out of the bed. We spent every last possible second wrapped in each other, so we need to get dressed rapidly and quickly make our way out the door to meet in the lobby.

In the elevator, I find myself letting my hands grip her and pull her up against me while I'm smashed in the corner. I run my finger across her forehead to push away a loose strand of her dark hair, still tangled from our lovemaking, and slide my finger to tuck it behind her ear. She smiles at me and I lean in to press a kiss to her lips, forgetting and honestly not caring the elevator is completely made of glass and therefore, see-through.

When the doors open with a chime, we clasp our hands together and I lead her out to where I know we're meeting before piling onto the bus. *The bus she'll be on again*, I can't help thinking with relief. I find the back of Cliff's head, and I walk toward him, realizing Darrell, Jasper, and Travis are not around him.

He's facing the front door of the hotel, and Prudence gasps behind me at the same time Cliff's spine straightens and pulls his body completely upright. I turn back to Prudence and her eyes are wide and staring past me. We reach Cliff right as he whispers, "Sylvie?"

Cliff doesn't even notice us, and Prudence tugs me gently, keeping me from walking right up next to him. "Hi, Clifford," the woman who I suspect is Prudence's mother says as she walks up to him.

Cliff's head shakes as if trying to confirm she isn't a mirage in front of him. "I didn't … It's been so long."

She walks up closer until she's standing right in front of him. "I wrote," she says with a lighthearted chuckle.

"I guess I need to be better about reading my mail, huh?" He puffs a half-hearted laugh.

I can't see his face, but hers has a closed-lip smile spread across it and her eyes are filled with unshed tears. Prudence steps in front of me and lets go of my hand as she walks toward her mom and I follow a few steps behind. She stops and stands between Cliff and Sylvie, and moves her gaze between them. When I'm standing next to Prudence, I realize this space is entirely too intimate for me to be here, and I turn to walk away and allow them the privacy they deserve when she juts out her hand and grips it around my wrist, stopping me.

I look up at her wide eyes pulling mine in. She tugs me gently and I timidly step to her side.

Sylvie peeks over at me and smiles enough to show her teeth now. She places a hand on my shoulder and gently squeezes. She's the sweetest woman I've ever met, and she hasn't even said a word to me yet. She instantly makes my body and my chest warm with the genuine kindness radiating from her.

"Hi, Macallister."

I smile and nod at her, only able to whisper a soft "Hi," with the overwhelming emotion of this moment. When Prudence tugs me again, I switch my gaze and she's trying to walk away with me in tow, so I allow my feet to step in time with her.

When we get outside, we stop and stand on the concrete sidewalk outside the doors.

"Did you know she was coming?" I ask.

She looks at me, her blue eyes still sparkling the way they were in the bed upstairs. "No, but I had a suspicion she might."

I nod. "Do you want to go back in? I can wait out here."

She shakes her head. "No. This should just be for them."

I turn my head to peek back through the glass. "What do you think they'll do?" I'm not sure what answer I'm looking for.

"Probably keep staring at each other," she murmurs and starts chuckling.

"Are you okay?" I turn my eyes back to her and I realize the gleam is moisture pooling.

She smiles and sniffs once. "Yeah, I am."

I believe her and I watch as one tear rolls down her cheek. I reach out to catch it and she presses my palm to her cheek, leaning into it and closing her eyes. I glide my thumb across her soft skin. I know she's happy because it's radiating out of her. I know she's mine from the way she leans into my touch. I take a step into her, keeping my hand on her face but using the other to grip her waist and pull her toward me.

Her eyes flicker up to mine and we stare at each other for an indiscernible amount of time. I'm so lost in the ocean of her irises, so captivated by the smell of roses surrounding me. She smiles, and I smile back at her.

Harvey pulls the bus into the roundabout next to us, and when the door hisses open, I grab her hand and pull her behind me. She hesitates at the first stair.

I turn back. "You coming?"

She tilts her head. "You sure you want me to get on this time?"

"Prudence, you better get on this bus," I tug her up to stand in front of me, pull her into me, and press my lips to hers.

Macallister, years later

EPILOGUE

As I watch the early morning light cast shadows across Prudence's cheek, I consider reaching over to trace the shapes with my fingertips. I don't, though, because she's still asleep and I know she's tired. Instead, I watch the patterns play on her skin and think back to that first day I met her.

Anytime I reminisce about that day, my heart does somersaults with the excitement of what it felt like to see her the first time along with the irritation of my behavior. I cringe at the replay of trying to prevent her from boarding that bus. I almost wish I could go back and reshape that recollection in my life. When I really think about it though, I know I never would even if I had the chance.

I couldn't because of the way her face lights up when she gets to tell someone that the first time we met, I was trying to kick her off Gnasher's tour bus, but her charm won me over. I love watching her tell the story, our story. The way her eyes sparkle, the blue like a welcoming pool on a hot day that I wish I could dive into. Her hand gestures, wild and sometimes over-exaggerated, but exactly her. The way she looks over to me at specific parts of the story with a knowing grin, a secret just between us.

Of course, my favorite part of the story is what gets left out.

The way we never let go of each other after that, even when things got difficult. Instead, we held on tight and built this life together. My favorite part of the story is everything she doesn't include because it would take ages to completely detail our history. It would take too long to explain why we never buy bananas, except for once a year when she gets the craving to make the banana pudding her grandfather made while she was a child. People would doze off completely if she went into detail about the many sea shanty vinyls she's found and added to what was once only my but is now our, collection over the years; and the specific one she loves to sing anytime I take too long in the shower.

Nothing is perfect, obviously, but sometimes I think our hardships are what does make us perfect, because there's no one else I'd rather navigate life with. Her resilience is astounding to me. Life gets complicated, especially when the rest of the world finally gets a hold of information as damning as being the love-child of a famous rockstar. Her paternity was exposed by *SubVox* after her old boss, Felicia, learned the truth. Apparently, that was the straw that broke the camel's back because the magazine came under a lot of scrutiny for the way they exposed Cliff and Prudence before they were ready, and *SubVox* suffered the consequences in the form of sales plummeting and eventually going bankrupt.

Prudence kept her head held high, and was even praised for her grace. She took it better even than I did. It seems backwards that what should have been her suffering was just one of the many times she helped me grow as a person. She's my missing piece, and sometimes I don't feel worthy. I knew taking on Cliff as a client would greatly impact my career, but I never knew how it would impact every facet of my life. I've thanked him more times than I can count, but he responds the same way every time.

"You can't thank me for something the universe set up." He isn't wrong. At this point, I thank him just to get the reminder.

Prudence shifts her body a little as she pulls the comforter up under her chin. When the sunlight streaming in through the bedroom window brightens, likely from a cloud passing, a beam directs itself onto her closed eyelid causing her to scrunch her nose and the corners of her eyes to crinkle. I can't resist anymore and reach out to lightly brush away the piece of hair that's fallen across her face from the movement.

The slow, upward spread of her lips is the only thing to indicate she's awake, rather than her eyelids that stay closed. "Morning," she rasps, her vocal cords still filled with sleep.

"Good morning, baby."

Her smile deepens at the scratchy sound of her pet name from my lips, my own voice still hoarse in the early morning. She peeks an eye at me. I mirror her in a frozen wink, which earns me the beautiful melody of her laugh.

I feel my cheeks as my growing smile presses them upward. "You know what I love about us?"

She regards me silently for a beat before furrowing her brow. "What?"

"That we love each other. Through every step, all I care about is that you're beside me. Through the good things, the challenges we face, and the little moments in-between, I can't help but think to myself 'who else could I do this with?' Because I don't care about any of it unless it's with you. You're my favorite person. There's no one else I can be myself with the way I can with you. I want to wrap around your body at every concert and drink up the way you see the world around you. I want to hold you when you sing along and feel the vibrations through my arms encircled around you. I'd never get over you, Prudence. I'd never even try. Without you, I think I'd cease to exist because our fibers have become so intertwined. So I thank every God that may or may not exist you never made me live without you."

Her blue eyes widen at me, scanning my face as the unmistakable sheen of moisture magnifies them even further. "Macallister," she breathes.

"Can I hold you?" I cut her off.

She smiles, knowing exactly what I want because we've done this so many times. She rolls over clumsily, then scoots back into me. I wrap my arms around her, pull her even closer, and bury my face into her neck so I can inhale her rosy scent, always more magnified after she wakes up. We stay like that for a minute or an hour. I'm not sure because I've lost track of time.

Her hips wiggle against my lap, and she giggles. "I think your lower half just woke up."

I smile into the nape of her neck before pressing a kiss to the warm skin and tighten my grip around her. "I just want to hold you right now."

"What about what I want?" Her tone is playful, and she grinds deeper into me.

"I'd give you everything. Anything you want." I mean it.

"You already have," she whispers and she pulls my hand up to her mouth and presses a kiss to my knuckles.

Fuck Me Sober

High,
I'm just a touch too high,
But you look so fly,
Cross my heart and die.

Hi,
Just a touch, too. Hi.
Time to paint the sky.
Thought you wouldn't mind.

I'm just an alien, orbiting your sun.
I'm just an idiot, looking for some fun.
I don't care if we're over,
Fuck me sober.

Chained,
Francis said we're chained.
Bet she feels big-brained,
When she makes me shamed

I'm just an alien, orbiting your sun.

I'm just an idiot, looking for some fun.
I don't care if we're over
Ooo! Fuck me sober

(Drum break)

I'm just an alien, orbiting your sun.
I'm just an idiot, looking for some fun.
I don't care if we're over,
You can fuck me sober.

Lyrics and music written by John Lipp

A Way

Lately I've been feeling
Complicated about this masquerading.
Clearly you've been feeling
Kinda funny, kinda scummy.
Well I'm sorry that I did it, honey

She comes, she goes.
We ebb, we flow.
Well she's right behind me yearning
While my cigarette is burning … away

Terror it comes pretty easy
These days, especially
Patience they say is a virtue.
Did I hurt you? When I say "I love you"
Then I skirt you

She toes the line
When the weather's fine.
Well I think she's finally learning
And all my wheels are turning … away

(Bridge)

She runs, she hides.
We die, we ride.
Well I can't hold back my laughter,
When she says, "Happily ever after"
My brain will take a licking
As I think about it sticking.
I can hear her stomach churning
And I can't imagine earning ... a way.

Lyrics and music written by John Lipp

She's Better

Anyone?
I'll take anyone,
Pruned the thorns from my side are they
Wires or vines?

Anyone?
I left everyone.
Do you play the game, or live up to your
Name?

I can't breathe
With your arms around me.
Fuck me, love me, hold my feet to the ground,
But she'll always be better when I'm not around.

Falling out
I've been falling out.
Remember Sunday?
What did you say?

I can't breathe,

With your arms around me.
Fuck me, love me, hold my feet to the ground,
But she'll always be better when I'm not around.

(Guitar solo)

I can't breathe,
With your arms around me.
Fuck me, love me, hold my feet to the ground,
But she'll always be better when I'm not around.

Lyrics and music written by John Lipp

Rate and Review

We hope you enjoyed *Dare You to Choose Truth* by Lauren Lipp. If you did, we would ask that you please rate and review this title. Every review helps our authors.

Rate and Review: Dare You to Choose Truth

Meet The Author

Lauren Lipp is a romance author and part-time poet. Despite being a Taurus opposed to inconsistency, she attended four different universities but eventually graduated from Colorado State University with a Bachelor of Arts in English. She was born and raised in Colorado, and still calls the mountains home. She's never skied but does drive a Subaru so she can be considered a true native. In typical millennial fashion, she has an infinite love of Harry Potter, early 2000s emo pop-punk music, and a good Rom-Com. She loves to write funny love stories and depressing poetry when she can find the time between chasing her two lively daughters and yapping her husband's ear off.

Other Titles from

5 PRINCE PUBLISHING

www.5princebooks.com

www.ingramcontent.com/pod-product-compliance
Lightning Source LLC
Chambersburg PA
CBHW020531020726
47494CB00006B/1723